Sonora, and the Eye of the Titans is a work of fiction. Names, characters, places, and events are either a product of the author's imagination or used fictitiously. Any resemblance to actual person, living or dead, events, or locations are entirely coincidental.

No part of this publication may be reproduced, stored, or transmitted in any form or by any means without written permission from the publisher. For information regarding permission, contact New Guy Publishing, Attention: Authorization Department, PO Box 3927, Ketchum, ID 83340.

This book was originally published in paperback by New Guy Publishing in 2011

ISBN-13: 978-1466428492
ISBN-10: 146642849X

Printed in the United States of America

www.sonoraseries.com

SONORA
AND THE EYE OF THE TITANS

Travis Hall

Acknowledgement

There are so many people who have been crucial in the success of this book. First of all, I would like to thank my mother and father for their unending support of my dreams. Without them, I would never have written this story. I would also like to thank Clarissa, for being the first to read my adventure, and give me the confidence to persevere. For my amazing brother Gavin, who gave me the tools to complete the final manuscript. A special thank you to Steve Cowden for an incredible cover design, and to Gorby for his help with the layout and icon design. To Abby and Emily for their help with the artwork. I'd like to thank Katie, Kyle, Barclay, Martha, Molly, Jarrod, and Jenny for helping to inspire and support me in my quest for adventure. And to all those in Sun Valley who have been an amazing part of my life, and with me in the final stages of my journey.

Prologue

"Faster, Kalia!" Tania shouted to her sister upon seeing the camouflaged streak of their pursuers. "We have to go *now!*"

Resonating from different directions, sounds of snapping twigs and rushing feet became louder. They had caught up, flanking Kalia and Tania's position. Kalia caught her shawl on a branch that hung below a large fallen tree. She stepped back and grabbed the cloth, forcefully liberating herself from the snag. The baby contained inside the shawl wailed from the sudden motion. As soon as she saw the men's beady eyes bob into view, Kalia seized her sister's arm, yanking her from underneath the tree. They continued their escape, aggressively weaving through the timber like slalom skiers as a barrage of multi-colored balls of electricity burst into the trees, blasting the two women with shards of bark and pine needles. The flying debris sliced through their skin, causing sporadic dark red lines of blood.

"I need time to open up the Gateway!" Tania yelled, pulling an apple-sized obsidian orb from her coat pocket.

Fear gripped Kalia as they approached Crystal Lake. Out of the corner of her eye, the men's silhouettes darted between the trees. Hooded shadows discharged streams of light, exploding and shattering the trees around them. Oncoming thunderclouds darkened the forest, inhibiting the women's ability to see. Only the occasional lightning strike illuminated the path ahead. Far behind, the sounds of war rumbled, but for Kalia and Tania, it no longer mattered. Their only goal was to protect the baby. Exiting the woods, they sprinted through a grassy field, stopping at the edge of an expansive lake that mirrored the flashes of lightning. As she calculated the time it took to open the Gateway, Kalia unwrapped the shawl from her shoulder.

"I need you to take my baby," Kalia said, gently placing the infant into Tania's arms. "I will try to fight them off."

The calm in Kalia's voice unsettled Tania. "You can't do this by yourself!" Tania said, tears pouring down her face.

"We don't have time to argue! That baby is the only hope we have now."

The full moon peeked through the thunderclouds, shining on the small patch of grass along the forest's edge. Kalia glanced back at her sister, whose tears sparkled on her cheeks. Fate had set its clock in motion. Days ago, her life had been so much different: joyous and full of optimism. One event, one singular evening, had changed the course of this world, and would now affect the fate of another.

"Ahhh!" She screamed and quickly sidestepped to her right to avoid a large tree crashing to the ground.

A large ball of turquoise fire billowed from the forest canopy. Streaks of red and yellow shot across the blackness of the woods, creating a deadly yet eerily beautiful display of colors. Kalia limped out of the forest as Tania read the last of the incantation inscribed upon the black orb. It glowed in Tania's, and then flew from her hand, landing in the shallows of the lake. The orb's surrounded Tania, linking her with the Gateway and initiating the portal's opening.

"Kalia!" She shouted, unable to move without breaking the link. "You can make it!"

Lightning streaked across the sky, followed by monstrous thunder that shook the ground. The hooded men closed in on the field, yelling adamantly to attack. A flaming blue ball whizzed between the trees, striking Kalia's lower back as she ran across the field. Her body arched, and then collapsed into the grass. As she stood up, her knees buckled. Looking across the field, Kalia saw the twinkle of her baby's eyes, held lovingly by her younger sister. Behind them, the water swirled rapidly, spinning upward, defying gravity like an upside down cyclone. There was only one thing left to do. Kalia concentrated. Her resolve was unwavering.

Tania stared at her sister as she got to her feet, watching as small lights appeared at the tips of Kalia's fingers. Electricity radiated from within her body, down through her arms, and into her hands. The electricity sparked from her fingers and balls of light expanded upon her palms. The unstable spheres of churning energy in Kalia's hands began to pulsate. Her body shook violently as she fought to keep control of the power in her hands.

The hooded men inched out of the forest's edge, unable to comprehend the sight of the large water tornado and the glowing figure in front of them. Kalia turned to the men and suddenly swung her hands together. A blazing sheet of fire, followed by a furious explosion, sent the men airborne. Their bodies flew wildly into the foliage. Noise reverberated across the lake, drowning out the thunder. Visibility became minimal, caused by the cloud of debris and dirt covering the area.

Tania had anticipated her sister's move and put up a protective energy field, but the force of the explosion was too strong. It lifted her off the ground, forcing her backward. Tania scrunched up into a ball, clutching the baby tightly in her arms. Luckily, the Gateway had opened, sucking them upward through the funnel of water and out of Sonora.

Chapter 1

Tryouts

"Allora... Allora!"

Mr. Swan stared down upon his star pupil, who raised her head looking guilty. A tall strong man, Mr. Swan stood over her with both arms crossed. Today, he was wearing a brown plaid shirt with black suspenders that held up his khaki pants. His curly hair hung down around his wireframe glasses. He remained silent until Allora sat upright.

"Are you back?" He asked with a disappointed look. Allora nodded, but, in reality her thoughts were on the cheerleading tryouts, which took place after school. "I might've expected this from your cohort sitting next to you, but..."

"Hey! Not fair," Katie said. Mr. Swan looked at her with raised sturdy eyebrows. "Okay, well maybe, but don't worry, Teach. It has nothing to do with you, or your fascinating lecture," she said with a wide smile, referring to the discussion of the last great Pharaoh of ancient Egypt. Mr. Swan looked at her disapprovingly. "She has been that way all day," continued Katie.

Allora promptly apologized for her mental disappearing act. "Sorry Mr. Swan, I've just been a bit distracted today."

"Is there something wrong, Allora?" Mr. Swan asked, still troubled by his student's lack of attention. And as if right on cue, the bell rang. "I'll hope for a little more attentiveness next time."

Amidst the squeaky shuffle of sneakers upon the over-waxed checkered tile and the clambering of overloaded backpacks banging against desks and chairs, Mr. Swan tossed out a casual reminder, "I expect those essays on my desk on Monday," Mr. Swan said, and then sat down at his desk. Allora and Katie quickly grabbed their things and made their way into the crowded hallway.

"Call me after cheerleading tryouts and let me know how it goes," Katie said as she was taken away by the herding students. "Good luck!"

Allora took a moment amidst the shrinking crowd as they fled the red and white colored walls of Sandy High School. As she made a beeline for the gym, months of practicing her routine flooded Allora's vulnerable memory. With only twenty-two spots open, Allora glanced around the locker room at the other eighty girls, who were quickly dressing into their athletic attire. Silence enveloped the room as the reigning varsity squad strutted in, rank and file. As if rehearsed, the squad marched in lockstep, executing precision breaks and turns in unison, to the center of the locker room. Looking around, their collective judgmental gaze penetrated even the most confident prospects. Each member of squad had her hair pulled back into the mandatory cheer ponytail, uniform perfectly starched, and each wore the same fake smile as her badge of unspoken supremacy. Jenny, the new captain of the squad, stepped forward and addressed the girls.

"Listen up skanks! As far as you all are concerned, from this point forth, I own you! Any questions?" She paused for dramatic effect while surveying her prey. "If — and that's a *big* if — you make it through tryouts, you will never work harder at anything in your pathetic little lives." The amateur prospects looked around the room at one another, dismal fear spreading across their faces. "If you're lucky enough to be selected from your grouping this week, don't make the mistake of thinking the hardest part is behind you. You'll have to prove yourself every single day before football season next fall, and every day thereafter. Get this through your heads: I am the queen of this squad and you are all my subjects. When I say jump, you jump. When I say back handspring, you'd better be flipping."

Allora leaned in to the freshman girl standing next to her and whispered, "And if she says suck my big fat toe, you better be on your knees ready to go." The bouncy shy blonde began giggling behind puckered lips, desperate not to be singled out. Jenny rushed across the room, stopping inches from the freshman's face. With a shake of her head, Jenny's hair swept across the young, now terrified girl, as if slapping her with a horse's tail. The freshman's eyes were firmly affixed to the cement floor, fearful of Jenny's full wrath. Adjacent to the freshman, Allora stood tall and unafraid, staring directly into Jenny's cold gaze.

"Did I say something funny?"

"Nope, just commenting on how excited I am your royal highness," Allora replied, with a wide grin.

"Who do you think you are?" Jenny questioned.

Allora leaned forward, not intimidated by Jenny's authoritative gestures. "Well, I guess if you're the queen, than I'm the court jester," Allora said, with a mocking smile.

The room erupted with laughter. Even the varsity girls, clustered in the middle of the locker room, couldn't hold back.

"Shut up!" Jenny said, projecting her voice throughout the locker room. The silence that followed was eerie.

"Just because you're my boyfriend's childhood pal doesn't mean I have to make this hurt for you any less than I would otherwise." Allora drew back her grin as Jenny eased in closer. "We will see who's laughing after today," Jenny said in a soft whisper that only Allora could hear.

Jenny slowly stepped back, turned, and stomped out of the locker room with her posse trailing close behind. Everyone looked at Allora as if she was live meat ready for the slaughter. Jenny's spite was unpredictable. This wasn't the time to relish on the confrontation. Allora needed to focus so that she would be mentally prepared for the routine. She finished getting dressed and followed the other girls out toward the football field.

Allora sat down on the soft green turf, extending her arms to stretch her thighs. On the fifty yard line Tanner, and Katie's brother Dax, were talking and staring at the mob of girls. Tanner moseyed across the field. Wearing only his football pants and a tight cut-off shirt, Tanner's muscular features, were extenuated in the afternoon sun. Allora was surprised how flustered she felt when he walked up.

"I'm surprised to see you at the gauntlet," he said, referring to the intense tryouts that most girls left in tears.

"Yeah ... well ... obviously, I'm a lot tougher than you think," she replied, getting up from her leg stretch.

"I guess so," Tanner said, remembering that this was the girl who used to throw him off the jungle gym when they were little. "Well, good luck," he said, giving her a wink, and jogging back to the football team to finish warming up.

Allora felt strange as she watched Tanner run back to his team. Her knees wobbled, her heart beat faster, and she could feel a tingling sensation in her stomach. Tanner had never had this effect before. The feelings quickly evaporated as the cheerleading coach made her way out onto the field.

"Okay girls, let's begin," Coach Laurent said, motioning the girls to line up in six lines, evenly spaced, and facing a long table along the track.

She pulled out a pink clipboard, and a long pen with a miniature pom-pom attached to the top. Jenny sat down next to her, pulling out an almost identical clipboard and pen. The coach instructed the girls to do basic moves to assess their balance, stamina, and poise. Allora fell into the first grouping. She was eager to set the high mark, confident her styling would impress Coach Laurent. As the group of girls came forth to claim their practice pom-poms, Jenny managed to slip a "special" pair into Allora's hands, shooting her victim a savage smile as she passed by. Immediately, Allora realized something wasn't right with her pom-poms, but she had no time to examine them before the music started. Allora executed the routine brilliantly, every move crisp, every step perfectly timed. After receiving an approving nod from the judges, Allora approached the table confidently, but as she tried to set down her pom-poms, she realized what Jenny had been smiling about all along.

"Allora, we're waiting on you," Coach Laurent remarked impatiently.

Jenny could not control her sinister laughter. She ran behind the bleachers to avoid incriminating herself.

"Coach, I can't get them off!" Allora screamed, flailing her hands back and forth to try and pry the strings of plastic from her hands. She put all her effort into keeping her composure, but as the groundswell of laughter grew louder, spreading across the practice field and spilling over to the football practice, anxiety and humiliation overcame her.

"Let me see," Coach Laurent said, grasping Allora's hands and folding them outward. She examined the handles and found the adhesive substance bonding the plastic to her skin. "This looks like industrial strength super glue."

"Please get them off," Allora whispered through tears of embarrassment.

"Allora dear, I don't think I can without tearing the skin," Coach Laurent said, hopelessly turning over Allora's hands.

"I just want to go home; I want it to be over, just let me go home," Allora whimpered, choking on her own tears.

By now, Allora was thoroughly embarrassed. The football team crowded close by, curious about the commotion.

"I'm going to get Coach Hale's help," Coach Laurent said, parting the crowd and running to the middle of the football field.

Allora stood alone before her peers, cheeks glowing red, naked with embarrassment. Her day, her tryout, everything she'd worked so hard for the past few months, had been ruined by a prank. Scanning the mob, Allora's humiliation was drowned by a surge of anger. In an instant, Allora knew who the perpetrator was. Jenny parted the group, strutting up to Allora as though she had just won an award. She placed her hands on her hips, oozing with pride at her accomplishment. Allora could feel her whole body filling with rage.

"I told you I would thoroughly enjoy this." Jenny glanced over to Tanner, and then back to Allora. "Oh and this little 'thing' between you and my boyfriend," Jenny mouthed, raising an eyebrow. "That's over."

Unable to restrain the fury inside, Allora's whole body shook. A faint swell of electricity crawled up her spine, moving through her torso, and into her arms. The pulsating energy flowed into her palms as she extended them away from her body, and let out a tormented scream. Suddenly, the pom-poms burst into flames. Only the gawkers immediately surrounding Allora witnessed the horrific phenomenon, but in mere moments, panic spread among the several dozen surrounding onlookers. Allora didn't realize what was going on until she felt the heat from the flames. The plastic was melting in her palms, consuming her fingers in intense heat. Drops of liquid fire dropped onto the ground, creating pools of flames on the track. Throwing Allora to the ground, Tanner and Dax began slapping at the fire with their shirts. With the flames smothered, Dax pushed away the onlookers in order to give Allora some much-needed space while Tanner remained by her side. In obvious agony, Allora lay on the ground in the fetal position with her back to the audience.

"What can I do, Al?" Tanner asked, softly. "How can I help?"

"It hurts, it hurts, it hurts...." Repeating these words over and over as tears escaped her tightly shut eyelids.

"What the hell happened here?" Coach Hale said, pushing through the crowd.

"Coach, she's a freak!" Jenny said. "We were just waiting for the Ms. Laurent to get back and next thing you know, her hands were on fire. Coach, there's something very wrong with that girl."

"Jenny, shut up," Tanner fired back. "She needs a doctor! She's in a lot of pain, Coach. We need to get her to a hospital."

Gently brushing Allora's hair from her tear-soaked cheeks, Tanner placed one arm underneath her knees, positioned his other arm under the small of her back, and pulled Allora toward him. She reacted instinctively, hugging his neck. She held on tightly, burying her face into his chest.

Tanner carried Allora's feeble body to a patch of grass at the edge of the track, away from the gawkers. Within minutes of receiving Coach Laurent's call, two paramedics arrived and took over Allora's care, urging Tanner from her side. Visibly shaken and scared for his friend, Tanner's unwavering attention didn't go unnoticed by the crowd of his peers, teammates, and above all, his girlfriend. Coach Laurent rounded up the remainder of the spectators and herded them into the gym as Allora was given an intravenous mixture of pain medication and fluids. Slowly, she eased into a deep peaceful sleep.

Chapter 2

Confusion

Lying prone on the bleach white linens covering the bed, Allora slept peacefully. A plastic bag of hydrating vitamins hung against the back of the bed, and a long tube ran into a needle, feeding the liquid into her body. A blanket covered the flower patterned hospital gown the nurses had dressed her in. Standing at the foot of the bed, Milly and Aunt May remain steady for a long minute of reflection. This event had taken them completely by surprise.

"We need to leave," Milly said.

"We don't know the whole story," Aunt May argued. "That fire could have started any number of ways. She isn't even of age!"

"There were plenty who could Focus before the age of eighteen."

"Yeah, but she just turned sixteen. That's impossible."

The faint sound of Allora's breathing echoed against the whitewashed walls of the hospital's intensive care unit. The two women stood idly, contemplating their next move. Plans had been put in place for this, but they weren't mentally prepared. Milly's heart beat faster, thinking about the potential consequences of her daughter's tragic event.

"If we've been compromised, then I need to contact Sumatra," May said.

"No!" Milly said. The sharp noise caused Allora to stir in her bed.

"Ssssshhhhh!"

"You cannot contact Sumatra," Milly whispered. "It's too risky! No. We need to lay low until this blows over."

"This isn't going to 'blow over.' We can't keep doing this. They need to know the truth. This is no time for half-measures — we need Sumatra."

"And you want another Shifter in town. If we summon him, any number of agents could pick it up. Don't you remember what happened last time?"

"Don't you dare bring Ben into this," Aunt May snapped.

Ben's name hadn't been said in a long time. Old wounds that never healed split open, surfacing guilt, anger, and fear. The death of their little brother was an unbearable tragedy that none wanted to relive.

"Once Allora wakes up, we are leaving. If she was strong enough to produce fire, the energy signature would have traveled for miles. And you know He has eyes and ears everywhere. They would have surely sensed it, and right now, we have almost everyone here in the hospital. Dax, Katie, Bell, and Tanner are in the waiting room. There could be agents in the area, and they could easily follow the energy trail here."

"So it's even more imperative that we contact Sumatra!" Aunt May whispered.

"No!" Milly yelled, rousing her daughter from her slumber. "This is my responsibility, not yours! I'm the Keeper!"

"What' going on?" Allora asked, perplexed by both the sudden rousing and her abnormal surroundings. As she scanned the room, Allora's memories slowing surfaced. She eyed the tightly wrapped dressing upon her hands, remembering the horrifying fire that had engulfed them. Not entirely awake, Allora rubbed her eyes. A strange energy filled the room. Fear and anxiety emanated from the worrisome woman as Milly knelt beside the bed, placing a hand on her daughter's bandaged arm. They held each other's silent gaze.

"Honey, I'm sorry. Are you okay?"

With her defiant teenage streak of pride intact, Allora replied, "Yeah, I'm fine. Sore, but I'll be alright."

Milly gave her younger sister an ominous nod and quietly excused herself from the room. The tension between the two was palpable.

"Aunt May, what's wrong with Mom?"

Trying to mask her concerns with a smile, a weak "Hello darling," was all Aunt May could muster before her eyes began to well up. She sat down on the bed. "Your mom is just worried about you, that's all."

Even as Aunt May spoke, Allora knew the words weren't true. The medication was wearing off and the throbbing pain in her hands and forearms felt as if she'd stuck her hands into a light socket. Allora couldn't understand why everyone was so distraught. It's not like someone died, she thought to herself.

Milly charged back into the room. "Get her dressed, we have to go home. —now!"

Aunt May helped Allora with the arduous task of getting dressed. Adamant about getting out of the hospital, Milly hurriedly undertook the discharge process, arranging to have Allora wheeled to the car. Allora found the sudden and immediate departure from the hospital alarming. With the abnormality of the day's events still fresh in her mind, Allora yearned for the safety and comfort of her own bed.

On the ride home, Bell, Allora's little sister, elucidated about the different treatments for severe burns. She had read up on the subject a couple months previous, and went on and on about various antibiotics to fight infections and anti-inflammatory creams that decreased swelling and pain. Allora was rather impressed by how much her sister knew about the subject. Everyone else in the car remained silent.

The minivan took a left at the wooden mailbox, and drove between two large pine trees. The long gravel road curved to the left opening into a large meadow. At the end of the driveway, a one story house sat in the middle of a field, surrounded by forest. In the middle of the house was an angled roof with a tall brick chimney extending upward. Milly pulled the van into the garage and turned to her daughter. "Lora, you should get right to bed.

You're going to need your rest."

Spent from the afternoon's events and devoid of any energy to disagree, Allora nodded. The incident at tryouts had exacted a heavy toll, and Allora needed some time alone to figure things out. She closed the wooden door to her room and leaned against it. As she glanced around her sanctuary, Allora saw only what she had always seen, yet the room somehow felt unfamiliar. The assortment of random gemstones on her shelves, the imaginative drawings of fantastical creatures on her wall, and even the funky amour built by her aunt—they all seemed foreign. Allora lay on the bed and looked up through her skylight at the bright stars. Her mind raced between the tryouts, the fire, and her mother's strange behavior at the hospital.

How did my hands catch on fire? she reflected. *Did my skin have some sort of reaction with the glue?*

It didn't make any sense. Obsessively reflecting over what happened left her fatigued. Like the shades of a window, Allora's eyelids drew down, and then... slowly, Allora fell into a deep... deep... sleep.

~~~~~~~~~~~~~~

A pounding headache greeted Allora when she woke. As she say up, the incisive pain in her hands quickly increased in severity. This was followed by an extremely difficult itch on her back that she couldn't reach. She ran into her sister's room, crashing through the doorway and jumping onto Bell's bed.

"It itches so badly!" Allora said, dancing up and down, unsuccessfully reaching for the itch with her wrapped hands. "Please, Bell, please!"

Bell was bouncing from her sister's frantic footwork, but she finally got to her knees and used both hands to scratch her sister's back.

Moaning with relief, Allora pleaded, "Keep going. Don't stop."

"Can't you get some sort of back scratcher?" Bell asked, yawning from her interrupted sleep.

"That's why I have you." Bell stopped scratching and left the room for the shower. "Hey, I'm still itchy!" Allora yelled down the hall.

"Find yourself another slave," Bell yelled back, closing the bathroom door.

Allora went down the hall, wearing a tank top and pajama pants. She found her aunt in the living room, reading the newspaper. Allora ran to Aunt May and begged for relief from the discomfort. Her aunt gave in, and Allora was able to get a good long back scratch. Aunt May used this time to question her niece about the previous day.

May waited for Allora to settle in front of her before saying, "So, I didn't know that you were interested in cheerleading."

Allora knew from the start where this was headed but decided that a back scratch was worth any interrogation. "Yeah, I wanted to do something active and I'm not really good at any other sports." That was only partly true.

"So, how did the tryout go?"

"I'm guessing that you really want to know how my hands caught on fire."

"Well... it was on my mind."

Allora could only tell her what she knew. Aunt May took it all in, listening intently to the details leading up to the fire.

"Honestly, Aunt May, I have no idea. One minute I was standing there humiliated, and the next thing I knew, the other girls were screaming. I looked down and my hands were on fire."

Aunt May stared at her niece with a blank expression as if stirring a distant thought that hadn't been explored in decades. She sat rigid, in a somewhat catatonic state. An awkward minute passed without a word.

"I'm going to be fine," Allora said. "My hands will heal. It was probably the sun catching the flammable glue on fire... or something."

Even though her niece recalled the events casually, Aunt May still felt uneasy.

"Breakfast!" Milly shouted from the kitchen.

Allora slowly and painfully got up from the floor. She turned to her aunt, who sat unmoving in the upholstered chair.

"Aunt May?"

"Go ahead and get breakfast," she said, pushing her niece toward the kitchen. "I'll be in there in a minute."

After Allora rounded the corner of the room, Aunt May went to the bookshelves that lined the wall. She scanned the titles until she found a large, brown leather-bound book. She pulled over a stepstool to help her retrieve it from the top of the bookshelf. She blew the dust off the cover, opened the book, and meticulously flipped through the pages, searching for a specific subject. Each page was old and stiff, cracking as it turned over. After a few minutes, she found the chapter on "Detectors." A sense of urgency crept into her mind as she read.

"We're in big trouble," Aunt May said to herself.

She placed the book back on the shelf, and retreated to her room where she paced back and forth in an inner struggle to make a difficult choice. Deep down, she knew this day would come, and it didn't make the choice of going against her sister any easier.

"There is no going back," Aunt May said.

With the affirmation made, Aunt May snuck out her bedroom window, silently tip-toeing across the front lawn, and then disappeared into the woods. She arrived back home in the late afternoon to find her sister stomping down the driveway.

"I can't believe you went behind my back."

Aunt May stared Milly straight in the eye. "I did what was necessary," she said, pushing past Milly and heading into the living room.

"No, what you did was disobey a direct order!" Milly said, causing both of her daughters to peek around the hallway.

"I'm not one of your soldiers, and this isn't the war," Aunt May insisted. "This isn't all about you. We have a duty to those individuals in this community who we swore to protect."

Allora walked toward the arguing woman, with both hands still wrapped tightly with white cloth and burn dressing. The sun was starting to set against the canopy of trees, casting a bright orange glow through the window, spotlighting the living room where they stood.

"What's going on?" Allora asked.

Realizing how loud their argument had been, Milly tried to backpedal.

"Just an old argument. This is none of your concern, Allora. Now, take your sister and go to your room."

Ever the defiant teenager, Allora stepped forward. "*No.*"

"Excuse me?"

"This has to do with me, and I know it," Allora said.

"Go to your room, now." Milly pointed sharply toward the hallway.

Allora felt confused and scared. Her own family was keeping secrets. Since the death of Uncle Ben, her family had become so reclusive. Every time she had tried to inquire about his death, Aunt May and Mom had become silent or defensive. There was something more to her family, and now it was more pronounced than ever.

"I'm not a little girl anymore," Allora said. "This is my life, and I have the right to know."

"You will go to your room and stay there or you will be grounded," Milly said.

"This has something to do with my hands catching on fire, doesn't it?" Allora asked, ignoring her mother's order. "Why don't you ever tell me anything?"

"That's enough!" Milly said. A shockwave of energy broke from Milly's body. The forceful wave pushed Allora into the couch and caused Aunt May to brace herself against an armchair. The entire room shook, causing books to fall from the shelves. The metal fire rods crashed into the wall, and ash blew out from the fireplace, choking the air with a gray-black cloud. Milly breathed in deeply, closing her eyes, struggling to control her anger.

"What just happened?" Allora asked.

"Oh, god!" Milly placed her hands over her eyes. "What have I done?"

Aunt May grabbed her sister by the shoulders.

"It's alright. It wasn't enough to detect."

Then, she took Allora by the hand, and ushered both of the girls to their room, leaving Milly to reflect over her actions.

"May...." Allora said, trying to get some sort of answer as she was shoved into her bedroom.

"This isn't the time, Allora. Things have become much more complicated. I need you to be patient. All will be explained to you shortly."

"But—"

The door shut before Allora could get any more information. *What secret are they keeping? What am I? How did my mother do that?* Questions led to more questions. She paced around her room, aggressively trying to comprehend the last twenty-four hours. The stress and anxiety was too much. Rolling off the bed, she pulled open the window sash, and squeezed through the opening. After circumvented the rhododendron bush at the base of the window, Allora quietly crossed the field, escaped the property, and headed east down the darkening road. With her home behind her, Allora walked a mile before turning left on Norman Court. At the end of the cul-de-sac, a discreet trail zigzagged down a steep hill. The sun was going down, which made traversing the way more difficult. The path was full of tree roots, and yet even in the fading light, the trail was so familiar that Allora never tripped. After several hundred feet, she came out of the woods where it opened up to a rocky clearing.

It was quiet, except for the constant swishing sound of flowing water. It grew louder with each step she took. The briskly moving water glistened against the day's last beams of light. Water tumbled over large rocks into a pool at Allora's feet. The sound of the rushing river was soothing. Allora sat on a flat rock by the pool and thought back over the events of the past

few days. She could not help but think that all of them were somehow connected. She stared up at the full moon inching its way up into the freckled
indigo sky. A brilliant sunset was ending in the western hills.

Suddenly, a cracking noise reached across the rocky riverbed. Startled,
Allora jumped backward, losing her footing on the slippery rocks. Pulling
herself up, she scurried across the rocks and propped herself up against a
sizable boulder. She fell silent, listening for any sign of movement. The constant thump of her heart beat loudly against her chest. Her panic increased
with each passing second.

"How am I going to fight like this?" she whispered, glaring at her finger-
less white limbs. There was only one thing to do. Gripping the end of the
wrapping with her teeth, she peeled back the bandages from her right hand.
I would rather fight with burnt hands than be defenseless. The sound was getting closer, which made her un-spin the bandages even faster. Surprisingly,
there was no pain. She pulled back the last layer, presumptively cringing at
the thought of grossly burnt skin. In the light of the moon, Allora gasped at
the sight of no burn marks. *What is going on?*

There was no time to reflect. Unwrapping her other hand, which was
also burn free, she grabbed a large rock from the creek bed. A quick glance
around the side of the boulder didn't reveal anything. Then, the sound of
pebbles grinding under the weight of a foot reverberated on the opposite
side of the boulder. More footsteps followed. She squeezed her fingers
around the rock in her hand, waiting to strike. The sound stopped. The
intruder was directly to the right of boulder.

Beads of sweat trickled down her forehead and a chill moved down her
spine. The footsteps started again and a dark figure glided past. She made
her choice and leapt onto the dark figure, knocking it to the ground. She
raised the rock over her head while the body underneath her turned over.
The figure screamed. The light of the moon revealed the intruder's face.

"Tanner?" Allora asked.

"Allora?" Tanner answered, equally shocked.

She pushed off of Tanner's chest and stood over him. He gradually got to his feet and brushed off the dirt from his shirt.

"Are you crazy?" Tanner asked, still shaking from the surprise attack.

Allora wasn't about to take the blame for the situation. She glared at Tanner and said, "Yeah, well, what are you doing sneaking up on me like that?"

"What!" Tanner said angrily. "I wasn't sneaking up on you. I didn't even know you were down here."

After a minute of silence, Allora decided to give in.

"I'm sorry." The events of the last few days were making her paranoid. "What are you doing down here anyway?" she asked.

"This is where I go when I want some time to think to myself."

"Well, I guess you'll just have to deal with me, because I'm not going anywhere," Allora said, lifting her chin and crossing her arms.

Tanner lowered his shoulders, releasing his tense muscles. His scrunched forehead released the anxious expression, reflecting on the previous day.

"Are you alright?"

Allora lowered her chin, uncrossed her arms, and walked past Tanner to the water's edge. She picked up a smooth, flat rock from the creek bed and skipped it across the water, trying to think of what to say.

"You mean with my hands," she said, holding them up.

"What the...." Tanner grabbed her hands. "There isn't even a mark on them."

"I know," she said. "I just found that out a few minutes ago when I was trying to kill you." Noticing Tanner's bewildered look against the moonlight, she pulled her hands away from his judging eyes. "Don't look at me like that."

"I'm sorry. I didn't mean to. It's just... that day... what happened?"

"Your delightful girlfriend decided it was a good idea to put superglue on the handles of my pom-poms during tryouts," Allora said. "Next thing I knew, people were screaming and I was on fire."

"I had no idea... I'm so sorry," Tanner said. "She can be pretty mean sometimes."

"Mean? Yeah, that's an understatement."

Tanner stood there, rubbing the back of his neck and blinking in the semi-darkness. "I'm not really sure why I date her."

The comment took Allora off-guard. They stared at each other for a minute in silence. The moonlight elucidated Allora's soft facial features. They stared into each other's eyes, unconsciously moving closer. Their bodies softly touched, each feeling the other's heat as it escaped from the increased circulation. Then, Tanner's cell phone rang.

Allora stepped back while Tanner awkwardly searched his pocket for the device.

He flipped open the phone. "Its Dax," he said, giving an awkward half-smile. Allora watched Tanner's face, seeming to be relieved for the interruption. She decided to act accordingly, choosing to ignore the previous exchange. After a few grunts, he said, "I'm with Allora right now. Uh huh... uh huh... okay, I'll tell her. Later dude."

"So what did he want?" Allora asked.

"Dax and Katie are up at the rock quarry and they wanted to know if we want to go up there. I guess a bunch of people are camping. Apparently, Katie called you a bunch."

"My mom took my cell phone away from me."

"Well, do you want to go?" Tanner asked.

The idea sounded like fun, but Allora had snuck out. If her mother found out, she would be grounded for life. At this point, she was so angry that she didn't care if she got in trouble. How many opportunities did she have to go camping with her classmates?

"Okay, let's go."

The two hiked back through the forest and up to the street where Tanner's car was parked. Allora paused, staring up with glassy eyes at the large full moon in the night sky. A hazy fog surrounded the white sphere. For a moment, Allora felt an ominous sense of alertness. Not a chirp, a shifting of branches, or even the familiar whistling of wind sounded in the darkness.

"Hey, you alright?" Tanner asked.

Allora snapped out of her trance and jumped into the passenger seat.

"Yeah, just fine," she said. She stared out the window at the mocking moon as Tanner drove the car onto the main road and headed east, toward the mountain.

Chapter 3

Rover

At mile marker fifty-four, Tanner veered his black Ford Bronco onto an old, abandoned timber road that stretched high into the wooded hills of Mt. Hood National Forest. After a jarring ten-minute drive through the thick forest, a distant orange glow grew from the darkness. A grand bonfire illuminated a rock quarry. Flames stretched ten feet tall, and the light seemed to dance against the rocky half-bowl-shaped hill.

Allora looked out over the edge of the quarry onto the moonlit forest valley. Dots of yellow sparkled in the distance, reminding Allora of her home. A stern fight with Milly seemed inevitable. Before tonight, she had never snuck out. But the revelations of her family's secrets were too stressful to stay in her house. Tanner pulled up alongside Katie's blue Cherokee. Noticing the infamous bright yellow Volkswagen with Pioneer Cheerleading plastered all over the rear window, Allora cringed. Tanner noticed too.

"I had no idea she was going to be here," said Tanner. Allora raised an eyebrow, questioning his remark with her stare. "We can go if you want," he said.

She let out a sigh. "I'm going to have to see her at school anyway."

Allora opened the door, stepped outside, and warily walked to the bonfire. Katie saw the duo and ran over.

"Hey! You made it!" she said. "I almost went to your house to pick you up, but I didn't want to get caught by your mom."

"Why didn't you tell me Jenny was going to be here?" Allora asked quietly.

"She didn't show up until a few minutes ago. I'm sorry. It's not like I invited her. You can thank Dax for that one."

Dax walked up behind his sister.

"Yeah, yeah. I know, that's my bad. I told Brandon we were thinking of going camping at the quarry. I should have known he would tell the whole school."

"Speak of the devil," Katie remarked as Brandon strutted over.

He wrapped his arm around Dax's shoulder. "Hi guys!"

"Hi Brandon," everyone said with hint of antagonism.

"Hey, what's with the attitude? This is a party."

Tanner turned around just as Jenny leapt onto him, wrapped her legs around his waist, and gave him a forceful kiss. She pulled herself away but still held onto him, with her arms hanging from his neck. "Hi, baby," she said.

"Gross," Allora muttered.

"What is the freak doing here?" Jenny demanded, pointing over Tanner's shoulder.

"Weird, I was going to say the same about you," Allora snapped.

Tanner pulled Jenny's arms off his shoulders, took a step back, and said, "Hey Jenny, back off."

Jenny's eyes opened wider.

"Excuse me!" she said, mimicking his body language. "Now, *you're* defending that freak!"

Everyone around stopped what they were doing to watch the confrontation. Jenny pushed Tanner and marched toward Allora. Katie stepped in front and raised her chin, stopping Jenny in her tracks.

"I dare you. Go ahead. I've been waiting for a reason to kick your ass."

Jenny was intimidating, but she didn't stand a chance against Katie. The two stared each other down like two gunfighters, each waiting for the other to draw. Jenny clenched her fists, but kept them stiffly by her sides. Suddenly, a loud rustling of branches projected down from the tree line at the top of the rock quarry. The unwelcome interruption shifted everyone's attention upward. The group fell silent. Nothing moved besides the shadows from the dancing flames.

Out of the darkness, a deafening screech pierced the silence. It echoed into the quarry, where the petrified teenagers stood motionless, grasping one another for some sense of reassurance. Allora turned toward the twins. Dax's and Katie's faces suggested knowing, quiet confidence instead of fear.

"That did not sound friendly," Tanner said.

Katie grabbed her brother's arm, and said, "Sumatra was right."

"Who is Sumatra?" Allora asked.

"This isn't exactly the time for explanations," Dax said.

A foreboding air surrounded the quarry.

"Shut up!" Jenny whispered loudly.

Katie ignored her and turned to Dax. "Where is your staff?"

"Crap, I left it in the car," Dax replied as he hastened to his truck.

"Real smart," Katie yelled.

Katie's disappointment in her brother's lack of preparedness was obvious. Panic spread throughout the group like a disease.

"Should we get out of here?" Brandon asked.

"You guys know what made that noise?" Tanner asked. "That didn't sound like anything I've heard before."

Again, Katie ignored the others. She confronted her friends. "Tanner, Allora—if something comes out of those trees, I want you to run as fast as you can into the forest. Head east, and don't look back."

"I'm not going to leave—"

"*Allora!*" Katie snapped. "We don't have much time. It's imperative you follow my directions."

The look in Katie's eyes was terrifyingly authoritative. It was as if a military commander had taken over; possessing her petit blonde best friend.

"I can't find it!" Dax said, frantically throwing junk out of the bed of his truck.

Katie walked a half step, and then spun back around.

"Oh, and whatever you do, don't let the Rover put its palm on your forehead."

"What the hell is a Rover?" Allora asked.

A dark, shadowy figure leapt from high above the crowd, landing on the hood of Jenny's car. The windows exploded outward.

"*That* is a Rover!" Katie said, fearlessly running toward the strange creature.

It was small, standing just a few feet high. Squinting her eyes in the firelight, Allora noticed that the creature's skin was scaly, with a dark brown-green color, like a reptile. Its eyes were golden with vertical irises like a cat. After briefly surveying the chaotic scramble of humans, the creature grinned, baring sharp, pointed teeth. Before Allora could move, Jenny knocked her to the ground, attempting to escape. From the rocky floor, Allora noticed Katie pulling knifes from her waist as she charged the creature. Dax found the handle of a short stick and pulled it from the bed of his pickup just as the creature sprang forward, hitting him in the chest. With the wind knocked out of him, Dax flew limply across quarry into a pile of dirt. Before the creature could mount another attack, Katie pulled back a knife, gripping the steel blade with her thumb and forefinger, and flung the weapon violently toward the Rover. The flash of her knife slashed through the crisp air, striking the creature in the side, sending it flying off the gravel lip at the quarry's edge. A high-pitch squeal trailed into the night, followed by a chorus of earsplitting screeches from the valley depths.

Suddenly, an identical creature flew over the line of cars.

It launched forward, striking Jenny in the back. The impact forced her forward, hurling the impudent cheerleader into the road. Her forehead crashed into hard dirt, knocking her unconscious. The creature crawled along her torso, maliciously pulled back her head by her hair, and placed its palm upon her forehead. The firelight showed a lanky reptilian like creature with a long skinny torso, sharp razor teeth, and five locks of hair pulled back against its flat skull.

Unhappy with its prey, the creature picked up a rock and raised it above Jenny's head. Allora's fast-moving foot clipped the Rover's side and sent it rocketing into the fire before it could do any damage. The creature hit the logs, catching the embers and scorching its scales. It yowled and ran wild. Allora turned around to see a larger creature charge at her. There was no time to mount a defense. Inches from her face, the creature yelled upon taking one of Katie's knives in its side. The creature pulled the weapon from between its scales, green blood spread thick upon the knife. It squealed and ran toward the cars. Upon reaching the quarry's edge, it let out another deafening screech, causing the other creatures to abandon their attack and follow it into the woods.

"Nice kick," Katie remarked, placing a throwing knife into her belt. "You should have tried out for the soccer team instead of cheerleading."

"Ha, ha," Allora replied.

"Well, I'm just surprised you didn't let the thing whack her on the head," Katie said, glaring at the unconscious blonde sprawled on the ground.

"And let it kill her? If anyone is going to whack Jenny on the head, it's going to be me."

Tanner and Dax strolled up.

"Where were you two?" Katie asked. Tanner pulled a tire iron from his side, showcasing the tool with a somewhat guilty half-grin for not getting back in time to fight. "And what about you?" Katie asked, putting her hands on her hips, clearly disappointed with her brother.

"That stupid thing knocked the wind out of me," Dax admitted.

"Did you at least grab your staff?"

"Yep," Dax said, pulling a handlebar from his waist. With a flick of his wrist, the short handle extended out from both sides to over five-feet long. Meanwhile, Katie began placing her throwing knives back into the sleeves wrapped around her waist. Perplexed by her friend's weaponry, Allora grabbed a burning stick from the fire.

"Okay, what's the deal with the ninja weapons? And why do I feel like you both know what's going on here?"

Katie opened her mouth, but wasn't able to give an answer. Jenny awoke, and Tanner picked her up by her arm, wiping the dirt from her face.

"Hey, you alright?" he asked.

"Am I alright?" she questioned mockingly, between sobs. "That stupid animal attacked me! Where were you?"

Jenny pulled her arms away from his grip. The rest of the students were running down the dirt road. They had decided to forget their cars and try to make it to the main road to flag down someone driving by. Brandon popped up from behind a large pile of branches.

"Is it gone yet?" he said, walking to the others.

From the depths of the forest valley, a screech echoed, yet this one was different. The deep pitch suggested something larger than the creatures they had just fought.

"I'm outta here!" Jenny said, running to catch up with the other students. "Wait for me!" she yelled after them.

Brandon jogged to his car.

"I wouldn't go over there," Dax said.

"I'm not leaving my car here!" Brandon said, moving to the quarry's edge. "I just got it detailed."

Allora and the others watched as Brandon frantically searched his pocket, trying to locate his keys among the random debris that filled them. He fumbled through receipts and coins, seeming to become increasingly frenetic.

"Brandon!" Katie yelled.

Just as he got to his car, a shadowy, human-shaped figure appeared back-lit by the light of the moon. Brandon finally pulled the keys out of his pocket, but dropped them. His hand shook as he picked them up and shoved the key into the lock. The others watched in horror as he froze, then reached up to touch a spot of moisture that had appeared on his shoulder. He slowly twisted his neck around to look directly into a face full of jagged teeth, dripping saliva.

A gut-wrenching scream followed. The creature picked him up and threw him twenty feet, knocking the boy out cold when he hit the ground. Then, it moved toward the fire where Allora, Tanner, Dax, and Katie were preparing their stances for an attack. Despite their fear, they stood their ground.

"You two need to get out of here," Katie said.

Allora moved forward with the fire stick held high. "No way!"

As the figure moved closer, they could distinguish some of its features. Like the smaller creatures, it had reptilian scales and no hair. Its beady, catlike eyes flickered, glowing gold. A slithering, snakelike tongue slipped in and out with every step it took. Dax placed his staff into the ground like a vaulting pole, pulling his body up as the creature sprang forward. As he came down, Dax swung the staff around, twisting his body and striking the Rover with the blunt end of the wooden staff. The Rover shook off the pain, positioning itself on all fours like a lion prepared to strike. Hissing and staring intently, the Rover pushed off, moving rapidly. Katie pulled back, launching a barrage of knives. The creature skillfully flipped, dodging the flying silver, and snapped around, kicking Dax in the chest. Dax flew backward, just missing the dying bonfire. Catching Katie's flying kick, the Rover twisted around, blocking another strike from the quick blonde. The Rover made an offensive downward thrust, but Katie blocked it and pushed her hand forcefully into the creature's chest. It cringed, reclaimed its balance, and spun around.

The glow from Allora's weapon lit the dark battle as the other three took turns attacking. The Rover easily blocked and countered every strike. After throwing Tanner into a car, the creature struck Allora in the gut, pushing her along the ground. Dax joined his sister, swinging his staff into the Rover's side, then twisting and trying to catch the back part of its knee. Noticing the move, the Rover jumped high, and twisted downward onto Dax's collar bone. Katie tried to thrust her knife into its abdomen, but the creature arched his back, grabbed her wrist, and smacked the steely weapon from her grasp. She tried to counter, but the creature had the upper hand, and flung her into the air. Katie's body crashed into the windshield of the yellow Volkswagen. The Rover leapt high, ready to exact a final blow. The other three were sprawled sporadically on the ground, trying to regain their composure. No one could help. Katie had but time for a brief scream until death, when a blue surge of light crashed into the creature's upper back. The explosion of energy forced it over the quarry's edge, and into the forest valley below.

All four teens gathered themselves, holding different parts of their body where the creature had struck. They looked up to the top of the quarry where the light had come from. Nothing was there. Upon meeting next to the fire, they all checked each other's wounds. Suddenly, the figure of an old man appeared from the shadows.

"Thanks for taking so long," Dax said.

"Did it identify any of you?" The old man asked.

"No," Katie answered.

The old man was somewhat short with gray silvery hair pulled back into a ponytail, a long cream-colored tunic buttoned down the middle, and baggy drawstring pants.

"Allora? Tanner? We should go. Now," the old man said.

"Who are you?" Allora asked.

"There is no time. We must leave here before it comes back."

"What about them?" Allora asked, motioning to the siblings.

"Katie and Dax have other responsibilities. Your path is with me." Allora gave Katie an inquisitive look of bewilderment, only to get a nod from her best friend. He parted the group, and headed east into the woods. Frightened, they stood still, unsure of whether to follow. The old man turned back and said, "I will explain everything. That Rover may return, and I can't be sure how many he might bring with him."

Smoke billowed from the dying fire while they contemplated their move in the pitch black of the forest. Katie and Dax quietly disappeared down the hill at the edge of the quarry. Allora grabbed Tanner's hand, feeling a sense of urgency, and then they slipped into the dark woods. The old man's silhouette was fading as they ventured further into the dense forest. Low hanging branches obscured Allora's vision, and she ended up tripping on a fallen log.

"I can't see a thing. It's way too dark."

As she said this, the old man's staff began to glow, dimly lighting a path that wound up the mountain. Most of the journey was done in silence. After Allora's bizarre couple of days, she wondered what could possibly come next. The full moon was dipping into the western mountains, indicating the coming end to the night. Neither she nor Tanner took notice of how long they had been walking. Being an athlete, Tanner didn't have much trouble with the hike, but Allora was growing tired. Dancing had kept her in shape, but the arduous hike required more stamina than she was used to. Instead of complaining, she chose to get her mind off of the physical exertion by breaking the silence.

"Where are we going?" she asked. The old man didn't respond, maintaining his stride along the path. That didn't deter Allora. "Can you tell me anything?" The old man, however, made no changes in his movement. Allora waited for a few more minutes, and then she stopped. "I'm not moving another inch until you tell us what is going on," she said.

Not noticing Allora's sudden stop, Tanner ran into her. The old man halted his progress a few feet ahead, turned slightly, and quietly said, "We must not stop. It's not safe here. I promise you that we will explain as much as we possibly can... soon." With that, the old man continued his quick pace up the mountain.

"We?" Tanner said.

The old man resumed his unrelenting pace up the mountain, his staff's blue light becoming faint in the distance. Tanner and Allora had to run to catch up. The sun hadn't yet made it above the horizon, but the morning dew was forming on the leave, and the birds began to chirp. The old man began to slow down. Just as they were about to climb over the top of an embankment, he turned around.

"We are here," he said softly.

Chapter 4

Sas

The old man led them over the edge of the rock embankment and onto a large stone outcrop. They proceeded slowly along the wide slab to the mouth of a cave. Something felt strangely familiar about this place, but neither Tanner nor Allora could articulate the feeling. A natural archway of thick vines lined the cave rim. Sharp, pointed rocks protruded inward, making the cave look like the mouth of a beast. On either side, moss-covered trees hung low, blocking their progress as they tried unsuccessfully to walk to the dark cavern. Tanner accidently broke off one of the low-hanging branches. A low growl echoed deep within the cave.

"That doesn't sound too friendly," Allora said.

Another growl escaped the black cavern.

"Oh, I assure you Ms. Sona, there is no danger here," the old man uttered softly.

A shadowy figure appeared in the depths of the opening. Slowly, the figure ducked under the hanging jagged stones and exited the cave. The silhouette of a man moved out into the light of the glowing staff, and when they saw the tall, hairy beast, both Tanner and Allora gasped.

"The first reaction has got to be the best one," the creature said in a soft, jovial tone. "Don't you think?"

The old man nodded his head and laughed. Allora and Tanner gripped each other tightly, terrified at the sight of the hairy gargantuan. What stood before them was eight feet tall with beady eyes, lanky limbs, and long brown fur covering the entirety of its body.

Finally, Allora said, "Oh my god, are you Sasquatch?"

The creature looked at her, smiled, and then said, "Well, yeah, but you can call me Sas for short." Tanner was frozen with his mouth opened wide. Timidly, Allora took a couple of steps forward, fascinated by the towering beast. She slowly moved closer and pulled the hair on its arm. "Ooowww!" Sas said, rubbing his arm. "Why'd you do that?"

"Sorry. I had to make sure you weren't wearing a costume," Allora said. "I don't like practical jokes."

"Well, you could have just asked," Sas said. "Anyway, I'm glad you all are here. It was getting a little boring up here."

They were still stunned that one of the most legendary mythical creatures in the world was standing before them. Allora couldn't quite wrap her head around the situation. How could the infamous Sasquatch be so melancholy?

"I thought you were just a myth," Allora said.

"I don't present myself to normal humans. The only reason Earth people know about me is because sometimes I get careless, and overly curious. Everyone makes mistakes, you know?"

Now, Allora was confused. "Well then how is it we are standing here in front of you?"

"Sas, wait?" the old man called out.

"Because you two aren't human."

~~~~~~~~~~~~~~

Milly slowly twisted the brass knob to her daughter's bedroom. Silence was normal since Allora never got out of bed before ten in the morning on a Saturday. After quietly entering the room, Milly gently sat down onto the bed, next to the long hump where she assumed her oldest daughter was sleeping.

"Honey, wake up," Milly began, placing a hand on the hump. "We need to talk about what happened last night." There was no movement in the bed, but Milly continued anyway. "You see, there are things about your past... our past... that are a little odd, and... well... it's difficult to explain." Milly's eyes welled with tears. A flashback of emotional turmoil seeped into her thoughts. Fighting back the tears, she continued. "You see, we aren't exactly from here."

Just then, Bell slid past the door wearing elephant-patterned pajama pants, a Care Bear T- shirt, and an expression of intrigue. Her mother's comment caused a complete change of direction, and she spun around, leaning into the doorway. "What do you mean we aren't from here? I'm pretty sure I've lived in the same house all my life. The same room, in fact, which I think should change sometime soon..." she said, surveying her older sister's much-larger room.

"We have lived here all of your life, but we are not exactly from here."

"Well, obviously. Grandma and Grandpa live in England," Bell said, moving around the room.

"No, that's not what I meant."

Bell stopped when she noticed something out of place, in the area where her sister's head should have been. She walked around the bed.

"What I've been trying to tell your sister is—"

"You mean a stuffed animal?" Bell interrupted.

"What?"

Bell pulled back the goose-down comforter to reveal a fluffy brown bear and a column of pillows, posing as a body. The repetitive shuffling of sheets caused Bell to back off from the bed while her mother became increasingly frantic.

"You didn't think Allora would be that quiet with us in her room this early in the morning, did you?"

Irritated from sifting through the empty bed, Milly ran out of the room, "*May!*"

Sitting at the kitchen table, unsuspectingly reading the newspaper, May quickly jumped from her chair.

"She's gone," Milly said.

"What are you talking about?"

"Allora... she snuck out last night!" Milly paced back and forth, contemplating every potential punishment she could muster.

"This would never have happened if you had just told her the truth."

"We're not going into this again."

"Do you really think it matters now? Imagine what's going through her head. This has got to be frightening for her."

"And what should I say? 'Hey, Allora, your whole family is from another world, has the ability to manipulate molecules, and oh, by the way, there are strange mythical beasts trying to kill us?' Yeah, that is going to make things much less difficult," Milly said.

"We're aliens?" Bell asked, having slipped into the kitchen.

She stood, petrified by her family's cavalier conversation about their otherworldly origins. The shocked expressions on the two women's faces suggested they had forgotten Bell had been in earshot of their argument.

"Honey... I... Aaaaaah...." Milly had no retort for her blunder. Aunt May burst out laughing. "This isn't funny, May! My oldest daughter is missing, there is no way of knowing whether she is safe, and now my youngest thinks we're aliens."

"Sorry, but we kinda are," Aunt May murmured with pursed lips. She could see her sister becoming more fearful for Allora's safety.

"You're not helping," Milly said, turning her attention to her youngest.

"Bell... it's kind of hard to explain."

"How about you start at the part where we are from another world," Bell insisted.

Milly glanced over to Aunt May for assistance.

"Hey, don't look at me. You're the one who said it. This would have been a lot easier if this was explained last night, like I said."

May sat back down, crossed her arms, and shot a smug look at her sister. The argument from the night before still festered in the room. Aunt May had been adamant about full disclosure of their origins. The comment left Milly speechless, and unable to counter her argument. Instead, she turned back to her youngest daughter, knelt down, and grabbed her hands.

"Bell...." Milly paused, thinking back to a home world she hadn't seen in decades. "Have you ever had a dream that felt so real you had to pinch yourself just to wake up?" Bell nodded. "And in that dream, were there strange animals and beautiful landscapes not seen anywhere on Earth?" Bell nodded again. "Those dreams are of the world our family is from. They are a remnant connection that we all have."

"I always knew it felt real," Bell said, excited and yet, strangely, not surprised. Bell glanced back at her mother. "What's this place called?"

Milly took a deep breath. She was about to say the one word she hadn't said in over a decade. The name of her world had been locked away as a distant memory; a painful memory of betrayal, dishonesty, and death. Now, she had to face the reality of her family's past and the consequences of their actions so long ago.

"It's called Sonora."

Are you joking?" Allora asked, unable to comprehend what was said. "You mean we are from another world?"

Sas realized what he had done. "Uh oh...."

"It's alright, Sas," the old man told him. "They would have found out soon enough."

Allora felt like she was the only one kept from an inside joke. She couldn't make sense of her surroundings and it made her angry. She wanted answers.

"What is going on? Am I the only one who's lost?"

She spun in a circle, trying to find someone who could explain it to her.

"Actually, I'm as lost as you are," Tanner said, not moving his eyes away from Sas.

"You mean you have no idea what they're talking about either?"

"Nope, no idea," Tanner said. "Are you saying I'm from another world also?"

The old man moved in front of them, tapping his staff, projecting four balls of light into the air. He swirled the staff, and the balls of white light shot to the outer parts of the area, illuminating the rock slab. At this point, Allora and Tanner were so numb from the peculiarity of the past few days that they didn't even react to the mystical display.

"Both of you came here from Sonora when you were infants," the old man explained.

Allora never liked to be left in the dark. Now, she felt as though her entire life was false. But, she wasn't mad. Throughout her adolescence, she felt unlike those around her. Growing up in Sandy was difficult, because none of her classmates could relate to her odd personality. Katie had been the only one she was able to talk to. Then, an epiphany lit her consciousness as she connected the recent events.

"Katie and Dax!" she exclaimed.

"Yes, they are also from Sonora," the old man confirmed.

Bewilderment rapidly changed to anger as she realized how long Katie had kept the secrets of their mutually strange existence. Meanwhile, Tanner was marveling at how well the creature spoke.

"How do you know English so well?" he asked.

Sas had moved behind a tree, next to the mouth of the cave, and was rummaging through a bush for an item of seeming importance. In answer to Tanner's question, he popped his head up and said, "There are so many campers and random humans that come up here. I picked up on your language by constantly listening in on their conversations. Let's just say I've been around these woods for quite a while. Plus, the old man there taught me a few things." The expression on Sas' face changed. He shook his head and then continued his thought. "I'm still learning it, though. Like last week when this group of young humans was up here. They had a campfire and one guy said, 'Yo dog, wasssuppp.' That was something that I hadn't heard before." Sas looked at the children with confusion. "Why would you call another human by an animal's name? It doesn't make sense. Humans are really quite strange."

They all chuckled. Even Allora, who wasn't in a very good mood, cracked a smile. The old man had been quietly leaning on his staff the entire time, as if watching a theater production. Allora turned her attention to him. Her unanswered questions and the frustration of not knowing who she was kept eating away at her. The constant babbling of this creature was making things worse, since he would not stop talking about unrelated random subjects. Allora finally got to a point where she couldn't take it anymore.

"Am I going crazy? Is this actually real? I've got an eight-foot-tall hairy mythical beast telling me I'm an alien, an old man with a glowing staff, strange creatures trying to kill me, and just a few days ago my hands burst into flames."

Sas stopped talking. Everyone stared at Allora, who was breathing heavily, with anger, fear, and confusion seeping from every pore. To her, the atmosphere seemed too jovial for what had happened in the last days. Why weren't they more freaked out about what had almost killed them? How could they act so normal under the circumstances?

The old man broke the silence. "I think it's time for them to hear their story."

Sas hesitated. "Are you sure? You know how Milly is, and if she finds out I told her daughter about Sonora, she'll kill me."

"You know my mother?" Allora asked.

"Okay, I'll tell you what I know, and then I'll leave the rest up to Sumatra."

"Who is Sumatra?" Tanner asked.

Sas gestured over to the old man. "That would be Sumatra."

So much had gone on in the past few hours, and the old man's name had been the last thing on their minds.

"Starting this story is the hardest part," Sas said, looking up at Sumatra for guidance. "I'm not sure where to begin."

"How about you begin by telling them about where they are from, and who they are?"

"Well, you all are from a place called Sonora. Some believe it to be another world entirely, but mystics believe Sonora is a world parallel to Earth. The idea is that the events occurring here have an effect on those that happen in Sonora, and vice versa. I just love that phrase, 'vice versa,' don't you? I just heard it from some campers last week." He shook his head and continued, "Sonora is a much different world, though. One trip there and you'll know what I mean. It is full of all kinds of creatures, including the infamous warlocks such as myself," Sas said, putting his hand to his chest, beaming with pride. "You'd be amazed by how many different creatures live there."

"Wait, you're a warlock?" Tanner asked.

"Yes, as a matter a fact I am," Sas said.

"I thought that warlocks were supposed to be scarier," Tanner said, trying to hold back his laughter.

"I'm pretty sure I saw you screaming when I arrived," Sas said.

The quarterback wasn't one to back down. "Maybe an initial reaction, until I heard you speak." Tanner continued, "I thought warlocks were supposed to... well... be warriors. Hence the name."

The mood of the conversation changed suddenly. Sas stood up from where he had been sitting and slowly stepped toward the young man. Tanner moved backward and swallowed hard. Sas bent down, looked his subject directly in the eye, and studied the boy before him.

"You have no idea what war is," Sas said in a deep, soft voice. His eyes slanted downward. He looked calm, but very serious. "You will soon find out, though, and you will wish otherwise. Your future is a painful one. Tread lightly, for you will need the warlocks for what is to come." Sas slowly stepped back and returned to searching the bushes for some lost item.

Tanner put his head down. His eyes glazed over and he contemplated the warning. All his life, Tanner was the one who had it all figured out. He had dreamt of graduating, playing football, and hopefully making it as a professional athlete. Now, he felt clueless, confused, and scared of his future. This creature seemed to know more about his life than he did. Tanner felt the soft touch of a finger upon his palm. Allora inched her fingers in between his, interweaving them at her side. Her soft touch eased his confusion. She knew exactly how he felt, and her compassion showed as her eyes tried to relieve his anxiety.

"Can you continue?" Allora asked Sas. "I need to know what I am."

"Of course," Sas replied. "Earth's history has labeled your species by many names. Some have called you witches or wizards, others have called you gods. I stick with the title of Titans, which are those Sonorians who came from the world's capital, Titanis."

It didn't make any sense to Allora. If anyone else besides an eight-foot Sasquatch had told her, she wouldn't believe them. The problem was that it created more questions than answers.

"I don't understand," Allora said. "I don't feel any different."

"That's because you haven't reached the age of maturation. Your body hasn't absorbed the necessary hadrons needed to demonstrate your magical abilities," Sas explained.

"What are hadrons?" Allora asked.

"Sumatra, you want to take this one?" Sas asked. "I'm not really an expert on the subject. I was never very good with that science stuff."

"We will discuss that later," Sumatra said. "Why don't you tell them about the night they arrived here?"

"Okay... So, Tanyon was the first to show up," Sas said, sending puzzled looks throughout the audience.

Tanner spoke up, "Who is Tanyon?" He asked.

"Well, that would be you, mister," Sas explained. "That was the name given to you at birth. Tanner is the name that they gave you when you came here." Light started to illuminate the rock slab upon which they stood. Above, the sky turned a bluish tint, an indication that the morning sun was fast approaching. "Where was I?" Sas asked himself, looking up at the blue morning sky as if trying to recover a distant memory. "Oh yes! I remember it vividly because your aunt was so frantic. I hadn't seen anyone come through the Gateway in a while. I ran to the exit location and found Lizi on the ground crying. Her face was cut up and her clothes were burnt all over, but she seemed alright."

"Why was my aunt hurt?" Tanner asked, upset that his aunt had never told him about this.

"She will have to tell you about that," Sas said in a tone suggesting compliance. "It's not my place."

Tanner wasn't happy about this but decided to remain quiet, partly because he wanted hear the rest of the story, but mostly because he was a little frightened to challenge the beast after their last confrontation. Sas cleared his throat and carried on with the story.

"Allora, you arrived a couple of hours later. You both were so small. Afterward, I put your families up in my cave until we could figure out what to do. Then, we set off down the mountain to find homes for you guys to live in. Of course, Katie and Dax came ten years later."

Sas got up from his seat and quickly disappeared into his cave. Tanner and Allora thought back to the rock quarry and how their two best friends seemed to know exactly what was happening.

Allora swung back around and yelled into the cave, "That's it?" She wasn't satisfied with the short story.

"Why don't you two come with me," Sumatra said, gesturing with his staff to follow him up a dirt path to the rocks above.

Allora followed Sumatra and Tanner up the trail.

~~~~~~~~~~~~~~~

Sas came back out of the cave, having finally found what he had been looking for, but his intended audience had left the area.

"What? Where did everyone go?" He said with a frown. "I didn't really think my storytelling was that bad, was it?" Sas was about to go back into his cave when he heard a sound echo from the forest. He crouched, sniffing the dew-filled morning air. His nose picked up on a rancid mix of reptile and moldy vegetables. He knew exactly what type of creature produced that putrid smell. "Rover," he said under his breath.

Crouching down on all fours, Sas prepared to attack. The bushes shuffled from side to side, and a silhouette appeared in between the parted branches. Leaping forward, Sas connected with the intruder's rib cage, crashing into the moss-covered trunk of a fallen tree. He twisted the body over and pinned its limbs to the ground. Beneath his furry legs lay Dax's body, surprised by the sudden impact of the beast.

"What are you—" Dax yelled, coughing and gasping for air, "—doing!"

Katie parted a bush, finally making it up to the edge of the rocky outcrop. Noticing what happened, Katie burst out laughing.

"Oops... I thought you were a Rover."

"Why would you think that?" Dax asked, pulling himself out from under

Sas' furry legs.

"You have a Rover's smell. Sorry."

Katie hiked up the last few feet and stood on the slab at the edge of the cave entrance.

"Hey, maybe you should be a little more prepared, bro," Katie said.

"Prepared for a two-ton orangutan?"

"You do tackling drills in football practice, don't you?"

Dax ignored his sister's comment and limped to the cave. "Where are Tanner and Allora?"

"Sumatra took them up to the lookout to tell them about Sonora," Sas said.

"So, now they know," Katie said.

Dax turned to his sister. "What are we going to tell them?"

"How about the truth?" Katie exclaimed.

She was tired of keeping secrets from her best friend. Years of lying about where she came from had taken its toll.

"We can't tell them everything, especially Tanner," Dax said, not happy with what they must do, but he knew there was no other choice. "You know what Dad said. We have a responsibility greater than our friendships. We must never forget that." Katie gave in to her brother's request. There was more at stake, and if they failed in their mission, dire circumstances would have deadly results.

"What are you two hooligans babbling about?" Sas asked.

"None of your business, Chewbacca," Dax replied.

"Chewbacca? What is that? Is that candy?" Sas said, licking his lips. "I love candy. My favorite is Sugar Daddies."

"You're weird."

"Yeah, well you get stuck up in the mountains by yourself for centuries and then see how weird you are."

"He has a point. Besides, I kind of like him," Katie said, smiling at the goofy creature. "He's like me, except hairier."

"Thank you, Ms. Katara. I like you too."

Sas had been up in the mountains of the Northwest part of America for over one hundred years. Sasquatch was known as a Guardian. It was a position that he earned from his father, who had taken over for his father, and so on. The Guardian of the Gateways was a very prestigious honor, only bestowed upon someone by the previous Guardian. There were thirty-one Guardians roaming the mountains of Earth. Some of the well-known warlock Guardians earned human names, such as Yeti in the Himalayas, his twin brother Abominable Snowman, and of course, Sasquatch.

The role of the Guardian was to protect the Gateways against unauthorized passage to Earth. Sonorians couldn't pass through the Gateways unless they had a key, which was an ancient artifact linked with the Gateway's cosmic energy path. The Guardians moved among the mountains in relation to the changing Gateway locations. The secrets to discovering the Gateways' locations were known only by Guardians and an organization of powerful peacekeeping Sonorians called Keepers. The exclusivity of this information had kept a balance between Earth and Sonora since the wars of the Gods, when humans were but slaves. Ever since Allora's family and friends had arrived, the delicate balance between the two worlds had shifted. Sas' obligation to guard the Gateways had become even more crucial to the stability of the two worlds. He could sense that it was only going to get worse. Much worse.

Chapter 5

Sunrise

Mt. Hood rose up in the sky, like the set of a Broadway play as the curtains are opened. It briefly blocked the sun from illuminating the forest valley, hiding the orange orb in the Eastern horizon. As they finished the steep incline, Sumatra, Allora, and Tanner moved out onto the rocky overhang just as the sun began peeking around the side of the mountain. The sun's rays warmed their skin. A blanket of pine trees extended as far as the eye could see. The viewpoint acted like a watchtower, giving the sentry a clear view of the entire forest. This surely was the reason Sas had chosen this location to be his home.

"Beautiful, isn't it?" Sumatra said. He let the children have a moment in peace before returning to the story of their origin.

Tanner and Allora surveyed the landscape, nodding their heads.

Sumatra began, "I'm sorry that so much has been kept from you both. Your families decided it was best to wait until you were older to explain the truth about where you come from. It wasn't until your episode at school that we decided it was time," Sumatra said, directing this last comment to Allora.

"How did you know what happened at school?" Allora asked.

"Your outburst at school sent out a traceable energy signature that was detectable for miles," Sumatra explained. "I knew that if there was a creature from our home world in the area, it would have sensed the energy output, just as I had."

Guilt crawled into her skin and permeated her pores.

"This was not your fault," Sumatra said. "You had no idea. None of us knew you were capable of doing what you did at such an early age. What you did is very rare. Most Sonorians don't even have the capabilities to Focus energy until they are at least eighteen years of age. And to produce an element like fire is quite extraordinary."

"This all seems kind of strange. Are you trying to tell me I can conduct electricity?"

"Not electricity. It's pure energy. Everything in nature contains energy. Most Earth creatures, such as humans, just don't have the mental capacity for energy absorption. You, however, are Sonorian. Our minds and bodies have that capability. But harnessing such energy is a skill that takes time and a lot of practice."

"How was I able to do it, if most my age can't?" Allora asked.

Sumatra turned around to look Allora in the eye. "There have been a few early maturations, but they are rare."

"So, no one from this other planet has my abilities?" Allora asked.

"Very few. And it's not just another planet." Sumatra's audience was visibly puzzled. He continued his story. "Sonora is a world that exists on a parallel dimensional plane of this world. They used to be the same world. Essentially, they are the same planet, but separated across the galaxy on the same dimensional place." The perplexed expressions upon Allora's and Tanner's faces were an obvious sign of confusion. "But to most this is just a theory, and not necessarily popular amongst the Sonorian elite. It is where we all come from, and as Sas said, it's a world full of magical creatures, like you and I. Long ago, our two worlds were separated by an ancient powerful magic, which created the Gateways between the worlds. Before the creation of the Keepers, Sonorians passed through the Gateways without restraint."

"What are the Keepers?" Allora asked.

"The Keepers are a primordial organization that kept the secrets of the Gateways and the history of our two worlds hidden to safeguard the human civilization. The Keepers, along with the Guardians, protect the Gateways against unauthorized passage between worlds."

"I don't understand. Why are the Keepers able to dictate who can go through?" Tanner asked.

"That is one of the reasons why you are here. Some believe this world shouldn't be guarded and magical creatures should have free rein over the human world, which was the case during ancient human civilizations on Earth. I'm sure your history teacher has told you of the ancient civilizations of Greece, Rome, and Egypt. Those humans were manipulated into thinking Sonorians were Gods. These so-called Gods were treated as such, while their human counterparts suffered as slaves. It's really a matter of free will. Humans were subjected to the rules and obedience these Gods commanded. Can you see how that might've been bad?" Sumatra asked.

Tanner realized what could happen if the Gateways were open. Sumatra knew Tanner had the same inner struggle that many in Sonora had been through before.

"What did you mean; one of the reasons why we were here?" Allora asked.

"This is a subject that must be addressed by your families. I have probably said too much already."

Allora gave Sumatra a look of protest, but he stopped her before she could say anything. "This is non-negotiable."

"But—" Allora argued but her mouth shut close without intending to.

She grabbed her mouth, trying to figure out why she wasn't able to speak. Sumatra had shut it closed with the wave of his hand. Allora let go of her mouth, calmly breathed through her nose, and stood with her hands crossed.

Tanner decided it was better to ask permission. "Sumatra, can I ask one more question?"

"Yes, but I can't promise I will answer it," Sumatra replied.

Tanner paused for a moment, not sure if he really wanted to know the answer. "Were my parents really killed in a car accident?" he asked, reluctantly.

Sumatra placed his hand on the young boy's shoulder. The gesture was intended to comfort him for an answer that would just create more questions, "No, they didn't," he said.

Tanner chose not to continue the inquiry. The old man's tone suggested that he wasn't going to tell him anything further, and he thought it would be better to discuss it with his aunt.

The force holding Allora's mouth shut was released, and she let out a breath. She forgot about the forced silence when she saw how upset Tanner had become after hearing the old man's words.

Allora compassionately rubbed his arm, and whispered, "Are you okay?"

Tanner let out a breath and laughed listlessly. Allora did the same, realizing it was a stupid question. The old man moved away from the ledge, headed down the trail, and waved for them to follow.

"Come. We have much more to discuss, but I want the other two to hear it."

"Other two?" asked Allora.

They descended the steep hill to find Sas, Katie, and Dax standing in a circle at the entrance to the cave.

"Oh, there you are," Dax said. "Took you long enough."

Allora made her way to the area in front of the cave. She wasn't sure how to feel. Katie had been her friend for the past six years, and they'd had told each other everything. She wasn't ready to forgive just yet.

Sumatra was the last to make it down the path. He walked across the cave opening to inform Sas about the previous events. The explanation of the Sonora was far too important not to be talked about first, but the fact that a Rover was roaming around the woods was highly significant.

"The children were attacked last night by a Rover," he said, calmly.

Sas' eyes popped open. He stepped back from Sumatra and said, "That's why you two smelled so funny! Why didn't you tell me earlier?"

"Sas, I needed you here to explain their origins before we got into the subject of the Rovers. It wouldn't have made sense to Tanner or Allora," said Sumatra. This didn't appear make the Sas any happier. "I hit him with a hadron burst. He's probably far away by now."

"I'm a Guardian, and I need to know if one of the King's agents is lurking in my forest, attacking humans."

The conversation perplexed Tanner and Allora.

"An agent?" Allora asked.

"The Rover you encountered is a creature from Sonora," Sas said. "Rovers are reptilian creatures that can break apart into smaller creatures to act as spies. The smaller creatures are its arms and legs. They have scales for skin and small, sharp teeth. The fingers and toes pull back to reveal a face on the palms, and soles of the feet." The creature's distinctive features had been embedded into the children's memory the instant they had seen it. "The trick is to find the main body when the limbs are separated, because the torso can't move very fast. It can only extend four very short legs and is therefore vulnerable. When the Rover puts itself back together, it is very quick and strong. Not someone you want to mess with unless you know how to defend yourself."

"But why would it want to attack us?" Tanner asked.

"Because, we are outlaws of Sonora—" Sas replied.

"Sas!" Sumatra interrupted.

Allora's mind quickly went to images of old Westerns and tales of bank robbers. "So you're telling me I'm like the daughter of the Al Capone of Sonora?"

"No. What he meant to say is that we left Sonora because the situation there became too dangerous," Sumatra said. "When we all came here, it was because malicious individuals had taken over the world, and persecuted anyone who opposed them. This included the entire Keeper organization, which Milly and I were a part of."

The morning light had now fully illuminated their location, and the sun was warming the cool air. Sumatra knocked his staff against the slab of rock at his feet, and the glow from the four surrounding balls of light subsided.

"I will have to go into more detail later. Right now, I need to go tell your families where you all are. Sas, I need you to make sure Dax and Katie weren't followed."

"We took every precaution," Katie insisted.

"Sas, check anyway," Sumatra said, directing the order to Sas.

"Before I forget..." Sas said, awkwardly sidestepping toward the pile of objects he had removed from the cave. He quickly rummaged through a potato sack.

"Aha!" he said, pulling out a beige rolled-up piece of parchment.

He handed the item to Allora, his face somber as he placed it into her hands.

"Uncle Ben asked me to give this to you when you were ready for it," Sas said, unable to hide his grief.

When she was ten years old, her mother had arrived home one night with bloodshot eyes from crying. Her uncle Ben had died from a supposed avalanche on Mt. Hood. Since Allora had grown up with no father, Uncle Ben had been the only male presence in her life. His death had left a gaping hole in her heart that she had never been able to fill.

Holding back her emotions, Allora said, "How do you know my uncle?"

"Your uncle never died in an avalanche," Sumatra said, moving closer to the young girl. "He was killed by one of the same agents you encountered last night. He died to keep us all safe."

"Your uncle was one of the most brave and selfless individuals I've ever had the privilege of knowing. He told me to wait until you were older, and when you were ready, to give you that parchment."

Allora stared down at the foreign object in her hands. It felt light and worn. The edges were uneven and torn. She slowly unrolled it, exposing a sequence of numbers.

8 5 3 2 1 1 0

On the other side there was a poem inscribed delicately. The writing was intricately done, but barely legible. At the bottom, it read, "The Eye of the Titans," in beautiful cursive. Allora looked up for answers but Sas seemed in no mood to explain. Wiping the tears from her cheek, Allora read through the poem.

At last you come to the cavern of gold.

Grand monuments to the gods of old.

Do not take more than you seek.

For penalty of greed will destroy the weak.

Before she could inquire further, Sas turned and retreated into his cave. "Follow me," he yelled back.

Tanner grabbed Allora's hand and dragged her through the dark opening. Katie and Dax followed. The path was only slightly illuminated by a faint light at the end of the tunnel. Allora and Tanner inched into a chamber, where sunlight shone a spotlight through a crack in the ceiling. Sas stood, staring intently at the rock wall in the corner of the cave chamber. There was nothing special inside. It was a hollowed-out moist cave, with no distinctive character suggesting someone lived there.

Sas faced the far wall, slowly swinging his arms in a strange circular motion and expelling electricity from his palms. The gritty stone wall glowed as Sas repeated his circular motions in different patterns. When he stopped, light shot outward. The piercing light imploded into stone, which then formed an almost fluid exterior, which shimmered strangely.

"This way," Sas said.

The tall, hairy creature sank into the wall and disappeared. Allora and Tanner were speechless. They remained motionless, unable to comprehend the impossibility of their surroundings. Undeterred, Katie and Dax followed Sas, vanishing into the wall. Tanner moved closer, apprehensively placing his finger into the substance. It felt cool and smooth, like putting a hand into wet cement. Tanner pushed forward, engulfing himself into the vertical wall of liquid stone. Then he, too, disappeared. Allora was left alone, still hesitant about proceeding. A hand popped out suddenly, causing her to jump backward. One finger, bending at the knuckled, motioned her to follow. Finally, she obliged, moving slowly through the sparkling wall.

Chapter 6

Truth

Upon reaching the other side of the mysterious wall, the teens' mouths dropped at the sight of an intricately designed cavernous chamber, lit by large glowing orbs that hung from the ceiling. Along the walls lay a myriad of trinkets, knick-knacks, and various objects commonly found in the rubbish. The junk seemed to be arranged in a peculiar manner, forming a vast and eccentric sculpture. Soda cans, metal spatulas, barbeque grills, tent poles, magnets, car doors, hats, lighters, water bottles, and other objects had been placed together to form an array of grand art, which lined the path into a grand hall full of cascading waterfalls.

A shadow moved across the expansive rock ceiling as Sas moved out from behind a strange, aqueduct-type system. Made of sheets of aluminum cans, it began at the top of a small waterfall and ended in an luminous aluminum bowl. Sas motioned the group over.

"I'm sure you all are thirsty. This is a natural spring. It is safe to drink from, and you can wash up over there," Sas said, pointing down the path toward the back of the cave, where the water emptied into a large, crystal clear pool. "I've gotta go."

He left, disappearing through the wall and leaving the four friends to explore the cave alone.

After a moment of silence, Tanner said, "How could you guys keep all of this from us?" Dax pulled the top of his head out of the water, flung his hair back, and began walking up the short incline.

"We had no choice."

"That's your excuse? You always have a choice," Allora insisted.

"That's not fair, and you know it," Katie protested. "As soon as we got here, your mother made it very clear not to say a word about where we came from."

"My mother?"

"Yeah," Dax snapped. "She has been at the center of all of this. We all take our orders from her."

Allora felt even more betrayed. Nothing could have prepared her for the shock and confusion she felt. Sitting down on a torn motor home couch, Allora tried to absorb what was happening. The alternate reality of who she was began to sink in, just as she was sinking into the cushions. Just a week had passed, and Allora had gone from worrying about finals to worrying about mythical assassin creatures from another world. And all along, it was her mother who had kept the secret hidden.

"Mom, how could you do this to me?" Allora whispered to herself.

~~~~~~~~~~~~~~

Milly could sense something wrong. Whether it was motherly instinct or just plain intuition, she felt a deep sense of worry. As a mother, Milly held the delusional belief that she could protect her children from her past. When she had arrived on Earth, creating a safe environment to raise Allora and Bell had become her ultimate objective. Her entire focus was on keeping their pasts hidden and staying under the radar of the agents placed on Earth to search for those who opposed the ruling class of Sonora.

Keeping this secluded Sonorian rebel utopia was a delusion, and a delusion Milly tried to hold onto for as long as she could. Now, the world she had created in this small Earth community was becoming a nightmare. Not knowing the whereabouts of her eldest brought back the lingering memories of the night her younger brother had died. "May..." she said, bursting with emotions. "I can't lose her."

"Sis, we won't," May said, grasping her sister. "Allora is a smart and resilient young woman. Plus..."

May trailed off when she saw the floorboards begin to spin. They melted downward, an act that was followed by the appearance of a gray-haired old man.

"...I made sure Sumatra was keeping an eye on her."

The floor underneath Sumatra solidified, leaving no mark or indication of his strange entrance. Milly quickly snapped off questions. "Where's my daughter? Is she alright? What happened?"

"Allora is fine," he said, his tone suggesting another detail that he was more reluctant to mention. "She and the other three are waiting in Sas' cave right now."

From the beginning of their seclusion on Earth, Milly had put the entire community on her shoulders. She had been the leader and first line of defense against any who would try to harm the Sonorian rebels. Her responsibility had made her blind to their old world and the struggles many still faced at the hands of the ruling class of Sonora. This stubborn isolationist attitude wouldn't allow the children to be ready for an inevitable confrontation. Sumatra knew this, but had been so far unable to convince Milly of their predicament. They had argued over the matter, and had not been on friendly terms since.

"We have a problem," Sumatra began.

"No kidding," Milly replied, unhappy with the stalled explanation.

Sumatra calmly ignored her sarcasm. "We have a Rover in the area"

The words had barely left his mouth before May jumped in. "I knew it!"

"How do you know?" Milly asked.

"There was an incident in the woods at an abandoned rock quarry. Allora, Tanner, and most of their friends were there."

Milly's eyes popped open. ""Did anyone get hurt?"

"One of the Earth kids got knocked out, but he's going to be fine. I got Tanner and Allora out of there safely and took them to the lookout."

Pacing back and forth, Milly absorbed the information. A gut-wrenching feeling of fear filled her body as she relived her most painful memories.

"I think it's time, Milly," Sumatra said, gently placing his hand upon her shoulder. "There is no more denying her destiny. She is far more powerful than we ever imagined. If we don't act now, there will be no safe place for any of us. Even here on Earth."

She had been dreading this moment, but Milly finally gave in to the realization of her daughter's inevitable fate. For so long, she had rejected the thought of having her daughters involved with their war. However, Sumatra was right. The malevolent agents of Sonora would stop at nothing to kill the children of the rebellion. Putting off their training had left them completely vulnerable. Milly sat down onto the sofa. Looking up at her sister, she exhaled loudly. May sat down, holding Milly's hand; her soft compassionate eyes knowing the gravity of their situation.

"Can I see my daughter now?" Milly asked.

Sumatra nodded, shifting his body to create a circular motion with his staff. The floor melted downward, and they all disappeared into the portal.

~~~~~~~~~~~~~

"You are supposed to be my best friend! That means we don't keep any secrets!" Allora was in Katie's face, unable to get over Katie's betrayal.

"You're not listening to me," Katie snapped back. "You don't understand the situation."

"Well, then, why don't you explain it to us?" Tanner asked, forcefully.

"It's not our place," Dax said.

All four were arguing as the ground gave way. Sumatra, Aunt May, Milly, and Bell popped in, followed by Tanner's Aunt Lizi.

"Mom," Allora yelled, and ran to hug her. Milly grabbed her daughter, held her close, and sighed with relief. However, the reunion turned ugly.

"How could you sneak out like that?" Milly started.

"How could you keep all of this from me?" Allora responded.

Tanner got into a similar argument with his aunt, and pretty soon, they were all arguing with the exception of Sumatra. Annoyed, Sumatra slammed his staff into the ground, causing a forceful wave that pushed the group backward into the couches and chairs that lined the edges of the metal sculptures. After silencing the room, Sumatra addressed everyone.

"This is no time for arguing," he said softly. "We are on the precipitous. Our lives, and the lives of those we fight for are in danger. If we have any hope of survival, we must work together or else everything we have worked to protect will be destroyed."

Sumatra turned toward Allora and Tanner. "Milly and Lizi kept our past a secret because they wanted you two to grow up without the fear and anxiety we all experience on a daily basis. They wanted a normal life for you. For the past sixteen years, we have been hunted by the forces of the Sonorian hierarchy. Last night, you met an agent of the Sonorian Royal Guard. They will stop at nothing to kill or capture any of the old rebellion, which challenged the authority of Sonora. We are that rebellion, or at least a part of it."

"No!" Milly jumped up from her seat. "This is not the old days. These are only kids. They are not going to be coerced into fighting."

"Well, why not?" Tanner asked.

"Because we don't want any of you to get hurt, or even killed," Aunt Lizi said.

Allora fought back tears. "So, we are just supposed to go about our lives as if everything is normal? And what if one of those creatures attacks us again?" Thinking back to the previous night, Allora cringed at her feelings of helplessness. She felt completely vulnerable against such a powerful opponent. She didn't want to ever experience the feeling again.

Milly could clearly see the fear in her daughter's eyes. It was the same set of emotions she experienced the night they came to Earth. Against her stubborn nature, Milly reluctantly gave in to the idea of preparing the children.

"Alright, Sumatra... May... I give my consent." Allora wasn't sure what it meant, but she could tell her mother was nervous about the decision. "On one condition... Any training must be done in the outer realm."

Allora asked, "What's the outer realm?"

"You'll find out soon enough, honey," May answered.

"Only the basics," Milly snapped. "There will be no advanced Keeper training!"

"And what about when they are ready?" Sumatra said.

"I will be the judge of that," Milly told him.

There was a general consensus among the adults. It was a compromise many had been waiting for since the last time an agent had entered the area. That was the night Allora's uncle had been killed. None wanted to relive the painful events of that evening, and they had been split about the children's training ever since. Milly had denied any training, but secretly, Sumatra had told Dax and Katie to instruct Allora and Tanner on the fundamentals of hand-to-hand combat. They were rudimentary lessons, but it had given them a base for instruction on more complex fighting tactics.

Milly walked across the room, tripping on an old, broken hubcap lying on the ground. She winced and said, "I wish that dumb furry Guardian would get rid of this junk."

A large figure jumped out from behind a pile of tires. "It's not junk!" Sas said.

"Have you been hiding there the whole time?" Milly asked.

"I came in a few minutes ago," he said. "I didn't want to interrupt your conversation."

Sas joined the rest of the group, purposefully not looking Milly in the eye.

"And I guess you're responsible for telling them all about Sonora?" Milly asked, giving Sas a judgmental, disapproving stare. Since youth, Milly had been able to invoke fear in any individual simply with her eyes. Her commanding stare changed. She looked to her daughter and grabbed Sas' arm.

"Since you are so willing to tell them of their past, it will be your responsibility to make sure they have a future," Milly said, turning to face the tall, hairy creature. "You will be their bodyguard. If they are not at school or at home, it will be on you to make sure they are safe."

Sas nodded quickly. There was no debate. Milly's order was direct and forceful, as if spoken by a military officer. Even Allora knew when not to rebel against her mother. The brief silence was filled with the sound of cascading waterfalls splashing into the cave pool.

"Were you able to track it?" Sumatra asked.

Sas shook his head. "I lost the trail."

Gasps followed.

"Isn't that good?" Allora inquired. "I thought we don't want the thing around."

"Allora—" Sumatra stopped short, receiving a discreet glare from Milly.

"We need to leave," Milly ordered.

"But I want to know more!" Allora protested.

Ignoring Allora, Milly grabbed her other daughter, who had remained speechless the entire time, and motioned the others to follow. She made a circling motion with her hands, opening a portal into the ground. Swirling light escaped the vortex, causing Allora to marvel at her mother's gifts.

"Seriously, you have to teach me how to do that!" Allora said.

Milly and Bell disappeared into the ground, while Aunt May whispered something into Sumatra's ear. Then, she winked at Allora and followed the other two into the quicksand-like portal. An overwhelming feeling of trepidation engulfed Allora's mind. The faces of the people she held closest revealed a quiet unease, which she had never seen before. In that moment, she felt a kinship to Pandora from the Greek story. Her episode at the cheerleading practice had opened up a Pandora-like box of evils. Why didn't anyone ask questions about Pandora, the woman? Why had she opened the box? Was it really her fault? And yet she was known throughout centuries as the one woman who brought about the evils humankind had to fight daily.

A curious excitement about her special abilities turned into angst. Allora was too smart not to see the terror in the eyes of those in the cave. Before she exited through the portal, she took one last look at Tanner, feeling even closer to her childhood friend. Smiling slightly, Tanner's simple stare was enough to settle Allora's nerves. But nothing could free her from the responsibility of her new life. A powerful burst of emotion had opened a box of evils. Pandora's guilt was now her own. Soon she would have to make the dreadful decision to either wither at the overwhelming obstacles ahead or fight against the fateful connection to the Greek myth. With that, she stepped backward and shot through the portal.

Chapter 7

Sheriff's Visit

Instantaneously, Allora flew out of the portal, crashing into the couch with both feet pointing skyward; the blankets clung to her due to the static electricity from the energy the portal created. Allora pulled her head back and sneered at her snickering family. Milly, Aunt May, and even Bell had gracefully landed on both feet.

"How did you not fly out of that thing?" Allora asked, swinging her feet to the carpet.

Disoriented from portal travel, Allora tried to focus her eyes. The room spun around as she sat in a daze.

"You've got to tighten your muscles so you don't get off balance," Aunt May answered. "Porting can be tricky sometimes."

"Can you go feed the animals?" Milly asked. "I didn't get a chance this morning."

Allora made no effort to acknowledge her mother's request. Mother and daughter stared at each other without emotion, unsure of how to address each other. Being lied to about her past made Allora angry, but a part of her could understand why the truth was hidden. Allora quietly left the room, walked through laundry room door, crossed the gravel path past the garden, and unlatched the chicken coop.

When Allora entered the coop, the chickens swarmed, pecking at her feet as she sprinkled feed throughout the area. The ordinary routine task of feeding the animals seemed so odd and insignificant after her ordeal. How could she live a normal life with the knowledge that she had assassins trying to kill her and a connection with a strange home world she'd never seen before?

Allora closed the gate, and two dogs leapt up onto her chest, snapping her back to reality. She stepped backward, losing her footing and falling to the ground. The dogs took advantage of their opportunity, ferociously licking their owner's face as if they had experienced centuries of separation. Allora pushed their heads aside, laughing as she tried to escape the slobber.

"Rex, Cody!" she yelled, still laughing at how excited they were to see her.

Finally able to sit upright, Allora took some time to play with her Labrador retrievers. They had an odd power of being able to calm her nerves and make her smile. Whenever stress was overwhelming, Allora spent time with her dogs, and all of the worry would go away. This made her think about school. She had completely forgotten about finals the following week.

Studying for her finals was never too difficult, though. Allora had never received anything less than an A-minus on her final grades. This semester would be no different; even with the distractions of assassins, strange creatures, portals, energy bursts, and stories of alien worlds. There was one more distraction that Allora had forgotten about: the old parchment she had received from Sas slipped out of her belt and landed on the ground as she went to the back door.

The parchment hadn't been torn, creased, or weathered from rolling around with the dogs. Allora had assumed the parchment material would be fragile. Picking it up from the ground, she decided to inquire about the item. She walked through the laundry room and found her aunt in the kitchen.

"Aunt May, what's the Eye of the Titans?"

The reaction from her aunt was frightening. With bug-eyes and held breath, Aunt May charged Allora, clasping her hands on her niece's mouth. Milly turned the corner from the living room.

"What was that honey?" Milly asked, entering the kitchen. "I didn't quite hear your question."

Aunt May gestured with a finger against pursed lips, suggesting silence.

Sensing the fear in her aunt's eyes, Allora leaned around her aunt's body. "Oh, nothing Mom," she said. "I was just wondering..." Allora tossed around ideas, trying to improvise a question. "...when we could go back to Sas' cave."

Allora watched as her mother analyzed the two women and their peculiar body language.

"You're going to have to wait for a while before going back there. It's not safe right now. We need to act normal," Milly said, directing the latter comment to her sister, who glanced back over her shoulder.

Milly gave her sister a questioning stare, and then went to her bedroom. Once the area was clear, Aunt May grabbed her niece and pulled her close.

"Where did you learn about the Eye of the Titans?" Aunt May whispered.

"Sas told me about it," Allora answered, unsure about informing Aunt May about the parchment.

"Listen to me very carefully," Aunt May ordered, pausing to regain her composure. "You are never to utter those words in front of your mother."

Allora didn't understand.

"Ever," Aunt May said quietly.

"I got it," Allora snapped back.

Allora had never seen her aunt so serious before. The tone of her voice was one of sheer fright. It was as if the Eye of the Titans was forbidden, evoking fear, anger, and trepidation. Aunt May gently grabbed her niece's shoulder in an unspoken apology, and then left the kitchen for the seclusion of her bedroom. Placing her fingertips on the torn edges of the parchment, Allora couldn't comprehend why her aunt was so scared. Was this Eye of the Titans something to be feared? And why couldn't she mention it to her mother?

Allora sat down on the living room couch and thought about her life. With so much happening in the last twenty-four hours, Allora had forgotten about her lack of sleep. Heavy eyes and the soft couch cushions allowed her to fall asleep quickly.

Not even a minute had passed before a loud, hollow bang jolted her awake. Allora glanced back and forth. Then, the bang happened again. It was a knock on the door.

"Allora, can you please get that?" Milly asked from down the hall.

Allora rolled her sleepless eyes, reluctantly getting off the couch. Unhappy about being awoken, she twisted the front door knob and aggressively swung open the large wooden door. Her eyes opened wide, adrenaline kicking in. Her eyebrows raised and her heart skipped a beat as soon as she saw who was standing in her doorway.

"Uh... hi, Sheriff Newton," Allora said.

Sternly staring back, the sheriff asked, "Is your mother home?"

"Yeah, she's here," Allora said, turning her head without taking her eyes off of the officer. "Mom? Sheriff Newton is here," she yelled.

Allora could hear her mother's footsteps coming quickly down the hallway. She had a very distinctive walk. Milly came into the room and walked up behind her daughter.

"Hello, Sheriff, won't you come in," Milly said softly.

Allora was afraid. She had no idea what the sheriff was doing here, but she figured it was because of what had happened at the quarry. The other students must have called it in once they got back. Allora wasn't sure what to do. She had never been a good liar, and the police always made her nervous. Allora made a break for the hallway and was about halfway down the corridor when her mother noticed the escape.

"Allora, you need to be here for this," Milly said, motioning her daughter to have a seat on the couch next to her.

Reluctantly, Allora walked over and sat down. She wasn't very happy with the situation, but she couldn't do anything about it. Allora looked at her mother, trying to silently tell her that she was crazy, but Milly just smiled back.

The sheriff took off his hat and placed it on the coffee table. Then he said, "Milly, this whole business at the rock quarry is not good. I had half the town calling and asking me whether there were strange animals roaming around attacking people. I mean, what is going on? Is there something I should know?"

Milly sat up straight. "Sheriff, the creature that attacked the kids the other night was a Rover."

Allora spun around. "Mom! What are you doing?" Why was she telling the sheriff about this creature from another world?

The sheriff ignored Allora's outburst. "Do we know if there were any others?" he asked.

"No, only one Rover," Milly answered. This made Allora spin back around toward the sheriff. She looked back and forth between them until Milly said, "Honey, Sheriff Newton is just like us. He's from Sonora as well."

Allora sat back in the couch and inhaled rapidly as if a large boulder had been removed from her stomach. "You realize you almost gave me a heart attack," she said, still surprised. "How many more are there?"

"Many more. We will discuss that later," Milly said, directing her attention back to the sheriff.

"Were you able to keep it quiet?"

"Yeah, I blamed it on a family of cougars spotted in the area. Fortunately, they bought the story."

"Well, that's good. We believe the Rover wasn't able to identify any of the children. Sumatra did hit him with an energy burst, so he does know that Sonorians are here. My guess is he will find others to help him search the area."

"Well, that's *not* good." The sheriff put his head down for a moment of thought. Then, he said, "I'll have to increase our patrols."

Both adults stood up and shook hands. "Thanks Newt. I appreciate all of the work you're doing," Milly said.

The sheriff nodded his head and went out the front door. Milly watched his patrol car roll down the long driveway and onto the main road. When she turned around in the doorway, her daughter was standing a foot away.

"Alright, now who else is from Sonora?" Allora asked with arms folded tightly across her chest.

Milly directed Allora to sit on the couch. "There is something I need to tell you," Milly said, looking straight into Allora's eyes. "Allora, that creature's sole purpose on this planet is to find the children of the rebellion and kill them. Specifically, the Rovers are after the children of the Keepers, which means you and Bell. I didn't know if I should tell you, but I believe you are old enough to know the truth." Milly's words hit Allora like a ton of bricks. This wasn't exactly news Allora wanted to hear.

"Why?"

"It's complicated."

"This whole thing is complicated, Mom."

Milly smiled, acknowledging the obvious truth behind Allora's words. "I need you to be careful. Make sure you control your emotions. The Rover is able to detect any sudden outburst of energy, which is what you did at cheerleading tryouts. And, please don't take off in the middle of the night. It's not safe."

"What about the sheriff and all the others who are in town? You said there were Sonorians all over," Allora replied, trying to convince not only her mother, but also herself.

"Yes, but that doesn't mean you are completely safe. There are guards set up on the perimeter of town, as well as those guarding you while you are at school, but by yourself, you are vulnerable. This means you need to be with someone with the advanced skills to take on a Rover."

"You mean Katie and Dax?" Allora asked.

"Yes and no. Katie and Dax were sent here by their father to be your guides into the life of a Sonorian. Katie and Dax are too young to be your guards. They, like you, have only a small amount of experience with the necessary training to protect oneself, let alone another," Milly said, watching as her daughter became angry, hearing the truth about her friends. "You shouldn't be mad at her, Allora. Katie was forbidden to say anything to you. We made it perfectly clear to the both of them when they arrived. She became your friend, not because she was asked to, but because you two shared something far beyond friendship."

Allora was still not convinced. She felt betrayed and wasn't going to let Katie off easy. Of course, she didn't tell her mother this. Instead, Allora sat with her head down, thinking about her best friend.

"Who's Sonorian at my school?"

"Well, Mr. Swan is your main protector at school," Milly answered. Allora's eyes lit up. Her favorite teacher was Sonorian, and now she had someone to confide in, considering she wouldn't want to speak to Katie right now. "I'll let the rest tell you themselves."

The sun had set and the stars were beginning to twinkle against the night sky. Allora searched the window for a glimpse of the moon, thinking back on the full, ominous sphere that had foreshadowed a nightmarish evening at the quarry. Milly could see her daughter's eyelids trying to stay up.

"I think it's time for you to go to bed. You have school in the morning and you got no sleep last night," Milly said, directing her daughter to the hallway.

"Goodnight, Mom," Allora said, smiling at her mother.

It was the first time in a long time she had done so. Most evenings ended with yelling or silence.

At school the next day, Jenny accosted Tanner about leaving her when the creatures attacked. Her high-pitched angry squeaks were heard throughout the hallways. Allora hadn't come to terms with Katie's dishonesty, so she avoided her friend as much as possible. Tanner wasn't speaking with Dax, either. Allora was looking forward to Mr. Swan's class. There were so many questions that she wanted to ask him, including questions regarding the odd piece of parchment, which was hidden in the back of her closet. She walked into her first period history class to see an old, gray-haired lady sitting at Mr. Swan's desk.

"Who are you?" Allora asked.

"I'm Mrs. Olson, your substitute teacher. Mr. Swan is away for finals week," the old lady replied.

Allora wasn't happy with Mr. Swan's absence. She had so much to ask him. Where was he? How could he leave at a time when Allora needed him most? The rest of class was a waste of time. The substitute didn't know much about history, so the kids took advantage of it and goofed off the entire time. Katie tried to get her friend's attention, but Allora was still ignoring her.

The end of the school year came quickly, and luckily, their lives remained drama free. Allora went to graduation and said good-bye to some of her friends. The last week of school was uneventful. Finals week went smoothly. Allora hadn't ever had trouble with her tests. She felt bad for Katie, though. Allora had always been there to help her friend through finals week, but she was still angry. When she saw Katie in the hallway during finals, Allora almost said something to her but chose not to and walked off. On the last day of school, Allora found Tanner walking toward her in the empty senior hallway. Tanner moved in close, while Allora stood still, holding a textbook against her chest.

"Hey," he said awkwardly.

They hadn't spoken much since the night at the cave. The reality of their new lives was still sinking in and they didn't really know what to say to each other.

Allora responded, "Hey."

The next few seconds went by without a word. Both of them tried to think of something to say, but the words couldn't be found.

Tanner finally asked, "So, how are finals?"

Allora gave him a look of bewilderment and said, "Good." She decided that small talk was not what they needed. "Tanner? Can we just be like we used to. I mean we haven't even talked about what happened to us," Allora blurted out.

"Yeah, I'm sorry. It's just that I have been so confused by everything," Tanner said.

"And you don't think that I haven't?" Allora said. "I'm just as confused as you are. Remember, this is all new to me, too."

Tanner's body gave in to Allora's words. He let down his emotional wall. "Allora, to be honest, I'm so scared right now, and there are creatures out there right now trying to find me. I just don't know what to do. I've never been this scared in my entire life."

Allora grabbed his hand and looked into his eyes, "I'm scared too. My mother told me that they are also looking for me for some reason. I think that it has something to do with what happened sixteen years ago."

The two teenagers moved closer together, Allora's hand still grasping Tanner's. They stood there for what seemed to them to be an eternity, gazing into each other's eyes. Their lips became abnormally dry. The gap between them slowly grew smaller; their hearts beat increasingly faster. Electricity surged between their bodies.

"Tanner!" Jenny yelled from down the hall.

The two teenagers let go of the other and stepped apart to try to hide what they had almost done. Jenny marched down the hallway to within inches of the pair.

"What are you guys doing?" Jenny asked.

Steam seemed to be pouring from her ears in anger.

"Ah... I had something in my eye, and Allora was nice enough to see what it was," Tanner blurted out.

Allora nodded in agreement. She wasn't about to admit what they had been about to do. She didn't even believe it herself. Was she actually falling for Tanner? She shook her head in disbelief.

She started to walk down the hall. "Well, you two have a good summer. I'm glad I got that thing out of your eye," Allora said, awkwardly shuffling, as Tanner had a minute ago. "Okay, well... bye!"

She made a quick break for the door and left the school.

Chapter 8

Training

The summer dragged on, and the agony of boredom was further intensified by the scorching heat. Oregon was known for its temperate climate, but lately the weather had become more erratic. A hand held fan in one hand and a glass of lemonade in the other, Allora tried to cool down from the hot and humid air. Sweat accumulated in her belly button while she sat on the hot leather couch. The freezer contained the only solution to her suffering, but when she stood up her skin stuck to the leather, requiring extra force to escape the insufferable cowhide.

After reaching the kitchen, she pulled open the freezer door and let out a gasp of relief as the cold air cooled the beads of sweat covering her body. The soft breeze from the icy freezer chilled her body as she leaned farther into the compartment. After getting some ice for her lemonade, she looked out the kitchen window. For the entire summer, she had been cooped up, forbidden to venture from the confines of the house. It had been a lonely summer.

Milly could feel her daughter's frustration. She sulked around the house like a caged tiger cub, unsure of her environment but yearning for the chance to prove herself. Milly's internal struggle was fierce, knowing the tumultuous situation in her home world and the significant role that her daughter would play in the future. For so long, she had denied it. With the selfish protective nature of a mother bear, Milly wanted to keep Allora from a destiny that was sure to be painful, difficult, and perilous. But without Allora, no one would be free from the evils of their past.

Milly picked up the phone. Each number she dialed brought her daughter closer to the inevitable path that she dreaded for so long.

~~~~~~~~~~~~~~~

On an early summer morning, Milly shook her daughter awake, knowing the sleeping beauty would soon turn into a conscious grumpy beast.

Allora looked through the slits of her eyelids at her clock. "Mom, it's five in the morning, and its summer. What are you doing?"

"Rise and shine. Today is your first day of training with Sumatra," Milly announced, pushing her daughter's limp body to wake her up. "Come on, honey. Take a shower and get dressed. Tanner, Dax, and Katie will be here in a half hour. You don't have much time."

Reluctantly, Allora slid out of bed. She stumbled to the shower like a zombie. Mornings were never pleasant. Allora was more of a night owl; the alarm was her relentless enemy. Unfortunately, her entire family loved mornings, so it was hard to stay in bed. After putting on a tank top and shorts, Allora heard a knock at the front door.

"Your friends are here," Milly yelled from the living room.

Allora slowly moved toward the front of the house, turning the corner of the hallway to see Tanner, Dax, and Katie standing in the front entryway with the same half-asleep look as she had.

"We've created a protected path to the portal, which is about a mile up the hill. Just take the normal path through back meadow. You guys should be safe. Sumatra will be waiting for you," Milly said, grabbing her daughter and kissing her on the cheek.

Too tired to protest, Allora sauntered out the back door. Outside, the sun was inching above the horizon as the four teenagers made their way through the backyard. Morning dew covered the grassy field, and the birds chirped their songs as the group reached the forest path. Tired silence was interrupted half a mile into the woods. Katie scurried quickly up to the front of the group, slid up the path, and blocked Allora's way.

"Okay, I'm tired of this," Katie said, grabbing Allora by the shoulders. "You've been ignoring me for way too long. If you want me to say it, I will. I'm sorry."

Allora knocked Katie's hands off her shoulders. "You're sorry? That's all you have to say? Our friendship is based on lies, and all you have is 'I'm sorry,' " Allora said.

"That's not fair!" Katie said. "I couldn't tell you about Sonora. I didn't have a choice."

"You always have a choice," Allora replied.

Dax made it up to the confrontation. "Neither one of us could tell you about where we were from. It would have put all of us in danger."

Hearing this caused Tanner to jump into the fray. "Oh and we would've screwed it all up, right?"

"That's not what I meant."

Tanner moved next to Allora. "Then what exactly did you mean? That Allora and I are just two screw-ups who can't keep their mouths shut?"

"What? No. We just—"

"Let's go," Tanner said, not allowing Dax to finish his sentence before grabbing Allora and proceeding up the hill.

Dax threw his hands up in the air.

The awkward tension followed them all the way to the portal site. A mile up the path, Sumatra came into view, standing upon a boulder. Next to the boulder was a large, odd-looking bush that moved without the wind. The strange flutter of the branches suggested something abnormal existed within it. Without saying a word, Sumatra faded into the bush. Realizing it was the portal, everyone followed, landing on what felt like a golf green. Enormous oak trees situated in a perfect grid-like pattern surrounded them. Each tree had been planted in a line as if in an orchard, and yet it seemed too perfectly designed to be real. To their right was a round dirt area with a small wooden bench where a multitude of colored robes lay. Sumatra instructed them to put on the robes. Allora grabbed a purple robe. Tanner put on a blue one, Dax a green robe, and Katie a white. Once they were all dressed, Sumatra lined them up in front of him.

He smiled. "Do you all know why you chose the robes you did?" The four of them glanced down at their robes. None knew the significance of their choices and just returned puzzled looks back to the old man. "You all picked a certain color robe without fighting or even realizing they were different."

He paused to let them contemplate their actions. Allora had always liked purple. She had never really known why that was, but it had always been a part of her life. What did a preference of color have to do with her training?

"Sonorians have always embodied a distinctive color based on a number of factors, mostly having to do with emotions. Just like a ruby is red, or a sapphire is blue; it is a part of you. This color is also what is produced when you perform a burst of energy," Sumatra said, as his staff lit up, creating a blue ball of energy at the top. The ball grew, shrank, and then disappeared. He continued, "The colors represented by your robes will be the color of hadron you produce when you mature."

"How do you know this?" Dax asked. "We haven't been able to produce hadrons yet."

Sumatra gave him a knowing smile. "Call it an old man's intuition."

Before they began their physical training, Sumatra gave the teenagers a lesson in hadron focalization. "The spirit of energy is very ancient and requires knowledge, strength, patience, control, and understanding. Hadrons are everywhere. They are what give you your gifts. They are in the trees that surround us. They are a part of you and me. They are all that is, all that was, and all that will be. Hadrons connect every living thing." As he said this, Sumatra closed his eyes and put his staff in front of him. Silence was followed by a rustling of the trees, and the oak trees began to glow with a tint of blue. A small, faint trail of blue light formed upon the tree branches, wove its way down the tree trunks, and slithered along the ground like a snake, absorbing itself into the base of Sumatra's staff. Once all of the blue light was absorbed into the staff, Sumatra open his eyes, spun around, and sent a hadron burst into a straw-filled dummy that had suddenly popped up from the ground behind him. The dummy exploded, sending pieces of wood and straw raining down. The children's eyes were wide in amazement. Sumatra swung around to face them.

"It is essential you understand your limits. Nature is willing to let you use its hadrons, but you must do so with respect. There is a balance in nature, as there is in all life. If that balance is interrupted, nature will try to balance itself back in order to survive. If you are greedy with the use of hadrons, there will be consequences." His tone was soft, but the words were sharp and meaningful in the context of his teachings.

Sumatra was about to start the physical part of their training when Allora interrupted to ask him a question. "Sumatra, why was I able to produce fire? And why am I able to do it before I'm eighteen?"

Sumatra's pause was deliberate as he debated whether to explain this phenomenon. "What you did was a very rare kind of energy focalization, of which only a few Sonorians are capable. I've never heard of anyone doing it at your age. Allora, you are what we call a Fermion. There are four stages of magical development. The first is Beson, second is Meson, third is Baryon, and the last is Fermion. Most don't reach the last stage. Those special few who do reach it have the ability to produce and manipulate certain elements in our environment. The elements, of course, are earth, wind, water, and as you found out for yourself, fire."

"I don't get it," Allora said, staring down at her hands. "How am I at the last stage if I've never even been to the first stage?"

"I don't know," Sumatra admitted. "I'm as confused as you are. Your situation is unique. I've heard of Sonorians being able to focus hadrons at a young age, but never at the level that you showed. Most Fermions at your age have only been heard of in ancient text, and not much is known on the subject because those ancient texts were burned or lost ages ago. The only person I know of who would have had an answer is no longer with us." His face reflected a painful memory as he spoke. Allora chose not to pursue any other answers. Instead, she stood there waiting patiently for another lesson.

Sumatra waved his hand, and four fighting dummies popped up from the ground. Sumatra instructed the four to each take a position in front of a dummy. Then, they were instructed to begin with basic maneuvers, performing a routine of kicking and punching. Katie and Dax had a thorough knowledge of martial arts technique, which made the instruction easy to execute. The other two had a more difficult time.

After they had been doing basic fighting instruction for hours, their hands, legs, and arms were becoming sore.

"How much longer are we going to do this?" Allora asked. She had been under the impression they would be training in how to focus hadrons, not kung fu.

Sumatra glided next to Allora. "Continue," he commanded.

The rest of the day was the same basic instruction. At sundown, Sumatra ended the session and sent them back through the portal. Again, the trip home was carried out in silence, although it had more to do with exhaustion than bitterness. As soon as Allora got home, she iced the sporadic bruises on her limbs and crashed on the couch.

Milly came into the living room and found her daughter asleep in an awkward position on the couch, with one leg hanging off the edge. She lifted Allora's legs, extended them out into a comfortable spot, and covered her with a blanket. Milly sat down and brushed the hair from her daughter's forehead. She remembered when she had gone through the same training. It was a long and difficult journey, but she knew her daughter could handle it.

The next morning, Allora felt herself moving back and forth. She assumed it was her mother shaking her awake until she slowly opened her eyes to see the face of an attractive young man staring back at her.

"Hi," Tanner said softly.

Their eyes met, each wondering what the other was thinking.

"Hi," Allora responded, unsure of what else to say. In that moment, she felt safe. His presence was soothing. She began to feel a strange sensation as she stared back at Tanner. Realizing the feelings of the moment, her eyes darted back and forth, searching for a distraction. Awkwardly, she stretched her arms and legs, which were completely sore from the previous day.

"I should... uh... probably go get ready," Allora mumbled and, not realizing she had only underwear on, she pulled off the blanket that covered her.

Her eyes grew wide when she looked down and realized how exposed she was. Quickly, she snatched the blanket, covered herself back up, and escaped to the bathroom. Tanner made a similar departure to the kitchen, clumsily tripping over one of the family dogs lying next to the fireplace. Katie and Dax arrived a few minutes later, unaware of why Allora and Tanner were acting so uncomfortable.

After a quick breakfast, they took off toward the portal and traveled through to the same orchard. The week continued with more of the same basic training. Sumatra taught them the vulnerable locations on the body and how to exploit these weak spots. Every day the four woke early in the morning and went to the orchard to train. A couple of weeks went by before Sumatra decided to change the training routine. On the morning of the fifth week, the four arrived to find no dummies. The old man was waiting for them to change into their robes as usual, and then he instructed them to take their normal positions in a line facing their instructor. They remained still, with their arms clasped behind them.

"Today, we train on something that has a little more mobility. You will be partnering up and training against each other," Sumatra said, causing mixed reactions. "Katie, you will be matched up with Allora. Tanner, you will train with Dax."

Reluctantly, they took up fighting positions facing each other. The emotional rift between them was obvious. Sumatra stood between the two sets of partners.

"Your objective is to attack, as well as block the other's attacks," he said.

Allora stood there thinking about what she would need to do to catch Katie off guard. She knew her opponent was much more skilled, but Allora was also ready to show Katie how much her lies had hurt.

"Begin," Sumatra said.

Katie advanced, preparing to strike. Allora moved around, getting ready to block. Katie swung her leg upward to strike from above, but Allora saw the leg streaking toward her head and pulled her arm up, blocking the kick. Katie turned the opposite direction, sending her fist into her opponent's other side. The move worked, causing Allora to wince at the pain. She recovered and mounted her own attack, sending a punch into Katie's midsection with a force that expelled the air from the blonde girl's lungs.

Katie hadn't anticipated the swift counter-attack. "I see you haven't let any of it go, have you?" she said, standing up straight.

"What, Master Katie?" Allora responded. "Can't take a little competition?"

At this point, Katie decided not to hold anything back. She was tired of her best friend's stubbornness, and the frustration from weeks of being ignored motivated her to work harder. Katie dug her foot into the dirt and lunged forward, swinging violently to confuse her opponent. The move had the desired effect, sending Allora's arms up to block a punch while Katie's leg struck her in the shins. Allora knelt down, but quickly threw up both arms to block another attack. Katie was obviously more gifted in the art of combat, but surprisingly, Allora was able to match most of her advances.

Dax and Tanner had a similar situation. Dax was able to blindside his partner, but Tanner was effective with his counter-attacks. Every time one of them landed a punch or kick, the other became increasingly angrier. Their motions grew progressively slower, but they continued fighting. Finally, after about an hour of constant sparring, they all collapsed in exhaustion, their bodies bloody and bruised.

Sumatra looked at them, leaning on his staff. "So, have you four had enough of fighting each other? Have you gotten all your frustrations out yet?"

The four of them sat on the ground, breathing hard. Shame at their immaturity spread among the group.

Sumatra maintained his stern demeanor. "As long as you are fighting among yourselves, you will never be able to defeat those who seek to do you harm." His words hit them hard. Sumatra walked between the pairs of exhausted teenagers. "We will end the session on this. Individually, you may be strong, but together, you four have the chance to become an incredible force, capable of many things. That is a choice you must make together."

With that, Sumatra disappeared through the portal. The kids put their robes on the bench and remained in the orchard.

"I'm sorry!" Katie and Allora said at the same time.

They laughed and hugged, feeling the relief of forgiveness. Meanwhile, the two boys just shook hands and nodded their heads without saying a word. The peculiar exchange perplexed the girls.

"That's how boys make up?" Allora asked.

"Yeah, we don't need to say anything," Tanner said. "It's a guy thing."

Dax acknowledged by nodding his head again.

Katie looked over at Allora. "Boys," she said, rolling her eyes.

The silence between them had been hard, and now they were all relieved to have their friendships back.

"Sumatra's right," Allora admitted.

They all agreed. Training had introduced them to the difficulty and seriousness of combat. Allora wrapped her arm around Katie, and they disappeared into the portal. Their faces were bloody, their bodies were bruised, and they were completely exhausted, but they were all smiles. They had each other again.

Chapter 9

Summer Camp

A blue, pulsating ball of energy shot through the warm summer air, singeing the ends of Allora's hair and narrowly missing striking her shoulder. The perpetrator stood idly, preparing his motions carefully, seeking to debilitate his opponent. Allora grinned arrogantly, taunting him into further action. She slid along the fine gravel, which gently floated toward the man. He absorbed a ball of energy within his hands and shot it forward. The streaking light zoomed past as Allora again swung around, mimicking her last move. A searing explosion of pain indicated her mistake. She keeled over onto her knees, panting and rubbing the spot on her lower back where her opponent had struck.

"Confidence is good; arrogance is not, my young Sonorian," Sumatra said, unable to restrain a smirk.

Allora writhed in pain. Getting hit with a hadron burst was an agonizing experience. It was like a jolt of electricity zapping her body, coupled with a hammer striking down on her chest.

"Lucky shot," she muttered.

"You're lucky I didn't use a large burst, or you would've passed out."

Sumatra had Allora, Katie, Dax, and Tanner dodging hadron bursts, deflecting flying apples, and training with various weapons. The weapons training was the hardest part, but also the most exciting. They worked with staffs, swords, flying daggers, scimitars, and ranged weapons. Each day they chose a different type of weapon, so as to be efficient with all types. Yet, they all had their favorites.

For Dax, it was the staff. Katie's weapons of choice were the double short swords. Tanner really enjoyed training with broadswords. Ranged weapons, such as throwing knives and javelins, were Allora's favorite; she enjoyed the composite bow the most.

On the day they trained with ranged weapons, each was required to hit a dummy with a bulls- eye painted upon its chest area. Allora was especially gifted at the use of a bow. Almost every shot hit directly in the center of the bulls-eye. When they switched to the flying daggers, Allora was just as accurate. Even if Sumatra was impressed, he never showed it, remaining unemotional as he walked in between his students. Occasionally, he gave instructions, but they were short and simple. A slight nod of his head indicated success.

Sumatra often said, "Experience is more important than anything said out of my mouth."

Weeks passed, and they all became increasingly efficient and skilled with the weaponry. Their lessons eventually changed from dummies to partner duels. There were a few cuts and close calls, but no one was seriously hurt. Sumatra explained that they needed actual experience fighting a real person so when the time came they would be prepared for another attack.

The end of August was approaching, and the weather had been getting hotter. They were all looking forward to the end of the week because it was when they would leave for summer camp. Allora had to argue with her mother to allow her to go this year.

"Thank you, thank you, thank you!" Allora yelped.

"On two conditions: you must not go out at night, and you must stay in the camp at all times," Milly ordered.

Allora happily nodded her head and raced off to her room to pack.

The next day, Milly dropped Allora off at the school, where hundreds of kids waited for the buses to arrive. Katie and Dax were on the curb with an excessive number of bags in front of them.

"Wow, got enough stuff?" Allora said.

"Ha, ha. Very funny." Katie said placing her hands on her hips. "I need all of these bags. This one has my makeup," she said, emphatically pointing to a small brown suitcase the size of a bowling ball. "This one has my really nice dresses. This one is my accessory bag. This is my workout clothes bag. This is my bag for all my stuff I'm taking to the lake. This would be my 'I don't care what I'm wearing bag,' which I will only be using when I'm in the cabin. And this is my bag with clothes for my friend Allora who never brings enough stuff to wear and eventually has to ask her friend Katie." She cocked her head to the side, smiling mockingly. Allora mimicked the smile, but secretly agreed with her best friend.

Just then, Tanner rolled up in his car. Allora noticed the big blonde hair of her nemesis arrogantly sliding out of the passenger seat. The sight of the pompous cheerleader was enough to make Allora cringe. She had almost forgotten how much she despised the prissy elitist. Tanner followed Jenny, waving at the football players and then falling in behind his girlfriend. Jenny strutted to Dax, gave him a hug, and then glanced over his shoulder. Pulling down her expensive designer bug-eyed sunglasses, she devilishly grinned at Katie and Allora.

"Could you two get my bags out of the car?" Jenny said, a condescending smile plastered across her face. "Thanks."

Jenny spun around, facing the opposite direction as Allora angrily moved forward with her fist cocked back, like a viper ready to strike. Katie reluctantly grabbed her best friend's body as Allora struggled to enact vengeful punishment. The summer training had given Allora a sense of pride and the confidence to defend herself. Not noticing the aggressive display, Jenny left and headed to the other side of the parking lot where the cheerleaders were congregating.

"She was only kidding," Tanner said, not looking like he believed the words as they escaped his mouth.

"Aaagh!" Allora screamed, snatching her bags and stomping off in the opposite direction.

Katie glared at Tanner, crossing her arms.

"What?" he asked, shrugging his shoulders with his hands outstretched.

"Sometimes I think all boys are clueless," Katie muttered, marching to console her friend.

Tanner turned to Dax.

"Hey, don't ask me. I'm one of the clueless ones."

Tanner rolled his eyes and stood there trying to understand what had happened.

A line of large yellow buses pulled into the school parking lot. Everyone grabbed their bags and filed into designated vehicles. Allora and Katie were assigned to a different bus than Tanner and Dax, but Allora didn't mind because she didn't want to spend the trip to camp in the same bus as Jenny. The eagerness was palpable as the youth-filled buses left the safety of the school and formed a long yellow caravan toward the wonder of the mountains. It was especially exciting for Allora, Tanner, Dax, and Katie because of the how stressful and exhausting the training sessions had been. Most of the summer had been about responsibility, growth, and adult issues. This trip would allow them to have fun and forget about the outside world. It was a chance to be young, without the constant worry of their new lives beating down upon them.

Camp Big Lake was located in the Cascade mountain range, at the edge of Mt. Jefferson. The camp sat on a large freshwater lake created from mountain runoff, which made it cold. Most of the campers didn't mind the chilly water due to the scorching summer heat. The view from the camp was amazing. Pine Valley Viewpoint, at the top of the bluffs, had a picturesque lookout where the mountain opened up on one side and a valley of Douglas fir trees stretched out on the other side. The view wasn't on any of their minds as the buses traveled east. Camp Big Lake was where everyone from

Sandy High School went to socialize, have fun, and be themselves away from their parents' watchful eyes. Every summer, they all came back from Camp Big Lake with the best stories, and this year was shaping up to be no different.

The bus pulled onto a gravel road and stopped at a wooden lodge. The old log cabin looked as if it had been built over a hundred years ago. Camp counselors lined up facing the buses, readying themselves for the arrivals. Splintered wood, a stained metal roof, and cracked concrete steps greeted them as they filed out of the buses. The head counselor started barking orders through a bullhorn as they exited the bus steps.

"Please make sure you have all of your belongings," said the head counselor.

The campers were instructed to find their name on a large list plastered on a wooden post, and then line up with the counselor associated with the first letter of their last names. After saying her long good-byes to Katie, who was going to cabin "H," Allora split off from the others and found the "S" counselor.

The girls' cabins were located on the east side of the lake, while the boys' cabins were to the south. Camp rules were very clear on the separation of boys and girls. After lights went out at ten o'clock, campers weren't supposed to leave their cabins, though this rule was broken every year. The junior boys had a tradition of playing pranks on the girls. This was Tanner and Dax's year, and they had no intention of letting it slip by without planning something great.

Allora, having found a decent bunk at the back of Cabin S, unpacked her bags and lay down on the bed. Directly across the aisle was Rebecca Sweeny, a sophomore with dark brown hair, glasses, and way too much energy. Diagonally left of her, a freckled, red-haired girl named Kami Summers placed a shirt into a dusty drawer. She was always really nice, but quite shy. At the opposite end of the cabin, Nancy Williams was unloading her stuff onto one of the beds. Nancy was one of Jenny's best friends. She was a little bit taller than Allora and had long blonde hair that was always perfectly straightened.

Nancy looked up from unpacking to see Allora staring back at her.

"What are you looking at?" Nancy asked.

Allora gave her a look of disgust. "Not much, obviously," she said. The quick retort was followed by an orchestra of giggles from the other girls. None in the room liked Nancy or any of the cheerleaders, who acted as if they owned the school and everyone else was just visiting. "Why are you even in Cabin S?" Allora asked.

"Unfortunately, they didn't have enough girls for Cabin W, so they stuck me in here with you losers," Nancy said.

Allora looked behind Nancy to see Jessica Sandall placing her shirts into a drawer. Jessica had been a victim of Jenny's wrath. During gym class, Jessica had knocked Jenny to the floor in a game of basketball, so Jenny had put itching powder on her towel after class was over. When Jessica had gone to dry off, she had begun itching uncontrollably. The embarrassment of being completely naked and unable to stop itching while the entire locker room erupted with laughter, had been enough to keep her home for weeks. The prank had gone unpunished because no one had the guts to report Jenny. Jessica was finally getting over the embarrassment, but the feelings of bitterness still lingered. This summer camp was her first time back with her classmates. So far, it had been without incident. Jenny had moved on to other victims.

Jessica finished putting away her clothes, but when she got up, her leg knocked one of her bags off the bed. It hit the hard wooden floor, causing the latch to snap open. Makeup and accessories exploded out of the carrying case.

Nancy turned around when she heard the commotion, and laughed uncontrollably.

"Ahhhh... did the poor baby drop something?" Nancy said.

Allora quickly made her way over to help Jessica pick up her stuff. "You alright?"

"Yeah, I'm fine," Jessica replied.

"Well, aren't you two just precious," Nancy said. "This is good for both of you. It'll be training for when you become my servants after high school. Because that's the only job you two are good for."

Allora's face turned bright red with anger.

"Since you're such pros, why don't you two unpack my stuff as well? That way I can go find people who actually matter."

Nancy departed, while fury seethed from Allora's pores. The arrogance of this girl was unbelievable. Allora and Jessica picked up the last of the bag's contents and placed it on the bed. Letting Nancy get away with treating others so disgracefully was not an option. Allora stepped to the front of the cabin. There were a few incoming sophomores whom Allora didn't know, but she didn't really care, either.

"Girls," Allora began, addressing the rest of Cabin S, "I'm tired of Jenny, Nancy, and Tanya treating people like crap. They think they can just push everyone around and get away with it." Allora paused for a second to see if the other girls agreed. Once she had them nodding their heads, she continued. "They need a little lesson in humility. Later this week, I'm going to play a prank on little Miss Nancy Williams. Who's in?"

All of the girls in the room raised their hands. Allora crossed her arms and smiled. Now she had to come up with a plan to enact her revenge.

That night, the camp met at the mess hall for dinner. Chicken, rice, and beans were served, followed by pudding for desert. After the meal, the head counselor proceeded to introduce the camp counselors, read the camp rules, and give an overview of the activities for the week. Then, they started singing a song, at which Allora could only roll her eyes. Afterward, everyone went to the amphitheater for the inaugural campfire, where the counselors performed a skit about campers getting attacked by a monstrous Sasquatch. The idea that the bumbling buffoon was a vicious beast kept Allora smiling all the way through the night. The campfire went on for about an hour, and once it was over, everyone went off to bed so they could get up early for the next day's activities.

The counselors rang the morning bell at 7:30 a.m. to wake everyone up. At 8:00 a.m. the campers filed into the large mess hall to eat breakfast. Katie and Allora sat down with their trays, which were full of fruit, oatmeal, and eggs. They were discussing how they wanted to go water skiing when Tanner and Dax jumped into the seats next to them.

"What's happening, ladies?" Dax asked in a cool, macho tone.

Katie looked up at her brother and dropped her spoon. "You realize how stupid and creepy you sound?" Katie said.

"Shut up," Dax replied, sneering at his sister.

Tanner ignored the siblings. "So, Allora, what are you up to today?" he asked.

Allora stopped eating her eggs. "I really want to go water skiing, but I also want to hit up the archery range."

Dax asked, "Didn't you have enough of that kind of stuff at the orchard?"

"You should always continue your training, even beyond Sumatra's instructions. Don't you remember what he said before we left?" Allora said.

"Yeah, but this is supposed to be our vacation. It's our break. We should be having fun!" Dax replied, eyeballing the group of girls cute walking by at that moment. Dax sat there smiling at the girls while his sister just shook her head.

"Well then, we will leave you two horny boys to your so-called fun," Katie said, getting up from her seat with her tray. Allora followed her, laughing at the boys' reaction. The girls kept laughing as they emptied their trays and went to change into their bathing suits. They had compromised on the activities for the day. First, they would sit out for a couple hours and tan. Then, they would go water skiing. And finally, they would practice their archery skills at the range. It was a beautifully sunny day, without a single cloud in the sky. When they arrived at the lake, the sun was almost at its peak position in the sky and the temperature had hit ninety degrees. Many of the other girls had the same idea. The dock and beach were crowded already. They found two lawn chairs and settled in with after applying their sunscreen thoroughly. The peaceful stillness, along with the soothing warmth of the sun, caused both Allora and Katie to nod off. The girls were lying on their stomachs when they were awakened by the sound of the dock bending and crackling from the weight of running bodies. They pulled their heads up in time to feel cold water splashing up from the dock's edge. The frigid wall of water caused both girls to gasp as they searched the dock's edge to find the perpetrators who had interrupted their nap. Two heads popped up from underneath the water. It was Dax and Tanner.

"You're dead!" Allora yelled.

Katie wasn't happy about being splashed either. "Don't you two have better things to do?" she said.

"What, than messing with you guys?" The boys exchanged sinister smiles. "Nah!"

They soaked the girls from head to toe. This meant war. The girls retaliated by leaping forward, trying to jump on top of the boys, but they were able to swim out of the way. The four of them splashed around for a few minutes, until they heard someone loudly clearing her throat on the dock.

"Having fun, children?" Jenny said, standing in front of Nancy and Tanya, all dressed in their best bikinis with no intention of getting into the icy water. Each wore the same pompous superior look. Meanwhile, Katie and Allora gave one another knowing stares, communicating their devious plan with their eyes. Just as the boys had done to them earlier, they began splashing the pretentious girls on the dock. Jenny and the rest of her entourage screamed and ran away, soaked from the attack. Tanner, Dax, Katie and Allora laughed uncontrollably and remained swimming around until their bodies became numb from the cold water. Allora swam over to the beach and got out, while Katie grabbed their towels from the dock. Then they went down the beach to the other dock, where the water skiing lessons were taught.

After two hours on the boat, the girls went off to the archery range. The instructor was amazed by Allora's talents. Katie was pretty good, but she needed a lot more practice. Allora pulled back the bow and sent the arrow soaring in a perfect line toward the middle of the target. The instructor wanted to test her skills, so he asked Allora if she could hit a moving target. She had never done it before, but was always up for a challenge. The instructor stood in the middle of the range. All of the other campers watched intently as the instructor motioned with his head. Allora grabbed an arrow out of the quiver, placed it in the bow, pulled the arrow back to the anchor point, and rested it on the shelf. Feeling confident with her positioning, she nodded her head to the instructor, who then tossed a square board in the air. Allora's eyes focused on the middle of the spinning plank of wood, following it until the object reached its highest point. Then, she let go, feeling the tight pressure release from her hands. Spectators crowded around, watching as the square piece of wood left its original trajectory and sailed to the back of the range. Once it hit the ground, the archery instructor jogged to where it had landed, picked it up, and ran back across the range. The arrow had stuck exactly in the middle of the target. Everyone cheered, while Katie—and even Allora—couldn't believe how accurate the shot had been.

"You are incredible," the instructor said, causing Allora to blush. The young brunette boy was good looking, with a strong, muscular build. He walked up to the wood barrier that kept the campers out of the archery range and handed the arrow to Allora. He smiled back at her, winked, and then went back to retrieving arrows from the targets. Allora maintained her gaze on the cute instructor until Katie bumped her shoulder.

"What?" she said defensively. Katie smiled even bigger. "What!" Allora exclaimed.

Katie shook her head, unable to wipe the smirk from her lips after seeing her friend flirting with the cute instructor. The harassment continued all the way to the mess hall. Allora had to laugh about it. She was still in disbelief about hitting the moving target so accurately.

That night, Allora woke up all the girls of Cabin S, except for one. Nancy Williams slept soundly, her obnoxious snore annoying the rest of the cabin as they congregated around her bed. Some had to cup their mouths with their hands to keep from laughing out loud. The giggles stopped when Nancy rustled in her bed. Eyes darted around, unsure whether to hide. The girls remained motionless until Nancy stopped moving. After a few seconds of stillness, the snoring resumed, and they moved closer, taking turns using an eyeliner pen to draw on the sleeping girl's face. Most of them just made a few lines, but when it was Allora's turn, she took it a little farther.

Chapter 10

Pranks

The camp bell rang profusely, rousing the girls of cabin S from their slumber. As they dressed out of their pajamas, none glanced in Nancy's direction for fear of ruining the previous night's shenanigans. Nancy looked around the room, wondering why the other girls were acting so strange. The stifled giggles made her even more confused.

"What?" Nancy asked the girls, who were trying to stay busy.

None acknowledge Nancy, which made her angrier.

"Seriously, you people are weird," Nancy said after only receiving more stifled giggles.

Normally, the girls went to breakfast before they took showers. They were counting on that pattern this morning as they watched Nancy exit the cabin and walk toward the separate building that housed the bathrooms. Everyone crowded in the cabin doorway, anxiously watching as Nancy paused to stretch. She made a move toward the bathroom door. They all held their breath, knowing that if Nancy saw herself in the mirror, it was all over. Nancy grabbed the bathroom doorknob, yawned, and then decided to eat breakfast first.

As Nancy disappeared down the hill toward the mess hall, all of the girls of Cabin S exhaled, and then followed their unsuspecting cabin mate. When

Nancy stepped into the mess hall, campers began spinning in their seats. Then, fingers started to point toward her. Every step she took was followed by more and more people looking and laughing.

Katie was enjoying a bowl of oatmeal when Allora sat down across the table with a huge grin plastered on her face. The mess hall was getting louder. Katie finally got a glimpse of Nancy, and then brought her attention back to her best friend.

"Did you...?" Katie asked.

Allora grabbed a piece of toast off of Katie's plate and took a bite. She maintained her grin while Katie slowly realized what had been done. Meanwhile, Nancy was at the end of the mess hall, yelling at the increasing laughter. Allora's grin grew as the mess hall filled with spectators. Jenny and Tanya arrived to see their friend, frantically pushing over underclassmen.

Jenny walked over to Nancy. "What is wrong with... whoa!"

The counselors entered the hall and moved through the crowd to see what had happened. Jenny pulled out a pocket mirror and lifted it up for Nancy to see.

Nancy screamed and ran out of the mess hall. The laughter stopped when Jenny turned and faced the crowd. She had a way of intimidating anyone. Both Jenny and Tanya left to help their friend, who was running to the bathroom. As soon as they disappeared, everyone started to laugh again.

"I can't believe you did that," Katie said, unable to stop smiling. "I just want to know how you convinced the other girls to go along with it."

"I didn't have to. Nancy's attitude was all I needed to convince them," Allora said.

She felt victorious. Jenny, Tanya, and Nancy were so mean to everyone at the school. Allora saw it as retribution for all their evil deeds.

"I mean, there was a drawing of a—"

"I know," Allora said, interrupting Katie before she was able to name the vulgar drawing on the side of the cheerleader's face.

"Were you the one who drew the—"

"Yes. Yes, I was."

Katie's grin vanished as she contemplated the consequences.

"You realize what might happen if they find out it was you?"

"They're never going to find out it was me," Allora said. She grabbed Katie's toast again and bit off another piece. "Besides, what can they really do? We're trained fighters, remember?"

Allora spent the rest of the day at the crafts center while Katie played soccer. Allora reveled in her victory all day. Girls told her how awesome the prank was. She was just a little worried by how many girls knew she had been the instigator.

After Allora was done sewing her small change purse, she walked to the soccer field.

"Katie! Let's go. I'm hungry!" Allora yelled.

Katie was darting up and down the field.

"Hold on. I'm about show Jarrod what a heater looks like," Katie said, avoiding the slide tackle from an oncoming defender.

She closed the gap between her and the goalie. Katie stepped right, kicking the ball in the air. As the ball sailed up, she spun to her left and did a roundhouse kick toward the floating ball. It shot toward the left-hand corner of the goal. Jarrod leapt up with an outstretched hand, but the ball was flying too fast. It hit the post and bounced into the net at the back of the goal. Katie jogged to the goal and stood over Jarrod, who was lying on the ground, smiling.

"Okay, okay. You win," Jarrod said. "You are the best soccer player at our school."

Katie strolled over to Allora, who was confused. "Jarrod bet me I couldn't get a goal on him. If I won, he had to admit that I was the best soccer player in our high school," Katie said.

"What happened if he blocked it?" Allora asked.

"I would've had to kiss him," Katie said.

Allora questioningly glared at her friend.

"What?" Katie said, pausing for a moment. "He never was going to be able to block it."

Both of the girls laughed and marched off to dinner. That night, Nancy wasn't in the cabin when they went to bed. In fact, Allora hadn't seen her all day. The girls of Cabin S laughed and talked about the prank until they fell asleep.

Allora's dream formed to the image of a field. The grass was green, soft, and yet foreign. It was quiet, with only the sound of the wind to keep her company. The sun was out, the sky was clear, and mountains filled the distant landscape. It was a very peaceful place, but for some reason, it felt peculiar. The ground suddenly began to shake violently. All around Allora, the ground cracked, breaking off and falling into a flowing river of fire. She could feel the burning steam escaping from the crevices. The mountain ranges crumpled, and all that was left was a small slab of rock beneath her feet. Then, she turned around to see an old man. His skin was wrinkly, the white hair on his head was thin, and he was hunched over on his staff. The old man wasn't looking at her; instead, he stared at the orange molten liquid below. He floated in the air, hovering a few feet away.

Finally, he looked up. His eyes were unusually blue, with a commanding stare that penetrated to Allora's core. She could feel a considerable amount of hadron energy emanating from the strange, supernatural man floating in front of her. It was the same type of energy she had experience during cheerleading tryouts. His demeanor became somber as he floated closer.

"You must decide the fate of our world, Allora. You are the key."

The words struck like a sword, piercing her thoughts and bursting into her imagination with ominous images of death, destruction, and pain. There was no time to analyze what the man said or the horrifying feelings it had created. The ground shook violently and then plummeted into the river of fire. She woke to someone restraining her arms. Allora tried to struggle, but the figures in the dark were too many. A cold sweat had permeated her skin, an obvious effect of the nightmare. She tried to scream, but they muzzled her with duct tape. All she could see was the light from a flashlight shining in her eyes.

"Make it tight, girls," a voice said while Allora's hands, feet and knees were bound by rope. "I don't want her escaping from this one."

The voice was familiar. She had heard it many times. It was a voice that caused most girls to run and hide. As she was carried out of the cabin, Allora saw the faces of the girls of Cabin S. They stood by, idly doing nothing, to her dismay. Seeing the weak, pained faces of the other girls was nauseating. How could they stand by as their "friend" was forcefully taken? Allora heard the voice address the rest of her cabin.

"If any of you try to help, I will come for you too!"

Allora wasn't sure where they were taking her, but she wasn't looking forward to it. The camp was quiet except for the sound of bullfrogs trumpeting in the shallows of the lake. She looked up at her captors. They were, of course, Nancy Williams, Tanya Brown, Madeline Jones, Emily Bowen, and, of course, Jenny Thompson. All of these girls were seniors on the cheerleading team.

When they stopped, Allora was placed upright. They pushed her back against a cold steel pole and tied her to it. The evil voice took shape before her, with a smug look of victory, smiling greedily and relishing in the moment. Allora pulled at the restraints, trying to break away from the ropes. She wanted to attack, but was unable to break free. Jenny stepped in closer to her victim.

"You really think you could have gotten away with it?" Jenny asked.

"Untie me and then we'll see what I can get away with," Allora replied.

"Girls, what do we do with a smart-ass girl like this?"

Nancy stepped up beside Jenny. Red, blotchy skin indicated how aggressively she had scrubbed her face to remove the markings.

"Let's draw on her face like she did to me," Nancy said.

Allora was so angry she didn't even notice the lack of clothing on her body. She was only covered by her underwear. Adrenaline had been keeping her warm. Now, the wind blew softly down from the mountain, sending chills up Allora's spine and forming goose bumps on her skin.

"No, Nancy," Jenny said. "We are just going to leave her here."

Jenny moved closer to her prey.

"You mess with one of us, you mess with all of us."

"I'm going to kill—" Allora yelled, but couldn't quite finish her threat before Jenny forcefully pressed the duct tape back over her mouth.

"Ah, ah, ah. We wouldn't want to wake up the rest of the camp, would we?" Jenny said, flicking Allora's forehead. "Come on, girls. Let's give Allora time to herself."

Anger spewed from Allora's slight body as she watched the cheerleaders laugh their way back up the hill to their cabins. Allora surveyed the area. She was tied to the flagpole right in front of the mess hall. Again, she tried to free herself from the rope, but the girls had been efficient with their knots. Her mind raced back to the dream she had been having prior to waking up. It was an incredible nightmare. What did that old man mean? His words echoed in her head. You are the key.

About an hour went by, and then Allora heard something move in the woods. Her heart began to beat faster. Milly had been adamant about not leaving the cabins at night. Allora continued staring at the woods. Jerking her head from side to side, she tried to search for the source of the sound. It grew louder. It was now in the bushes next to the mess hall. Allora started to panic. Then, she heard the same noise behind her. She pulled at the restraints as hard as she could, but they wouldn't budge. The rope burned her wrists, creating lines of red skin. The sound changed to swishing water, as though someone was moving in the lake. A cold fear enveloped her body as wet footsteps closed in. The muffled sound of her struggle reverberated in her ears as she thrashed against the steel flagpole. Drops of water splashed against the hard dirt. Allora's conscious mind couldn't grasp the idea of death, and soon released her from reality. Her eyelids dropped, and the floor gave way as she fainted to the cool, damp ground.

A deep, soothing voice called out her name. "Allora...."

A soft, wet hand pulled at the ropes on her back, and suddenly she fell forward. The impact roused her awake. Between fuzzy blinks, a human-looking figure, clear blue and tall, disappeared into the moonlit lake. An apparition of sorts, the creature dropped into the depths as if disappearing in a dream. Allora lay there, unable to comprehend the strange occurrence. She got up from the ground, dusted the dirt from her body, and slowly tip-toed back up the hill, periodically glancing over her shoulder at the dark lake. The water seemed undisturbed, as if the last moments had never tran-spired.

During the walk back, she talked to herself quietly, wondering if what she had seen was real. She was almost to Cabin S when a bunch of boys popped out around the corner of the cabin. One of the boys smacked into her, and she looked up to see Tanner. Right then, she remembered that she was only in her underwear and tried to cover herself with her hands, but it wasn't really working.

All of the boys were surprised to see Allora, and even more surprised that she was half naked.

"What are you doing?" Allora and Tanner asked at the same time.

"Why are you out so late?" Allora jumped in.

"I was about to ask you the same question," Tanner said, trying to look at Allora's eyes while he talked to her. The boys around him weren't trying so hard, though, and Allora noticed.

"Hey! Boys! Up here!" Allora whispered harshly, pointing to her face. At this point she was too tired and too upset to care whether they saw her in her underwear. She had way too much on her mind to even explain any of it. She deduced that the boys were out to play a junior prank on the girls. "Can you guys not prank Cabin S? I'm not in the mood to wake up to something bad. I will kill each and every one of you if I do." She stormed off toward her cabin.

Tanner couldn't help but watch her walk away.

Dax smacked the back of his head. "Hey, snap out of it. We have a mission, remember?"

Tanner turned around, focusing on the task at hand. "Okay, you guys know what to do. Let's get it done as fast as we can, and then make a break for our cabins. Remember, if we get caught, you are all on your own. Ready... break!" They dispersed quietly through the camp, carrying out the mission they meticulously planned the night before.

The girls woke up in their cabins as usual. Allora was a little apprehensive about it because of what the boys had been up to last night, but decided not to ruin it for them. Allora didn't tell anyone what she had seen. Instead, she went to Jessica's bunk to ask her where Nancy had gone. Allora wanted to confront her, but when she had arrived at the cabin, Nancy wasn't asleep in her bunk.

"She left last night to go bunk somewhere else," Jessica said. "Are you okay? What did they do to you?"

Everyone else was waking up and wondering the same question. They all hung over their beds, trying to listen in on the conversation.

"It was nothing. They tried to tie me up to the flagpole all night, but they didn't exactly do a very good job with the knots," Allora said.

The girls appeared to believe the lie. They felt bad for not doing anything, but they all knew that Jenny was true to her word. If one of them stood up to the senior girls, they would become the next target. That wasn't enough of an excuse for Allora, but she didn't say anything. There was no point in blaming anyone else. She let it go and wondered what the boys had done the previous night.

The girls were busy talking and making their usual trek down the hill. All of them filed behind the senior girls, who filed behind the cheerleaders. As they walked down the small hill from the girls' cabins, there were a few points where the steps dropped and they had to jump down.

Allora hung back for a little while, still unsure of what the boys had done. She found Katie and told her to wait there as well. Just as they did every day, the cheerleaders jumped down the exaggerated step. Instantly, all of the cheerleaders dropped into the ground.

The boys had dug a large hole in the ground and had set up a garden hose to feed water into it from the bottom, creating a large mud bath. Many of the girls weren't paying attention, and they proceeded to run into the girls in front of them, who ended up in the muddy pit as well. Screams echoed through the camp as brown faces popped up from the pit. This continued until the girls at the back of the line heard the screams and stopped. The boys jumped out from behind the bush where they had been waiting and began rolling on the ground, laughing hysterically.

Jenny looked over to where the laughter was coming from. Her whole face was covered in mud. "Tanner!" she screamed. "You are so dead!"

Tanner couldn't stop laughing, even with his girlfriend drenched in mud. All of the cheerleaders looked like weird, earthy brown creatures.

Dax leaned toward Tanner and whispered, "Maybe this is what the girls of Sonora look like?" They both burst out laughing.

Allora and Katie ran around the other direction, toward the lake, to see what was going on. They stopped after turning the corner and put their hands to their mouths in shock and amusement. Both of them started chuckling slowly, and then burst into laughter. Everyone was laughing now.

"This isn't funny!" Jenny yelled, trying to get out of the mud pit, only to slip and fall back in.

The counselors overheard the commotion and ran over from the mess hall. Holding back laughter, they pulled the girls from the mud-filled hole. The head counselor wasn't happy with what was going on, but everyone could tell that even he was trying to hold back a smile.

After the boys' prank, camp went by like normal. Before they knew it, it was the end of the week and camp was over. Allora spent the trip back with Katie, Tanner, and Dax. They shared stories and reflected over how much fun the week was. This year's camp would be legendary. Allora saved the story about the strange creature from the lake for when they would be alone and able to discuss the subject. The bus wasn't very private. Soon, they were back in Sandy and safely in their homes.

Chapter 11

Upperclassmen

At the edge of the driveway, Bell's bright yellow bus disappeared over the distant hump in the road, heading off to the first day of school. Left waiting, Allora reflected on her summer and the harsh reality of her life. She felt confused, scared, and unable to comprehend how to deal with everything. Strange, almost alien feelings were awaking inside her. As Allora stood alone in a confused state of emotional turmoil, a distant blurry figure appeared, moving quickly through the trees like an animal on the hunt. She felt an unfamiliar cold breeze fill the air. Hair on her neck rose, and goose bumps formed on her arms. Allora clenched her bag tightly, unsure whether she should stay still or run for her life. She picked up a stick from the side of the road as another cold chill blew through. For reasons she couldn't explain, the wind didn't feel like a mountain breeze. Twigs and branches snapped under the weight of the oncoming figure.

"Whoever's there, this isn't funny," she said, gripping the stick tighter.

Something blurry streaked between the tree trunks, accompanied by the sound of more breaking twigs. It was so close Allora could almost see the shape of a human. She dropped her book bag, put her right foot back, and took a batting stance with the stick clenched tightly in her hands.

"Show yourself!"

A car flew over the hump in the road, pulled over, and stopped. "Practicing for softball season?" Katie joked, not noticing Allora's fearful stare.

Allora threw the stick into the ditch, grabbed her bag, and leapt into Katie's Jeep Cherokee.

"Whoa! I don't think I've ever seen you *this* excited to go to school before."

"Just go!" Allora said.

Katie slammed the accelerator, causing the Jeep to spin out. White smoke blew out from the tires as the car jerked forward and sped down the road. A good distance from Allora's house, Katie slowed the speeding car.

"What's going on?" she asked, frantically.

Allora spun around, fingers gripping ferociously into the leather headrest, staring intently at the forest. No matter how hard she stared, nothing materialized. She spun back around, and forcefully put her seatbelt on.

"There was something in the woods," Allora answered.

"What?"

Allora controlled her breathing, trying to negate a panic attack. "Watch out!" The road had curved, and since Katie hadn't been paying attention to the road, she had to slam on the brakes to avoid hitting a tree. White smoke from burnt rubber billowed on both the sides of the car, and the pungent aroma of worn brakes filled the interior. The girls breathed heavily, trying to regain their composure.

"Whoa..." said Katie.

"Yeah," Allora answered, aware of what could have happened.

Katie allowed her friend to take a minute, then said, "Now... what just happened?"

"I saw... no, I felt... something..." Allora couldn't articulate anything. She wasn't even sure if any of what she had experienced was actually real. Katie lifted her eyebrows and cocked her head. "I don't know, alright?" Allora exclaimed in frustration.

Katie put the car in reverse, gassed it out of the gravel ditch, and backed onto the road.

"With everything that has happened to you, it's okay to be a little paranoid," Katie said, after pulling onto Main Street.

"I'm not paranoid!" Allora snapped. "I can't explain it. Whatever was in the woods wasn't natural."

Katie wasn't about to argue. She knew what happened to those who got into a verbal sparring match with Allora. Besides, her mind was on something a little more important, at least as far as she was concerned.

"What?" Allora snapped again, unsure why her friend was grinning so adamantly. "You don't believe me, do you?"

"No, this has nothing to do with what you saw in the woods."

Allora paused, waiting for some sort of explanation. "Well... spit it out!"

"Okay, I was going to wait, but I can't." Katie bit her lip, and then said, "Tanner broke up with Jenny yesterday."

"What?" Allora exclaimed, and then pushed her lips together, trying not to show any emotion. "Why did he break up with her?"

Katie could see the giddy struggle playing out in her friend's mind.

"Now don't be mad at me, but I kind of told Dax what Jenny and the other girls did to you at camp," Katie admitted, a little ashamed because she had been asked to keep it a secret. "And... well... Dax told Tanner."

"Katie!" Allora yelled.

"I know, I know, but you should have told him. He needed to know what that heinous evil troll did to you," Katie reasoned.

Allora sat back into the seat. She wasn't going to fight Katie on this one. Secretly, Allora had hoped Tanner would find out. She just hadn't wanted to be the one to tell him. "You're right," Allora admitted. "But why? It's not like she hasn't done worse things to other people."

Katie thought for a minute. "It's probably because of what's out there right now. I mean, something really bad could have happened to you. You're really lucky. It also could be because Tanner totally has a major crush on you."

"No he doesn't," Allora said softly.

"Well... you obviously have a crush on him."

"No I don't!" Allora snapped.

Katie laughed. "Why do you think Jenny has it in for you? She didn't tie you up just because you wrote on Nancy's face. Remember, you weren't the only one who did it."

Then, Allora remembered what had happened to her that night. "Oh my god, I totally forgot to tell you," she said, and then told Katie about the odd creature who had released her from the flagpole.

It was difficult to explain what had happened since she hadn't seen who untied the ropes. Allora finished the story as Katie pulled her Jeep into a parking spot. On the first day of school, students had to get their class schedules in the main lobby area. Allora and Katie compared their schedules and found they had most of their classes together. Mr. Swan was teaching Advanced World History, and both were in his first period class.

"How did I get into Advanced World History?" Katie asked. "I suck at history!"

"Good question," Allora said.

She had a lot of questions. Maybe now, Mr. Swan could answer a few. They got to the door of his class to find a lady with curly short hair and glasses surveying the students as they lumbered into the room. Allora double-checked the room number. The sheet said room 202, Mr. Swan, Advanced World History. After confirming it was correct, she took a seat in front of two familiar faces.

"What are you doing in here?" Allora whispered to Tanner and Dax, who slouched in their seats with their legs extended out.

Tanner didn't know how to answer the question because he hadn't even signed up for the class. He shrugged his shoulders as a response.

The curly-haired lady walked to the front of the class. "So, Mr. Swan is away. I will be your substitute. I'm Ms. Benfield," she said.

Allora wasn't satisfied with her explanation of Mr. Swan's absence. "Where is Mr. Swan?"

"Miss, you will raise your hand in my classroom," Ms. Benfield ordered. Allora rolled her eyes and put her hand up. "Yes, Ms. Sona?"

"First of all it's Allora, and I shouldn't have to repeat my question," Allora snapped back.

"I will not tolerate rude behavior from students," Ms. Benfield replied. "You will repeat your question and say please."

The abrasive retort piqued everyone's interest because they all knew Allora's reputation for battling oppressive teachers. Allora was about to blow. She hated when authority figures tried to control her.

She took a deep breath. "Where the hell is Mr. Swan, you pretentious tramp? Please," Allora said, leaning back and smiling. The whole class erupted in laughter.

Ms. Benfield wasn't laughing. She marched down the aisle to Allora's seat, grabbed her by the ear, and dragged Allora to the door. Katie was not going to let the substitute teacher get away with abusing her friend.

"Hey, you evil bitch!" Katie said, standing up in protest. "You're hurting her!"

Ms. Benfield maintained her grip on Allora's ear and motioned to Katie.

"Fine, you can join your friend in the principal's office," she said.

Allora could have easily gotten out of the teacher's hold, but it would have meant possible expulsion, so she resisted. Ms. Benfield let go of her ear and pushed them both into the hallway.

She pointed to the front office. "Go! You will not disrespect me like that and get away with it." She slammed the door.

Allora made an inappropriate gesture in the skinny door window, which the whole room of students witnessed. Ms. Benfield spun around, but Allora had vacated the window before being caught. The two girls decided to avoid the principal's office, and instead they roamed the halls for the rest of the period, gossiping about the horrible substitute. They had made it around the back of the school to the end of the sophomore hall when they saw three sophomore girls standing around a petrified freshman with glasses, tightly holding her books.

As Allora and Katie moved closer, they saw that the young girl against the wall was Bell. Allora watched as the sophomore girls knocked her sister's books out of her hands. Fueled by anger, Allora ran up and knocked over the first girl.

"What do you think you're doing?" Allora said in a threatening manner. "The only person who gets to push my sister around is me."

The tallest of the girls stepped forward. It was Suzy Moore. She was on the girls' basketball team, and a well-known bully.

"I should ask you the same thing," Suzy said, pushing Allora backward.

"Hey!" Katie yelled. She stepped between them, placing her hand on the Suzy's shoulder. "You do not want to start this. Trust me."

Suzy grabbed Katie's hand and squeezed it. Then, she pushed her into the lockers. This set Allora off. She stepped forward to attack, dodging Suzy's punch and placing a fist into the right side of the tall girl's lower abdomen. Then, she spun around with one leg extended, kicking the girl's knees, sending her plummeting to the ground. Suzy wiggled on the floor in pain as the other girls tried to sideswipe Allora. Katie deflected the attack, moving to exact her own vengeance. Before they could do any serious damage, Allora and Katie froze, their bodies tight, unable to move a muscle. The sophomore girls knew they were outmatched and took the opportunity to quickly retreat. Allora's eyes darted back and forth, trying to find the reason for her immobility. Sumatra had done something like this, but he couldn't be at the school. As much as she tried to move, nothing seemed to work. All of a sudden, Katie and Allora fell to the ground. They moved their limbs, trying to figure out what had happened. Then, they saw two black stiletto shoes step onto the carpet in front of them. Both turned their eyes upward to see a figure standing rigid and stern, with hands on her hips.

"Hi, Principal Winters," they said in unison, their monotone voices revealing their guilt.

"Bell, you can go to your class," Mrs. Winters said to the frightened freshman still pressed against the lockers. Bell looked at her sister and moved her lips as if to say, "I'm sorry," then she took off down the hall.

Allora picked herself up, followed by Katie. The two girls were embarrassed, not because they were beating up the sophomores, but because they had gotten caught. Mrs. Winters directed them to march off to the front office. Once they got there, they sat down in seats facing Mrs. Winter's desk, waiting for the principal to join them. Mrs. Winters sat down in her chair, placed her arms on the desk, and clasped her hands.

With a look of disappointment, she said, "It seems as though you two have been busy today. The first day of school and you have gotten kicked out of class and beat up some underclassmen. And it's not even second period yet!" She sat back in her chair and took a deep breath. "Both of you have been given a great responsibility, and it will only become more difficult as you get older."

Allora was confused. "What do you mean?"

"I, like you, am from Sonora as well," She said. Mrs. Winters disregarded their surprised look of bewilderment, and went back to the previous discussion.

"I know you could have hurt those girls, even worse than what I saw, but you have to understand that using force to create fear and intimidation is not what we stand for. You are much better than this... I expect better than this."

"But they were picking on my sister," Allora argued. "I had to do something."

"What you could have done was use diplomacy and reason. If that doesn't work, then there are ways to debilitate your opponent without physically harming them. Straight aggression comes from fear and hate. These emotions are especially strong for some Sonorians, and it can lead you down a very dark path. You must be cognizant of your emotions, but you must not let them control you. I would have hoped that Sumatra had given you some sort of wisdom."

Silently, the girls listened to every word their principal said, but they didn't quite understand all of it. They nodded their heads in agreement to satisfy Mrs. Winters, and then quickly made a break for the door.

Just as they were about to run off, Mrs. Winters halted their escape. "Oh, and you both owe me detention tomorrow. And plan on volunteering to set up for the football games all season long. I'm sure Mrs. Mondrach could use your help."

Again, they nodded their heads, accepting their punishment, and then they went to their second period classes. After fourth period, Tanner, Dax, Katie, and Allora met in the middle of the hall. Allora turned to Tanner.

"I heard that you broke up with Jenny," Allora said, looking to make sure Jenny wasn't around.

"Yeah well, I heard what she did to you that night at camp," Tanner said, causing Allora to blush a little. "Why didn't you tell me what happened?"

"Tanner, I'm fine," Allora responded. Even though she played it off like it was no big deal, a part of her enjoyed the fact that she was the reason they had broken up. "It was just a stupid prank."

Tanner became serious, softly taking hold of Allora's shoulder. "You could have been seriously hurt. Remember what Sumatra said? There are far worse creatures in the woods than what we encountered at the rock quarry. What Jenny did was inexcusable."

Tanner's hands were firmly grasping Allora's shoulders. Her eyes gazed up at his. In that moment, Allora felt completely at ease. Her heart felt like it had fallen into the back of her body. Her limbs were numb as she stood there, paralyzed. Tanner was inches away from Allora's lips, when both of them caught a glimpse of someone out of the corners of their eyes. Tanner let go of Allora and pivoted toward the front double doors.

Dax moved over, noticing the figure stepping through the heavy metal doors. It was a long- haired, beautiful brunette girl with sparkling blue eyes. The wind pushed through the door, tousling her hair. She wore a short denim skirt and a tight spaghetti-strapped tank top. Her long legs were accentuated by her black designer high heels.

She walked by, glaring at Katie and Allora as if trying to project her dominance. Then, she winked at the boys who were now bent over with their mouths to the floor. They both smiled back and watched as she strutted to the front office. Seeing the boys' hormonal reactions led Allora to slap Tanner on the back of the head, while Katie hit Dax. The girls left, rolling their eyes as they walked away. The boys remained perplexed.

"What was that for?" Tanner asked as Allora exited the school.

"Yeah," Dax added, rubbing the back of his head.

Allora spun around. "For being an idiot," she said.

"I just felt like smacking you!" Katie added as the doors closed.

Ignoring his sister, Dax walked up next to Tanner and said, "Dibs."

"You can't call dibs when you haven't even met the girl," Tanner replied.

"Guy code says, you see a girl, you claim her, and she's yours," Dax rebutted, grinning emphatically.

"That might have been the guy code if we were cavemen. Are you going to club her and take her back to your hut, too?" Tanner said, grinning when Dax didn't have a comeback.

Outside the school, Katie said, "She must be a new student," as she climbed into the driver's side of her car.

"Did you see the way she was dressed?" Allora said, not liking the reaction the new girl had gotten from the boys—especially Tanner. She didn't express that to Katie, though. Allora still wasn't sure how she felt about him.

"She better not be good at soccer, because if she is, then I will have to break her legs."

They looked at each other and laughed.

"I'm sure she's a nice girl," Allora said, not really believing it herself.

Katie pulled into Allora's driveway and dropped her off. Allora went inside, waving good- bye to her friend. She grabbed a cold soda out of the fridge, flopped onto the couch, and spent the rest of the night alone, reading a book in her room, happy to have some time to herself in a safe, quiet place.

Chapter 12

New Girl

After school the next day, Allora and Katie plopped down into their seats in detention, sitting at the back of the almost-empty classroom. This wasn't a new environment for the two troublemakers. On several previous occasions, they had received detention for talking back to teachers in class.

Katie and Allora sat in detention, watching the clock tick slowly around to end another minute. Mrs. Slade, a freshman social studies teacher, was at the front of the class, quietly reading a book, not paying attention to anyone in the room. Allora looked around to see Sam Prior sitting next to the window. He was a part of the skater posse, as they called themselves. Most wore DC shoes, grew their hair long, wore ripped jeans, and sported some sort of offensive T-shirt. This was the reason Sam was in detention. He wore a shirt that said, "Suck This," and had a hand pointing to his crotch. The fashion statement hadn't gone over too well with Principal Winters. Behind him, in the corner, was Betty Salazar. She was one of the drama students. Betty was in detention for punching one of the other girls in the school play. The play was West Side Story, and the scene called for the group to act out a fake fight. Betty was very big on getting into character. She thought that actually punching the girl would make the play more real. The drama teacher, however, disagreed.

Katie scooted her desk forward, inching closer to Allora.

"Do you know what we are supposed to do on Friday for the football game?" Katie whispered.

Allora leaned back and turned her head slightly. "I think we've got to set up decorations, the snack stand, and clean up after the game. Or at least that is what I had to do two years ago."

"You've done this before?" Katie asked.

"Yeah, you remember freshman year when I got in the fight with the English teacher over that thing we were supposed to write about?"

Katie shook her head.

"My English teacher played a video of some woman flushing toilets and we were supposed to write an interpretive essay on why it was considered to be art," Allora said. The teacher in front put her head up because of the whispers going on between the two girls. "I refused to do the assignment and told the teacher that he was an idiot. He sent me off to the principal's office and she gave me the same punishment."

"There is no talking in detention," Mrs. Slade said, snapping her fingers. "Now zip it!" The girls stopped talking and remained silent for the rest of the hour. They arrived at school the following day, dreading the eventual confrontation with Ms. Benfield. The thought of having to apologize was revolting. Allora walked into her history class to see a different substitute teacher putting her name on the chalkboard.

Allora sat down next to Katie, saying, "I wonder where the other teacher went."

Tanner leaned forward from his seat behind the two girls. "Principal Winters fired her."

"Really?" Allora asked, enthusiastically spinning around in her chair. "But why? I really liked her!" Allora said, sarcastically.

"I was in the office after school, and Ms. Benfield came into Mrs. Winter's office. Then I heard some yelling. A few minutes later, and Ms. Benfield came storming out of the office," Tanner said.

Allora spun back around.

"Good morning, students. My name is Ms. Norman. I will be your substitute teacher until Mr. Swan returns. I don't know when that will be, but let's hope we can get through as much material as possible before he gets back."

Someone opened the classroom door. A girl poked her head in and then swung the door open. "Hi. I think that this is my class," the girl said. It was the new girl, and she look just as beautiful and confident as she did the previous day.

"You're a little late, darling," Ms. Norman said.

"I know. I'm so sorry. I'm new here."

"Well, what is your name?" Ms. Norman asked.

"Kim."

"Well, Kim, go ahead and have a seat so we can get started," Ms. Norman said, directing her to an open desk near the front.

Kim took a seat in Allora's row, on the other side of the class. She strutted across the room, like a princess in front of her court. An obviously audacious individual, Allora felt strange as she watched the new girl take her seat.

Ms. Norman began the class by talking about the Roman Empire, discussing Gaius Julius Caesar and his great military victories in Gaul. The Battle of Alesia was especially fascinating to Allora. In it, Julius Caesar and the Romans were outnumbered five to one. They erected fortifications and traps to slow down the attacking Gallic army. Eventually, the Gallic army was defeated by Caesar's cavalry, which outflanked the Gauls. Then, Ms. Norman discussed the dictatorship of Caesar.

"Soon after the victories in Gaul, Caesar was ordered by the senate to disband the army and come back to Rome. Does anyone know who was leading the Roman senate at this time?" Ms. Norman asked the class.

Allora was about to answer the question when the new girl interrupted her. "That would be Pompey, Ms. Norman."

Allora glared at Kim, unhappy with being upstaged. History was her subject. She had always been the top gun when it came to history trivia.

"Good job, Kim," Ms. Norman said, and then continued with the story. "Caesar chose to take one of his legions and march with them to Rome. This ignited a civil war, since no Roman army was supposed to be in Rome. Does anyone know what happened to the Roman senators who defied Caesar?"

Allora was again about to say the answer, but Kim got to it first. "Most of the senate was pardoned, but a few of the more treacherous Romans were killed," she said.

"So what happened to Caesar?" Ms. Norman asked.

Kim smiled and said, "He became a great Roman dictator."

Allora jumped in. "Actually, he was a tyrant who wouldn't give up his power over the Roman Empire, which is probably why he was assassinated."

"Which was an obvious tragedy," Kim responded.

"A tragedy? And what about the thousands of people the Roman Empire oppressed, killed, and raped? The Roman Empire burned, pillaged, and murdered its way across Europe."

"A necessary evil, when you think about the barbaric and obviously weak people that the Roman Empire destroyed," said Kim.

A few minutes later, the bell rang to end class.

"Alright class," Ms. Norman said, cutting off the argument. "Great discussion today. I will expect those papers on the history of Caesar on my desk on Monday."

Allora marched across the room, eager to confront the new girl, who was busy putting her notebook away.

"How can you think one man with absolute power is great?"

Kim turned her attention to Allora. "Because, one man making all the decisions is efficient. Look at what he was able to accomplish in such a short amount of time. The Roman Empire controlled half of the world," Kim said, putting the rest of her stuff in her bag.

"Yeah, and they killed thousands, if not millions, of people," Allora argued.

Kim moved closer to Allora. "To make an omelet, you have to crack a few eggs," Kim said, giving Allora a sinister smile.

Katie walked up as soon as Kim exited the classroom.

"I don't think I like that girl very much," Allora said.

~~~~~~~~~~~~~~~

Thursday came, and it was now the last full football practice before game day. Tanner and Dax stretched on the field while the cheerleading squad was busy practicing their routines. In the equipment room, Allora and Katie received an extensive tour from Mrs. Mondrach, who was the parent volunteer for the Pioneer Club. Most of the funding for equipment, uniforms, and setup costs for the games came from the club's fundraising efforts.

"So, here is the area where you can make signs. You guys will need to make one big one for when the football players run out onto the field," Mrs. Mondrach said. Her son Robert was the first string running back.

"I thought the cheerleaders made that sign," Katie said.

"Not this time," Mrs. Mondrach replied. "They need as much practice as possible."

Mrs. Mondrach was explaining where the long tables went when Kim walked out of the girls' locker room wearing a cheerleading outfit. She ignored Allora and headed toward the rest of the cheerleading squad.

"We're going to go get some water from the fountain, Mrs. Mondrach," Allora said, yanking Katie by the arm and pulling her to the field.

"Okay, girls, don't be too long," Mrs. Mondrach replied. "I still need to show you where the chairs go."

Allora and Katie made it down to the field to hear Coach Laurent introducing the new girl to the rest of the cheerleading squad.

"Everyone, this is Kim. She is a transfer student from Florida. She's been a varsity cheerleader since she was a freshman, and I hope you will all welcome her with open arms," Coach Laurent announced.

Jenny pushed her way through the squad.

"But coach, she wasn't here for tryouts," Jenny said. "There is no way she should be allowed to make the team. That isn't fair to all the other girls who tried out for the squad."

"It also wouldn't be fair for us to rob her of her senior season," Coach Laurent said. "Besides, Jenny, when you see how talented she is, I think that even you will change your mind."

"Not likely," Jenny said, only loud enough for the rest of the squad to hear, causing them to giggle.

Hearing this, Kim lined up next to the girls, facing the field. She started running, performing a few cartwheels, three back handsprings, and finishing with a double full back flip. The cheerleaders stood on the side of the field with their mouths wide open.

Tanya walked up next to Jenny. "Wow, she may even be better than you."

Jenny turned, put her leg behind Tanya, and pushed the other girl's shoulder, causing her to fall over.

"Nobody is better than me," Jenny said, stomping off to the girls' locker room.

Allora was also amazed by Kim's talent. Her amazement changed to jealousy when she saw Tanner strutting over to Kim.

"That was amazing!" Tanner said, causing Kim to blush. "I'll have you know this squad has won state almost every year I've been here. With you on the squad, you girls are going to be unstoppable."

"Thanks, hotshot. You're not so bad yourself." As she said this, she gently stroked Tanner's chest flirtatiously. Then, she stood on her toes and gave Tanner a kiss on the cheek. "Good luck tomorrow."

Jenny watched the sensual exchange and erupted like a volcano. Coach Laurent was oblivious to what was going on. She was looking at a chart full of cheerleading routines when the cheerleading captain charged past her. Jenny pounced on the unsuspecting new girl. She dragged her to the ground, and the two girls began pulling each other's hair. Screams filled the area as the girls became more ruthless. Hair pulling turned into biting and scratching. The entire football team started yelling and running over to the fight. Coach Laurent finally got through the crowd of students and tried to pull them apart, but they both had iron grips on one another. Tanya and Nancy moved in to help, while Tanner and Dax both tried to grab Kim. Allora made it through the horde in time to see the two girls get separated.

Coach Laurent got to her feet, snapping back her head. "What the hell is going on here? You two, my office, now!"

Jenny stomped off while the coach kept Kim next to her. The three of them marched off to the gym, leaving everyone talking excitedly about the fight.

Dax was the first to comment. "Buddy, you really know how to incite a riot, don't you?" he said. "That was the best chick fight I've ever seen! It's too bad I didn't have my camera, because that definitely would have been perfect for YouTube."

"Shut up," Tanner replied.

"Seriously, dude, you have a gift."

"I hate you."

"I'm just saying, you may want to think about calling one of those talk shows. You know, the real trashy ones where the guy has, like, five girl-friends that don't know about each other."

As Dax continued to hassle his friend, Allora remembered an important message that she was supposed to pass on to the other three. She grabbed all three and pulled them to a spot on the green turf where no one could hear.

"I forgot to tell you guys," Allora said. "Sumatra told my mother that he wants us to stop by his place after we get done here."

"Do you know why?" Tanner asked.

"I'm not really sure," she said. "My mother left a note on my bed saying he wanted to speak with us. When I went to ask her about it, my aunt said she was going to be gone for the day." Allora paused for a second. "We should probably listen to her. It may be important."

After practice, they hiked through the forest to the portal and jumped through. Usually, they landed in the orchard where they had trained all summer, but this time was different. When the world reappeared, the four teens were standing in a grand hall of arching wood, filled with weaponry. Swords, spears, bows, arrows, and more lined the stone walls. At the end of the hall, the kids could make out the image of an old man sitting cross-legged on the ground in front of a large fireplace, which was lit. As they walked down the corridor, flames began to dance out from the fireplace. Each flame danced along the stone floor, crawled up the pillars, and lit the candles, bringing light to the entire room. The kids gawked at the display.

Once they were a few feet from Sumatra, he got up and looked at the children. "Thank you for coming," he said, moving away from the fire, walking in between the children and out into the corridor.

"How did we get here and where are we? I thought that the portal went to the orchard," Tanner said. Everyone had the same question on their minds.

Sumatra turned around to face the kids. "That's very difficult to explain. You would need to understand the intricacies of time and space. If you know how, you can change the direction of the space fold, and therefore change the destination. But you also have to be very careful. The outer realm is nothing to play around with. If you get it wrong, you could end up sending half of you to one location and half to another." The kids cringed at the thought. "The reason I had you all come here today is because I believe you to be ready for your weapons, or at least temporary ones." As he said this, he went back down the corridor, waving his hand for everyone to follow.

They made their way to the middle of the grand hall. The hallway split into four directions. In every corridor, weapons were stacked against the walls, reaching high above. "I want you all to spend some time here and find the weapon that fits you. I'm sure that you all have an idea of the type of weapon that best suits you, so go on and take a look."

With that, they all split up.

Tanner found the section with the long swords. He walked down the hall, running his hand along the cold steel swords hanging on the racks. He went past the Roman spatha, the European rapier, and the Scottish claymore. After a while, he stopped in front of a two-handed German long sword, called a zweihander. The straight blade was double-edged forged steel. Normally, this type of sword was about eighty-five inches long and weighed fifteen pounds. The particular sword that Tanner picked up was a little bit smaller, which made it far easier to use.

Katie wasn't that much farther down the hall. She was holding a Japanese katana. "Sumatra, can we pick out two weapons?" Katie asked.

"Yes, Katara," Sumatra said, while Katie pulled two swords from their sheaths. The single- edged, beautifully crafted, moderately curved swords glistened when she swung them in the air. She made fast swooshing motions and then placed them back into their sheaths.

Dax was in a completely different hallway, looking at the staffs. He made a pass through the entire row of staffs and found one that he liked. He picked it up and twirled it around in his hands. "That particular staff is made of a rare type of dogwood," Sumatra said, catching Dax by surprise. The ends of the staff were rounded; the wood was very smooth and surprisingly light.

Then, Sumatra headed toward the ranged weapons, where Allora was eyeing a composite bow that hung out of reach. Suddenly, the bow lifted itself from the wall and fell into Allora's arms. She looked to her left, and then her right, and found that Sumatra was holding up his staff. "How did you do that?" Allora asked.

Sumatra smiled. "I will teach you when you get older." He waved his staff, and a quiver of arrows appeared from down the hall, flying toward them. "These are especially efficient, strong arrows that will fly true. They are made from hickory, and the feathers are that of a Bennu bird. It is said to possess the soul of the ancient Egyptian sun god, Ra. I think that they will be perfect for you."

The teens met back in the middle of the grand hall. Once there, they showed each other which weapons they had chosen. They were all very proud of their choices. Sumatra let them reflect over their new gifts before he said, "Now that you have your weapons, I must tell you about their power. Each one is old and was charmed by an ancient mage. They're imbued with hadrons that will flow through you and back into your weapon. They can be very powerful, but you all must use them wisely. You four have a responsibility like no other before you. I hope that you are able to embrace your destiny." Sumatra went to a wide circle in the middle of the hall. "I will be gone for a little while, but make sure you still continue your training without me. I will assess your progress when I return." Then, he was sucked through the portal.

Chapter 13

Friday Football

The first game of the season was always crazy. Everyone was dressed head to toe in red and white. The football players always had their jerseys on, and the cheerleaders wore their uniforms to school. The whole town was fanatical about Pioneer football. The previous year, Sandy High School had made it to the semifinals of the state championships, only to be beaten in the last quarter by Lake Oswego High School. Now, they were playing against the Lake Oswego Lakers again in the first game of the year. This had been on Tanner's mind ever since the coach had announced who their first opponent of the season would be. He had played a magnificent championship game, but a fourth quarter interception had led to the game-winning touchdown.

The memory ate away at him all day. Allora found Tanner pacing back and forth in the parking lot next to his car. "Are you thinking about making a break for the border?" Allora playfully questioned, trying to cheer him up. She could tell that he was stressed out about the game.

Tanner kept pacing. "Allora, I can't do this." He was becoming increasingly agitated. Allora walked over and grabbed his shoulder. The touch of Allora's hand helped to calm him down.

"Hey, look at me," Allora said. "You are an amazing quarterback. Think about all that you have accomplished. This is only a game." This was the first time that Allora had ever seen Tanner so insecure. She knew that football meant a lot to him, but she had no idea how much pressure he was under. "Go down there and play as if it were a pickup game with your friends."

Tanner smiled at her. "You know, you would think that I would be more nervous about weird mythical creatures trying to kill me than a football game."

They both laughed. "Yeah, well I'm not sure which one is more scary: creatures from another world, or Pioneer fans," Allora said.

Tanner put his arm around Allora's shoulder, and they walked to the football field. They descended the concrete stairs next to the gym, stepping down onto the track. The field was completely surrounded by large trees, making it seem enclosed in a bowl. At the far end was a slope of matted grass and dirt. Katie was waiting for Allora down at the equipment closet next to the bleachers. She watched as Allora walked by with Tanner's arm wrapped around her neck. Then, Tanner ran off to join his team for a pregame talk.

Allora didn't smile back at her friend, who was giving her a huge grin.

"Not a word," she said, pointing at Katie.

Katie shrugged her shoulders. "What? I didn't say a thing," she replied, unable to wipe the grin from her face.

The two of them went through the entire checklist that Mrs. Mondrach had given them. She had gone over everything twice so that the girls wouldn't have any excuses if they messed up. When Mrs. Mondrach showed up an hour before the game, she was surprised to see that the girls had accomplished everything to her exact specifications. The signs were all made, the tables were set perfectly, and all of the decorations were in their correct places.

"Well, girls, you have done a great job. I will let Mrs. Winters know how fabulous you are," Mrs. Mondrach said, and then left to perform her pregame duties.

Allora and Katie found seats in the student section of the stands, at the edge of the running track. They still had a while before the game started, and figured they might as well get good seats. Slowly, students started to file in and fill the stands behind them. Allora watched as the cheerleaders practiced their splits, flips, and stances. The only fun part about it was watching Jenny and Kim bicker. Their dislike of Kim was about the only thing that Jenny and Allora had in common.

Eventually, the football players went into the locker room to listen to Coach Hale give the pregame speech. The cheerleaders lined up across from each other, creating a corridor into the field. Four of the cheerleaders held up the sign that Allora and Katie had made earlier that afternoon. About ten minutes before that start of the game, the Sandy High School Pioneers charged through the red double doors from inside the locker room and crashed through the large sign held up by the cheerleaders. The crowd roared to life, and the deafening sound reverberated through the packed stadium.

At halftime, Allora stood, unable to watch the cheerleaders do their dance routine. "I'm going to go over to the concessions stand and get something to drink. You want anything?"

"No, I'm good." Katie responded.

Allora walked down the track, past the rambunctious junior high kids. Memories of being fourteen circulated through her mind. She reflected on how carefree her life had been. Things had been simpler back then, and yet it had seemed so important at the time. Allora bought a Diet Coke, her favorite, and moved to the exit, where a group of junior high kids came screaming out of the woods, toward the stadium. Their parents rushed down the hill from their seats. Allora slowly walked past them so she could hear what they were saying. One of the girls was crying uncontrollably as she told her mother about a monster in the woods. The little girl was terrified. Between gasps of fright, she kept repeating the same two words.

"Red eyes... red eyes... It ha... ha... had red eyes."

Her mother carried her away. Allora thought about following them to find out more, but that would have been too suspicious. She rushed went back to her seat and told Katie what had happened. As she finished the story, the cheerleaders lined up and the football players jogged out onto the field. Allora wanted to tell the boys, but she knew they had enough on their minds. Tanner walked past her, looked up, and winked. Allora giggled.

"When are you finally going to admit that you like him?" Katie asked.

"I don't know what you're talking about," Allora said.

Katie wasn't going to let Allora off the hook that easily. "Come on. I see the way you two look at each other—it's so obvious. He is single now. You should totally go for it," Katie said, just as Tanner threw a sixty-yard pass to Dax for a touchdown. The crowd exploded, but the two girls remained seated. "When are you going to stop lying to yourself and admit that you like him?"

Allora sat there contemplating what Katie said. Was she lying to herself? Every time that she was around him, a strange feeling formed in the pit of her stomach. She knew she cared about him a lot, but were those feelings changing to something more? All around her, people were cheering, but she hardly noticed the sound. Deep down she was scared to get hurt. She was strong when it came to everything except love. Katie saw that her friend's mood was quickly changing for the worse. She grabbed Allora's arm and shook her.

"Hey. We can't be in a bad mood for this game. Our boys need us."

Katie pulled Allora up and started hollering at Tanner and Dax, who were standing by the water cooler.

"Nice catch, Dax!" Katie yelled over the crowd.

"Thanks, sis!" Dax yelled back, grinning.

At the end of the game, Allora and Katie stood in the middle of the field as Tanner and Dax walked out from the locker room. The Pioneers had won in the fourth quarter, and the girls could tell the boys were exuberant as they met them in the middle of the field.

"I told you there was nothing to be worried about," Allora said.

Tanner gave her a half smile. "Yeah, I'm just glad Dax doesn't have butterfingers."

Dax shoved him playfully. All of a sudden the lights shut off. They all began to laugh at each other, because it had caused everyone to jump. Darkness set in as the bulbs dimmed, turning orange and then fading away. They looked around to find that the field was completely empty of people. Just then, a snap echoed from the woods surrounding the field. The stadium was now engulfed in complete blackness. They stared toward the edge of the trees, where the noise had come from. Nothing happened for about a minute, until two dark red eyes appeared between the trees. Allora remembered the little girl from earlier in the evening. The eyes gradually grew bigger, as it slowly made its way to the edge of the field. Something grabbed Tanner by the shoulder, causing him to spin around to attack. Everyone else spun and screamed, ready to pounce on the intruder. A light came on, revealing that it was Kim. She had her cell phone out, and was clutching it to her chest.

Kim caught her breath. "Oh my god, you scared the crap out of me. What are you guys doing?"

"I was about to ask you the same thing. Why did you sneak up on us like that?" Allora demanded.

"I wasn't sneaking up on you. I needed a ride home and everyone left before I could ask someone. I saw you guys down here and thought that you could help me out."

Allora stepped back, a little ashamed for assuming that Kim was up to no good. They all turned back around to see if the red eyes were still there, but they had vanished.

"Yeah, we should probably get out of here," Tanner said with a bit of urgency.

They all stole a few glances behind them while they walked to Tanner's car. Dax took the front seat, as usual, which meant that the three girls had to squeeze together in the back. Allora wasn't too happy to be so close to Kim. She felt a weird vibe whenever she was around the girl.

Tanner pulled out of the school lot and onto the main road.

"So where do you live?" he asked.

"River Road," Kim replied.

"That's really close," Tanner said.

"Yeah, probably close enough to walk," Allora said.

Allora didn't look at Kim's reaction to her comment. She guessed that it was a fake smile, followed by an angry glare. It was a look that Allora had given when she heard a smart-ass comment directed toward her. Seconds later, the car pulled onto River Road. Tanner went all the way down to the end of the street.

"Stop," Kim said. "We're here."

The car pulled up to a two-story yellow house with large bushes surrounding the property. Allora knew who lived there.

"Hey, isn't this the Nelson's house?" Allora asked.

"They're my grandparents," Kim said, opening the car door. "On my mother's side." She got out of the car. "She's in Europe for work, so she asked me to come stay here to take care of them." With that, she closed the door and waved them good-bye. But she remained standing in the driveway and watching as the car rolled back toward the main road.

"That girl is strange. Really strange," Allora said.

"I don't know. I kind of like her," Tanner said.

Allora wasn't too happy with that, but she didn't want to argue with him. Instead, Allora changed the subject. "Okay, what the hell was that thing in the woods?" she said, lowering her voice as she spoke.

"I don't know, but whatever it was, it looked unnatural," Dax said.

"We should ask Sumatra," Katie said.

"Remember, he's gone right now. Oh, and we are not telling my mother. She will flip out and chain me to my bed," Allora commanded.

Tanner pulled the car into the Allora's driveway, and she got out. They were all exhausted as their emotional day finally came to an end.

Chapter 14

Swan's Return

"What's going on?" Mrs. Ferris demanded, perplexed by the sudden departure to the dank, secluded high school basement. The eerie echoes of the old pipes softly clanked and clamored against each other on the ceiling. An ancient furnace filled the air with a pungent burning odor.

"I found the second piece!" Mr. Swan whispered.

"Really!" Mrs. Ferris exclaimed, enthusiastically.

Mrs. Ferris gasped at the sight of a rat, scurrying along the edge of the concrete floor. "Couldn't you have told me this upstairs?"

"That's the problem...." Mr. Swan inched closer, knowing the danger in their situation. "It's no longer safe to talk about it in school."

"How do you know?"

"They somehow knew I was going to Peru. There was a Chenoo waiting at the base of Manchu Picchu when I arrived."

"How did they find out?"

"I don't know. I was able to fight it off, but I'm almost positive I was followed back," Mr. Swan said, with guilty apprehension. "It was most likely a—"

"*No!*" Mrs. Ferris yelled.

"Shhhh!"

Mrs. Ferris pulled back, again whispering in the dark of the basement, "Where is your proof?"

"I ported back, and the residual of someone else came through only minutes afterward. I could sense their hadron levels... it was someone very powerful."

"Why the hell did you port?" she asked.

"I had to! It was the only way I could get out alive, with the...."

Mr. Swan paused, his senses picking up on the muffled sounds of voices. Out of his peripheral vision, he saw a shadow dance along the wall near the doorway. Grabbing Mrs. Ferris, he moved toward the back corner, hiding behind stacked crates of milk cartons. Footsteps grew louder as two sets of feet walked toward them. They held their breath in frightened anticipation. One pair of feet stopped on the other side of the crates, followed by eerie silence.

Then, one of the individuals spoke. "We only need two crates of milk, right?"

"Yeah, I don't think these kids will drink any more than that."

Mr. Swan let out a sigh of relief, realizing it was only the cook and the custodian. The two left with their supplies, leaving Mr. Swan and Mrs. Ferris in the dark, catching their breath.

"Why in the hell do they keep milk down here?" Mrs. Ferris asked.

Mr. Swan ignored her question and went back to their discussion. "It's now even more imperative that we find the last piece."

"You know where it is?"

"I think so, but I can't get to it," Mr. Swan said, glancing back at the closed metal basement door. "If I was followed, then my identity is compromised. I need you to go."

"Me?" Mrs. Ferris asked. "I can't do it. I'm just a science professor. I never got the training you received."

"We don't have a choice!" Mr. Swan yelled, pulling back as he realized how loud he was becoming. Silence followed. Both of them thought about the importance of the task.

"What about the kids?" Mr. Swan asked.

"Milly would never allow it." Mrs. Ferris snapped quietly.

"You have a better option?" he asked.

Again, they stood contemplating. Neither could think of anything better.

"But how will you get around Milly?"

"You'll see." Mr. Swan grabbed the door, then remembered one last thing. "Oh, and I also think you should consider giving them a lesson on glues... they will most likely need it."

He left the room. Another rat ran across the floor, causing Mrs. Ferris to quickly follow behind him. "I hate making glues!" she proclaimed softly.

~~~~~~~~~~~~~~~

"Do you know what the Eye of the Titans is?" Allora asked.

Mr. Swan turned pale, yet his body suggested an odd fervor. He leaned forward. "Where did you learn that term?"

Allora was about to speak, but Mr. Swan's sudden gesture suggested against it.

"Wait," Mr. Swan said, pressing his finger toward her lips. "Not here. We aren't safe."

He glanced over his shoulder at the open door, where screaming students zoomed past as they socialized before their next classes.

"Bring the other three to my classroom after fourth period. We'll talk then."

Afraid and confused, Allora complied with her teacher's request. Escaping the classroom, she could sense something strange in the hallway. She looked back at Mr. Swan's room, but he had mysteriously vanished. There was no other way out except through the doorway, which Allora now occupied. Shaking off the strange moment, Allora joined the herd of students.

Why is everyone so freaked out about the Eye of the Titans? she thought to herself as she arrived at English class.

Waiting anxiously throughout the class, Allora watched as the small hand of the clock struck the nine, causing the bell to sound. Most of her classmates were eager to leave the confines of the school, while Allora was anxious to stay. After grabbing Tanner, Katie, and Dax, they all found Mr. Swan pacing at the back of the room. Seeing them walk in, Mr. Swan gestured toward the front.

"Close the door and come sit."

They did as instructed, sitting in the front as Mr. Swan moved around his desk and retrieved an item.

Allora began, "So, what is this Eye—" Mr. Swan gestured for silence again.

In front of Allora, Mr. Swan placed a round, white gel-like ball on the table. They crowded around, trying to get a glimpse of it. The ball had a strange metallic tint and seemed to swirl with an odd, flowing glint against the light of the dim room.

"You guys should probably stand back," Mr. Swan suggested.

When he pointed his finger, a green spark shot out and struck the peculiar white ball. It exploded, sending clear goo to cover every surface of the room. This included the individuals standing in a circle around the desk. They tried to speak, but no sound came from their mouths. No one could hear anything. Mr. Swan struggled to hide his smile. He had been afraid that this might happen. Again, he pointed his finger, sending green sparks toward each student. The clear goo fell toward the floor, collecting into a small ball at each student's feet.

"What was that?" Allora said, not at all happy with the teacher's weird contraption.

Mr. Swan collected the small balls and put them together to form one medium-size clear ball. "It's called silencing glue," he said, gently placing the ball into his desk drawer. "If you look around, that goo is forming to the interior of this room, creating a soundproof space." As he said this, the clear gel formed to the walls and disappeared. "Mrs. Ferris is still trying to perfect the formula."

"So we can say whatever we want and no one can hear except us?" Katie asked.

"That is correct," Mr. Swan answered.

Katie went up to the wall to see if she could feel anything, but it was completely normal. "That is so cool," she said.

"Why is all of this necessary?" Allora asked.

Mr. Swan became uneasy, choosing to lean against his desk in order to explain himself. He took a moment to collect his thoughts, wondering which parts he should refrain from mentioning. Allora bent her knee, crossed her arms, and raised her eyebrows.

"Allora... it's complicated."

"Why is everyone treating me like a baby?" Allora asked. "I've shot fire out of my hands, traveled through portals, and fought random alien creatures. I'm pretty sure complicated is turning out to be a normal occurrence."

The other three chuckled at Allora's sarcasm. Even Mr. Swan smirked.

"Alright, but this has to be our secret. Your mother would kill me if she found out."

After receiving nods from each of his four students, he walked past them and stopped at the back wall. Placing an open palm on the wall, Mr. Swan began rotating his hand. A green glow escaped the edges of his hand while he continued rotating it clockwise, and then counterclockwise. Awestruck, the students remained watching until he finally finished and placed his hand at his side. Green lines slowly dissipated on his palm, while a green glowing circle formed on the wall. A bright flash burst out from the green lines, and then pulled back inward.

Mr. Swan reached his hand into the wall, just as they had done at Sas' cave. From the depths of the liquid wall, he pulled out a rolled parchment. Eyes wide, Allora shoved her hand into her bag, wondering if he had somehow stolen her copy. The familiar sheepskin she had received from Sas still remained in her book bag. Puzzled by what Mr. Swan had, she moved in closer to look at his copy. She anxiously waited as he unrolled the ancient beige parchment.

Finally reaching the end, Mr. Swan placed a book on the top to keep the parchment flat.

"Hey, I've got one too!" Allora said, excitedly pulling the parchment from her school bag.

Mr. Swan didn't seem surprised. "Yeah, Ben gave that to Sas for safe keeping. I've been trying to find the other two pieces to complete the riddle."

Mr. Swan's copy was completely blank.

"I don't get it," Allora said. "Why doesn't this one have anything on it.

Again, Mr. Swan's hands began to glow, filling the room with a green hue. A soft light escaped his palms, covering the blank pages. Suddenly, ink emerged onto the parchment, slowing forming intricately artistic lettering. Cursive writing blanketed the pages in large bold lettering, with four lines of words.

"Whoa!" Tanner said. "I don't think I'll ever get used to that."

Mr. Swan stared at the writing, grinning with excitement.

"I've waited decades to look upon this script," he said. "We already exposed the other parchment when the first one was discovered. The ink reacts to hadrons. Very unique stuff."

Allora couldn't help but notice an odd, unfamiliar look in Mr. Swan's eyes. At first, he was in a state of exuberance, but it changed quickly. A cold energy began to filter into the room. A long minute passed as Allora continued to feel as though there was another presence in the room, like she had just entered a haunted house.

"Mr. Swan...?" Allora said.

He stopped staring and looked up.

"I'm sorry," he said, embarrassed by his behavior. "I've just been searching for these artifacts for a very long time. Don't mind me...." He moved back, allowing for the others to take a glance. "Allora, why don't you read it?"

Allora inched forward, unsure about what she had felt. The cold sensation passed, but the feeling of peculiarity still remained.

"Okay," she said, staring down at the beautiful scripture.

> *"Heed the warnings of the path you take.*
> *For one false choice will be the last you make.*
> *Be careful to step with winged feet.*
> *For one wrong move will send you deep."*

There was something powerful about what was contained in this writing. First, Allora's aunt had blown up about even mentioning the Eye, and now Mr. Swan was reacting none too differently. The Eye of the Titans was just a group of words, and yet it brought out so much emotion. Somehow, this Eye had to do with Sonora, and the turmoil that had led to her family and friends coming to Earth. Determined to get to the answers, she confronted her teacher.

"Now, what is the Eye of the Titans?"

Mr. Swan leaned against his desk, taking a deep breath before beginning his story.

"Do you all know the story of the Titan Wars?" he asked.

Remembering the story of Greek gods and Titans, Allora asked, "Wasn't that just mythology?"

"The story you were told was mythology, but the war was real..." he began. "The Titans were, and still are, the rulers of Titanis, which is the main capital of Sonora. Back when the Gateways to Earth were discovered, the Titans treated humans as slaves, and Earth as its own colony. This was at the initial evolution of humans as intellectual creatures, who started to think on their own. Separate Sonorian colonies formed in different parts of Earth, and wars were fought over that land because of the Earth's resources. But soon, the rulers of these colonies became entrenched with the humans, teaching them their ways, educating the humans in technology, religion, math, science, and language. The Titans of Sonora became infuriated. Since the Gateways were permanently open, a large Titan army was released on Earth, starting one of the largest and most devastating wars for either world."

The four kept leaning forward as if they would enter the story themselves. Somehow, they all felt a familiar kinship to the story, as if it had occurred in a recent dream. Each word their teacher spoke drew them closer to the characters, closer to the emotions and pain that had consumed those involved.

Mr. Swan continued, "To quell the onslaught of the invading army, the Sonorian colonists formed a secret army called the Guardians. Most of the main leaders of the Guardians you know." The puzzled looks made Mr. Swan smile. "They are Zeus, Hera, Hermes, Aries, Poseidon, and the rest of the 'Greek Gods,' " he said, with mocking hand-signaled quotations, suggesting the inaccurate use of the word "God."

"Why were they called 'Gods,' then?" Tanner asked.

"Well, if you were a human at that time, and a group of aliens arrived who could create energy from their hands, wouldn't you consider them 'Gods' as well?"

They all laughed.

"Those Sonorian colonists around Earth joined the Guardians to battle the Titans for the freedom of Earth and the humans."

"So what happened?" Allora asked.

"That is why we're here today. No one knows what happened, because all of the true texts and stories were destroyed, or hidden away in secret locations to preserve the truth. I've been trying to locate them, but I haven't been successful just yet. Most of what is known was passed down through verbal telling of the stories, and that is why you have those mythological stories of the war and the leaders of the rebellion told from a human perspective."

"And the Eye?" Allora asked.

"Well... the Eye is said to be a myth, but most of us believers know it as one of the artifacts used to defeat the Titans and bring order to the two worlds," Mr. Swan said with authority and exuberance. "It is said to be more powerful than any known artifact. I believe it is real, and those pieces of parchment prove it is."

Allora's mind was moving fast, picturing an item of great power that could be used to protect the people she loved. Finding this artifact could be the solution to those who sought to do them harm. And it might be used to return her life to a sense of normalcy. This life she has been thrust into was becoming overwhelming. The threat of constant danger was exhausting, and this Eye could be her saving grace.

"So how do we find this thing?" Allora asked, thoroughly intrigued.

"Well, that's the problem. We need to find the last piece of the puzzle; it is the most important piece, because it explains the geographic location of the Eye."

"Do you know how to find the last piece?" Tanner asked.

"No," he said. The disappointed faces of his students indicated their passionate interest in finding the artifact. "But... I believe I know who might."

"Who is it?" Allora asked eagerly.

"Sas."

Allora was a little confused as to how the bumbling creature would know the location of the last piece. She wondered why he wouldn't have already told them, after giving Allora the first piece when they first met. "How would he know where the last piece is?"

"Because his father was the one who found the first," Mr. Swan said, pointing to the parchment lying on the desk. "Sas' father died mysteriously, but was said to be searching for something that could be used in the wars in Sonora. This was before the turmoil that landed us on Earth." Mr. Swan's expression turned sour, unable to mask the emotion he felt at the memory of a painful past. Even though they were curious, none of the teenagers chose to inquire further. Instead, Allora remained focused on finding the last piece of parchment.

"So, you believe Sas' father told him where it was hidden?"

Mr. Swan reverted back to the moment, shaking off the pains of his past.

"Not necessarily," he answered. "I believe the location of the last piece is exactly where Sas' father died."

"If Sas' father died trying to find this thing, why would we want to go looking for it?" Dax asked.

"Because, for one, this artifact is one of the only chances we have of protecting the people of our community, and legend has it that Sas' father was betrayed...." Mr. Swan broke off, as though he wasn't meant to tell the story. "It's better to ask Sas about this."

"Why haven't you asked him?" Allora inquired.

Mr. Swan fidgeted around uncomfortably.

"Sas and I haven't really seen eye to eye on this topic for quite some time," Mr. Swan said. His vagueness was disconcerting. "This is not a matter that needs to be examined further." His tone was direct and stern. Allora closed her mouth, swallowing the numerous questions she had intended to ask.

Rolling up the precarious pieces of parchment, Mr. Swan moved to the back of the room, facing a blank space. He motioned his hand in circular patterns, twisting his open palm as though opening a safe. A green glow of his palm shot forward, spreading into a large, liquid circle upon the wall. He placed the weighty documents into the liquid wall, and then sent another open palm spark into the wall, solidifying the area.

"I've created a safe to protect the directions to the Eye," he said, walking back to the front of the classroom.

"Do we get to learn how to do that?" Dax asked.

"Maybe when you're able to focus hadrons," he answered. "Now, I need you four to talk with Sas. That last piece is critical."

Mr. Swan sent a wall of green throughout the room, pulling the silencing glue from walls and collecting it into a ball again. He motioned for them to go, and then sat down at his desk. Before Allora left, she glanced through the small door window to see Mr. Swan staring blankly out the classroom window. His distant gaze was eerily emotionless, as though his entire past was now coming into focus. It was as though he had blocked out his painful memories and was now converging on an answer to an agonizing question. Allora walked away from the window, wondering whether she would ever find out the truth to the past that they seemed to all share; a past that she wasn't sure she would ever understand.

Chapter 15

Silencing Glue

An arrow sliced through the air, leaving a faint glow as it shot from the end of the bow. The shooter saw the trail of clear violet, reveling in her new abilities. The steel-tipped arrow penetrated its target with extreme precision; the tail end protruded from the target, wobbling up and down, indicating the powerful force with which it had hit the enemy—this enemy being a six-foot-tall straw-filled dummy that Allora was shooting at with her composite bow.

The trail of light slowly dissipated, leaving Allora in awe at the wonders of her new life. While amazing, her new life presented overwhelming complications that made those incredible moments of magic seem infinitesimal. A part of her wanted to give it all up for the normal life she'd had before the incident at cheerleading tryouts. For weeks, she had been battling a crisis of identity. The human girl within was fighting for normalcy, while the responsibilities of this new life seemed to be taking over, like a virus with no cure.

As she watched her closest friends sparring with inanimate dummies, the potential consequences of their new lives were inescapable. What would she do if one of them was killed? How could she live with the tragedy of watching one of her best friends die? The thoughts made her sick, and she almost keeled over.

"Hey, you alright?" Tanner asked as he left the sparring dummy to prevent Allora from falling over.

Allora shook her head, not able to discuss her thoughts.

"We've got our first puker!" Dax said, laughing and sparring with a fighting post called a muk yan jong. "Don't be embarrassed, Allora. I've puked many times during practice, especially when Coach Hale makes us do suicide runs."

"I'm fine," Allora said, backing away from Tanner, trying to act tough. "I'm just not feeling very well."

"Maybe we should call it a day," Katie suggested.

"We need to be prepared," Dax insisted. "I'm pretty sure that monster in the woods isn't calling it a day."

Reminders of the red-eyed creature were unwelcome, but no one wanted to take it lightly. Images of the malicious red eyes were permanently plastered to the forefront of their minds. Even the thought of facing this unknown creature caused chills throughout their bodies.

"Look, I've got physics homework, *and* I have to find a Halloween costume before Friday, so I need to call it a day," Katie said.

"Oh, yeah! Halloween!" Tanner said, remembering the earthly holiday. "Are you guys coming to the party?"

Allora shook her head, but Katie jumped in. "Of course we are!"

"Katie..." Allora said, suggesting her reluctance to participate in the popular social event, which most had been looking forward to for weeks because of the absence of Robert Mondrach's parents. Allora thought about Mrs. Mondrach coming back early from their vacation.

Katie ignored her best friend and insisted they would be there. After placing the equipment in a large wooden shack, they went through the portal and down to Allora's house.

"Don't forget about Mrs. Ferris' room after school tomorrow," Allora yelled, before the others pulled out of her driveway.

The next day, they all met in the junior hallway, making sure they weren't followed to Mrs. Ferris' room, which was empty when they opened the door. After entering the classroom, a lady with curly red hair popped up from behind a counter. Mrs. Ferris was a short, stocky woman with large glasses that took up half of her face. She carried a glass beaker in one hand and bottle of some sort of liquid in the other. The science teacher was humming, not realizing that she had company. Dax closed the door, causing a loud bang. Mrs. Ferris jumped up, letting go of the glass beaker. It flew into the air and then shattered on the tile floor when it landed.

"Sorry, Mrs. Ferris. We didn't mean to startle you," Dax said, feeling guilty for closing the door so loudly.

"Oh, kids, don't worry, it's not your fault. I put up the silencing glue before you got here," Mrs. Ferris said, walking over to them. "I heard that my first batch didn't work out very well in Mr. Swan's class. Sorry about that. I've perfected it. The new formula should skip biological creatures when it expands now," she said, lifting the broken glass with a wave of her hand and gesturing the floating pieces toward the trashcan.

"You have got to teach me how to do that!" Dax said.

"Yeah, then you won't have an excuse for having such a messy room," Katie said. Dax sneered at his sister.

Mrs. Ferris pointed to the back of the room, where four pots had been placed on the burners in the lab. "You'll get your chance. Today you will be making your own batches of silencing glue."

The exuberance was palpable, and yet Dax's excitement suggested something more mischievous. Allora could almost imagine the types of pranks he was thinking about at that moment. Mrs. Ferris led them to their stations and then walked to the shelving on the far side of the wall behind them. She pointed to the wall, and a small red spark shot forward. All of a sudden, everything on the shelves melted into the wall. Containers of ammonia and vinegar disappeared as if consumed by small black holes. The four teens stood up in shock, watching as strange contraptions, bottles, cauldrons, potions, human skulls, rolled parchment, animal skins, and odd colorful orbs materialized from inside the wall. Mrs. Ferris grabbed a handful of items. Once she walked away, the weird objects were absorbed back into the wall, and the regular lab material reappeared.

Mrs. Ferris was so busy placing the items on the lab stations, she didn't notice her students' shocked reactions to the magical display.

Allora picked up one of the bottles, which said, "Balumar Family: Signature Slug Sauce."

She shrugged, put it down, and picked up another. It was a very small glass bottle with very small writing that couldn't be read with the naked eye. Seeing Allora uncork the container, Mrs. Ferris yelled, "Stop!"

Allora froze, unsure why her teacher had snapped.

Mrs. Ferris carefully took hold of Allora's wrist, and like a puppeteer, directed the cork in Allora's hand back into the walnut-size glass bottle. A hard sigh followed, suggesting something dangerous about the innocent-looking container.

"That is Tiranis extract," Mrs. Ferris said. "It is made from the Tiranis plant, which is the stickiest substance on Sonora. One drop can deform the skin and glue you to any substance for years. You must handle it with extreme care, and use gloves."

Allora slowly lowered the bottle to the linoleum countertop and inched away as if the bottle were a ticking bomb. Mrs. Ferris neatly arranged the necessary items on the rest of the stations, and then went to the blackboard.

After the instructions were written on the board, Mrs. Ferris told them to begin. Allora started by boiling two cups of slug sauce, then slowly poured in a half cup of liquid spider web, followed by two teaspoons of crushed lilac powder and a tablespoon of dragon's blood. She let that cook for ten minutes until a shallow film formed on the top.

"Um... Mrs. Ferris?" Dax said, as the liquid boiled over the rim of his pot. "I think there is something wrong with my mixture." An extremely large greenish-yellow bubble grew from the pot.

"Oh no—don't touch it!" Mrs. Ferris said, sprinting to the back shelf and extracting a potion from the inner wall.

The bubble grew larger, engulfing the lab station and ballooning so big that it hit the ceiling. Mrs. Ferris pulled out a smoky liquid from the potion bottle, like a rabbit from a hat, and magically pushed the contents toward the monstrous bubble. It exploded, covering everyone with a slimy film of greenish goo.

"How much lilac powder did you put in there?"

"Two tablespoons," Dax replied, wiping the slimy goo from his face.

Mrs. Ferris shook her head and got towels from a drawer.

"Teaspoons, you moron!" Katie yelled, irate from having her nice clothes ruined. Dax apologized.

Mrs. Ferris threw each of them a towel. "It's alright, Dax. You're not the first to make that mistake. When the lilac powder mixes with the dragon's blood, it causes a reaction with the slug sauce."

"You mean I'm covered in slug boogers?" Katie exclaimed.

Everyone laughed at Katie's discomfort, watching as she aggressively wiped the green goo from her clothes.

"How were you able to do that?" Allora asked, referring to the potion retrieval.

"I just used a small amount of hadrons to counter gravity and raise the bottle's molecular contents."

Mrs. Ferris almost laughed at the confused faces of her goo-covered students. They looked like creatures from a Sonorian swamp.

Since they had to wait for the glue mixture to settle, Mrs. Ferris gave them some background on hadrons.

"A hadron, essentially, is a wave particle. Electricity or light might be an easy comparison, but hadrons are far more complex. They grow inside of us as we get older: inside our blood, our cells, our brains, and the rest of our organs. When we choose to, we can absorb them, move them, focus them, and expel them, depending on our level of ability. Sonorian scientists are still trying to understand what they are, so I don't expect you guys to have a complete understanding." She paused for a moment, washing the green goo from her towel.

"Human scientists are even worse, though. They call hadrons, 'dark energy.' It's kind of funny, because it's not really dark...." She thought for a moment. "Wait, let me correct myself. It can be dark, depending on how you define 'dark.' There are plenty of 'dark' Sonorians out there. But hadrons are definitely not simply dark energy. The humans are trying to understand hadrons. They have this machine in Switzerland called a Large Hadron Collider which is supposed to replicate the forces of hadrons. I think they might be angry to know I have four small hadron colliders in front of me," she said, giggling at her own joke.

"Why can we focus hadrons and humans can't?" Tanner asked.

"That would have to be a question for someone much wiser than me. Humans do possess a small amount in their bodies, but they can't conceptualize them yet. You've heard me say that human beings only use ten percent of their brains?"

They nodded their heads.

"Well, their minds aren't ready for hadrons just yet. Some in Sonora fear that the humans will eventually be able to harness hadrons and be a threat against Sonora itself. Personally, I think the idea is completely ridiculous."

"Do you think you could use some of those hadrons to get this horrible stuff off my clothes?" Katie said, scrubbing her jeans with a towel.

"You're such a drama queen," Dax said.

"These are designer jeans," Katie replied. "If I can't get this stuff out, you're a dead man."

Mrs. Ferris ignored the siblings and inspected the other pots.

"Well, Allora, it seems you are the only one who was able to mix a sufficient batch."

Katie continued to wash her clothes in the sink, while everyone else crowded around Allora's pot. A soft white layer of what looked like cream had settled at the top of the liquid. Mrs. Ferris carefully scraped the top layer, scooping up the white foam and placing it into four petri dishes. She handed out goggles and gloves and instructed Allora to gently pick up the Tiranis extract. Allora uncorked the bottle, holding it with straight arms.

"Hold it very steady, Allora," Mrs. Ferris said, unnerved by the rare substance.

Her fingers magically pulled the substance from the bottle, slowly pulling the weird, thick liquid into four parts and gently lowering each part an inch from the four foam-filled petri dishes. With a flick of her fingers, the Tiranis extract dropped into the foam, and four enormous plumes of sparkling smoke exploded from the dishes. Filling the air, the smoke smelled of lilac and skunk. The odd aroma was delightful and yet vile at the same time. The thick smoke gradually dissipated, and the four petri dishes came into view. The liquid swirled around, forming four small white sparkling balls.

Mrs. Ferris took them, and placed one in each of the students' hands.

"Now, use these when you're discussing anything about Sonora. You never know when someone could be listening in on your conversation. They are reusable, but if you need more, just come find me."

"Got any more cool things on that crazy shelf of yours?" Dax said.

"Not for you, Dax. Who knows what you would do with some of that stuff," Mrs. Ferris said, pushing them out of the classroom and into the hallway. It was a little early, but she had many things to do.

They decided to go get costumes for Mondrach's Halloween party. The prospect of just being average teens for the night was exciting.

Before they left, Allora went to the bathroom, opening the door to sounds of crying. She inched her way inside, curious as to who it was. Quietly, she peeked around the corner to see a blonde girl slumped over the sink. Her mascara ran down her face; drops of black collected in puddles in the white porcelain sink. She was rubbing her cheeks with a damp towel when Allora walked up. The blonde girl raised her head, and an image of Allora's nemesis formed in the mirror.

"What are you looking at?" Jenny sneered at Allora, still trying to wipe the mascara from her cheeks.

Allora pulled her head back and stood against the wall. She wasn't sure what to do. This girl had caused her so much frustration and anger. She had humiliated her in front of the whole school, as well as tied her up in the middle of the night, half naked. However, Jenny was in here all alone and in obvious pain.

"I bet you're enjoying this, huh? Big bad Jenny gets her heart broken. You happy now?" Jenny said, leaning back over the sink. The sounds of her sniffles echoed in the tile bathroom around them.

"Actually, I just wanted to say I'm sorry," Allora said, not sure why those words came out of her mouth.

"What? You're sorry?" Jenny asked calmly. "Why should you be sorry? Especially after what I did to you? I humiliated you. I should be the one apologizing. I don't get it. Are you patronizing me? Is this some type of joke to you?" Jenny's mood seemed to change from confusion to anger. She stood up straight, looking defiant.

"No, I'm not. I'm sorry because I know what it feels like to lose someone you love," Allora said. Jenny eased back down, letting go of her aggression, looking almost guilty for questioning Allora's apology.

Allora gave in to her own vulnerability, unsure why she was about to divulge her most painful experience.

"I grew up without a dad. My uncle took on the role and raised me like a father would. But when I was ten years old, he went missing. My mother said he had died while mountain climbing on Hood. It was devastating, and one of the hardest times of my life," Allora admitted. Her eyes began welling up with tears, her body remembering the emotions as if it were yesterday. Jenny put her arms around Allora, pulling her in for an embrace. Shocked by the oddity of the moment, Allora wasn't sure how to react. Eventually, she gave in, reciprocating Jenny's hug. The girls held each other as if they were long-lost friends. After they pulled apart, neither girl said a word. Jenny half smiled at Allora, and then left the bathroom. Allora stood in the middle of the bathroom for a while, reflecting over the peculiarity of the exchange. Who knew Jenny was just as insecure as any other teenage girl in the school? One small gesture of forgiveness had completely changed their relationship.

Allora walked out onto the pavement of the parking lot to an angry best friend. "Where were you? What were you doing? You took almost half an hour. We were worried about you," Katie said, appearing exasperated but relieved.

"I'm fine, Katie," Allora said, walking up to the car.

"Give her a break. She was probably just taking a big number two," Dax said, causing Tanner to crack up laughing.

"Really?" Katie said. "You're sick."

"Hey, sometimes I take longer than Allora did. Especially after they have mystery Mexican taco meat for lunch," Dax replied. Tanner laughed even harder as they jumped into his car.

"You know, sometimes I wonder if we are actually related," Katie said to her brother.

The car pulled away and headed toward Ruth's Costume Shop.

Chapter 16

Halloween

Fall arrived, changing the leaves to a vibrant variety of beautiful colors. Allora took time away from feeding the chickens to notice the landscape. It was a nice break from the flurry of activity in her home. Halloween was in full effect, with the house covered in fake spider webs, boiling pots of dry ice, skeletal bones, candy-corn-filled trays, creepy monsters, and other elaborate decorations. Milly and Aunt May had been busy all week long, preparing the house for their most celebrated of holidays. This was the first year Allora hadn't questioned the extravagance of her mother's love for Halloween. Every year, Milly went all-out to make the girls' Halloween an amazing event.

While Allora and Katie were getting ready, Milly told them about why Halloween was such an important tradition for Sonorians. The origin of the human tradition came from the time of the Celts and Irish thousands of years ago. Supposedly, on October thirty-first, the ghosts of the dead would return to Earth. As Milly told the story, she began to laugh.

"Of course, humans didn't realize those ghosts were just Sonorian tricks they played on the humans. That's when they created the game 'Trick or Treat.' If you weren't able to scare the human, then you had to give them a treat," Milly explained. "Over time, humans took it over as their own tradition."

"What other influences have Sonorians had on Earth?" Allora asked.

Aunt May yelled from down the hall, "Milly, I need your help putting up this large plastic spider."

"Well, you don't think the tooth fairy was human, do you?" Milly said with a smile, and turned to help her sister in the living room.

"I didn't know there were fairies in Sonora," Katie said, putting her witch's cape around her shoulders.

"A tooth-stealing fairy... I knew there was something fishy about that," Allora said, placing her pointy black witch's hat on her head.

"Girls, Tanner is here," Milly yelled, holding up the plastic spider decoration.

Allora and Katie looked into the mirror one last time to review their outfits. Both had the same costume, except for the shirt. Katie wore a white tank top, while Allora wore a purple one. They both had short black skirts, long capes, and pointy black hats. They had spent hours working on their makeup, and had put black eyeliner on to look more exotic. A quick application of lip gloss and they were ready for Mondrach's party.

Allora finished touching up and walked into the living room with Katie close behind. Tanner was standing next to the fireplace in a shiny knight suit. He looked comfortable in his costume. It wasn't a full suit of armor, since that would have cost a lot, but it had plated metal, making it look real. Tanner also had the sword he had received from Sumatra, which hung in a sheath on his back. The outfit was masculine and eerily familiar to Allora. She couldn't understand it.

"You're smart to bring your sword, Tanner," Milly said. "Now, you all need to be careful. Halloween is usually off limits in regards to any acts of aggression, but the Royal Guard rarely plays by the rules."

"We know, Mom," Allora said, a little perturbed by her mother's constant worrying.

"I put extra guards out there anyway," Milly said, and then returned to helping her sister with the decorations.

Allora said her good-byes and they all went out the door to Tanner's car.

"Where is my brother?" Katie said, looking around for a guy dressed in a Merlin costume.

"Right here!" a voice said from behind the car, grabbing Katie by the waist. Katie swung around instinctively, hitting her brother on the side of the head, sending him to the ground.

Katie realized the guy on the ground was her brother. Although he was in pain from the blow to his head, Dax couldn't help laughing. "I guess all that training has really paid off. You should have seen your face, though. It was priceless," Dax said, getting on his hands and knees.

Katie responded to her brother's comment by kicking him in the stomach. "Do that again, and I'm kicking you in the balls," Katie said, stepping around Dax and getting into the car. Allora followed, laughing as she jumped into the passenger seat.

Dax slowly picked himself up. The kick had hurt much more than the punch to his head. He opened the car door and inched his way into the seat, all the while glaring at his sister.

"I guess next time you'll think before you act. You shouldn't scare a trained individual such as myself," Katie explained.

"Oh yeah? Next time I'm scaring you with a cattle prod," Dax replied.

Allora rolled her eyes at Tanner, who had to suppress his laughter as he pulled onto Greenburg road. The conversation in the back was entertaining and continued all the way to Mondrach's house. A multitude of cars lined the driveway. Robert Mondrach's parents were in Hawaii, leaving him home alone for a week. He had decided to use this to his advantage, and throw a Halloween party. What he hadn't prepared for was the amount of people who would show up. Luckily, his house was secluded from his neighbors, and it backed into the woods.

The four teens got out of the car to the sound of muffled music, bumping from inside the two- story home. Through the living room window, they could see the house packed with their classmates. They moved through the crowd to find Robert in the kitchen.

"Dude, I thought this was supposed to be a small get-together," Tanner said, walking up to Robert.

"Yeah, so did I!" Robert responded, putting plastic cups into a trash bag. He was obviously flustered by the number of people in his house. "It's not so small, is it?"

The entire school had shown up for the party. Princesses, comic book heroes, M&Ms, and even a Sasquatch were there. The Sasquatch took off his mask to reveal Brandon Stringer, the wide receiver on the football team. He had a jug of red punch in one hand and playing cards in another.

Mondrach's parents were wealthy. They had six bedrooms, a game room, a swimming pool in the backyard, and even a weight room. Allora, Tanner, and Katie went to the game room, while Dax went to the pool to talk to a group of sophomore girls. Katie and Robert played on the billiards table, while Tanner and Allora threw darts.

"I don't think this is very fair," Tanner said after losing for a third time.

"I can't help it if you suck with ranged weapons," Allora said, jabbing Tanner playfully in the side.

"You're just going to have to give me a few private pointers," Tanner replied affectionately. "I'm going to get a soda, you want anything?"

"Yeah, can you get me a Diet Coke?"

Tanner left the room, weaving his way through the crowd.

Katie came up behind Allora. "Heads up, crazy blonde just got here," she whispered.

Allora jerked around to see Jenny strutting down the hallway with Tanya and Nancy trailing behind. They were dressed in bright pastels, scantily clad, with fake wings attached to their backs. Glitter sparkled on their skin, and their makeup was way overdone.

Robert walked over to them. "What are you guys supposed to be?"

"We're pixies," Tanya said, moving in closer. She'd had a crush on Robert for years. He didn't feel the same.

Jenny found her way to Allora and stopped in front of her. The room fell silent. Gossip from the incident at camp had circulated through the entire student body. Everyone assumed, with eager anticipation, that there would be a fight.

Jenny lifted her cheek as if to smile. "Thank you for what you said the other day," she said, confusing the curious spectators who watched eagerly, hoping for a dramatic fight. "I didn't get a chance to say I'm sorry earlier."

"That's okay," Allora responded. "You didn't have to say anything."

Then, someone in the back started clapping. The girls turned to watch as a petite, beautiful brunette slid her way out from behind a zoot-suit-wearing gangster. It was Kim. She was dressed in tight black leather with tall boots that went past her knees. She had a long, flowing cape and a pointy witch's hat.

"How precious," Kim said, slowly moving toward Jenny and Allora. "You know, Jenny, I think you're losing your edge. I thought you were supposed to be queen bitch." Kim was now within a foot of Jenny. "Not that impressive, if you ask me."

Jenny was about to take a swing, but Allora grabbed her wrist. "Try me," Kim said.

Just then, Tanner walked back into the room. "Did I miss something?" he said to a quiet yet giddy crowd. They were finally getting their drama fix. Tanner's entrance made it even more exciting.

Kim turned toward Tanner, placed her hand on his chest, and gave him a long kiss. "Nope, you didn't miss a thing," she said and sauntered toward the kitchen.

Jenny stormed off in the opposite direction, followed by Nancy and Tanya. Allora stomped over to Tanner. "You're unbelievable," Allora said, forcefully taking the Diet Coke from Tanner's hand. Then, she took off toward the door, pushing Dax out of the way. Tanner remained standing, completely confused.

"What just happened?" Dax asked, stopping next to his friend, who was just as confused. "I always miss the good stuff."

"I have no idea. One minute I'm getting soda, and the next thing I know I'm getting kissed by the new girl, and then yelled at by everyone else."

"Wow, tough life, bro," Dax said.

Allora was fuming outside, wondering why she was so upset. It wasn't like Tanner was her boyfriend. He could kiss whomever he wanted. Maybe she was angry that he had kissed Kim while Jenny was in the room. That was rude, but then, why was she upset by Jenny getting hurt? She had apologized, but did one apology erase all the mean things she had done over the years? The inner debate went on while she walked off the porch, landing on the side of the house.

Allora walked by a rose bush.

"Pssst!"

Allora jumped back. A furry head popped up from the top of the bush.

"Sas!" Allora exclaimed, putting her hand to her chest, relieved it was a friend. "What are you doing? You scared me half to death."

"How does someone get scared half to death?" Sas asked, but Allora stood there, not laughing. "Okay, sorry," Sas said, coming out from behind the bush.

"Why are you here? There are a ton of people who could see you."

"I know, I know. I had to come and warn you. I have been tracking a Wraith, and I believe he is close by," Sas said, swiveling his head around and surveying the area.

"Does a Wraith have red eyes?"

"How did you know that?" Sas asked.

Allora wasn't sure how to respond to this information. She already knew a something was in town, but she wasn't sure whether to let Sas know they had seen it. Instead, she chose to keep that information from him. The presence of a Wraith could cause her mother to keep her inside the house for the rest of the year.

All of a sudden, a figure moved behind Sas. Allora whispered, "Someone's coming!"

"What do I do? They will see me move?" Sas said.

There was nowhere to go.

"Just act normal," Allora commanded, unsure what she was going to say to the intruder.

The figure moved into the light. Allora blinked her eyes. The figure was really hairy. It was another Sasquatch, but this one was much shorter, and didn't look as real. Then, the hairy thing took off its head. It was Brandon.

"Hi, Allora," he said, his speech slurred. Brandon came closer, stopping next to Sas.

Brandon looked down at Sas' feet and then looked at his own feet. "Am I seeing double?" He pulled his head upward but had no other reaction to the creature standing next to him.

"Ah...." Allora faltered, not sure what to say.

"Cool costume, dude! We are so like twins," Brandon mumbled.

Sas looked very uncomfortable trying to think of what to say. "Yeah, I got it on the internet," He mustered, unsure if he got the term right.

"That's awesome. So much better than my costume," Brandon said, pulling strands of hair from the creature's leg. Sas winced at the pain, obviously agitated by the pesky human. Brandon began swaying from side to side. "I'm heading to the barn to find more plastic cups. You guys need anything?"

"Nope," Allora said as he walked off. "Don't you need a flash..." Allora started to say, but couldn't get through her sentence before Brandon stumbled inside. The sound of crashing garden tools, pots, and broken glass followed.

"Ouch!" Allora said. "You think he's alright?"

"Yeah, sure," Sas said. Then he froze as if he heard something else. "I gotta go. Be careful, Allora," he said, and ran off toward the woods.

Kim came hopping down the porch steps just as Sas disappeared behind the trees.

She looked around suspiciously. "I thought I heard you talking to someone." Allora wasn't sure how to respond.

"I was talking to—"

Brandon fell out of the tool shed. "I'm okay," he said, getting to his knees.

Allora turned to Kim. "Brandon... I was talking to Brandon." She walked across the lawn, and helped Brandon to his feet. She put his arm around her shoulder, and dragged him back to the house.

"I'm hungry," Brandon mumbled.

"Let's go get some candy corn," Allora said, dragging Brandon past Kim, who stood by with her arms crossed. Allora left Brandon in the kitchen gorging himself, and met back up with Katie in the game room.

"I think it's time we left," Allora said to the other three, who were playing pool.

They all could tell Allora needed to talk to them, so they said their goodbyes and left the house. Tanner turned the car key in the ignition, but the car didn't start. He kept turning the key, but nothing happened. Dax jumped out of the car to look underneath the hood. A few minutes later, he came back to Tanner's window.

"The spark plug is gone," Dax said. Tanner jumped out, infuriated.

He stared down at where the missing spark plug should have been and slammed the hood, causing both girls to exit the car.

"What now?" Allora asked.

"Well, I don't think anyone else wants to leave the party," Dax said. "I guess we should just walk."

"I don't think that's such a good idea. I just spoke to Sas and he told me a Wraith is out there right now looking for us," Allora said. Everyone just stared back. "You know, the red-eyed monster thing in the woods."

"When did you talk to Sas?" Katie asked.

"That's why I asked you guys to leave," Allora explained. "Sas found me outside and told me he was tracking it. He came here to warn us."

They stood in silence, thinking about what to do. No one wanted to meet the Wraith on their way home, but they had no other choice. Their parents didn't know they were at a party by themselves. If they got picked up at Mondrach's house, everyone's parents would know they had lied about where they were going.

"We have no choice but to walk back. I have my sword, Dax has his staff, and Allora has her throwing knifes," Tanner said. Allora pulled up her skirt a little to reveal the leg band she had hidden. Six small knifes hung in pockets on her thigh. Tanner couldn't help but look down. Allora recognized this and quickly covered herself, and Tanner awkwardly looked away.

"Why didn't you tell me you brought knives?" Katie exclaimed. Allora shrugged her shoulders. "Great. So, if we get into a fight, I'm going to be chopped liver."

"Sis, all you need to do is talk, and it will probably run away screaming," Dax said. Katie glared at her brother while the other two started down the road. "I know I would," he added. Katie ignored the comment and caught up with the others.

"Let's go, Dax," Tanner said, awkwardly looking away from Allora, who hid a smile from the others.

As they hiked along the dark, eerie road, Allora pulled a knife from the band and held it in her sleeve. She wasn't about to be attacked without a weapon. Tanner gallantly moved ahead, with his hand on the hilt of his sword. Dax followed closely, holding his staff in front. Allora's house was two miles away, which seemed much farther in the cold, black night. They walked in silence, periodically glancing at the dark woods on either side. Occasionally, Tanner would stop when he heard a noise, scanning the murky area. Allora looked out upon the trees, but visibility was low. The moon was absent, and with no streetlights, the walk home was dark and ominous.

Every step was one closer to her home, and yet each step felt wrong, like they were walking into a trap. Allora felt the woods watching their every move. Her intuition pleaded against moving forward. A chill ran up her spine, causing a spasm. It didn't feel right.

Tanner stopped suddenly. Allora pulled out her knife. "What is it?" she whispered.

"I thought I saw something move up ahead. I couldn't tell because it was like a shadow without a body."

Dax walked up to the front. "What's the holdup?"

"I don't have a very good feeling about this," Tanner replied.

"Now ya decide this. That doesn't really help us, does it?" Katie said loudly.

"Ssshhh!" the others exclaimed.

Allora watched as Tanner's eyes opened wide. His terrified expression caused Allora to quickly jerk around, just in time to see two red eyes speeding toward them. Pulling the knife behind her head, Allora moved her arm forward, but the dark figure was too quick. It hit Allora on her side, tossing her into the ditch like a ragdoll. Tanner and Dax ran forward, leaping to attack. Katie tried to spin around but tripped over her own feet and fell backward into the ditch, alongside Allora. The Wraith pulled out two swords from sheaths attached to its back, catching both boys' downward swings. The boys stepped back, finally able to get a good glimpse of the creature.

The Wraith was the same height as the boys, with humanlike characteristics, except its skin was jet black. It had muscular features, and long, pitch-black hair pulled back in a tight ponytail, which flowed in the wind like mist into the night. Dark red eyes penetrated the cores of its opponents, creating fear in any who faced it.

The Wraith pulled back, stepping sideways, encircling the boys while they mimicked the creature's motions.

"Well, well, well. Looks like we have ourselves a couple of warriors," the dark creature said in a deep, condescending voice. "This should be fun. Give me your best shot."

With that, the boys launched themselves at the creature, swinging their weapons aggressively. Allora was mesmerized by the fight. The boys' skill was incredible, but they were no match for the creature. Every attack was blocked and thrown off by the black crystal swords wielded by the Wraith. Allora picked herself up. Right then, Tanner was able to knock one sword from the creature's hand, but it motioned its arm forward, sending Tanner flying through the air as if an invisible force had struck him. Dax pushed forward, swinging his staff as well as his body. He hit the Wraith solidly in the side, knocking it to one knee. Dax pulled the staff over his head for a downward thrust, but the creature pulled his sword up just in time to block it. Then, the Wraith punched forward, launching Dax into a tree.

Allora had just enough room with Dax out of the way. She held up her knife, and as she did, her body began to tingle. Warm electricity flowed, absorbing into her hand. The knife glowed purple as she hurled the weapon. It streaked through the air, leaving a magical trail lighting the night. Seeing the purple streak, the Wraith put up his hands, but only in time to create a hadron energy field to block the attack. The knife hit the invisible field and exploded, showering the Wraith with purple sparks and knocking it into the trees.

"That was amazing, but we have to get out of here," Katie said.

Tanner was helping Dax to his feet. "I agree," he said. "We have to go through the woods."

They were bruised and battered, but the adrenaline was pumping through their veins, along with the hadrons slowly growing inside of them. They ran as fast as they could. The woods were dark, but their eyes had adjusted. Behind, they could hear the Wraith in fast pursuit. The sound of crunching leaves and breaking twigs grew louder as they ran. They made it to the edge of an open field.

"It's gaining on us!" Tanner yelled.

They all stopped, not sure what to do. Allora pulled out another knife,

Tanner unsheathed his sword, and they stood back to back, preparing for an attack.

"Guys, we're in trouble," Katie said.

"Yeah, and he does not look happy," Dax said, watching the Wraith as he sprinted through the woods, exploding the small trees that stood in his path. His eyes bobbed up and down as he leapt over a log.

"What's that?" Allora asked, seeing a dark figure moving toward them from across the field.

Barely seen through squinted eyes, the figure was covered in fur and moving quickly.

"It's Sas!" Tanner yelled, seeing the familiar features of their friend.

Sas leapt over the four and struck the oncoming red-eyed creature as the Wraith exited the woods. The impact sent both creatures crashing into a large tree, shattering the trunk. The Douglas fir began to fall toward where the four teens stood.

"Move!" Dax yelled.

They ran in opposite directions to avoid the deadly falling evergreen. Allora rolled along the grass as the trunk smashed into the ground. The branches smashed her into the grass, covering her body. Sharp branches cut into her skin. Pain pierced her body as she pulled herself from the cocoon of needles. The pain subsided when she thought of her friends. Were they hurt? What if the tree had crushed them?

Frantically, she scanned the dark for signs of life. A hand reached upward from the ground. Allora grabbed it and pulled Dax out of the tree. In the dark of the night, Allora could see black streaks of blood on his face, neck, and arms.

"Where are the others?" he asked.

Without saying anything, they trudged through the fallen tree, climbing over the trunk to where they assumed their friends would be. They swam through the sea of branches, searching for a hand or foot. Dax was able to find Tanner, who was barely able to stumble from being buried by the tree branches. He moaned as he got to his feet. The signs of blood were easily discernable.

"Where is Katie?" Allora asked, a fearful pitch in her voice.

A muffled yell came from a few feet away. They ran to the area, sifting violently through the thick undergrowth. When they pulled back a large branch, Katie's face appeared.

"Took you guys long enough," Katie said, softly.

The foliage had slammed her into the ground, leaving her breathless from the impact. Simultaneous sighs of relief came from everyone.

"My leg is pinned," Katie said, pointing down her body.

After a group effort, they were able to pull her out. Everyone had been bloodied, but they were content that nothing worse had happened. Before they could think, sounds of movement echoed across the field. They had almost forgotten about the Wraith.

"I lost my sword," Tanner said.

"I lost my staff, too," Dax added.

They stood, ready for whatever might spring from the woods. A figure jumped out, landing firmly in front of them. It was Sas.

"Where is the Wraith?" Allora asked.

Sas looked disheveled, with obvious signs he had been in battle.

"I don't think that he'll be back anytime soon," Sas said proudly. "But we shouldn't wait around to find out." He moved his hands in an extravagant circle. Green sparks swirled into his arms, focusing at his palms as he suddenly slammed his hands into the ground. A shockwave of earth flowed outward from the impact point, causing the dirt to push upward. The wave of dirt raised the four momentarily, and then dissipated through the field. Sas stood over a swirling circle of dirt.

"Time to go!" he said, motioning to the portal.

"I thought they can track us through a portal?" Katie asked.

"Not these types of portals. Now, hurry up!"

Without hesitating, they followed his orders, quickly jumping through the portal of earth. Allora tightened her muscles, trying to stay rigid as she shot through the streaking gray portal. Landing on two feet, Allora reveled in the successful port. A grandiose cave, sparkling knick- knacks, and the sounds of multiple waterfalls gave away their location. Sas had ported them to his cave, arriving only seconds after they did. After landing next to the portal, Sas pulled hadrons from the ground and stuck his arm into the portal. Suddenly, the ground stopped swirling and froze. As he pulled his arms from the cement-like ground, a green light escaped the closing portal.

"What did you do?" Allora asked.

"I locked the portal, inhibiting any from tracing portal's exit point," Sas answered.

"I've never heard of anyone being able to do that," Dax said.

Sas grinned. "We Guardians have abilities that other Sonorians, or even Keepers, are not privy to."

Sas moved around a large pile of pots and pans, taking a drink from the natural fountain of spring water. Following his lead, the other four gulped the fresh liquid as if they had been walking in the Sahara desert. The fight with the Wraith had drained most of their energy.

"We need to get you four home and tell Milly what happened tonight," Sas said.

Allora nearly choked on a mouthful of water. If Milly found out about the attack, Allora assumed she would be put under house arrest. A life of imprisonment was worse than any attack from a Sonorian assassin.

"Wait!" Allora grabbed Sas' arm before he was able to create a portal to her house. "You can't! My mother will never let me out of the house again."

"But Allora, this is something that can't stay a secret," Sas said.

Allora was desperate to withhold this information from her mother. "And keeping my entire past a secret was okay?" While slightly underhanded, she intended to make sure Milly never found out about their evening. "And it was acceptable to keep the truth about my uncle's death from me?"

"That's not fair, Allora," Sas said, flooded with guilt.

She kept a thoughtful stare, glaring mercilessly.

Writhing uncomfortably, Sas gave in. "Alright... but if anything else happens, I'm spilling the beans."

Allora smiled overtly, wrapping her arms around the reluctant creature. While the night's events had been disturbing and unsettling, a life spent locked up in her house every night was even scarier. They all called their parents. Milly was averse to letting Allora stay in the cave, but after a short debate, Allora was able to talk her way into staying. Sas showed them a large pile of sleeping bags, which made for decent beds, and they all settled in, talking quietly about the fight that almost cost them their lives. Then, they fell asleep, exhausted from the tumultuous Halloween they would never forget.

Chapter 17

Sas' Father

An excruciating headache woke Allora in the middle of the night. The sharp pain was like someone taking a pickax to her brain. Five minutes of throbbing pushed Allora to escape the confines of her sleeping bag in search of a relief from the headache. Her friends snored softly as she walked through the maze of junk piles to the dark blue lake at the bottom of the path. In its depths, she could see small bluish lights, swimming through the water. Every few seconds, the small lights would brighten, creating a sparkling orchestra of blue light.

"They're called Botaqua Bugs."

Allora jumped backward, sliding on her rear, searching the dark cavern for the source of the intrusion. Two beady eyes were perched on a ledge behind a large pillar of rock. The eyes darted around the pillar, turning into a familiar figure.

"They clean the water," Sas said, jumping down from ledge to the water's edge. "Great natural filtration system." Sas noticed Allora clutching her chest from fright. "Sorry, I didn't mean to scare you."

"It's alright," Allora said, clutching her head.

Her headache was becoming worse, and all she could think about was the pain.

"What's wrong?" Sas asked, helping Allora to her feet.

"I've just got this horrible headache, and I don't know why."

Sas left the pool, disappearing behind a pile of black inner tubes. He came back a minute later and handed her two white pills.

"Are these supposed to be magic fairy pills or something crazy like that?" she asked, hoping for something powerful.

"Nope, just aspirin," Sas said, moving toward the edge of the glistening pool.

Allora shrugged, took a drink from the waterfall, and swallowed the pills, happy to have something for the pain.

"Sometimes when you expel a large amount of hadrons, like you did tonight, it depletes your body of water and energy, causing painful headaches. It's a common side effect," Sas explained.

"That and a fifty-foot tree landed on me."

"Yeah, that could've had something to do with it," Sas said.

They both laughed. The pool twinkled in the dark cave as they stared quietly at the serene water. A flutter of bats sounded in the dark crevices of the cavern. Allora thought back to Mr. Swan's request. She assumed it would take some maneuvering to get the necessary information from Sas.

"What was your father like?" she asked.

The question caught Sas off guard.

He turned. "Why would you ask about my father?" Sas' tone was rigid and apprehensive.

Allora had to choose her next words carefully. She didn't want Sas to become defensive and choose to close off, which would destroy any chance of finding out the location of the last piece of parchment.

"I never had a father," she said. Sas' body language became less tense. "I just figured that it was something we could talk about."

"I'm sorry," he said. "I get a little suspicious of those who ask about my father."

The slight verbal maneuver had worked. Allora felt a little guilty for using the absence of her own father to manipulate her friend, but finding the Eye was far too important to be passive in collecting the necessary information.

"He was also named Sas, as he was the original Guardian who had met the native humans who lived in this area. I took his name out of respect; an honor to his legacy. He was an amazing Guardian. He was taller, bigger, and far more skilled than I could ever be. He had been the Guardian Council Leader during a very tumultuous time. When he died...." Sas teared up, feeling the same pain he had felt the day he was told of his father's demise. "When he died, it was a great loss for everyone."

"How did he die?" Allora asked.

Sas became suspicious again, searching Allora's eyes for malicious intentions, but none could be seen. He stared back at the blinking blue lights in the slightly rolling water, caused by the cascading waterfall at the back of the pool.

"My father was searching for something," he began. "Something of great importance. When he left, he told me he had found what he was looking for, but that it wasn't a safe time... I never quite understood what he was talking about."

"What happened the day he died?"

"Allora, this isn't a subject that I can talk about," Sas admitted. "It's also very dangerous. Whatever my father was searching for, it was so important that those involved would kill for it."

Allora was determined. She knew the consequences were severe, but there was no distinction between dying from Royal Guard assassins or some other way.

"I think I know what your father was searching for," Allora admitted. Sas perked up, facing the small human. "I need to know where your father died. It may be the only hope we have to stop whoever's out there trying to hurt us."

"So, this really wasn't about your father, was it?" Sas asked.

Allora put her head down. Dishonesty wasn't part of her nature. After a few awkward silent minutes, Allora turned around to go. Before she could leave the area, Sas said, "Mount Saint Helens."

Allora stopped in her tracks and came back to the water's edge.

"Before he left, he told me that the secret lies in the lava tubes."

Allora smiled and hugged her hairy friend. He reciprocated reluctantly, wondering whether he had made the right decision to give away the secrets of his father's death. Watching Allora saunter back to the large pile of sleeping bags, Sas thought back to the night his father had died. The news had been tragic, but what bothered Sas so much was the way he had died. Sas' father had been ambushed by a platoon of Shifters. The only way the Shifters would have learned of his father's quest was if someone from the Guardian Order had committed treason and informed the other side of what his father was looking for. Sas had never found out exactly what happened that day, because the consequence of his father's battle with the Shifters had caused Mt. St. Helens to violently erupt.

Chapter 18

Hadrons

"Mom!" Allora yelled down the hall. "Where is my bow? The guys are going to be here in a few minutes, and I can't find it." Allora rummaged through a pile of clothes in the corner of her room. She had a tendency to misplace her stuff.

"I put it in the garage," Milly yelled back.

As Allora sifted through the many boxes lining the garage wall, one of them caught her eye. Written in large block letters was her uncle's name. The box hung out over the edge of the top shelf in the corner, asking to be rediscovered. She stared at the box, feeling fear and curiosity at the same time. Knowing her family's real past had made her wonder about Uncle Ben. Milly never talked about him and would change the subject every time Allora inquired. It was the same way with her father. Allora's curiosity won, and she pulled the box down from the top shelf. Right before she pulled back the lid, someone yelled her name from inside.

"Allora, your friends are here."

She stopped, staring at the dusty lid for a minute.

"I'll look at you later," she said, shoving the box into a discreet corner of the garage.

Allora grabbed her bow, left the garage, and joined her friends. Sumatra had intended something special for their training, but they never assumed they would be going anywhere but the orchard. When they arrived through the portal, their sight came into focus on top of a flat hill of unnaturally green grass. Rolling hills of green blanketed the landscape, with nothing else in sight. Majestic and surreal, their destination caught everyone off guard.

"Sumatra is totally obsessed with grass. I'm starting to wonder if he was really just a landscaper in Sonora," Katie said, causing everyone to giggle.

"Very perceptive, young lady," Sumatra said from behind Katie's position. Katie jumped back.

"Why can't you just appear like a normal person?" Katie asked, catching her breath.

Sumatra ignored Katie's last comment and walked to the edge of the hill. "Beautiful, isn't it?" Sumatra said. "All of the places I've shown you are exact replicas of areas in Sonora. They are the places where I trained when I was just a little older than you are now."

Sumatra turned to face the others. Then, he pulled his legs upward as if gravity didn't exist. His legs crossed over each other, and he was suspended in mid-air. Then, he lowered his body onto the finely cut grass.

Tanner, Dax, Allora, and Katie sat down, trying to understand what they had just seen. A small breeze swept through the gaps in the hills, blowing gently on their faces. They sat in complete silence, listening to the wind as it passed through the valley.

"The wind, like everything, has a purpose. It has an energy that can grow and shrink. The focalization of hadrons, works in the same way. It can come as gently as a cool breeze or as strong as a destructive tornado. One must understand the power of hadrons before one can use them," Sumatra said. He whirled his hands, creating a small black dot. The dot grew, encompassing everything above them. The blank blue sky transformed to blackness. It was completely dark, except for a small light in the middle of the sky. The light began to grow larger with every second.

"This is how our universe was created billions of years ago. It started with one complete energy source. This pure energy source grew, imploded, and then created a supernova that expelled that energy into our known universe. Humans called it the Big Bang."

Just as he said that, the entire sky exploded with light. The small ball seemed to eat itself and then expand into millions of small pieces of light, rocketing across the black canvas above.

"Mystics call it the 'day of divine creation.' What we do know is this expulsion of pure energy created life in some capacity. Hadrons were the source that came to produce that life. They evolved, adapted, changed, and grew into what life is today. Mrs. Ferris would argue one way, and mystics would argue another. To me, it doesn't matter how we were created, but what we do with our creation."

The black sky folded itself toward the middle and then disappeared.

"Hadron focalization is an exercise of the mind. It takes practice, concentration, persistence, and a complete confidence in yourself. It won't be easy. I don't expect you to even be able to create a spark today. Allora may be able to because she has already done it, but Allora, you were able to do it under duress, which is a lot different from when you are calm. Emotion plays a large part in focalization and what is created from your hadrons."

Sumatra closed his eyes and put his hands out with his palms up. His fingers glowed. Blue sparks shot out from his fingertips, creating a small, circular ball of energy in his palms. Allora could feel the ground move underneath her, as if hundreds of ants were crawling beneath her body. Sumatra opened his eyes. The balls of energy shifted with his change of expression.

"This is what happens when emotion is involved with hadrons," he said, changing his expression to that of anger. Sparks of electricity escaped his palms, striking the ground furiously. None of the sparks hit anyone because Sumatra was able to control them, but the sporadic patches of blackened grass were very close. "Anger and fear can cause erratic behavior with hadrons. They can also be used as a strength as long as you are able to control your anger and fear. If not, you can easily succumb to the dark side of hadron focalization. Power can be seductive. It can manipulate and change someone. Even the most benevolent individuals can succumb to a more malevolent way of life."

Sumatra's body language was communicating more than he led on. The teenagers could tell there was more to his words, a personal experience that struck him to the core. The balls of energy in Sumatra's palms dissipated, and then he closed his fist as if thinking about something painful.

"I think it's time for your instruction. I want you all to put your palms out in front of you." They imitated Sumatra's motions. Their palms rested on their knees, and then they raised them to the sky. "Now, I want you all to close your eyes and clear your minds of thought. You must be completely aware of your surroundings without your sight. Feel the energy that is flowing constantly around you."

Allora sat in the grass, listening to Sumatra's words. The feeling he spoke of was familiar to her. A warm yet cool sensation ran through every vein in her body. The warmth of the sun penetrated her skin; the cool breeze flowed through her, and the rocky earth moved underneath. It was as if she was a part of everything around her. A perfect orchestra of living energy moved within her. Allora was in a sea of receptivity.

Once she was in a state of clear awareness, she began to focus her thoughts and the flowing energy to her hands. The accumulation of hadrons surged through her body, flowing rapidly into her hands, and collected in small purple balls of circulating energized molecules. Amazed by the instant imitation of the instruction, the others moved in closer to watch. It was as if Allora had known how to do it all along; even Sumatra was surprised and impressed by his student.

Allora opened her eyes and looked down at her hands. The purple hadron balls quickly vanished. She was able to focus the hadrons, but couldn't sustain it for too long.

"Your mind can be your greatest weapon, as well as your strongest opponent," Sumatra said, smiling. "With your eyes closed, you were able to create and focus hadrons with ease. When you came to the realization of your creation, the hadrons dissipated. The conscious mind wants to believe that this ability is impossible, and it wants to keep you from the power within. The constant struggle between what is impossible and possible can only be resolved by the constant connection with the belief that anything is possible. Only then can the true inner power be realized. Only then can you four become what you are destined to be."

Sumatra walked over to the other side of the hilltop. "I'm going to leave you here to practice. I'll be back later." Then he disappeared through a portal.

"What did he mean by 'destined to be'?" Tanner asked the group.

"No idea. I'm starting to think the adults are keeping secrets," Allora said, looking at Katie and Dax. "I think it's about time that you two tell us about why you were sent here."

Katie looked at her brother for approval, and he nodded to let her know it was okay. Katie swallowed and then began, "Allora, our parents aren't really... well... our parents." Katie said.

Allora's eyes grew wider. "What?"

"Jarrod and Maureen are friends of our real father."

Neither Tanner nor Allora could come up with anything to say. Katie and Dax's fake parents were like family. At this point, Allora couldn't even be angry. She was numb to all of the secrets in their lives.

Katie let it sink in, and then she explained more. "Our real father is the High Commander of the Western Army of Sonora, and he sent us here for two reasons. First, if we were captured by the Royal Guard, then the king would have leverage over our father, which would mean the resistance movement would be in jeopardy. Of course, Dad couldn't risk that. Even if that meant we grew up without a father," Katie said with contempt.

"Katie, you know he was just trying to protect us," Dax interjected.

"It still sucks, though," Katie answered back, crossing her arms.

Dax put his hand on his sister's shoulder and smiled. "You've always had me."

Katie's demeanor eased after seeing her brother's genuine expression. Dax took over the story for Katie. "The second reason we were sent here was to back you two up. Our dad wouldn't give us all of the details. He told us all would be revealed when the time was right. He said our destiny resides with you two, and that destiny is not given, it's chosen."

Katie said, "The commander can be pretty vague sometimes."

"We know about as much as you guys do about our Sonorian past. Our father had to keep our existence a secret for ten years before we were sent here. We grew up learning two things: how to fight, and how to blend into Earth culture. We didn't much like the latter."

"That's probably why I'm so bad at history class," Katie said.

Allora wanted to ask a question, but didn't know if it was entirely appropriate. She decided to do it anyway. "What about your real mother?" The siblings looked at each other with remorse. Allora could tell that it was a subject that was painful. Allora pulled back. "I'm sorry. It's really none of my business."

Katie stopped her. "No. I think that the both of you should know," she said. "Our mother, Tamara, was captured by the king's men, and tortured for information about the location of the resistance. Dad said our mom was tough, and never gave in." Katie's emotions welled up, her eyes filling with tears. Dax gently placed his hand on her shoulder. She regained her composure, rubbing the tears with her sleeve. "They were able to save her, but she had been beaten, badly. We were only a couple of years old, but the memory is as vivid today as it was when...." Katie couldn't finish.

"She died from internal bleeding and malnourishment," Dax said.

Allora held her crying friend, holding the back of Katie's head against her shoulder. "Whatever our future holds, promise that we will all be together when it happens," Allora said.

Katie pulled herself away. Her eyes were red from the tears. Quietly sniffling, she nodded her head, along with the others.

"It's imperative we learn how to use hadrons," Dax said, changing the subject.

"Dax is right. If we're going to have any chance of protecting ourselves or anyone else, we need to be able to focus hadrons," Tanner said, shifting his attention to Allora. "Got any tips?"

Allora thought for a minute. Comparing the sensation was difficult. It was unlike anything she had ever experience. An idea popped in her head.

"You know that feeling you get when you're around someone you have a crush on, or the feeling you get when someone you care about is in trouble?"

"Like butterflies in your stomach?" Katie asked.

"Yes, that's it!" Allora exclaimed. "That's exactly the sort of feeling you get, except it's more intense. And you have to focus on the feeling, bottling it up into one central location. Then, you push it with your mind into your hands."

They all closed their eyes and practiced. Allora watched them as they wiggled and scrunched their faces. For hours, they practiced without much progress.

They were about to give up when a blue spark shot out of Tanner's finger, hitting Katie on the back. Katie arched her back from the impact and fell forward onto her stomach. "Hey!" she yelled.

Tanner was too busy with his surprise to notice. He stared at his hands, and Dax patted him on the back.

"Nice work. Not only did you produce hadron energy, you also shocked my sister, which I've been wanting to do for years," Dax said, laughing while Katie got up from the ground.

"It wasn't that much, though," Tanner said, as Allora walked over from helping Katie up.

"At least we're getting somewhere," Allora replied.

"Yeah, at my expense," Katie said, rubbing the place the where Tanner's spark had hit.

Sumatra popped into the field. "How are we doing?" he asked the group.

"Well, Tanner was able to shock me," Katie said, still unhappy that she had been caught in the crossfire.

"Sorry, Katie."

"That's great," Sumatra said. "Now, you all must not practice this unless you have gone through the portal. This is very important." Sumatra became very serious. "You are unable to track energy trails in the outer realm. The use of hadrons in your hometown could have dire consequences, as you all have experienced. They obviously don't know you four are there or else they would have sent an army to capture you. But they do know that Sonorians are in town. We must be very careful moving forward. I need to leave, so if any of you have further questions, you'll need to ask Kurt."

"Wait, who is Kurt?" Allora asked.

"You know him as Mr. Swan. His Sonorian name is Kurtimar, but he never liked it."

Just then, a figure appeared out of nowhere, obviously from passage through a portal.

"I still don't like it!" Mr. Swan said.

Allora was anxious to tell her teacher about what she had learned from Sas. Once Sumatra left, leaving them in the grassy magical field of rolling hills, Allora told Mr. Swan about her conversation.

"Mount Saint Helens?" Mr. Swan asked.

"Yeah, he said that the secret lies in the lava tubes," Allora said.

Mr. Swan walked to the edge of the green hill. Wind was blowing, moving in waves and flattening the medium-length grass. The four teens waited patiently, wondering what thoughts were consuming their teacher's mind. He remained quiet, searching his brain for an answer to Allora's message. Allora slid behind him and was about to tap his shoulder when he spun around with wide, excited eyes.

"I know exactly where it is!"

The others exchanged confused looks.

"I should have known there was something about that place!"

"Where?" Allora asked.

Mr. Swan proudly moved to her. "You will learn soon enough."

He became somber. "We have to be more careful than ever. The closer we get, the more dangerous it becomes. I can't ask you four to go any further."

"You don't have to," Allora answered with a smile.

Chapter 19

Ape Caves

"Make sure you don't forget your jackets," Mrs. Ferris instructed as the large group of students filed off the bus. "It's going to be cold down there."

Mrs. Ferris had scheduled a field trip to the Ape Caves, which were located just south of Mt. St. Helens in the national forest. Winter had brought with it a sharp cold front. A thin sheet of white covered the path as the parade of students made their way to the entrance of the caves. Descending into the dark cavern, Allora was reminded of the conversation she'd had with Sas. As they passed the stalactites hanging down from the cavern roof, Allora searched the area for anything that seemed out of place.

"I don't even know what we're looking for," she muttered quietly.

"Where is Mr. Swan?" Katie asked. "I thought he would for sure be here."

"Mrs. Ferris told me that Mr. Swan thought he was being followed," Allora said. "He thought it would be safer if he didn't go."

Katie locked arms with her, moving together through the narrow path. Allora surveyed her friend's outfit. She was wearing a puffy white coat, long pink stockings on her feet, and a pink Gucci cashmere scarf wrapped elegantly around her neck. The ensemble looked as though she had dressed for a winter fashion show rather than a trip into caves.

"Do you really think you dressed for the occasion?" Allora asked.

"Who says I can't look good while I go spelunking?"

"Spelunking?" Allora asked, shocked by her friend's use of vocabulary.

"Maureen has been forcing me to study S.A.T. flash cards," Katie answered. Her unenthusiastic tone expressed an aversion to studying. "I have no idea why she's making me do it. It's not like I'm going to college, anyway."

Allora flashed her look of disappointment, but was unable to inquire further.

"Alright, now what we have here is quartz," the guide began. "Quartz is created when rock, heat, and pressure mix to form small crystals. These lava tubes once had immense heat and pressure."

Katie and Allora stood in the back of the group, snickering at the park ranger's uniform. He had on large hiking boots, knee-high socks tucked into his pants, a fanny pack strapped around his waist, a tight green national forest jacket, thick horn-rimmed black glasses, and a highly starched flat ranger's hat that was too tall for his head.

"This is called the Ape Caves because they were discovered by a Boy Scout troop, which named it after a group of foresters called the Saint Helen's Apes. But most believe it was named for the infamous man-ape, also known as Bigfoot or Sasquatch, who is said to have roamed these parts."

"Did anyone ever see him down here?" Allora asked.

They all became attentive, moving closer to the front.

"Well, there was this one old lady," the guide said. "But I was told she was a little crazy, so I'm sure she was just seeing things. Okay now, let's continue the tour."

"Wait!" Allora yelled at the ranger, who was now moving down the path. The yell reverberated against the cavern walls. The ranger stopped. "I want to know what she said."

"Miss, we have a long tour, so we need to move on," he said.

"Can you just answer the girl's question?" Mrs. Ferris asked, which seemed to annoy the ranger. "Just for fun."

The ranger walked back up the short incline, laboring with each step as if bothered by the reversal of direction. He stopped short of where the girls stood, pointing aggressively down a narrow cavern, bending down while he pushed his horn-rimmed glasses against his face.

"The old lady said she saw a hairy man walking down that cavern." They looked at the open black cavern. A large rope was draped across the opening with a sign saying Keep Out. "But that area is restricted, so there is no way she would have seen something down there."

Allora and Katie leaned back, smelling the aftermath of the tuna fish sandwich the ranger had for lunch. They half-smiled back, grossed out by the weird, awkward gestures of the ranger. The tall, thin man snapped around, as if he were in boot camp, and went back to following the cavern path.

"Alright, moving on," The ranger said.

Allora, Katie, and Mrs. Ferris remained behind, quietly moving out of sight against a rock outcrop.

"We need to move fast," Mrs. Ferris whispered. "This tour won't last very long, and there is no telling what or who else may be down here."

Just then, Tanner and Dax showed up, running to a stop.

"Sorry were late," Tanner said between breaths. They seemed to have sprinted into the cave.

"Where were you guys?" Katie asked.

"Our bus got held up because of a car accident," Dax said, looking agitated. "The bus driver assumed the car had hit an animal, but when we passed by the accident, it looked like a crumpled heap of metal. No animal could have caused that much damage."

A bat screeched as it fluttered only inches above the group. A squeal followed, but it had come from the blonde girl all wrapped in pink and white.

"I hate bats!" Katie said, grabbing Allora's arm.

"Alright," Mrs. Ferris said, ignoring the girl. "We need to split up."

"We'll take that way," Allora said, pointing to the restricted area. She had a feeling about it.

After the others left to search other openings, Allora and Katie crawled underneath the rope indicating the restricted section, and then ventured into the dimly lit cave. Luckily, Allora had remembered to bring a flashlight. The further they moved, the colder it became. A slight stinging formed at the tips of their fingers, and their noses became numb from the frigid air. Pretty soon, only the small beam of the flashlight was visible. The only sounds were the occasional drip of water and the deep, smoky breaths from the two frozen girls. As they moved deeper into the cave, the walls began to narrow. Creepy shadows danced along the rock, caused by the flashlight beam casting over the sharp stalactites.

Allora and Katie pushed closer together, fearing the unknown that lay ahead. A quiet scurrying echoed in the dark. Allora frantically swung the light around, feeling her heart beat twice as fast. The beam of light projected a large shadow of a spider, seen on the wall as over ten feet high. Katie screamed. Their eyes narrowed, finally accustomed to the dark, and they saw the tiny spider dangling from the ceiling. Embarrassed, Katie walked ahead defiantly.

"I could have taken that spider!" she said.

Allora squinted her eyes in the darkness. Above Katie, something moved against the cavern ceiling.

"They are such awful little creatures," Katie said, shaking from disgust. Above her, a long thin leg clasped a stalactite, tightly wrapping itself around it. "Their webs are the worst. Eew!"

Slowly, Allora moved the light up, illuminating a grotesque figure. The creature had what looked like three heads joined at the ears, with one eye each. Its arms looked like razor sharp butcher's knifes, with fingerlike tentacles. The creature's body was thin, with more than ten long legs, which moved along the roof of the cave with frightening quickness. Covered with short fuzzy hair, this creature was like nothing Allora had ever seen. It crawled closer, hanging right above where Katie stood. Unable to react, Allora stood with her mouth open, frozen with fright.

"Not funny, Allora," Katie said. "I'm not turning around. There is no way you're going to scare me."

Katie defiantly stood with her hands crossed on her chest. The creature reached out with its butcher claw. Allora planted her foot and sprang forward with a jerk. The forceful lunge took Katie off her feet. The creature swung the cleaver-like arm downward, missing the feet of the flying teens. Rolling to a stop, Katie got to her feet in confusion.

"What the hell are you doing?" she asked, shaking the dirt and dust from her white coat. "You realize how expensive this thing is?"

Allora crawled on all fours, grabbed the flashlight, and projected it on their attacker. The light shined on the creature as it pulled its arm from the ground.

"Oh..." Katie said.

The creature let out a terrifying screech, arching its back in an obvious aggressive gesture. Allora grabbed Katie's arm, pulling the shocked girl down the only escape. Sprinting through the dark cave, the two girls randomly chose their path. The flashlight bobbed up and down with every step, only illuminating a few feet ahead. Unable to turn around, they heard the creature scurrying quickly along the ceiling and walls behind them.

"It's gaining on us!" Katie said. "What're we going to do?"

"*I don't know!*" Allora yelled back.

A new smell wafted into their nostrils as they moved deeper into the cave. The smell increased with every step. Katie glanced over her shoulder just in time to see an arm swinging at them.

"Duck!" she said, pushing Allora forward.

The momentum of the creature's attack caused it to become unbalanced. It slipped from the wall, crashing into the other side, and sent fragments of rock everywhere. It writhed around, giving the girls enough time to get to their feet.

"I can't find the flashlight!" Allora exclaimed.

The creature turned over, shaking off the rocks that pinned it. Katie grabbed her friend.

"No time!"

Katie pulled Allora into the blackness. Unable to see, their progress was slow as they fished around with their hands to protect them from running into rock.

"I can't see a thing. We needed that flashlight!"

"I'm so sorry," Katie responded. "Would you rather be an appetizer?"

The path turned abruptly, opening into a larger chamber that was slightly illuminated from a small crack in the high ceiling. Jogging through the chamber, Katie caught the end, almost crashing into the closed-off rock wall.

"Now what?" Allora said.

Katie frantically shuffled along the wall, feeling for some kind of hole or crack to escape through. Unable to find anything, they searched frenetically around the darkness, unsure of their next move.

"I'm too young to die," Katie said.

Allora could feel her friend's fear. Then, she remembered Sumatra's instruction. He had said there would be moments like this, that their emotions would dictate their ability to protect themselves in any situation. The sound of falling rock and growling echoed into the chamber. The creature was moving fast. It would be in the chamber in seconds. Focusing intently, Allora calmed herself, breathing deeply, pulling hadrons from the cave interior. A slow progression of energy surged within her body and focused into her hands. Two purple balls grew and surged with immense power. Katie stepped back, knowing what would come next.

The purple glow revealed the creature as it entered the chamber. It snarled and growled when it saw the glowing girl. Allora pulled her hands to one side, combining the two purple balls. She controlled the energy, swirling her hands over the weapon like she knew exactly what she was doing. The creature made its move, crawling quickly along the ceiling.

"Get ready to jump out of the way!" Allora said as she shot her hands skyward.

Anticipating its victim's move, the creature blocked the hadron burst with its butcher's knife. The force from the attack knocked it from the ceiling, and it crashed to the ground. Katie and Allora jumped in different directions as the creature slid along the dirt floor. It hit the wall at the end of the chamber. An explosion of rock filled the chamber with dust, choking the air. Allora coughed, sucking in the dirt and dust.

"Katie, look!"

Pulling her head up, she noticed a light coming from a crack in the wall. The light was reddish orange, further illuminating the dusty chamber.

"Is it a way out?" Katie asked.

"I don't know, but I think it's our only chance," Allora replied.

The creature was gaining its footing, but blocking their escape.

"So, how are we going to get to it?"

Allora only had a moment to figure it out. She remembered something from her childhood.

"Do you remember playing dodgeball in the gym?" Allora asked with a grin.

"You're kidding me!" Katie exclaimed. "That's your plan? Is that even going to work?"

"Only one way to find out," Allora said, moving to Katie.

They stood together, preparing for the creature's next move.

"So, I guess I'm the bait on this one..." Katie said, apprehensively.

"Get ready."

The hideous creature crept closer. Enraged by its elusive prey, the creature spat and growled. When the two girls were in elementary school, they had a way of winning every dodge ball tournament in gym class. One of them would lure someone by baiting that person to attack, and then the other would flank and strike. The move always worked. But, this time they weren't using rubber balls. Winning meant life or death.

Seeing the creature preparing to lunge, Katie sprang forward while Allora rolled to her right. Caught unaware, the creature swung at its first target. Katie rolled left, avoiding the swinging arm. The creature adjusted, moving to its right to counter the evasion. Meanwhile, Allora was able to get a clear shot at the glowing crack. Allora's hadron burst destroyed the remaining wall, and piercing light blanketed the cave chamber, causing the creature to wince and squirm. The light was blinding it. The creature swung violently, unable to see.

"Katie!" Allora screamed as a cleaver-limb crashed into the wall.

Katie jumped out of the way of the falling rock, and they both sprinted into the light. The violent swinging caused the chamber to become unstable. Once through the blown-out rock wall, Allora and Katie heard a deafening screech as the entire chamber collapsed on itself. They fanned the dust that blew out of the hole and sighed in relief. The adrenaline was pumping so much that they hadn't noticed the extreme temperature change.

"Do you feel warm?" Katie asked.

"Very warm," Allora replied.

They slowly turned, and gasped loudly.

"I don't think that this was the exit..." Katie said. In front of them was a sea of lava, flowing like a river within a grandiose lava tube. The red-orange landscape was eerily beautiful. Along the walls, cascading lava escaped out of holes, erupting in sparks as it hit the flowing river below. The unrelenting heat hit their faces, causing them to sweat. Every few seconds, bubbles of lava would burst, sending a wave of burning air throughout the cavern.

"I'm almost missing the cold, creature-filled cave," Katie said, sweating profusely.

She stripped off her dirty jacket and scarf, unable to stand the excruciating heat. A reflection from the lava caught Allora's eye. She focused on a small platform protruding from the center of the lava. Upon the top of the platform sat a shiny object. Squinting her eyes, she could make out a small black orb.

"We found it!" Allora said.

"Really?"

"Yeah!" Allora pointed at the platform.

She searched the area for some way to access the platform. Unfortunately, there was no way to get to it. The platform was about fifty feet away, with nothing between except for molten lava.

"Now what?" Katie said.

Allora noticed large boulders sporadically flowing along, knocking into each other as they floated on top of the lava. They were numerous enough to make sort of floating stepping-stones to the platform. Katie watched Allora's stare, moving back and forth.

"No," Katie said, shaking her head. Allora smiled. "No.... No way. Not going to happen." Allora jogged up the lava river, looking for the best rocks. "You're crazy if you think I'm going to follow you." Allora found the perfect path, calculating the best pattern to make it to the platform as it flowed down. The maneuver had to be perfect, or they would be dragged down the river. "You don't even know if those rocks will sink!" Katie continued to fight against it, but her friend's stubbornness was relentless. Allora backed up, and then sprinted to the edge, jumping forward.

The rock swayed, pushed through the lava by the force of her impact. It bobbed in the lava, but remained safely above the scorching surface. Katie moved the edge, but the heat was so intense that she was knocked back.

"How are you able to stand the heat?" Katie asked, following her friend as she floated down the river of lava. "I can't even get close to the edge. It burns my skin!"

Allora braced herself and leapt to another rock.

"I'm not sure," she said, preparing for her next jump. "Somehow, it doesn't affect me. Maybe it has something to do with my ability to produce fire."

With every jump, she got closer to the middle. The platform loomed in her sight. Allora leapt to the next rock, slipping on edge and falling forward.

"*Allora!*" Katie yelled, seeing her friend slip over the other side of the rock.

Grabbing a pointed edge, Allora was able to save herself from falling in. Her hair flipped down close enough to catch on fire. Pulling herself up, she madly beat the flames.

"You okay?"

Allora didn't have any time to respond. The platform was only a few feet ahead. If she didn't move quickly, her chance of reaching it would be gone. She hopped onto the next rock as if playing a game of hopscotch. Dancing from one rock to the next, she made a desperate leap, clutching the edge of the platform. Katie winced, watching as Allora swung her legs, trying to drag her body onto the granite surface. With her shoes melting beneath her, Allora heaved onto her stomach and finally reached the platform's surface. She collapsed, breathing heavily from the physical exertion.

She gave Katie a thumbs-up, and then crawled up a ramp to the top of the platform. Allora looked down upon a shiny obsidian orb within a bowl-shaped granite podium. The orb seemed to swirl with motion, and yet was made of seemingly solid material. Odd and beautiful, the object was an obvious abnormality for the site.

Is this it? Allora asked herself.

"What's taking so long?" Katie yelled, wondering why Allora hadn't grabbed the thing and returned already. The environment made her anxious. She began to search for an exit strategy.

"It's too easy," Allora answered.

"Easy!" Katie exclaimed, exploring the walls of the cavern. "I didn't think this was easy!"

Something was wrong, and Allora knew it. Why would Sas' father leave the artifact out in the open? And how was this orb the last piece? It was supposed to be a piece of parchment.

"Let's go!" Katie yelled, becoming more agitated.

Slowly, Allora picked up the orb between her thumb and forefinger. Fascinated by the small object, she stared at its mesmerizing surface. The interior of the orb swirled with silver-black liquid, yet the exterior was solid obsidian, shining against the orange glow of the lava. Suddenly, the platform jerked. Allora was caught off-balance. The orb slipped from her grip, falling toward the river of lava. She stretched out, diving down the platform's ramp, catching the orb on the granite rim.

Then, the podium descended and the whole chamber shuddered violently.

"Move!" Katie screamed.

Allora got to her feet as the walls burst open and a rush of water exploded into the chamber. She placed the orb in a zippered pocket, leapt to a rock, and proceeded to dance across the large rocks, moving fast. The water crashed into the boiling orange liquid, creating a terrifying hiss of hot steam. The cloud of steam enveloped the area, pushing hot air toward the girls. Bobbing on each jump, Allora picked up her speed. An eruption of magma, steam, and rock was building. Meanwhile, Katie had found a small hole, which seemed to extend back into the Ape Caves.

"Hurry up!" she screamed.

Erupting pockets of magma exploded toward the chamber ceiling as Allora reached the other side of the chamber. She sprinted to the cave opening, dashing through with Katie right beside her. Behind them, the lava had burst over the bank, flowing into the opening. They turned their heads to see the bright, ominous glow of the pursuing magma. It illuminated their path, but was gaining fast.

"Look!" Katie yelled, pointing ahead. "The path ends!"

Allora squinted to see the orange glow shining on a wall, but what caught her eye was the dark contrasting floor only a hundred feet away. Her eyes went wide, but she had only a moment to react. She pulled back her arms, absorbing a purple ball of hadrons within. Then, she shot it forward, bursting the wall and creating a hole.

"Aaaaaaaahhhhhh!" they screamed, leaping over the deep crevice and into the makeshift hole.

The lava flowed into the crevice, unable to reach the hole on the other side. The girls slid along the smooth cave rock, crashing through a thin shale wall. The crumpled pile of arms and legs de-tangled itself and they sat breathing heavily in the cloud of dust. Covered from head to toe in dirt, the girls looked like strange cave creatures. Their clothes were blackened from being burned and their hair was in disheveled messes. Once the dust settled, a group of onlookers stood with their mouths wide, perplexed by the odd entrance.

Katie and Allora awkwardly smiled at their classmates. Tanner, Dax, and Mrs. Ferris ran down the trail after hearing the commotion. They were relieved to see their friends alive. Allora smiled at them until she saw a familiar face wedging itself through the crowd of students.

"Hi Aunt May," Allora said. She had forgotten that her aunt had come as a chaperone.

"You're in big trouble, young lady."

Chapter 20

Parent Conferences

"And in breaking news, Mount Saint Helens has come back to life. At about three thirty-eight p.m. this afternoon, the quiet volcano spewed ash and lava from the interior of the crater. As we can see from a viewer submission, lava escaped the round dome in the middle of the crater. Ash and debris exploded into the atmosphere and is said to be traveling toward the Portland metropolitan area. The last eruption was in nineteen eighty. Far more extreme than we saw today, but this new eruption comes as a complete surprise."

Milly walked in front of the television screen, hands on hips, a bewildered stare directed toward her daughter.

"What the hell happened?"

"Nothing," Allora answered, unconvincingly.

"Nothing... nothing! That doesn't look like nothing," Milly said, pointing back to the television.

"We have Dr. Alexander Von Derau here from the United States Geological Survey. Doctor, what could have caused this eruption?"

"To be honest, we're not sure. There was only a slight earthquake before the eruption, and there were no signs indicating the normal sequences leading up to this kind of eruption. Plus, Mount Saint Helens isn't known for lava eruptions.

*Like the nineteen eighty eruption, the pressure builds and explodes with mostly
ash, but this was different. My colleagues and I are completely dumbfounded.
Something extraordinary happened here today, and we are going to get to the
bottom of it."*

Milly turned off the television. "I want to know, right now, what you and
Katie were doing in that cave."

Allora hesitated, knowing her mother would react badly. "We were
searching for a piece of a map."

"A map of what?"

"A map that would lead us to the Eye of the Tita—"

"*Stop!*" Milly yelled, preventing Allora from saying anything else. Aunt
May put her head down in silent anticipation of her sister's fury. This was
a subject that they hadn't spoke of in six years, since Uncle Ben's death.
Milly paced from front door to bookcase, trying to control her emotions.
She didn't want an outburst like before. After a minute, Milly addressed her
daughter.

"How did you find out about the Eye?"

"Mr. Swan said that—"

"I knew it!" Milly said, infuriated. She glanced over to Aunt May. "He's
never going to stop. And he's going to get someone else killed."

"What does that mean?" Allora asked.

"Your Uncle Ben was killed by a Shifter because he and Swan set off
a trigger, like the one you did today, that sent an extremely strong energy
signature, informing our enemies where we were," Milly said, becoming
angrier. "They compromised our community."

Guilt crept up Allora's spine, realizing she had once again put her friends
and family in danger. An inner argument arose, though. Were they supposed
to spend the rest of their lives hiding? Were they just supposed to cower
when these creatures were causing so much pain? How could her mother
be so docile and think they could remain isolated from this evil?

"And what am I supposed to do? Sit here and hide? I'm not a baby anymore, so stop treating me like one!"

"Well, then stop acting like one," Milly said. "You have no idea how lucky you are. You need to think, Allora. This isn't a game!"

"Well maybe if you told me the truth and stopped lying to me, I wouldn't have to go it alone," she snapped back.

"Don't you see, I'm trying to protect you!" Milly fired back.

"Protect me?" Allora said. "By sitting here and doing nothing. You're supposed to be this famous Keeper who could take on anyone, and yet I haven't seen you do anything." Tears burst from Allora's eyes. The scared girl inside couldn't take it anymore. She was afraid, and her mother wasn't there for her. Allora's exterior was a thick shell, but inside she couldn't hold back the fear she'd held onto every day since cheerleading tryouts. "I may be young and not understand what went on before I was born, but I'm not going to sit around and hide while my friends and family are being attacked." Tears flowed freely down her cheeks. "I'm scared, Mom. I'm really, really scared. But that isn't going to stop me from fighting." Allora took a deep breath for what she knew would be a spear to her mother's heart. "At least Uncle Ben stood for something. At least he was willing to do something to protect the ones that he loved."

The comment hit Milly at her core. A lone tear broke from its nearly-impenetrable emotional shell and crashed like a dumbbell to the hardwood floor. The weight of guilt upon her shoulders grew unbearable. Watching Allora leave the living room, Milly's tough facade collapsed in a flood of shame. Her daughter's safety had been her number one priority. It had been her identity for sixteen years. She had failed in her mission. Quickly, her self-deprecation turned to anger toward the one man who had defied her orders and infected her daughter with tall tales. The Eye was a myth. And it was going to get her daughter killed. Intending to put a stop to this deadly quest, Milly went to her room in anticipation of the parent conferences taking place that evening.

~~~~~~~~~~~~~~

Squeezing into the undersized desk chair, Milly waited patiently at the back of the room. She glanced around at the numerous maps hanging about the walls. Turning around, she could see a faint tint to a small area in the corner. The discoloration was a sign that only a trained eye could decipher. There was a safe located in the wall. Milly wondered what was in there. Was Mr. Swan someone she could trust? He had been her little brother's best friend, but he had a tumultuous past filled with unexplained secrets.

The room slowly filled with unassuming parents, waiting for their kids' teacher to arrive. The small talk dissipated when Mr. Swan entered the classroom.

"Welcome, everyone," Mr. Swan began, moving behind his desk to ruffle through some papers he had prepared for the presentation. "I'm glad you all were able to make it. For those who don't know, I'm Mr. Swan, your children's history teacher. Before we begin, does anyone have any questions?"

"I've got one," Milly said.

"Alright, Milly, go ahead," Mr. Swan answered, trying to sound surprised.

"What are you teaching our children?"

Mr. Swan pulled his head back, shocked by the simple, ordinary question.

"Well... we are reading Homer's great masterpiece, *The Iliad*, and learning a lot about the Greek culture."

"Oh, that's great!" one of the parents interjected. "I loved that story when I was in school."

"So, you're teaching our children about Greek mythology?"

Mr. Swan hesitated, wondering what Milly was pushing him toward. He knew how manipulative she could be. Her cunning was legendary, and he could see himself stepping into a trap. But there was no other way out.

"Yes, parts of the class are on Greek mythology."

"So, then, do you think it's alright to teach religious doctrine in our schools?"

Mr. Swan became tense as all eyes waited for his response.

"I believe Greek mythology has relevance to historical events," he said, trying to get at the real truth that Milly was pushing for, "and can explain certain outcomes that have implications to modern society."

"So does every other religion. But you think it's alright to feed our children these stories in order to feed their curiosity and endanger their lives!"

Some of the other parents looked skeptically at the teacher, wondering why this woman was making such brash accusations. But to the rest of the class, Milly sounded crazy. They remained seated, staring awkwardly forward and feeling sympathy for Mr. Swan, who seemed innocent in their eyes. These parents were unaware that these two had a storied past, going back decades. Pulling at his collar, Mr. Swan could feel his blue satin tie becoming tighter. His brow became sweaty as he contemplated an exit strategy.

"Can I talk with you outside?" Mr. Swan said, softly.

Milly grabbed her coat and marched into the hallway. The two squared off, like two boxers in a ring. Mr. Swan shut the door on the curious group, many of whom leaned over the desks for a glimpse through the narrow door window.

"What's the matter with you?" Mr. Swan whispered.

"Are you kidding me?" Milly said. "You sent my kid after that stupid artifact, knowing what happened last time!"

"Don't you realize how important that *stupid* artifact is?"

Milly shifted her weight. The hallway was quiet. She looked both ways to see if anyone was listening, and moved closer.

"I understand that my little brother died looking for it. And none of you even know if it exists or what it does."

"It exists," Mr. Swan said. "And if found, we can finally have a fighting chance."

"You don't know that," Milly said. "It's just too dangerous. I will not let someone else die because of it."

"You made a promise to Ben that you would continue the search."

Milly's mind burst into a memory of her younger brother dying in the deep forest. A picture of the blackened wound that had killed him was permanently imprinted in her head. His last breaths had been shallow and pained as he had begged his older sister to continue his search. While holding his hand firmly, with Mr. Swan, Aunt May, and Sas looking on, she had promised to find the Eye. Her promise had been the last words spoken before his eyes had rolled back, fading into death.

Milly fluttered her eyelids, looking upward to help stop the flood of tears that was ready to break through the dam. "My daughter's safety comes first."

"And what about the safety of our people? Of our world? And this world. Pretty soon, they will be at our doorsteps whether you like it or not. As we speak, his power and influence is growing. Our days of hiding in this place are over. We must find the Eye at all costs."

Swan was hoping that guilt would persuade Milly to join his cause. He had a strong sense of duty to the people on Sonora to continue the fight against those who wanted to suppress the rebellion. He was tired to hiding on Earth, hoping for someone else to win the fight. Mr. Swan was a military man in a teacher's body. He was going to do everything in his power to convince Milly to take up arms.

"The Eye is a myth; a far-fetched idea that my brother was obsessed with and which ultimately led to his death. Even if it were real, it isn't worth the consequences that it brings. I will not trade this artifact for the life of my daughter."

"When are you going to realize how special she is? Your daughter is meant for greatness. And right now you are holding her back."

"I'm holding her back because she doesn't understand how dangerous our world is."

"That doesn't sound like the Milly I knew. She was fearless, and defied her mother in order to become a great Keeper."

"Yes, and that girl was stupid and naive. Our world changed, and is more dangerous than ever."

"And what about the others? What about the people back home? Are you just going to forget about the war and pretend that it isn't happening?" Mr. Swan could tell that his words struck a chord within this woman's hard exterior. "You took a vow to protect the innocent, remember?"

Milly pulled back like a cobra ready to strike. "Don't you dare lecture *me* on the Code! It wasn't too long ago when your allegiances were in question." Mr. Swan bit his lip, stepping backward. Milly knew how to hit back, taking away any argument the man had. She had stabbed at the one part of his life that pained him most. "So don't try to give me a lesson on my responsibilities to the Order. You are only here on my good graces. If you hadn't been my brother's best friend, I would have thrown you out long ago. One more mention of the Eye to my daughter and I'll kill you myself. Is that clear?"

"Crystal clear," Mr. Swan said, stepping back in defeat. He swallowed hard, fighting back the urge to argue. There was no point and no argument to convince Milly to take up the quest to find the artifact. She was blinded by emotion, and stubbornly clinging to the idea that they would be safe on Earth. He knew otherwise, but couldn't explain the situation. Mr. Swan let go and went back into the classroom.

Milly stood in the quiet hallway for a moment. The woman who always knew what to do was now rattled. Lately, she had been second-guessing her choices, with no clear idea whether she was doing the right thing. As she drove home, her mind wandered to a time when she had been a warrior. In battle, she had known exactly what to do. As a mother, life had become much more complicated. Now that Allora was becoming a woman and developing her gifts, life was even more difficult.

How was a mother supposed to keep her child safe, while giving her the room to grow and develop? How was she going to allow Allora to become stronger, without worrying that she might die along the way? Still in deep thought, Milly parked the car and went into her quiet home. She went down the kids' hallway, stopping just inches from Allora's bedroom door. Unable to enter, she left the dark hallway, choosing to leave her daughter be and take some time to think.

Meanwhile, Allora lay on her bed, staring intently at the small black orb she had discovered in the caves. As she held it in her palm, the orb pulsated with a light, sparkling glow, as if it had a heart beat. The black orb was cold, and yet it projected small sparks from its interior. Her eyelids became heavy, and after an hour of staring at the object, she fell fast asleep, dreaming of what this small sphere might produce and how it could be used to find the tool needed to bring peace to her life.

Chapter 21

Ski Trip

Mesmerized by the crystal orb, Allora couldn't take her eyes off of the magical object, wondering how this round rock was the last piece of the map. She twirled the sphere in her fingers as Katie's Jeep drove down the long road toward school. Because of the incident at the Ape Caves, Allora had been grounded and hadn't been able to see her friends for all of winter break. Even Katie's incessant rambling was a nice change from the boredom of her home.

"I got these awesome diamond earrings from Jarrod. They are so beautiful. I think I'm going to wait till prom to wear them, though. I'm getting a white dress?" Katie said.

"I'm sorry to interrupt your fascinating story," Allora said, "but have you seen Mr. Swan?"

"I haven't seen him since school," Katie replied, and then went right back to her story.

When the girls, Dax and Tanner arrived at their first period history class, they noticed an unfamiliar face at the head of the class.

"Where is Mr. Swan?" Allora asked.

The old lady stopped writing her name on the board to address the four young students. "He has been assigned to a different classroom, honey."

Allora wasn't very keen on being called "honey" but let it slide because of how old the woman was.

"Why?"

"I don't know, darling," she said. "Principal Winters asked me to teach you from here on out, sweetie."

The old lady pinched Allora's cheek and then turned back around to finish writing her welcome message. The pinch almost set Allora off. Katie had to grab her arm to stop her from attacking. Leaving the room, the four congregated in a corner of the hallway, away from anyone else.

"You alright?" Katie asked.

"Yeah, I just hate having my cheeks pinched," she said, rubbing the spot. "And what's with old people calling you 'sweetie' and 'honey'?"

"Long break?" Tanner asked, feeling Allora's agitation.

Allora let out a sigh. She had been cooped up in her house for so long. "Sorry. I'm a little stressed out. Being stuck at my house without any answers as to what this thing is...." She pulled the small crystal orb from her pocket. "I just want to talk with Swan about what it is, because it's unlike the other two pieces."

"So, you two did find it!" Dax exclaimed.

"I told you," Katie said. "Why don't you ever believe me?"

"And you also fought off a giant bug and jumped through a river of lava?"

"Yes!" Katie yelled.

A few other students glanced over at the group, causing them to move in closer.

"We shouldn't be talking about this here," Tanner stated. "Remember, Swan said it wasn't safe at school. Let's meet after school at the orchard."

Allora shoved the orb back into her pocket, and then they all split off in different directions, choosing to talk after school. Allora went searching for Mr. Swan, but couldn't locate his new classroom. She wondered whether

her mother had something to do with his reassignment.

Allora met Katie, Tanner, and Dax in the parking lot after her last class of the day. They all went to Allora's and hiked up to the portal and jumped through to the orchard.

"Why are you so obsessed with this thing anyway? It's not like it has anything to do with us," Dax said. "It just seems to be causing more problems than solutions."

"You're wrong," Allora said. "It has everything to do with us."

"Allora has a point. If this artifact can help us fight off those stupid creatures, then we have to find it," Tanner said.

"And what if one of us dies?" Dax asked. He wouldn't admit it, but hearing the story about the caves and the peril that his sister had been in didn't sit well. Katie was the only family he had on this world, and he felt the need to protect her at all costs.

"Do you really think we can take these things on ourselves?" Allora asked. "We already have targets on our heads whether we like it or not. If this Eye can make us stronger, I'm going to do whatever it takes to find it."

"But you don't know anything about it," Dax argued. "And neither does Mr. Swan."

They all stopped talking. Dax was right. None of them knew exactly what this artifact could do, if anything. The unknown was frightening, and the idea that their quest was trivial made Allora and the others angry. They were putting their faith in an object they knew nothing about.

When they jumped back through the portal, they noticed the first snow of the winter season was falling through the forest canopy. The meadow behind Allora's house was covered in a thin layer of white. The sprinkles of white powder reminded the four of a more innocent time when they had been ignorant of their current reality.

"I realize that this year has been stressful for all of us," Katie said, staring from the edge of the forest. "I think it's time we have a little fun. If not, we are going to go crazy. You know what we need?"

Tanner smiled. "A ski trip."

Allora could conceive of only one response from her mother. "Milly won't let any of us do that, and you know it. She will convince everyone that skiing at the mountain is far too dangerous."

"That is why we have to do it on a school day," Katie said with a sinister smile.

Grinning profusely, they silently agreed upon the idea. Everyone in town went to the mountain in the winter. Every year, they would buy season passes and ski whenever they could. This year had been different for all of them. Since the attacks, their extracurricular activities had been limited to after-school sports and nothing else. Allora had asked her mother, but she had adamantly said no.

"Katie is right," Allora admitted. "We definitely need this. I don't think anything is going to attack us while we're skiing. Besides, no one will know where we are because we're not going to tell anyone, right?"

They all nodded in agreement. The plan was to meet at the local grocery store in the morning before school. Each one had to sneak their stuff out of the house and into the car the night before. Her ski supplies were in the garage. She had to beg Bell to distract their mother, which proved to be difficult because her sister kept asking questions.

"Why do I have to do this?" Bell asked.

"Because, I said so," Allora said, pushing her little sister toward the living room where Milly was reading a newspaper. "Now, just get Mom to go outside."

Bell did so reluctantly. Allora went to the garage and got her skis and boots. She had to make a second trip to get all of her ski clothes. As Allora was exiting the garage, she heard her mother and sister coming back into the house. She motioned to her sister to stop Milly. Bell turned her mother around, dancing in place while Allora ran to her room. She threw her supplies out her window, just as her mother was opening her bedroom door.

"Do you know why your sister is acting so strange?" Milly asked.

Sitting back on her bed, Allora shook her head. "No idea," she said, with a look of guilt. Milly stood there for a minute, trying to figure out what her daughters were up to. She gave up on it and slowly closed the bedroom door. Allora exhaled and lay back hard into her pillows.

The next day she said good-bye to her mother after breakfast, grabbed her stuff from the side of the house, and quickly packed it into Katie's car. Katie drove off toward the grocery store. They met the boys in the parking lot and packed Tanner's car with all of their gear. Then, they all drove up toward the mountain. A few miles up the road they could see the majestic white- capped mountain shining in the sunlight. It was a beautiful winter day and perfect for skiing.

It was only eight o'clock by the time they reached the parking lot of Timberline Lodge, at the bottom of the mountain. The girls dressed into their ski clothes while the boys went to get passes for everyone. The boys grabbed their snowboards, while the girls got their skis and poles. The four hopped onto the chairlift and took off up the mountain.

Allora took this time to close her eyes and relax. She felt the mountain breeze blowing through the trees, hitting her face. The air smelled of pine trees. The slopes were pristine white, which glowed in the brightness of the morning sun. The trees swayed as the mountain breeze danced down the canyon below them. The swish of passing skiers echoed in the canyon, along with the rumbling of the chairlift as it passed the stands that held it up. Allora was in her own personal heaven. The worries of the past year vanished. She was in a blissful state of peace. All she could think about was the feel of the snow beneath her skis. Thoughts of evil creatures were replaced by the anticipation of flying down the mountain with her friends.

Allora put the support bar up and they all pushed themselves off the chair. Dax wobbled and caught the front edge of Tanner's board, sending both flying forward. The people behind them tried to ski around, but couldn't make it. They fell over, smacking into the boys. There was a large pileup, causing the attendant to stop the chairlift. The girls stood a couple of feet away, cracking up with laughter as the boys pulled themselves up. Nothing could change their moods, though. They laughed along with the girls while they strapped in their back feet.

The first run felt amazing. In front, they could see blue sky and rolling white hills lining the landscape. Etched in the valleys were rivers and lakes, glistening against the rays of sun. Allora felt the fresh powder beneath her skis as she cruised, side to side, along the run. The mountain was surprisingly empty for such a beautiful day. Once they made it to the bottom of the run, they quickly got back onto the chairlift. This time, they went to the top of the Palmer chairlift. Allora couldn't hold back a smile while she sliced her skis into the fresh snow. It was a perfect day with her best friends, and it felt amazing to be a normal teenager.

Around noon, they all went to lodge for lunch. Allora got a sandwich and bowl of soup, while the boys got chili fries. "I'm not going to ski behind you two after this," Katie said with a disgusted look on her face.

"And why is that?" Dax asked.

"Because after you are done with that," she said, pointing to their meal, "you're going to be farting up a storm."

They all laughed. "I'm just glad that we came up here. I really needed this," Allora said.

"We all did," Katie said.

Allora thought back on one of Sumatra's talks. "Can we make a pact right now? Let's all agree that no matter what happens in the future, we will always have each other's backs," she said, putting her hand on the middle of the table.

"Agreed," Tanner said, putting his hand over hers.

Katie and Dax did the same. "Agreed," they both said at the same time.

The rest of the day was a lot of fun. They traveled around the mountain, making sure to ski on every run. The end of the day was quickly approaching, and they decided to take one more run. Allora hadn't had a chance to ski through the trees, so about a quarter of the way down she went off the main run, skiing between two large pine trees. She sliced through the trees as if she were on a professional slalom course. The rest of the group pushed on ahead, assuming their friend would pop out below. Instead, Allora caught her pole on a branch, which swung her toward the trunk of a tree. She extended her right leg against the snow, turning her body to the left. She missed the tree, but her right ski clipped the trunk, sending her sideways into the powder. She screamed, which caused her friends to stop.

"Allora!" Tanner yelled, hopping up the mountain as fast as he could. He stopped, and starting unfastening his board until he heard Allora yell back.

"I'm fine, I'm fine," she said, pulling herself up and walking up the hill toward her skis. "I just fell."

The sun was beginning to set along the western skyline. Allora could feel the air getting much colder. The light was fading, especially among the trees.

Allora's boot was almost clipped back into her binding when she heard a rustling through the trees. Her heart jumped, and a sense of alertness burst from her stomach and into her throat. Allora quickly put pressure down on her heal. The sound of the boot securing into the ski caused the rustling to stop. Allora looked through the trees, but she couldn't see anything. She remained still, listening to the wind. Out of the corner of her eye, she saw a large, furry creature peek its head around a tree.

"Sas?" Allora said in a loud whisper. The furry creature came out from behind the tree to reveal that he was, indeed, Sas. He slowly stepped forward. "What are you doing here? You could've been seen."

"I was just checking up on you," he said, uncharacteristically serious.

Allora was puzzled. "How did you know that we were here?"

Sas moved even closer. "I need you to tell me where the Eye is."

Allora inched away, moving down the hill as Sas came closer. Something was wrong. As he came down through trees, Allora sensed an odd energy about him. Allora pushed herself further away from the oncoming creature.

"We don't know where it is," she said. "You know that."

The furry creature bellowed, "I need you to give me the map!" His eyes were strangely unfamiliar, and as he came closer, Allora's inner alarms screamed at her to run.

"You're not Sas!" she yelled. Allora was able to push her pole into the snow and launch herself to the left of a tree as the creature leapt forward with its arms outstretched.

"Allora!" Tanner yelled from below.

The creature hit the tree that Allora had avoided, knocking snow from the foliage on top of itself. Allora came screaming through the trees, trying to find the spot where Tanner was waiting.

"Go, Tanner," she yelled. "Go!"

Tanner put his board forward and pushed off of the snow. He didn't have any momentum, so Allora extended her pole.

"Grab it!"

Tanner grasped the pole. "What's going onnnnnn...?" he said as Allora launched him down the mountain.

The Sas lookalike exploded out of the trees, hurling itself toward them. Allora sliced with her ski, changing her direction to the left. Tanner looked backward, confused by what he saw. The creature looked exactly like Sas, but something was off. Allora sliced back to the right as the oncoming creature leapt to her position. Tanner carved on his board, cutting across Allora to distract the creature. He launched himself over a jump as the creature dove to grab him. Tanner flew through the air, right over Allora's head.

Meanwhile, Katie and Dax stood at the bottom of the run, waiting impatiently for their friends. They had unclipped themselves and stood next to the chairlift. Then, they heard someone scream.

"That was Allora," Katie said, her expression quickly changing to fear.

The two siblings looked up the mountain, witnessing two small objects gliding down at an alarming speed.

"Why are they going so fast?" Dax asked.

Then, they both saw the reason. The furry creature flew into view. The two siblings couldn't understand what they were looking at. Sas was jumping down the mountain, trying to grab their friends. Allora zoomed past the chairlift attendant, who was trying to close up the lift for the night.

"Whoa, slow down," he yelled.

Tanner whizzed by at an equal speed, spraying the attendant with snow. The attendant was about to yell again, but a large, hairy creature's arm hit him. The attendant was launched in the air, landing right in front of Dax and Katie.

"We gotta go!" Katie said, throwing her skis on the ground and clipping herself in.

Dax took longer because he had a snowboard. Katie left without him, slamming her poles into the snow to gain momentum.

"Wait, I'm almost in," he said, pulling the strap over his boot. "Hold on.... Wait.... Stop...."

Katie didn't listen. She pushed herself past the ski lift and down through the trees, where the others had gone. The sounds of screaming pushed her to ski faster.

Allora was dodging the creature's every advance. Tanner was doing the same, unsure how they were going to escape. He yelled over to Allora, "Can you shoot a hadron burst at it?"

"I don't think I can get a good shot off without falling down," Allora replied, almost hitting a tree branch.

The snow beneath them became thicker, slowing their escape. The pursuing creature was gaining on them. It was only feet behind them, and the only reason it was unable to catch them was because of the trees blocking its every advance. The kids darted among the pines, making use of the only deterrent they had. Allora noticed that up ahead, at the bottom of the hill, the surface became flat, opening up into what looked like the bottom of a canyon.

Inches from Allora, the creature pushed off the powdery snow, flying forward. Tanner had to move fast. He brought his right foot upward, catching the snow on the edge of his board. Then, he made a diagonal cut sideways. The furry brown creature had Allora in its grasp when Tanner came soaring through the air, striking the creature on its side. It spun around in the air, crashing into the snow and hitting the base of a tree. Tanner tried to land on his board, but his balance was too lopsided, and he fell onto his back, tumbling down the remaining incline. Allora also became unbalanced, catching the sharp edge of her ski in the snow. The ski departed from her foot, and she followed Tanner as they both cascaded down the rest of the mountain in a flurry of white.

The creature stuck its foot into the snow, corrected the direction of the rest of its body, and continued the pursuit. Allora and Tanner made it to the bottom of the mountain, landing on a flat surface and sliding toward the middle of the wide opening. They tried to move, but the surface was completely iced over.

"Tanner! What do we do?" Allora yelled frantically, slipping on what seemed to be a frozen river.

"You have to hit it with a burst, now!" Tanner insisted. Allora tried to pull her hands up to focus, but she kept slipping. The creature was almost upon them. "Allora!" Tanner yelled, just as the creature planted its feet and jumped into the air.

The shadowy creature flew above the flat area, and the two waited for gravity to bring it down on top of them. Allora saw the panic in Tanner's eyes. Suddenly, a brown blur flew through the air, hitting the creature on its side. The two furry masses hit the surface with a mighty force. The impact sent shockwaves through the ground, and water exploded upward. Both creatures were knocked into the forest on the other side of the river, disappearing into the dense trees. The surface where Allora and Tanner lay broke apart. Tanner grabbed Allora's hand, pulling her up and then swinging her body to the edge of the ice. Allora glided along the surface, knowing that Tanner had sacrificed himself. She screamed his name, looking back as Tanner fell out of view, and into the cold river below. Allora ignored the screams from Katie who was almost down the hill. Allora moved along the edge, trying to find a branch to save Tanner. She ran down the riverbank, sweeping the snow from the ice. Tanner had been pulled by the current and was now under the thick ice. She knew she had to act fast. The piercing cold had likely pushed the air from his lungs, and soon he would be out of breath.

Allora pulled all of her emotions into a central location, and then her body exploded in fire, which escaped from her hands. A huge stream of flames glided along the ice, melting it instantly. Tanner came into view, his body bobbing in the river. The fire burned out, but Tanner still moved down the rapids, uncontrollably. Allora's body couldn't move, and she collapsed into the snow.

Allora pulled herself up, reaching her arm toward Tanner, whose lifeless body was almost out of sight. She tried to scream for him, but the words could barely be heard.

Something swam through the water down in the canyon below. Allora watched as Tanner's body was lifted above the surface and moved upstream.

Katie finally made it to Allora, who was getting back enough energy to lift herself up. Tanner was limp, but his body drifted on top of the water. He came to rest on the bank in front of the two wide-eyed girls. At that point, a creature pulled its head out of the water with the sunset to its back. The creature moved out of the water, and out of the glare of the setting sun. Once the two girls were able to see, they looked upon the strange creature with amazement. It had a humanoid figure, but with a jellyfish-type skin. The eyes were mesmerizing. They were bright crystal blue, but with no iris. It stepped onto the snowbank and knelt down next to Tanner.

Then it spoke in a deep, calming voice. "He isn't breathing."

The creature put its hand on Tanner's chest and closed its eyes. Its body began to glow blue. Veins of blue covered its body, pulsating and glowing in the dimming light of the sun. The blue veins began to snake their way toward the creature's heart, and then into its hand with a jolt. Tanner's body pulled upward, arching his back as if the creature had just shocked him. Tanner opened his eyes and pulled himself to a seated position. Allora and

Katie jumped on him as soon as they could. His shivering body convulsed as they held him.

"Tanner, we need to get you warm," Allora said, taking off her coat. Katie did the same thing. Both of the girls ignored the creature standing in the water to their left. They pulled Tanner's freezing clothes from his shaking body. He was in his boxers when Dax came crashing through the snow above them.

"Hey," Dax yelled, falling face-first into the snowbank. "Where is he? I'll kill him."

"You're too late," Katie said, taking off her coat. "You missed it."

Dax pulled his head out of the snow to see Tanner almost naked in front of him, and the girls, who were pulling off their clothes. "Whoa. Am I interrupting something here? I can come back," Dax said in his usual joking manner, unaware of what had just happened.

"Shut up, you idiot, and help us get Tanner warm," Katie yelled at her brother as she pulled her jacket over Tanner's arm. "He fell into the water."

Hearing the seriousness in his sister's tone, Dax pulled off his boots and pants. "I don't think that he is going to fit into your pants, sis," Dax said, handing his to Katie.

Katie sneered at her brother and snatched the black pants quickly. Tanner was fully clothed, but he was still shivering. Dax finally noticed the jellyfish creature quietly standing on the edge of the river.

"Who is he?" Dax said, pointing at the creature.

Katie opened her mouth, but couldn't get any words out before a brown furry creature jumped through the river toward the group. Everyone except Tanner, who was still shivering, turned and got into defensive stances.

"You're not going to get anyone today," Allora said, creating a ball of purple balls of hadrons in her hand. She felt a cold yet soothing hand upon her wrist. Allora looked over her shoulder and saw the jellyfish creature.

"It's alright," the creature said in a soft yet powerful voice. "That is the real Sas."

"How do you know for sure?" Allora asked.

"Trust me," the creature replied. "I know."

Allora still couldn't believe it. It looked like the same creature that had attacked her in the woods. She saw the look on the tall Sasquatch. It was one of worry and fear. Allora put down her hand and the ball of hadrons disappeared. Falling sparks absorbed into the ground around them.

Sas moved with a purpose, unlike Allora had ever seen before. "Is Tanner alright?" Sas asked, stepping onto the bank where they stood.

The creature stepped forward. "He should be. We have to get him to a safe, warm location, soon."

"Thank you, Baymar," Sas replied, causing Allora to look at the creature. She realized that this was the creature who had helped her escape the ropes at summer camp.

"Can you create a short portal?" Sas asked. "I don't have enough in me to do it."

Baymar thought for a brief moment. "I can only do one for the river's edge. That's the only spot that my eye can conceive that is close enough to town."

"Then do it," Sas said. "We have to get out of here. That Shifter is hurt, but he will definitely be back."

Baymar nodded. Then, he swirled his hands, pulling up the water beneath his feet. All around them the water shot up, as if it were a marionette being pulled by a puppeteer. Baymar tucked in his hands, and then thrust them out toward the snowbank. The snow swirled around in a circle, as if in a blender, and then pulled itself to the middle of the circle.

"Everyone, through the portal, now," Sas said.

They picked Tanner up and dragged him to the portal, then jumped in. They could feel their bodies getting sucked through the snowbank. They popped out in the river, where the water was freezing. Tanner was now in agonizing pain from the reintroduction to the piercing cold water. Allora kept a hold of him, but slipped on the rocks. Dax caught both of them, and they all made it onto the riverbank. Allora knew where they were. It was the same location she went to whenever she was upset. Sas and Baymar hadn't followed them. They made their way up through the forest and back onto the familiar street Allora had walked along her whole life.

The walk back to her house was long because they had to drag Tanner's weak, shivering body. Finally, they arrived at Allora's home and crashed through the front door in exhaustion.

Chapter 22

Aftermath

"What the hell happened?" Aunt May asked as they landed on the floor at her feet. Too tired to speak, they lay there gasping for air. They were soaking wet, half-dressed in their ski clothes. Milly sprinted down the hall, followed closely by Bell. Milly's eyes darted back and forth, contemplating the scene.

"You better not tell me that you were up at the mountain," Milly said, standing over her daughter with her hands on her hips.

Allora had more pressing issues to deal with.

"No time, Mom. We were attacked. Tanner... river... hypothermic..." Allora said between shivers and breaths. All four were freezing from landing in the river. Milly turned from a mother to a barking general within seconds.

"Dax, I need you to take Tanner into Allora's room and strip him down. Allora, you and Katie go get the blankets from the cabinets in the hallway and put them on Tanner. May, go get the mirror glue from your room. You know what to do with it. Bell, go put some hot water on the stove." They all moved quickly to begin their duties. "After you guys are done, there are three showers. Use them. Then, I want you all out here in the living room. You have a lot of explaining to do."

Milly went about making a large fire while everyone did exactly as she had instructed. Dax was able to get Tanner under the sheets while his body convulsed. The girls put the blankets over him, and then they went to the showers to warm themselves. Bell made tea, and then went to Allora's room. She spoon-fed Tanner the warm liquid. Milly walked into the room minutes later with a red bottle. Tanner's skin was pale blue, and he was still shivering, even with six blankets over him. Milly grabbed the spoon from Bell and poured the contents of the red bottle into it. Red, yellow, and orange poured from the bottle, swirling around magically. Milly fed Tanner from the spoon, and instantly Tanner's skin turned the colors of the liquid and then returned to its normal shade. He stopped shivering. Then, he turned his head and fell asleep.

Bell's mouth was wide open in amazement. Milly displayed the bottle to her daughter. "Warming liquid. Your aunt made it years ago. Pretty potent stuff," Milly said, getting up from the bed.

"What is it made of?" Bell asked, completely consumed by curiosity.

"The main ingredient is dragon saliva. You would have to ask your aunt what the rest of the ingredients are," Milly replied.

"Dragon saliva!" Bell exclaimed, giddy with excitement.

"Yes, they are Sonorian pets. Not as big as the stories have told. Pretty much the size of a large dog," Milly explained.

"Cool... can we get one?" Bell asked as Milly went to the kitchen pour tea for everyone else.

Allora pulled on the faucet, shivering as she sat down in the tub. She was too exhausted to stand. Beads of warm water hit her face, stinging her skin as she sat with her arms around her knees. Now in the safety of her home, she could reflect on the past few hours. Her mind raced, thinking about the power that had come from within her. The amazing display of fire had been exhilarating, but she couldn't get over the powerlessness she felt afterward. The terror of watching Tanner's body floating down the river was too much. Tears escaped from her eyes, but she couldn't distinguish them from the water streaming down her face. With all the showers running at once, the hot water didn't last long. The girls and Dax exited at the same time, putting on clothes that Milly had laid out for them.

Everyone met in the living room, dreading the explanation of their disobedience. It was warm from the fireplace on the far side of the room. They all sat together, staring into the fire silently as Milly brought them tea. She sat down with the rest of the group and gave them a stern look. Allora already knew she was in trouble.

Milly took a sip of her tea, placed it on the table next to her armchair, and said, "Now. Tell me exactly what happened."

Katie and Dax sat attentively listening to Allora recount the events from hours earlier. This was the first time they had heard the details of what had happened on the mountain. Milly was taking a sip of her tea when Allora mentioned the conversation at the riverbank. "Sas said it was a Shifter that attacked us."

Milly dropped her cup on the floor and stared at her sister, who glanced back with a an equally fearful look.

"Then what happened?" Milly said, picking up the porcelain remnants of her teacup from the floor.

Allora continued the story about how Tanner had become submerged under the ice and what she had done to try to free him. Her mother remained silent while her daughter told her about the river of fire. When Allora was finished, Milly sat back in her armchair.

"I don't think you know just how lucky you are to be sitting here," Milly said. "If Sas wasn't there...." Milly turned away at the thought of what could have happened.

Aunt May leaned in toward her niece. "What exactly did the Shifter ask you in the trees?"

"It asked me where the Eye was," Allora said.

"How do they know about it?" Aunt May asked her sister.

"They know Allora is Sonorian if they are asking questions about the Eye. It also means that they know we are looking for it." Milly paused for a minute, contemplating the consequences that might occur. "I don't like this."

"I don't either, but what can we do?" Aunt May asked.

The increasing number of Sonorian creatures in the area was alarming. Time was like a vise, slowing squeezing them into submission. The weight of a battle loomed just around the corner, and they weren't sure if they could win. Milly could only hope that everyone would be ready for the inevitable confrontation. Milly spent the rest of the night on the phone, informing the other parents and Sonorians in town about the day's events. They all thought it best to keep the children at the Sona house.

Tanner was asleep in Allora's bed, so she set up sleeping arrangements in the living room. Exhausted, everyone went to bed with their thoughts. Allora lay on the couch, staring up at the ceiling. Although she was exhausted, sleep evaded her. Her mind raced through time. One question crept in with every memory.

Why is this happening to me? she asked herself.

Before this year, she had begged for something new and exciting. Now, she could only hope for some sense of normalcy. Even the mundane tasks of her past would be welcomed.

After a few hours, she finally drifted off to sleep. Her dreams took her to a wheat field. She walked forward, and in the distance a short, brown-haired man stood with his hands behind his back. Allora stepped through the wheat, gliding the straws through her hands as she walked. The texture of the wheat touched her palm as if she was really there. The man became clearly visible ahead. The wheat field rolled with the wind. Allora walked along the top of a hill toward the man, who was standing on the edge of a cliff. The ground dropped off to a large body of water. Stopping next to him, Allora gasped at the familiar face staring into the distance. A peaceful smile hung above his chin as he turned to the young girl.

"Hi, Allora," the man said.

"Uncle Ben!" Allora said, grasping him around the waist. Her grasp was tight, as if trying to inhibit the moment from passing. It felt so real. Even the familiar smell of his aftershave was present when she buried her face against his chest. Flooded with emotion, Allora held on for dear life. He was the embodiment of a past that was filled with joyful memories. When he died, her life changed.

"Beautiful, isn't it?" he asked, his calm voice flowing through the valley like the wind.

Still holding onto his waist, Allora turned and looked upon the beautiful scene reaching to the setting sun. The two figures stood for what seemed to be hours, watching the sun dip into the water.

"How are you here?" Allora asked.

Uncle Ben pulled his chin down his chest, staring lovingly at his niece.

"I never left you," he said.

"I don't understand," she answered. "You died."

"I will always be with you," he said. "You must understand that you have all the answers you need. Trust yourself and you will find the path you seek."

As he said these last words, his body faded as if made of fog, and then disappeared into the wind.

Allora woke from her dream and sat up. Bewildered by the dream, she remained stuck in one spot, frozen by thought. She finally got up and walked into her room, only to find Tanner standing in his boxers. She shuffled back and forth awkwardly. Tanner stood in the middle of the room, almost laughing.

"Sorry, I... uhhhh... I forgot you were in here," Allora said, grabbing the doorknob. She closed the door behind her and leaned against it. She couldn't help but smile. Tanner had a perfectly toned body, with a six-pack stomach, large biceps, and long muscular legs.

"What are you doing?" Bell asked, walking into the hallway.

Allora jumped as if she had been caught doing something she shouldn't be.

"Nothing!" she whispered harshly. She stepped into the bathroom and shut the door on her sister.

After breakfast, Allora's friends all went home and Bell went off to Aunt May's room. Allora was alone with her mother, who was drinking her coffee and staring at her daughter.

"My guess is that you're going to ground me for a lifetime and yell at me for an hour about how irresponsible I've been," Allora said, frustrated by her mother's silence. Milly kept sipping her coffee, thinking about what she wanted to say.

"No, Allora. That isn't what I'm going to do. No matter what I do to protect you, eventually you are going to have to experience life and the consequence of your actions. I'm realizing that as much as I want to keep you safe, babying you is just going to keep you from learning how to protect yourself."

Allora was caught completely off guard. She had already created a rebuttal. Instead, she sat confused by her mother's lack of emotion. Milly had conceded the fight before it even began.

Milly set the coffee mug onto the kitchen table. "I think it's time you hear how your uncle died," Milly said, eyes gazing forward. Allora remained silent. "Ben and Mr. Swan had learned about the Eye of the Titans from Sas' father during the onset of the war that brought us here. They had intended to use its power to change the course of the war. Unfortunately, the other side had the same idea. They found the first piece on an expedition to Shangri-La in Nepal."

"I thought that was just a myth?" Allora asked.

"Nope, it's real. Shangri-La is the capital headquarters for the Guardian organization on Earth," Milly said. "Sas says that someone in the Guardian order had betrayed his father and gave away their location, which led them back here. The king had sent a Shifter, like the one you encountered yesterday. The Shifter learned of our community, and had intended to report back to the king. Uncle Ben caught up with it, and prevented that from happening."

"At the cost of his life," Allora said, thinking back to the night she found out about her uncle. Her mother had been hysterical when she got home. Allora was only ten years old at the time. After that night, the energy in their house was different.

"Yes..." Milly said, holding her daughter's hand.

Getting up from the table, Allora went to the garage to put away her ski clothes. She pushed the bag against the wall. The zipper wasn't completely closed, and a beanie fell out. Allora went to pick it up, her eye catching the box on the ground: her uncle's possessions. She sat down on the garage floor, pulling the cardboard flaps open. She sifted through old documents, sports memorabilia, and other objects. She pulled out the old Oregon Ducks hat that her uncle had always worn. The bill had been perfectly molded to her uncle's specifications. He had taught Allora his trick for molding a hat how he wanted. He wore it in the shower, and then gradually bent the bill in a half circle until it was perfect. She found her uncle's old coffee mug, which he always had on the kitchen table in the morning. It was see-through royal blue with his name etched into the glass. Allora slowly turned the cup over in her hands while she thought back to how they used to talk about sports in the morning over breakfast.

She rummaged around in the box, pulling out object after object. She finally reached the bottom. There was a small worn and tattered book lying against the edge of the box. The binding was made of leather, and the cover had a picture of what looked like an armored warrior. Allora opened it to the first page. The title read, *The Iliad of Homer*. Allora kept turning through the pages. A folded piece of paper dropped from the middle of the book. Allora placed the book on the concrete floor and picked up the paper. She unfolded it and began reading.

Dear Allora,

I'm writing you this letter in hopes that you will receive this book on your eighteenth birthday. I gave instructions to your mother to give it to you when you were old enough to realize who you really are. I don't think that I will be there when you find out. There is something that I must do, and it may be the key to our survival. I don't expect you to understand right now, but hopefully you will in the future. The next few years may be hard on you. I can't imagine the hardships that you may face. Allora, you must push forward. For some reason, you are the key to a grander vision that I can't quite see myself. The weight of responsibility can be trying. Lean on those around you for support.

I'm going to try my hardest to make it easier on you. I believe I have found what I've been looking for. This will be the reason for my absence. Let's just hope that I can find it. Remember, Allora, I will always love you.

Your Uncle,

Ben

When she finished, a tear broke off from her chin, landing on the paper. Allora sat for almost an hour staring at the words, rereading each one until she memorized it. Wiping the tears from her cheeks, she placed the book back into the box. Then, she shoved it back into the corner and left the garage. Placing the note into her pocket, she left the garage with a new sense of purpose. She made a proclamation to herself that she would finish her uncle's quest. Even though the road ahead was dangerous, she would not falter. She would find the Eye and bring a stop to those who would hurt those she loved. Her path was now clear.

Chapter 23

Planning

February arrived in a flurry of snow showers. Blankets of white powder and ice covered the roads, causing the cancellation of school. Allora was quietly reading a book next to the small, crackling fire when Katie burst through the front door. A chilly air and flakes of snow exploded into the room. The overly eager blonde wore a bright pink one-piece ski outfit with a matching pink headband wrapped around her forehead. In her hands was a plastic disc, which she had been using as a sled.

"Seriously! Why are you sitting inside when it's dumping snow outside? Get off your lazy bum and get your clothes on!" Katie said.

Annoyed by the cold intrusion, Allora was in no mood to be active. Almost losing Tanner had affected her more than she'd realized.

"Don't you remember what happened a couple of weeks ago?"

"Yes, I do," Katie said, sitting down next to her friend. She could see the pain in Allora's eyes. "But I'm not going to let it ruin my life. What are we supposed to do, live our entire lives looking over our shoulders and never being able to do anything?"

Katie had a point. But it still didn't change things. "I'm not in the mood, Katie."

The pink blob idly stood, wondering whether to remain with her friend, knowing there was more to this introversion. She decided against it. "Well... call me later?"

Allora nodded.

Katie left, leaving Allora to her thoughts, which were eating away at her mind. Flashes of Tanner's cold, lifeless body permeated into the forefront of her mind. Thoughts of death and the dangers ahead made her shake. Coming to terms with the loss of someone so close had such a familiar taste. Looking down at the worn leather seat upon which she sat, reminded her of how her uncle used to read to her while she sat on his lap. The emotions became too much, and her bedroom became the only sanctuary.

It wasn't long before the snow subsided and school closures ended. Allora walked into her first period history classroom to find a familiar face looking up at her.

"Mr. Swan!" she exclaimed, running up and hugging her teacher. Mr. Swan stumbled back, caught off guard by her excitement.

"It's nice to see you too," Mr. Swan said, with a surprised look upon his face.

Allora let go, looking up at her teacher. "I'm really glad that you're back," she said. "I need to talk to you about something important."

"Me too," he said.

"I have—" Allora began.

Mr. Swan cut her off. "Not now. Come here after school and we'll talk," he said, turning around to begin the lecture for class.

After school, Allora walked quickly to Mr. Swan's room and shut the door. He put his finger to his lips and proceeded to expand silencing glue to cover the room.

"I've had to be extra careful lately," Mr. Swan said, moving toward the far wall to retrieve an object from his secret location. "Are you okay? I heard about the Shifter attack."

"Yeah," Allora said, putting her head down. "I guess." She had a lot that she wanted to ask her teacher.

Mr. Swan pulled the object from the wall and walked over to his somber student. "Hey," he said, picking up her chin. "What's wrong?"

Allora took a while to ask the question. "How well did you know my uncle?"

"I'm guessing your mother told you what happened." Mr. Swan walked over to the window and looked out on the patches of snow. "You know, the hills where I grew up used to snow like it does here," he said, pausing for a moment. Then, he turned and leaned against the windowsill. "That's where I met your uncle. We grew up together. He was my closest and best friend." Mr. Swan's eyes rolled down, and he laughed. "Your uncle used to get me in so much trouble. One time, we captured a dryad, put it in a box, and gave it to your mom as a birthday present. When your mom opened the box, the dryad jumped out and attacked her. It was one of the funniest things I had ever seen. I think your mom still hates me for that one." He chuckled.

"What's a dryad?" Allora asked.

"Oh, they're tree nymphs. Small, shy creatures unless provoked. They can be especially fierce if you mess with their trees. Ben was an amazing man. He saved my life." Allora could see tears forming in her teacher's eyes. She didn't interrupt, though. Mr. Swan wiped his eyes and continued. "Your uncle and I joined the Royal Guard after we got out of preliminary school, what you would call high school, and we quickly moved up the ranks, until the wars began. We were arrested, but your uncle was able to escape. Ben found out I was going to be executed, only a couple weeks afterward. He cooked up an elaborate escape. We barely made it out of there alive. I told him he was an idiot and he could have gotten himself killed. He told me that he would rather die than see my death at the hands of the king."

"Why did the king have you and my uncle arrested? Didn't you just say you were a part of his royal guard?"

"The previous king," Mr. Swan said. "He was an amazing man. Kind, virtuous, fair, and he could throw an amazing party. There was a jealous General from the southlands who despised peace. He orchestrated a coup, killing the previous king and all those who opposed him, including all of your mother's friends and colleagues."

"So that's why she doesn't like to talk about it."

Mr. Swan nodded. "Before Ben died, he asked a favor of me. That if anything should ever happen to him, I would look after his nieces," he said, smiling. Mr. Swan grabbed Allora's shoulders and looked her straight in the eyes. "Listen, your uncle loved you more than anything. He wouldn't want to see you wallowing in self-pity. His death wasn't your fault. None of this is. You have two choices. You can either flounder in grief, or you can carry on your uncle's legacy and fight against those who took his life. We must never give up our mission," Mr. Swan said, standing up straight.

Allora was shocked by how blatantly honest Mr. Swan was, but it was exactly what she needed to hear. Her uncle wouldn't want her to feel sorry for herself. He would have told her to hold her head up high and not let anything stop her. Uncle Ben would have wanted her to finish what he started.

"Well..." Allora said, pulling the small black orb from her pocket. "This should be the last piece, but I couldn't figure out how to open it."

Allora placed the orb in his palm. He excitedly rolled it over, feeling the cold surface with his fingers.

"You found it!" Mr. Swan exclaimed. "Your uncle would be very proud of you."

Allora thought back to the note from her uncle. "So this is what he was looking for all those years?" Allora asked.

Lining up the pieces, Mr. Swan placed the orb along the top edge of the middle parchment. Then, he rolled the orb down along the edge while his palm glowed. As the orb slid along the perforated edge, it began melting onto the table, like pizza dough being rolled. Mr. Swan stepped away, and Allora watched as the melted orb flattened. The bright glow dissipated. The parchment was now one complete sheet, miraculously glued together; leaving no indication that it had been three separate pieces. The last parts of the directions were clearly written in the same manner as the other parts of the riddle.

> *A water-bound mass of wizard's past,*
>
> *Where phantoms raise their earthly mast.*
>
> *A witch's cauldron with secrets to bear,*
>
> *With stones you enter but do beware.*

Allora read it through. "Do you know what it means?" Allora said.

"I'm not sure," Mr. Swan answered. They debated it for a few minutes before Mr. Swan put it back into his safe.

Allora left the room and headed straight to the library. The words of the riddle festered in her mind while she searched for books on magical places. For days, Allora spent all her free time in the library, searching the Internet and reading books on different places around the world. Frustration boiled over after spending weeks among skyscrapers of stacked encyclopedias, fantasy novels, and research articles with no progress. She went home defeated.

Flopping herself down on the couch next to her sister, Allora let out a discouraged sigh. Bell didn't even flinch. She was too busy reading a book on molecular biology. Allora pulled out the piece of paper that she written the riddle down on. Staring at the words had no miraculous effect no matter how hard she ran the words through her brain. Bell finished the page she was reading and glanced over. She read the first line of the riddle before Allora noticed.

"A water-bound mass of wizard's past. What is that?" Bell said.

"It's nothing, Bell. Just some stupid riddle I can't figure out."

"Well the water-bound mass is probably an island."

"Yeah, duh. I figured that part out."

"Just trying to help."

"I'm sorry, Bell. It's just, I can't figure this stupid riddle out, and I'm really getting frustrated," Allora said, putting her hands over her face.

"You know, there is a wizard's island in the middle of Crater Lake. Remember, we went there a couple years ago. I read the entire visitor's guide." With that, Bell got up and left the living room.

Allora pulled her hands slowly down her face, with a bug-eyed expression forming.

"It can't be that easy," Allora said softly, slowly realizing her sister might have found the location of the Eye of the Titans.

Bell walked back into the living room with a glass of milk in hand. Allora jumped up from the couch and gave her sister a bear hug, causing Bell to flail her arms, which sent milk flying in the air and landing on the jumping sisters.

"Hey!" Bell exclaimed. Allora ignored her sister and ran to her room, covered in milk. She closed the door, grabbed the telephone, and dialed Katie's number. The voicemail picked up after a number of rings. Allora hung up and dialed again. She did this until Katie finally answered the phone.

"Okay, this better be important!" Katie yelled on the other end.

"Whoa! What's with the hostility? It's me," Allora said.

"Sorry, I was painting my nails. It's kind of hard to hold the phone while your nails dry."

"Well, too bad. I have some news. I found the Eye!" Allora paused in order to create some suspense. She was so excited to tell someone.

"Shut up..." Katie said. "No way!"

"I don't really want to say, over the phone." Paranoia had set in, mostly from reading too many spy novels.

"I'll have Dax tell Tanner, and we will meet you at your house tonight."

Katie hung up the phone.

Allora left her room and went to do some research on Crater Lake before the rest of them came over. Luckily, her mother had accumulated a pretty large collection of material on Crater Lake. Allora also took a look at the

Internet for more information. That's when she found an interesting article talking about sightings of Sasquatch decades ago.

"Sas was there," she said to herself while she sat at the computer. "It has to be the place."

Allora stopped reading the article when she heard Katie talking to her mother in the living room. She turned off the computer, grabbed the others, led them to her bedroom, and closed the door. Then, Allora projected a purple spark, striking a round clear ball, and glue exploded onto the walls.

"I can't wait until I can do that," Katie admitted.

Allora rummaged in her pocket and pulled out the piece of paper with the riddle on it. Then, she passed it around to her three friends sitting side by side on the bed.

"Is this the complete riddle?" Tanner asked.

"Yes, and I believe I know where it refers to," Allora said with a smirk. She pulled out the book she had been reading earlier. The book opened to a beautiful picture of Crater Lake.

"That," Allora said, pointing her finger in the middle of the picture. "Is a water-bound mass called Wizard's Island."

"And this is a rock formation called 'The Phantom Ship,' " Allora said, flipping the page and pointing to the picture of rocks jutting upward out of the water, "where phantoms raise their earthly mast," she said, repeating the next sentence in the riddle.

The other three glanced back and forth between the pictures and the words from the directions.

"You found it, Allora!" Katie exclaimed. They both screamed and hugged each other.

"I can't believe it's so close," Dax said. "How did they not find it before?"

"I'm not sure, but I found an article online that talked about sightings of Sas near the lake many years ago. Maybe they looked there before and couldn't find the entrance. All I know is that we have to go down there."

"You know your mom will never let us go," Katie said.

"That's why we have to make a plan to make the adults think we are doing something else."

"Why don't we tell them we're going to Sumatra's for training?" Tanner suggested. "We'll say Sumatra wanted us to go there for a whole night because he had a lot to teach us."

"That's perfect."

"We also need supplies. Flashlights, camping equipment, food, water, weapons, et cetera." Dax said.

"We'll need to be discreet. Food and water can be bought on the day we leave. I'm sure we can find camping equipment," Tanner said.

"I've got tons of flashlights," Katie said. They all looked at her. "What? So, I'm a little afraid of the dark. Don't judge me."

Allora chuckled. "And we already have weapons. There is one small issue.... We need the actual parchment from Mr. Swan's room."

"What? Why, that's going to be impossible. Mr. Swan guards that like it was his baby," Katie said. "We have no way of accessing his safe."

"I asked Aunt Lizi about the wall trick and she told me you can only access it with a specific hadron signature. That means only Mr. Swan can retrieve it," Tanner explained.

"I know. I asked my mom the same thing, but we need the parchment because it has important information on the back. I saw the numbers when I originally got the parchment from Sas. I'm assuming there is more on the other pieces. It's a combination of some sorts," Allora said.

"How are we going to get it, then?" Dax asked.

"I've already figured that out. We will need to make a duplicate. Then we'll ask Mr. Swan to see it. That's when Katie will distract him and we will make the switch," Allora said.

"How do I distract him?" Katie asked.

"I don't know, get creative. Flash him if you have to," Allora said.

"Flash our teacher! Are you crazy?" Katie said.

"Well, it would do the trick," Tanner said.

They all laughed. Katie just crossed her arms in protest. Allora went back to the subject at hand.

"Spring break is in a couple weeks. That will be a perfect time to go down there."

"When should we tell our parents?" Tanner asked.

"We should probably wait until a day before so that they don't have time to ask Sumatra themselves."

"Good idea, Dax. We can use my car to get down there," Tanner said.

"Okay, it's settled, then. We'll create the duplicate this week, make the switch next week, pack up the car, tell our parents, and head out the next morning," Allora said.

"Alright, I guess we have a plan, but I'm not flashing anyone," Katie said.

They all laughed again, and then left Allora's room to get a snack before they left.

The next day, Katie and Allora went to the craft store on Main Street to find a similar material as the parchment. Katie found what they were looking for in the back of the store. They spent days trying to copy the parchment. Most of it they had to do by memory. When they got stuck, Allora asked Mr. Swan to see it. She wondered if he was getting suspicious, but rejected the idea. They didn't have much time, anyway. The guys had accumulated a large stockpile of camping supplies, which they stored in the back of Tanner's car. Katie finished aging the copy just in time to make the switch.

"Okay, do we all know our roles?" Allora asked everyone while they were standing outside the school.

"Yes!" they all said at once.

They walked into the school together. It was lunchtime, and they figured it would be a good time to make the switch. Rounding the corner, Allora bumped into someone.

"Watch where you're going!" Kim said.

"Excuse me," Allora said in a sassy tone. Kim glared back at her and then turned her attention to Tanner, who stood behind Allora. Kim pushed Allora to the side in order to get to Tanner.

"Hi, Tanner," Kim said, seductively touching Tanner's chest. "When are you going to ask me out on a date?" She fluttered her eyelids in a flirtatious manner.

All Tanner could muster was, "Um... ah...." Dax smacked him on his back. "How about after Spring Break?" Tanner said.

Kim lightly dragged her hand along his body as she moved past Tanner. She looked back and said, "I can't wait." Then, she turned and walked out the front door. Both boys stared as she left.

"Dude, she is so hot!" Dax said, hitting his friend on the shoulder. "You are so lucky!"

Allora walked up and smacked Tanner on the back. "Hey, focus! We have a job to do."

She was partly angry at Tanner for accepting a date with Kim. Allora didn't like the girl.

Tanner rubbed his shoulder.

"Why does everyone keep hitting me?" he said, following the girls toward Mr. Swan's room. Allora opened the door to find Mr. Swan working on paperwork at his desk. They all walked into the room and shut the door.

"Hi, Mr. Swan," Allora said.

"Hi, guys," Mr. Swan said, looking up from grading papers. "What's going on?"

"I wanted to show everyone the new part of the parchment," Allora said. "They haven't been able to see it yet."

Mr. Swan got up from his desk.

"Of course. I haven't gotten very far with it. I've done research about different places, but nothing really pops out as an exact location," he said, walking to the back of the room and sparking the wall to retrieve the parchment.

The object melted its way out and flew into Mr. Swan's outstretched hand. He brought it over, placing it on the desk in front of the boys. Katie's role was to make some sort of scene to distract Mr. Swan while Allora switched the real copy for the fake one she had hidden inside her coat.

Katie moved toward the desk where the boys were. She shoved her brother to the side for a better view. That's when Dax pushed her over the desk behind them. Katie went flying, crashing into the ground and began to cry. She screamed at her brother. Mr. Swan ran over and knelt down to see if she was alright. Dax moved his body in order to block any view Mr. Swan had of the parchment. Allora pulled out the fake copy and swapped it with the real one. The exchange was quick. She moved back a step and eyeballed Katie to let her know that it had worked. Katie stopped crying. She got up from the ground and shoved Dax to sell the confrontation. Allora thanked Mr. Swan and they all left. Allora looked back to see Mr. Swan placing the fake copy into the wall.

Once they were out of the school, Allora spun around. "We did it!" she said, hugging Katie. "You really sold that fall. I didn't know you were such a good actress."

"Hollywood, here I come," Katie said.

Dax rolled his eyes. "Personally, I thought that it was a little dramatic," he said.

"Yeah, well, you didn't have to push me so hard. I'm going to have a bruise on my butt because of you," Katie said, pushing her brother with one hand.

"I had to make it look real," Dax replied, pushing his sister back.

"You guys. Check it out," Allora said, unfolding the parchment and turning it over. "Look at these shapes." She pointed to small black smudges with distinctive abstract lines. "What do you think it means?"

"No idea, but we shouldn't look at it here," Tanner said, taking the parchment and folding it back up. "We don't want anyone else knowing we have this. Mr. Swan isn't the only one we have to worry about, remember."

He walked to his car. "Okay, here's the plan," Tanner said, putting the parchment in the back of his car with the rest of the supplies they had packed. "We leave tomorrow morning. Make sure you guys tell the adults the story after you get home. We'll meet up at Allora's house like we always do. I'll park my car on the road up the street. Once we're through the woods, we will head to the car. We'll stop off at the grocery store, and then we'll hit the road. Sound good?"

They all nodded in agreement.

"Crater Lake, here we come!" Allora said.

Chapter 24

Road Trip

Allora slid out of bed before the alarm rang, and then marched to the shower with a strange determined energy for so early in the morning. As she got ready for the day, thoughts of the coming adventure down south kept her mind busy. She had a feeling of scared anticipation, like the feeling of riding up a roller coaster. Allora was preparing herself for an unknown road trip that could lead to her death or the deaths of her friends. There was no turning back though. Today would decide the fate of her world. Milly walked into the kitchen to see her daughter wide awake, eating breakfast.

"Who are you and what have you done with my daughter?" Milly said.

Allora tilted her head and lifted her eyebrows.

"I've gotten up this early by myself before," Allora replied.

Milly walked over to the coffee grinder to begin her usual routine in the morning. "Yeah, maybe when you were five and it was Christmas morning," she said, placing the cap on the grinder and starting the machine.

Allora ignored her mother and went back to eating her cereal.

The others arrived right at seven o'clock. Milly, of course, had to do her usual questioning to make sure they were actually going to training.

"So, Sumatra knows that you all are coming?" Milly asked, drinking her freshly made coffee.

"Yes, Mother. We talked to him earlier this week," Allora replied.

"And he is okay with you all staying at his cabin overnight?" Milly asked.

"Yes, Mother," Allora said, giving Milly a hug and grabbing her bag. "Stop worrying so much."

"It's my job to worry," Milly said, walking the kids to the back door. "Make sure you don't divert from the path. It's the only safe way through the woods," Milly yelled as they all moved through the field and into the forest.

"We know, Mom!" Allora yelled back.

They walked a few hundred feet up the path, and then Tanner turned right. They all were silent as they hiked through the trees. There wasn't a set path, but Tanner had found the way to the road because he had hiked into the forest last week to make sure.

Weaving through the thick forest, they found Tanner's car about a half mile down an old dirt lumber road that had been abandoned. The warm sun shone upon them, and excitement spread quickly among the group. Even with the task ahead, they were all smiles as Tanner drove the car onto the highway, heading southwest. When they arrived at the grocery store, they exited the car while peering at the parking lot for any sign of people they knew. If they were spotted, the trip would be compromised.

"Do you have a grocery list?" Tanner asked.

"Yeah, I made it last night," Allora said. "We need to get food, water, batteries for the flashlights, bug spray, and whatever else we can think of."

"I think that's good enough," Dax said. "Make sure you don't get noticed. We can't afford to have someone recognize us."

Allora ripped the list in two so that the shopping would go faster. Once they were done buying their supplies, they packed up the car and hit the road. Tanner took Mt. Hood Highway until he got to Boring, Oregon. Then, he turned onto Highway 211, which took him to the onramp to I-205. Twenty minutes later, they were on I-5 heading south.

"So, we have to go about four hours south to Roseburg and then go east on North Umpqua Highway," Allora said, sitting in front with the map. "A couple hours east and we are there."

"How did she get shotgun?" Dax said, frustrated by sitting in the back with his sister. "I thought we were boys."

"We are, but she has the map," Tanner replied. "The navigator has to sit up front."

Allora turned her head and stuck out her tongue.

"Oh yeah, that's real mature," Dax said.

"We can switch in Roseburg. I want some time to look at the back of the parchment before we get there, anyway." The intricate design of the symbols was important, but unlike anything she had ever seen before.

The car ride down was jovial. They talked about everything from the teachers they didn't like to their favorite celebrities. They played games and told stories about their classmates. Allora felt at ease. This was a stress release from the threat of death, another life on a strange world, and the responsibility she didn't understand or want. Allora put her head out the window and closed her eyes. The wind hit her face and tossed her long brown hair back against the window of the car. The sun pierced through the scattered white clouds, warming her skin. Spring had arrived with a bountiful display of colors. It was a nice change from the rainy, cold winter.

Roseburg came sooner than they expected. They had all lost track of time because of how much fun they were having during the car ride. Tanner got gas, while the others went to the bathroom. They reconvened at the car. Dax sat in front this time, while Allora hopped in the back. She pulled out the real copy of the parchment, which was sealed in a protective plastic casing.

Tanner drove out of the gas station and headed east, toward the lake. Allora unfolded the sheet, resting it between herself and Katie. She turned it over. The symbols were arranged in a line down the left side. In the middle were random numbers, arranged sequentially. On the right was a word that ran along the edge. Allora read it out loud. "Credo."

"So, what does it mean?" Katie asked.

"Mr. Swan told me that it meant, 'I Believe,' " Allora said.

"That's deep," Katie responded sarcastically. "Wonder how that plays into it."

"I'm sure we'll find out," Allora said, staring out the window.

Tanner turned the car south onto Crater Lake Highway. Tall pines, covered with patches of snow, lined the road to the lake. A mix of fresh pine and flower scents filled the air. A vibrant green peeked from the snow-covered trees. Tanner pulled the car onto Rim Drive and circled around the lake. They looked out the left-hand window, crowding against the glass. Tanner had to push Dax back so that he could maintain his grip on the steering wheel. Mounds of snow lined the road as they zigzagged through the forest, on top of the ridge. At the end of the road, the visitor center appeared at the end of a large parking lot. It was a grandiose building made of oak, built on the edge of the ridge.

They scurried out of the car and ran to the edge of a steep canyon. The picturesque landscape seemed surreal. They stood on a rocky outcrop, hanging on a wood fence, looking down a vertical to of hundreds of feet below. At the bottom of the bowl-shaped canyon was a majestic crystal blue lake, sparkling in the sun. Allora focused on one particular monument on the left side of the lake. Wizard's Island jutted out of the water. It sat there like a miniature volcano, rising from the deep abyss below. They couldn't contain their excitement. The Eye of the Titans was somewhere on that island, and now they were so close to finding it. The excitement subsided as they realized the gravity and pressure of their next step.

"This won't be easy," Allora said.

"Has any of this been easy?" Tanner replied.

They continued staring out at the imposing task before them.

"What now?" Dax asked.

"We wait," Allora said, feeling the weight of nervous anticipation. She pointed down to the boat dock at the bottom of the canyon. "That is where we will set out from. We'll have to hang around until dark, and then borrow one of those small boats to get over to the island."

They all turned around, heading for the car.

"Borrow?" Dax said, lifting his eyebrows.

Allora smiled mischievously. "Yeah, just for a little while. We'll give it back."

"That's going to be a difficult thing to explain if we get caught," Dax replied as they walked back to the car. "Sorry, officer, we were just borrowing the boat so we could sneak over to that island and find an alien artifact to help us defeat mythological beasts who are trying to kill us."

"Well, when you put it that way, it totally sounds believable," Tanner said.

Laughter followed as they all got into Tanner's dirty Bronco.

He drove to a secluded area of the woods down the road. The spot was a flat dirt clearing that stood on the edge of a cliff on the southeastern side of the lake. The view was amazing. They pulled out some chairs and set them up facing out over the cliff. It was around three o'clock in the afternoon. They had a couple hours until sundown. The plan was to kill time where they were until sunset. Then, they would leave the car and walk back toward the visitor center. Once they hiked down to the docks, they would find a boat and motor over to the island. Allora wasn't sure how they were going to obtain the boat, but she figured that it wouldn't be hard.

After eating some snacks, they sat thinking about the voyage across the lake. After about an hour of discussing the meanings behind the strange markings on the back of the parchment, Dax and Katie went on a short hike to clear their heads. Tanner went to the car to retrieve the equipment they needed for their expedition. Allora stood alone, watching the sun descend into the western horizon. The evening sky was clear, and the sunset was full of warm colors. Tanner walked up, dropped the supplies in the chair, and moved next to Allora.

"Beautiful, isn't it?" Allora said.

"Yes, it is," he said, gazing at her.

Allora twisted herself, noticing that Tanner didn't have his eyes on the sunset. Confused for a moment, she glanced up at Tanner. A minute of gazing upon each other felt like days. Allora caught Tanner's motion toward her hand. She felt the warm touch of his fingers, inching their way past her palm and curling in the crevices between her fingers. Nervous warmth flowed throughout her body, permeating her cheeks. The stubborn, independent, strong-minded girl gave way to a more innocent, shy young woman. It was as though Tanner had knocked down her walls with the touch of his finger. He stepped closer. Allora's eyes fluttered, still gazing into Tanner's. Her heart beat faster as they drew closer. The sun was submerging into the background as Tanner's lips inched closer to Allora. His chest lightly touched hers. His body was warm, and his heart beating in rhythm with hers.

Tanner's lips were almost upon hers.

"Whoa! Did I interrupt something here?" Dax said, coming out of the woods.

"You always do have great timing, buddy," Tanner said.

Allora let go of Tanner, embarrassed by the intrusion. Katie walked up behind Dax, slapping him on the back. "I told you to wait!" Katie said.

"You two were spying on us?" Allora said.

Katie shook her head. "Not exactly. We stopped on the edge over there to talk about tonight. We were only there for a few seconds. I told Dax not to bother you guys."

"Why? It's not like we were doing anything," Allora said, trying to play it off like nothing happened. She glared at Tanner.

"Yeah," Tanner said awkwardly. "Nothing happened."

"Dude, you are a horrible liar," Dax said.

Allora shook her head. "We don't have time for this. It's time to go."

They all took her lead, altering their moods to a more serious demeanor. As much as Dax wanted to harass the two, there were more important matters at hand.

Allora reverted back to her usual guarded personality. Even though these were her best friends, she felt embarrassed by her feelings. She was also confused by her feelings toward Tanner. Her mind and body began to swim with exuberance over the moment she'd had, but the logical side took over. Allora shook her head, changing her thoughts to the unemotional operation that required her complete attention. She moved with a purpose while everyone else hurried to keep up.

Tanner caught up to Allora. "I just wanted to—" he began.

Allora interrupted him before he could speak his mind. "Not now, Tanner. I have to be focused on our mission." She walked faster.

Tanner slowed down, unsure why Allora was so abrasive.

Katie sped past him, running up alongside Allora. She didn't say anything, knowing that Allora wasn't in the mood to talk.

Dax came up and patted Tanner on the shoulder. "Women... they're like the universe. You may come to understand one part, but there is so much more yet to discover," Dax said, laughing at himself and stepping past his bewildered friend to follow the girls down the hill.

Tanner marched forward. He had to keep his wits about him for what lay ahead. Night was coming fast. They had to hurry, because they didn't want to use their flashlights. Someone could see them, which would ruin the entire trip. They made it down the ridge to the water's edge. Moving along the rocks, they could see the docks ahead. Allora pointed silently to a small boat with an outboard motor attached on the end. As they reached the back of the equipment shed at the base of the dock, they heard footsteps. Allora held them up, causing Dax to run into Katie. Dax slipped on a rock and crashed into the water. The splashing sound initiated a response from the park ranger, who had been about to head back up the crater. Allora motioned for everyone to quickly get underneath the dock. Tanner was last. His foot barely made it under before the ranger got the edge of the dock. The park ranger knelt down, shining his flashlight underneath the dock. The light scanned the shore, searching the rippled water. Pinned awkwardly against the back of the dock, the four pushed each other closer, trying to become invisible. The rocks were wet and slippery and smelled of dead, rotten fish. Katie gagged, causing the light to jump from the water to the back of the dock. Allora thought that they would be caught. The light scanned the rock they were hiding behind, but suddenly retreated.

Then, they heard the muffled sounds of someone in the distance.

"Let's go, Harry!" the voice said. "What's taking so long?"

"I thought I heard something," Harry said.

Allora looked up between the cracks of the wood planks at the puzzled face of the park ranger.

"It's probably just an animal," the other ranger argued. "I'm not missing my wife's meatloaf so you can investigate a ferret sighting."

The park ranger remained, scanning the area again. Finally, he left and headed back up the cliff. They all let out a sigh of relief when they heard the man's footsteps disappearing up the dirt path. They stayed underneath the dock for some time, until they felt that the ranger was far enough away. Once they felt comfortable, everyone got out from under the dock. Tanner untied the boat.

"We should probably pull the boat along the bank so they don't see us paddling out into the middle of the lake," Tanner whispered.

"Good idea," Dax said.

Trekking along the edge of the water took a long time. The moon was now high in the night sky, beckoning them forward, as if a guiding light to their final destination. Stars glittered in the sky, scattered majestically in their usual patterns. With each passing rock, their task became more real. At certain spots along their journey around the lake, they were required to get in the boat and paddle along the edge of the water. Occasionally, a foot or hand would slip into the glacial waters, causing a sudden spasm of pain. They reached the point in the lake where the span of water between them and the island was shortest, and they headed out. The arduous work was forgotten as soon as they reached the island. Allora put her left foot onto a large boulder, holding the boat steady while the rest got off. Tanner helped her pull the boat onto the sandy bank while the other two looked around.

"Witch's Cauldron is at the top of the island," Allora said. "That's where the directions said to go."

With only the moon to guide them, the group hiked up the steep incline. They weaved through trees, sometimes crawling up the hill. A couple times they tripped over fallen branches. None wanted to pull out the flashlights, though. The experience with the park ranger had left them paranoid. Flashlights could be seen from anywhere along the ridge of the crater. The moonlight would have to suffice. Reaching the top, Allora pulled out the parchment.

"A witch's cauldron with secrets to bear," she said, repeating the riddle that she'd read numerous times. "With stones you enter, but do beware."

"What the hell does that mean?" Katie asked, surveying the barren rock-filled crater.

Witch's Cauldron wasn't anything spectacular. The incline of the bowl-shaped crater at the top of the hill wasn't steep. Steadily, they walked down the rocky slope to the middle, where a collection of boulders and rocks were scattered on the floor of the cauldron. There were small shrubs, but no sign of an entrance of any kind. They were all perplexed by the normality of the landscape. Nothing looked special or out of place.

"I don't get it," Allora said. "I thought that it would be clear when we got here."

"I think we all thought the same thing," Katie said sympathetically.

They spent almost an hour searching through the dirt and rock.

"Why don't we take a break?" Dax said, sitting down on a boulder.

Allora plopped herself on a boulder, along with the rest of them. Tanner had packed sandwiches, a bottle of water, and an energy bar for each. The nourishment was nice compensation for all of their physical exertion. The moon hung overhead as they chewed. Dax opened his bottle of water and drank about half of it. Then, he placed the bottle next to him on the rock in order to finish his sandwich. The rock, however, wasn't flat, and the bottle of water tipped over, dumping out the rest on the boulder.

"Oh, come on!" he said, getting up from his seat. "Hey, sis, can I have some of yours?"

"Um... no," Katie replied.

"Pleeeease," Dax begged. "I'm so thirsty."

"Maybe you should've been more careful, then," Katie said, grabbing her water from her lap before Dax could grab it. The two siblings were wrestling for the bottle when Allora noticed something.

"Hey, guys!" Allora said, pointing to the boulder. "Look!"

The siblings stopped wrestling on the ground. Both rotated their heads to see a thin light shining off of the boulder. The water had washed away some of the dirt that covered it, which had exposed some sort of reflective surface. The moonlight bounced off the boulder, pointing toward the other side of the cauldron. The beam of light was faint. Allora walked over and dumped the rest of her water onto the boulder's surface.

"Do you have some kind of extra shirt or towel in that bag?" she said to Tanner.

Tanner unzipped his backpack and withdrew a towel.

"I guess this is as good a time as any to use this," he said, handing the towel to Allora.

Allora wiped the dirt from the rocky surface. This revealed a shiny black surface below. Allora moved to expose a bright stream of moonlight reflecting off the rock. The end of the light stopped at a specific spot on the ground about twenty feet away. They all walked over and began digging into the ground. After a few minutes of excavation, they found something. Allora gently brushed the dirt away to reveal a magnificent black stone. It was a little dusty, but radiant. None knew what it was or what to do with it. Allora pulled out the parchment and turned it over. When the moonlight hit the surface, it exposed a compass etched in silver.

"Whoa!" Katie said, huddling closer to Allora. "Did you notice that before?"

"No, it just appeared," Allora said, staring like the rest of them. "It must have something to do with the moonlight or this area or something. I have no idea. This is my first time with magical parchment."

The shapes on the parchment were now surrounded by the same silver ink. This created very distinct shapes.

"Anyone have a suggestion as to what to do next?" Allora said.

"Maybe we need to arrange the stones according to how they correspond with the compass," Katie said, pointing her finger to the first symbol. "Look, the shape of this symbol and the shape of the rock are the same."

"Nice work, Katie. Let's try it." Allora positioned the parchment with the "N" facing the North Star. Secretly, she thanked her mother for forcing her into Girl Scouts for so many years. Then, she turned the black stone counter-clockwise. Allora could feel the stone grinding against the circular rock underneath. The stone moved as if she were winding up a toy. As soon as the rock was positioned like the picture, they heard a clink. The circular rock, along with the black stone, sunk into the ground. They scuttled along the gravel, crawling backward to escape the sinking ground. They sat there, wondering if something was going to happen. Nothing moved.

Allora turned back to the parchment.

"There are more symbols, which probably means there are more stones. See those boulders on the outside of the cauldron? Put water on them, and wipe them down."

They each picked out a boulder, dumped water on it, and wiped away the dirt. Beams of light appeared, angling to the opposite sides of the cauldron. Now there were five beams of light that crossed in the middle. The boys dug up the stones, while the girls arranged each one according to the position on the parchment. Finally, they were on the last one. The boys had wiped away the dirt and Allora was about to turn the stone.

She paused and looked up at her three friends standing in anticipation.

"Here goes nothing."

Chapter 25

Wizard's Island

Allora turned the stone to its correct position, according to the diagram. The round rock sank into the ground like the others. Again, Allora scurried backward to avoid the sinking ground. Nothing happened, to the everyone's surprise. The rock sank further into the ground, but the area remained still. No one moved, hoping for some kind of sign to show the next step. The still air was eerie. It was like waiting for the wick of a firework to burn in quiet anticipation, and then watching as nothing happens.

"Well, that was totally anticlimactic!" Dax said against the silent night.

Katie stood in the middle of the cauldron. Suddenly, Allora watched Katie fall backward and disappear into the ground.

"Katie!" Allora yelled, crawling frantically to the edge of a deep hole. Allora could only see a foggy mist escaping from the black void.

"Give me the flashlight!" she yelled to Tanner. Quickly, he tossed her a MagLite from his bag. Allora flashed the light around, but the dust blocked any visibility.

"What do we do?" Allora asked frantically.

"We go after her," Dax said, folding his arms.

"Dax, wait!" Tanner yelled as Dax jumped into the hole.

Tanner looked after him with a frightened yet determined stare. "We didn't come this far just to give up now," he said, winking at Allora and dropping into the dark hole.

"You guys are crazy!" Allora yelled, but no one was there to hear her. She paced back and forth, debating what to do. "Oh yeah, jump down into the creepy dark hole, Allora. That sounds like a great idea," she said out loud.

After a few painful minutes, Allora took a deep breath, folded her arms, and stepped down into the unknown opening. She screamed as she fell through a circular tube, spinning around and picking up speed. Then, the surface of the tube angled itself toward her and she felt herself sliding. The surface was completely smooth and slippery. It was like she was on a slide at a water park, without any water. Allora continued screaming as she rocketed through the earth. The tube bent, causing her to turn to the right. Allora coiled around, moving at an alarming speed. All she could do was keep her body straight. The steep angle of the slide eventually leveled out. Progressively, Allora slowed. She looked at her feet to see the end of the tube. Then, someone caught her as she slowed to a stop. It was Tanner. Her hair was shooting upward from the ride. Lights flashed in her eyes when she came through the end of the tube.

"Took you a while," Tanner said, helping Allora to her feet.

Allora smiled, happy to be alive. "I'm not doing that again."

Dax came bouncing over. "Are you kidding me?" he said, grinning from ear to ear. "That was the best ride I have ever been on! I say, once we get out of here, we do it again."

"Count me out," Katie said, hugging her dizzy friend.

"I thought you were a goner," Allora said, embracing Katie.

"That makes two of us," she replied.

Allora gazed around at the large, circular room. It was the size of a high school gymnasium, covered entirely in reflective obsidian. The floor and ceiling were covered with intricate artwork, carved into the hard obsidian. In the middle was a stone basin with flames that lit the room. Allora turned to Katie for an answer.

"We did that," Katie said, chuckling. "It had oil in the basin. Dax thought that it was water at first. The idiot drank it."

"I told you I was checking to see what it was," he said, putting up his arms. "I *was*," he said to Tanner, while the girls walked up to the basin.

"Right," Tanner said. "Oh, I believe you."

The light from the fire bounced off the walls. The magnificence of the room was overshadowed by their next obstacle. Sixteen doors lined the walls of the circular room, precisely the same distance apart from each other. Above the doorways, roman numerals were carved into the black stone.

"Sixteen doors and only one will lead us where we want to go," Tanner said.

Allora pulled out the parchment from inside her coat, unfolding it to show the back. The guys shined their flashlights for a better view.

"I'm guessing that the numbers on the back correlate with the roman numerals on top of those doorways," Allora said.

"You guess?" Dax said. "Don't you remember what it said? 'Heed the warning of the path you take, for one false choice will be the last you make.' That makes me think that guessing is a bad idea."

"We just need to think this through. The numbers are: eight, five, three, two, one, one, zero," Allora read out loud.

"Yep, I have the answer," Dax said, to the everyone's surprise. They all twisted around. "We're screwed."

Katie stepped to her brother and punched him on the shoulder. "You are no help!"

"Thanks for the pessimism," Allora said.

Meanwhile, Tanner was staring at the numbers intently. "Wait, I've seen this exact arrangement of numbers before," he said, wondering why he hadn't recognized them the first time he saw them. "I saw this in my geometry class. This is a Fibonacci sequence." He glanced up to see puzzled expressions on his friend's faces. "Do any of you pay attention in math class?"

"I hate math," Allora said. "It's my worst subject."

"I never really got along with my math teacher," Katie said.

"Don't look at me," Dax said, gesturing to himself. "You know I suck at math."

Tanner could only smile. "The answer is thirteen," he said. "That's the doorway we need to go through."

"Are you sure?" Allora asked.

"Yes, I'm positive," Tanner replied. He could tell the rest of them weren't sure, so he marched to the doorway and walked through.

"Tanner!" Allora yelled. "Why does everyone keep doing that?"

Tanner had disappeared.

"Okay, I'm not going last this time," Allora said, following Tanner's lead and stepping into the black doorway with her flashlight pointed in front of her. She felt a pulling force, like every molecule in her body was being stretched. Then, she landed on a flat stone surface.

"That was a portal," Allora said between struggling breaths. She swiveled her head up to see a long cave of majestic glowing blue. Her mouth dropped open. She ignored the siblings, who arrived seconds later. The sight was unimaginable. Feeling the cold of the cavern wall, she walked along the sides of the crystal blue tunnel. It was made of ice. The ceiling above curved in a half circle, with a wave pattern as if the current was frozen in time. The blue water around them seemed to radiate light.

"That must be the lake above us," Tanner said.

As they walked slowly into the ice tunnel, the ground became rocky. They pushed forward, still gazing up at their surroundings. It was like nothing they had ever seen before. At one point, Allora saw a fish swim up to the cave wall, and then dart away. Katie was so distracted by the cave's blue glow that she tripped on a rock and fell over.

"Why is it that I'm always the one falling over?" Katie said, rubbing her back, which had hit a rock.

Dax put his arm out to help his sister up. "Maybe it's because you're so clumsy," he said.

Katie grabbed his hand and got to her feet, sneering at her brother. Mist created an unusual ambiance throughout the cavern. Allora felt a slight chill as they moved deeper into the tunnel. They walked about two hundred feet, until the blue ice opened up to a dark, expansive cave. Dax lit the torches that hung on the wall to either side of them. This projected light across a reflective surface. The floor was obsidian, but it was arranged like tiles in a bathroom. Perfectly square tiles were arranged in a perfect formation. Allora's eyes rolled upward. Above the cavern, sharply pointed stalactites hung ominously. They were numerous, hanging over the tiled cavern floor. In front of them was a large reflective section that wasn't tiled like the rest.

"Well, what do you think?" she said, stepping onto the different block of obsidian.

"I'm not so sure that we should walk out there just yet," Tanner said, cautiously moving diagonally behind Allora.

The expansive field of black tiles seemed too easy. A slight sheen reflected the flicker of light from the torches. Squinting her eyes, Allora tried to see across the tiles without any luck. There was no other way but forward.

"What choice do we have?" she said, stepping onto the tile in front of her. Allora turned her head. "See, no big deal." She shrugged her shoulders.

That's when she felt a strong pull from behind. Allora was yanked backward as one of the stalactites shattered the tile she had just been standing on. Tanner had caught the motion from above. Luckily, he was able to grab the back of her shirt before the sharp tip of the calcium spear skewered the unsuspecting girl.

"That was close," Tanner said.

Allora breathed heavily, feeling a chill run up her spine as she thought about what could have happened.

"Yeah, you can say that again," Dax said, staring down through the space where the tile had been. "Look at this." Dax swirled his flashlight down through the hole. "The falling stalactite didn't even make a sound."

"So that's what the parchment meant by 'one wrong move will send you deep,' " Katie said, hanging over her brother's left shoulder.

"Now what?" Allora said, still a little frazzled.

"I think we should all run across at once," Katie suggested. "Those things on the ceiling take a few seconds to fall. We can make it."

"Yeah, and how do we get back across after we are done?" Tanner argued.

Katie scratched her head. "Didn't really think about that."

"I saw something weird happen when you first stood there," Dax said, moving toward the reflective surface that Allora had started from before she stepped forward.

"Watch my reflection," he said, stepping onto the platform. Suddenly, Dax's reflection split itself into many different reflections. They gasped at what they saw. The multiple reflections launched themselves forward in all different directions. The other three moved closer to see. The multiple small versions of Dax seemed to have minds of their own.

"You see," Dax said, twisting his head around. "I thought that I was crazy at first."

"So, then, which one do you follow?" Allora asked.

"Do you guys remember Mr. Swan talking about Hermes?" Dax paused for a moment. They all looked at each other. "He was the messenger of the gods."

No one had an answer. Dax shook his head. "Anyway, he had winged shoes that he used to fly around. The instructions say, 'Be careful to step with winged feet,' and if you look at that reflection of me,—" Dax pointed to the tile diagonally to his left "—it has winged shoes."

The small Dax in the tile did indeed have winged feet. Feeling confident with his theory, Dax stepped onto the tile. Everyone looked upward, half expecting the stalactite to fall. Nothing happened. Dax kept following his winged reflection, hopping from tile to tile. Allora went next. She was about to step on the same tile as Dax, but pulled up at the last second. She noticed that her winged reflection had jumped to the diagonal tile to her right, not the left. Now she was confused.

"Hey, Dax?" Allora said, watching Dax stop and spin around.

"Yep?"

"My winged reflection went to the tile on the right, not the left."

Dax thought for a second.

"The instructions are simple," Dax said, jumping to the next tile. "Follow the winged you."

"Alright, here I go," she said, stepping onto the right tile. Nothing fell down this time, so she kept going. Each one had a different path. Sometimes they would cross in between one another. As they moved, the light grew dim. By the time they reached the end of the tiled floor, they had to use their flashlights to see. Katie was the last to arrive. Darkness surrounded them. The only light came from the small torches behind them and the beams from the flashlights.

It wasn't long before the floor stopped. Ahead were two large wooden doors. Intricate drawings of warriors and gods were carved into the wood. Gold plating lined the edges. Bulky copper rings the size of tires hung where the two doors met. Tanner and Dax each pulled a ring backward, straining their muscles from the weight of the doors. The hinges creaked loudly. A cloud of dust burst from the opening crack between the doors.

Allora walked forward, fanning the dusty air with her hand. They stepped into a grandiose room. Once their feet touched the strange yellow floor, small round orbs lit up the room. Everywhere they looked, there was gold. Gigantic gold statues greeted them as they entered. Awestruck and fascinated, they proceeded slowly along the corridor. The statues stood majestically, grand and proud, like watchmen standing guard. Behind them, normal-sized gold men were evenly spaced along the wall. Half of the golden men were sunken into the wall, while the rest stood frozen with long spears at their sides. The detail on the gold men was incredible. Allora joined the others in the middle, and they all walked down the corridor together.

"This is amazing," Katie said, spinning in a circle. "I have found my new home."

"Look at these statues," Tanner said, walking up to one of the giant golden men to their right. The man held a trident. He was mostly naked, except for a small loose robe around his waist. He had a long beard and flowing hair. "This must be Poseidon."

Allora had moved another statue that looked familiar from her history books. Katie came up behind her. "Who is this?"

The statue was of a woman with hair braided to the sides. She wore a toga that came down to her lower thighs. Along her chest was a sash that held a quiver of arrows on her back. Her head was held high. An expression of strength had been molded perfectly upon her face.

"This is Artemis," Allora said, touching the feet of the statue.

Katie moved off to the next statue. It was that of the goddess Demeter. She had a long, flowing toga, with a round crown upon her head. A staff was angled up, held in Demeter's grasp.

"Come here," Dax yelled. They all moved forward to where Dax was standing. They looked up at a thin, naked statue of a man wearing a helmet. "See, wings for feet," Dax said, placing his hand on the golden wings that protruded from the statue's ankles. "This would be Hermes," he said proudly.

Something caught Allora's eye while they stood there. Turning to the left, she saw a light shining on a flat podium in the distance. Slowly, she began to walk to it.

"Allora?" Katie said. "Where are you going?"

Allora didn't say anything, but quickened her pace. Instantly, the other three forgot what they were doing and immediately ran after her. She slowed down, moving up the steps to the golden podium. It was spotlighted by an orb, hanging in midair, high above. Allora stepped onto the platform where the podium sat, and looked upon it. Nothing was there but sand upon a plain stone tablet. It seemed out of place in the elegant golden room. The sand was piled in a pyramid, and occasionally sparkled in the light of the hanging orb.

"Where is it?" Tanner asked, moving up alongside Allora.

Katie got up to the platform. "Or maybe someone was already here."

Dax was down below.

"You mean we came all this way for nothing?"

Allora pulled out the parchment again. The instructions weren't specific with regards to the next step. She motioned the other two to be quite. She remembered the Latin word on the back.

"Credo," she said out loud.

Nothing happened.

"Great!" Dax yelled, storming off to one of the golden men on the wall. "We do all that work to get here and have nothing to show for it."

Allora ignored him and kept thinking. She wondered if she was missing something. Why hadn't it worked? The questions circled around in her mind with no clear answer. The harder she thought, the further away her mind traveled. Meanwhile, Dax was busy trying to yank one of the golden spears free.

"What are you doing?" Katie said, descending the stairs to yell at her brother.

"What does it look like I'm doing?" he said, pulling at the golden spear.

"That isn't yours!" Katie crossed her arms.

"We did not go all this way to come home empty-handed," Dax said, pausing momentarily. "Think of it as a souvenir."

"That's it," Allora said softly, dropping the parchment. "I believe." She placed her hands, palms up, over the tablet and closed her eyes. They all looked at her like she was crazy, but Allora didn't care. She knew what she had to do. In a whisper, she said, "I believe I have the Eye of the Titans." She repeated those words over and over again.

Dax ignored the group and went back to prying the spear from the golden man's grasp. Allora kept repeating the words with her eyes shut. Her hands began to glow as the hadrons in the room flowed into her body. All of a sudden, the sand from the tablet began to filter through the gaps between Allora's fingers. More sand relocated to the air over the palms of Allora's hands. The sand hovered an inch above, distributing itself into a glowing circle, spinning into a core like gravity forming a new planet. Particles of sand condensed into a ball. Then, the whole thing caught on fire and released a powerful burst of light, expanding throughout the chamber. The light withdrew, speeding back into the core, imploding into a solid ball of black rock.

"I got it," Allora said, holding up an orb of obsidian.

They heard a loud *clank*. "I got it too!" Dax said, holding up his prize.

Just then, a decrepit skeletal hand burst out of its golden shell. It grabbed Dax on the wrist. He screamed like a girl and dropped the golden spear. Dax moved back to the platform while the man started to break through his gold casing. A deafening screech came from the former statue. Suddenly, all around them the golden men were breaking from their golden prisons. The creatures looked like skeletons, except they had translucent skin that had a slight shimmer. In their eye sockets were glowing red balls that pulsated. The creatures were neither dead nor alive.

"I told you not to touch it!" Katie said, backing into the platform. Golden shards crashed onto the floor, echoing loudly throughout the chamber.

Securing the orb inside her coat, Allora prepared herself for a fight. "Those are Baykok," she said, fascinated by the weird creatures. "Mr. Swan told me about them."

"I don't think that we have too much time for a history lesson," Tanner said, pulling Allora, and jumping down to join the others. "Run!"

The four sprinted down the long, golden corridor. Golden spears flew within inches of them as they ran. They had to dart back and forth to miss them. The army of Baykok had now freed itself from the golden casing, and began chasing the intruders. Allora shot a purple burst of hadrons, knocking one of the creatures into the statue of Poseidon. Two more stood guard in the doorway, blocking their escape. Allora twisted her body in order to get a good throw. She rotated 360 degrees, and then shot two purple balls into the creature's chests. Both Baykok flew back, striking the half-open wooden doors. The teenagers hurried through the dark part of the cavern, only to arrive at the reflective field of tiles.

"I guess it's time to test out your original idea, Katie," Allora said, between breaths.

They all ran ahead, darting across as fast as their feet would take them. Behind them they could hear the progressive crash of stalactites breaking the tiles. Katie slipped, falling and sliding along the ground. She looked up, watching a glint of light as the piercing stalactite made its way toward her. Dax stopped, grabbed his sister, and jumped out of the way of the falling rock. Katie kept slipping and falling stalactites kept missing her as she struggled to gain her footing. Dax continued to help his sister, frantically pulling her coat to get her on her feet.

"Move it!" Tanner yelled, as Allora and he reached the safety of the cavern opening.

After a few more steps, Dax and Katie leapt in the air, landing on ledge as the last of the stalactites crashed into the tile floor. They breathed heavily, feeling the adrenaline flowing throughout their body. Across the deep chasm, the Baykok stopped at the edge. They didn't have a way to get across the deep opening. All of the tiles had fallen.

Breathing hard, Dax and Katie got up from the dirt floor.

"I think we've had enough of these close calls," Katie said, shaking out her shirt.

"We may have another one pretty soon," Dax said, pointing across the chasm.

The Baykok had started forming multiple arms that grew out of their torsos, enabling them to crawl on the walls like spiders. The Baykok scurried along the cavern ceiling, moving quickly.

"I think that we should leave," Allora said.

They all turned and darted into the ice tunnel.

"The trip back seems to be much shorter!" Katie yelled.

Dax hurdled a boulder and helped his sister over. "It helps when you have hundreds of evil skeletons chasing you."

Tanner reached the obsidian cave first. He looked around. "I don't see an exit, guys."

They scanned the walls, searching desperately for some kind of way out. They held their breath when they saw small skeletons leaping over rocks in the distance. Red eyes glowed under the blue mist. The Baykok were moving fast. The four teens stood in a line, bracing for the inevitable attack.

"Now I know how General Mustard felt," Katie said, to the puzzled audience standing next to her.

"What?" Allora said.

"You know, Mustard's Last Stand, surrounded by Indians."

"That's Custer's Last Stand, General George Armstrong Custer," Allora said.

"And you call me an idiot," Dax said, pointing to himself.

"You are an idiot!" Katie yelled. "This whole thing is your fault!"

"Guys, we don't have time for the blame game," Tanner said.

The Baykok were within a hundred yards and closing in fast.

Tanner grabbed Allora by the arm. "Allora, we need you,"

Allora stepped forward. She took a deep breath, pulling in the hadrons like Sumatra had taught her. Focusing the energy, she generated one large purple hadron ball around her chest and sent it shooting down the ice tunnel. Baykok were thrown as the sphere blasted through. The hadron ball burst, causing shockwaves of energy that knocked them over.

"Oh no, that doesn't look good," Dax said, pointing to the large cracks forming inside the tunnel.

The force from the hadron burst had caused the walls of the tunnel to become unstable. The cracks grew, and an eerie snapping sound echoed into the cave. Suddenly, a wall of water crashed into the tunnel, flowing rapidly toward them.

"Oh god, what have I done?" Allora said.

The rushing sound was terrifying. Allora and Katie hugged each other with only seconds left. Tanner moved in front of the rest, performing the necessary motions that Sumatra had shown him. Blue hadron energy circled in front of him. Spray from the water hit their bodies. Tanner expelled the ball of hadrons.

It exploded, knocking Tanner back so he tripped over the huddled girls. Allora held Katie tightly, waiting for her watery grave. She opened one eye after a few seconds of silence. The two girls sat up. Tanner was wide-eyed, staring at what he had done. The rushing flow of the water was frozen.

"You know what you did?" Allora asked, grabbing Tanner's hand. He was too shocked to answer. He just shook his head. "Do you realize what you are? This means that you are a Fermion, like me!" Allora said, jumping on Tanner and giving him a hug.

Tanner was caught off guard by Allora's affection, but he didn't mind it. Allora was so excited to have someone who could share in her unique gift. Tanner was different, though. Allora was a fire Fermion, while Tanner turned out to be a water Fermion.

Dax walked around the large ice sculpture, staring at a Baykok frozen in the wall of ice. One of the Baykok had its face right next to Dax. He stared at the red-eyed skull and tapped the ice. The creature's eyes spun around. Dax fell backward, putting his hand down to regain his balance.

"Alright, can we get out of here," Dax said, moving away from the mound of ice. As he moved, he noticed a crack in the far wall.

Katie was on the other side, trying to find a way out. "Oh, and how do you propose we do that genius?" she said.

"How about we try this way?" Dax said, squeezing himself into the wall. Allora and Tanner got up quickly. They all rushed over to the far side of the cave to find Dax shimmying sideways up small, narrow stairs. The crack was wide enough for them to scurry in between the sides of the rock. As Dax got higher, the walls widened and the stairs became larger. About twenty yards up, Dax was able to climb normally up the stairs. He looked up to see a daunting climb ahead. The others followed him. Climbing up the stairs was painful, but the relief of escaping the caves gave them new energy. The rock walls were slanted and got increasingly taller as they climbed. Allora's legs burned.

"This is harder than the stairs we have to do for football practice," Tanner said.

"If Coach Hale knew about this, he would have us make a trip down here," Dax said.

The boys continued talking about their football season while they hiked. Allora was too busy with her own thoughts to pay any attention. She was thinking about the orb resting against the inside of her coat. Her thoughts were focused on her family and her future. She wondered whether this object would be the key to stopping the imposing unknown assassins that conspired to destroy everything around her. Hope was something she held onto. It was the strength that kept her going. Hope kept her striving to be stronger, faster, and more knowledgeable than her foe.

"What do you think, Allora?" Tanner said, twisting around. "Allora?"

She looked up, snapping back to reality. "What? Oh. Sorry, I was thinking about something. What did you say?"

"Are you okay?" Tanner asked.

"Yeah, I'm fine," Allora said. "Just a little tired, that's all. What's up?"

"Dax was saying that we should stop in Roseburg and get some food. You down?"

"Yes! I'm starving," Allora said. The thought of food caused her stomach to talk. "I could really go for a cheeseburger."

"I second that," Katie said.

"Hey, Dax," Tanner said, trying to find an end to their ascent, "can you see how much more we have to go?"

They had been climbing for a long time. Dax squinted his eyes in the dark, noticing the end to the steps. "I think I might see the top. It's probably another ten minutes away."

That said, they continued upward. The muscles in their legs were throbbing. Every step was daunting, with every movement more painful than the one previous. The last ten minutes turned into twenty. Their pace slowed to a crawl. Dax reached the last step and collapsed onto a flat, level surface. One by one, they all reached the top, only to look at a wall of rock.

"Great, we traded one dead end for another," Katie said, frustrated. "Only this time, we scaled a mountain for it."

Tanner felt around the wall with his hands. There wasn't that much space, which left a small area to search. Dax came over next to Tanner, followed by Allora and Katie.

"I was really looking forward to that cheeseburger, too," Dax said, leaning against the wall. He didn't hit rock, though. He kept leaning, without watching. His body tried to balance itself, but he kept falling sideways. Tanner noticed and grabbed him. Dax's momentum pulled Tanner with him, through what they had thought was rock. Katie went to grab Tanner, but the boy's weight was too much. Katie swung her arm around, grasping Allora by the coat.

All four of them passed through the rock, coming out into bright sunlight. Allora continued falling sideways, and then began to slide down a large boulder. She was now on her back, and picking up speed. Turning was out of the question. There was no room. Rocks jutted up on both sides of her. The rocks parted, leaving her room to twist her body. Allora flipped onto her stomach, right before the rocks' edge. She screamed, and then fell into a bush. The momentum sent her bouncing off the top of the bush and onto the other three, who had landed on the ground.

Allora rolled off, landing in the dirt. Dax was moaning at the bottom of the pile. He had taken the weight of everyone dropping on top of him. Tanner finally was able to move. They lay in the dirt, on their backs, while a tour group stood in a state of confusion a few yards away. The tourists grabbed their cameras and snapped a barrage of pictures. Allora pulled her head back, but none of them moved more than that for a few minutes.

"Are you guys alive?" Katie asked. Moans and grunts followed. It was the only acknowledgement they could muster. Allora could see the visitor center through a small gap, between the curious tourists.

"We made it," she said. The night was over and morning had come. The Eye of the Titans was now in their possession. They all shared a sense of accomplishment. Even though their bodies ached, they beamed with pride, for they had been through the gauntlet and come out alive.

Chapter 26

Eye of the Titans

Allora closed her eyes, feeling the warm, soothing rays of sunlight upon her face. It was a beautiful spring day without a cloud in the sky. The crowds of people at the visitor center turned to watch the four as they walked back to Tanner's car. Allora wasn't sure if it was because of the heavy layer of dirt that covered them, or because of how tiredly they walked. Exhaustion had set in. Allora felt herself falling asleep while she moved.

All of them stopped once they were within sight of the car. They wanted to get one last glimpse of Wizard's Island before they left. Allora thought it amusing that thousands of people walked upon the island, not knowing there was a golden palace below their feet. She put her arms around Katie and Tanner.

"We make a good team," she said. Tanner put his left arm around her and his right arm around Dax. "Yeah, we do," Tanner responded.

The island seemed so peaceful from where they stood. Crater Lake sparkled in the sunlight. The bright blue reminded Allora of the ice cave. As scary as the experience was, she appreciated the beauty and magic that was contained in the depths of the lake. She wondered what kind of things awaited her in the future. Notions of far-off lands, spectacular creatures, and beautiful scenery churned in her mind.

Tanner broke off from the group to prepare the car for the return trip. The siblings followed him, leaving Allora to reflect alone. The shimmer of the crystal blue lake was beautiful. Allora wrapped her arms around her stomach as she stood on the edge of the cliff. She couldn't help but dwell on the events in the cave.

Tanner noticed something wrong and made his way to Allora's side. He softly touched the lower part of her back. Allora could feel the warm energy flowing through his hand. The simple touch of his fingers was enough to calm her down. He had a way of knowing just what to do when she was upset.

"What's wrong?" Tanner asked, holding her hand as she turned around.

"I almost killed us in there," Allora said with her face pointed to the ground.

Tanner lifted her chin, catching her eyes as they darted up to him.

"We would not have been able to fight off those creatures. If it wasn't for you, we would have been killed." He lightly touched her shoulder, and left to finish packing the car.

In the cave, she had felt helpless to save her friends. Tanner always had a way of disarming her with his words. The problem was that he didn't understand. Allora turned back to try to explain, but Tanner had gotten in the car already. Allora took one last look at Crater Lake, and then got in the car and closed the door.

The ride home was much longer than the ride down had been. There was no energy in any of them. They stopped in Roseburg for a much-needed meal. No one talked while they ate. Everyone was too hungry to speak. After devouring their food, and cleaning themselves up a bit, they packed into the car and got back onto the interstate. Allora dozed off on the way back. Her dreams went back to the cave. She kept playing the event over in her mind. Focusing hadrons was new to her. During that moment, her emotions had controlled how she reacted. It was erratic, unspecific, and out of control. The feeling was unsettling. After five hours of driving, Tanner turned onto the forest road from which they had left, and Allora got out of the car and walked around to Tanner's window.

"Thanks for earlier," she said.

Tanner simply smiled.

He put the car in reverse and backed out of the old timber road. Allora stood watching the car move away. She picked up her stuff and walked through the forest back to her house. The orb was safely tucked into her coat pocket. The four had planned on examining it together. Allora thought it would be best if they did it in Mr. Swan's room, and the rest had agreed. Allora hid her gear next to her window, and then went to the back door. Milly was in the kitchen.

"How was training?" she asked.

"It was fine," Allora said while pulling off her shoes.

"Nothing eventful happened?" Milly said.

Allora quickly went through the kitchen, heading for her room.

"Nope," she said.

Short answers weren't anything odd for the teenager, so Milly didn't question her further. Allora closed her door softly, got her gear from outside the window, and put it in her closet. She tucked the orb into the far corner of the closet in order to protect it. Then, she placed a bag in front to conceal it. She needed to find a better hiding spot though.

The next day, after sleeping in, everyone met at Allora's house. They needed to go up to Sumatra's place so they would have an alibi. The events from the previous evening also suggested that they needed more training, especially since Tanner had been able to expel hadrons. He was eager to ask Sumatra questions about his Fermion power.

~~~~~~~~~~~~~~

"You're saying that you can manipulate water?" Sumatra said, shocked by the revelation. "Two Fermions in one location? I want to see it."

Tanner hadn't experimented since the night in the cave. Sumatra placed a bowl of water on a table in front of them. They were all gathered in Sumatra's cabin, staring at Tanner. He tried to focus his attention on the bowl of water, but nothing happened. Not even a blue spark came from his hands.

"I don't get it," Tanner said, frustrated by his inability to repeat the incredible feat. "They all saw what I did!"

Sumatra nodded his head. "I believe you, Tanner. Your body and mind are not ready for complete hadron focalization yet. These things take time. Sometimes, when you are young, certain events cause the power inside of you to take over. Patience and understanding will guide you to the inevitable gift that lies dormant for now. Do not be frustrated. The time will come."

The rest of the day, Sumatra taught them breathing techniques to control their power. Allora was very eager to learn this. Ever since the incident at the ice cave, she was afraid of her power. A lingering thought of seeing her friends die kept creeping into her mind as she tried to concentrate. She was also overwhelmed by everything that had transpired over the course of the year. It was enough to be a sixteen-year-old who was trying to survive high school, let alone having to deal with ancient mythical creatures in an underground golden cavern. The thought actually made her laugh because of how ridiculous it sounded.

During the week, Sumatra gave them more lessons in combat. They trained relentlessly. There was a new sense of determination to be ready for anything after what they had been through in the ice cave. Allora had Katie teach her tricks with a sword. The week went by quickly. It was almost time for school to start again.

"Remember, when you get to a certain level with your hadron focalization, you can use those weapons to focus your hadron energy," Sumatra said as they picked up their things to leave. "It's tricky, but it can be very powerful if used properly."

As they walked down the forest path, Tanner ran to catch up with Allora. "Hey, how are you?" he asked.

"I'm fine," she replied.

"You know, I'm here for you when you need me," Tanner said. Then he took off ahead to join Dax.

Allora kept going forward with a small smile on her face.

Katie heard the whole thing, and walked up next to Allora. "Wow, you've got it bad, girl," she said with a big grin on her face.

Allora tried to hide her exuberance. "I have no idea what you're talking about," she said, lifting her chin defiantly.

Katie rolled her eyes, shaking her head at her friend's persistent denial of her feelings toward Tanner. Before they reached Allora's house, the four made a plan to meet after class the next day to examine the orb. Even though Mr. Swan might tell their parents, they needed to show him. It was, after all, his quest to find the Eye of the Titans. Allora was a little worried that Mr. Swan might be angry they hadn't included him in their plan.

Once school ended for the day, were about to find out. Allora held onto the orb, which was situated inside her coat. She walked into Mr. Swan's room with the others were close behind. Dax closed the door while Allora motioned for Mr. Swan to get out one of his silencing balls. As soon as the jelly-type material covered the walls, Allora pulled out the orb from her coat.

Mr. Swan's face went white. He looked up to question what he was seeing, but the words didn't come out. He kept cocking his head up from staring at the orb to get some sort of acknowledgement that it was real. Allora nodded her head, but he still couldn't believe it.

"How... where... when...?" Was all Mr. Swan could say.

All four were now nodding their heads. "But you guys are just kids. The stories of the Eye's location were about intricate obstacles that would test even the strongest of Sonorians."

"Well, the stories were right," Tanner said. "It wasn't exactly easy."

"It would have been a lot easier if my knucklehead brother over here didn't try to steal that gold spear," Katie said, looking at her brother angrily.

"Hey, how was I supposed to know that an evil golden army of demons would rise up to kill us?" Dax said.

"Oh, I don't know, maybe because the directions said that greed would destroy the weak!" Katie said.

"Yeah, it said 'the weak,' " Dax argued. "I don't see any weaklings in here except you."

"Guys, let's focus," Mr. Swan said, turning back to Allora. "Who figured out where it was?"

"That would be Allora," Tanner admitted, proudly.

"I should have known," Mr. Swan said, proud of his best student. "Where was it?"

"Well, technically it was Bell who figured it out. It was at Crater Lake, below Wizard's Island in the middle of the lake," Allora said.

Mr. Swan smiled and shook his head. "You never cease to amaze me, Allora," he said. His proud demeanor changed when he thought of them going alone. "You all should have told me. Any one of you could have been killed." He put his hands on his hips.

Allora spoke up in the awkward silence that followed. "We knew that if we told you, then we wouldn't have been able to go. You always talk about stepping up the challenge of responsibility. We did exactly that."

"That also means taking on the consequences that come with that responsibility. Would you have been able to live with the consequence of Katie being killed? Or maybe Tanner?" Mr. Swan said.

Allora didn't have a response. Mr. Swan's words were like piercing daggers. The idea of one of her friends dying was becoming a constant thought that wouldn't go away. At that moment, she realized the four of them had jumped into the adventure of finding the Eye with complete reckless abandon. Had something happened to any of them, it would have been more than she could have handled.

Mr. Swan let his words sink in. Before he could speak again, Dax said, "What about me?" Mr. Swan looked at him with a perplexed expression.

"You named off everyone else dying except for me!" Dax said, crossing his arms.

Everyone chuckled. He had, once again, completely changed the mood of the conversation.

"Alright, let's take a look at this orb," Mr. Swan said, placing it in his palm. They moved around to the teacher's sides so that they could finally see the object that had been so difficult to retrieve.

"So..." Katie said, impatient with the lack of activity.

Mr. Swan laughed. "You ready?" he said, pointing his finger.

A small spark exited his index finger and shot into the orb. As soon as it hit the orb, Mr. Swan was shot into the air, crashing into the back wall of the classroom.

"Whoa!" They all yelled.

They ran to him, pulling him up from the ground.

"You okay?" Allora asked.

Mr. Swan shook his head, barely conscious. "Yeah..." His eyes fluttered quickly. "Wow, that thing is powerful." He staggered to the orb on the ground, picked it up, and handed it to Allora.

"Why are you handing this to me?" she asked. "Isn't it going to be safer with you?"

"Obviously not, since you guys were able to get the directions from me," he said, as Allora took the orb. "Besides, I don't think that I was meant to possess it. For some reason, it may only react to your hadron signature."

"It's time I taught you how to create your own hiding spot." Mr. Swan walked over to a blank wall and turned to face them.

"Okay, now, you need to place your hand upon the spot where you want to hide a certain object. Focus a small amount of hadrons to the palm of your hand. Once you feel the hadrons pulsating, you twist your hand and stop when you want to. Make sure to remember which way you twisted your hand, and at what angle you stopped," Mr. Swan instructed. "It's like the combination lock on your lockers. You spin your hand one way, and then turn the other. When you are satisfied with the combination, let go." Mr. Swan did so, and the wall started to swirl. He took the orb and placed it into the wall. Then he sparked the wall and it became solid again.

"So then, how do you get it back?" Allora asked.

Mr. Swan placed his hand onto the wall again. "You do the same combination with your hand," he said, twisting his hand in the same way as before. "You can even do it away from the wall, but you have to make sure to spark it while you are doing the combination." The orb slowly melted out of the wall when he was done.

Dax was the most excited. "That is so cool! Now I can hide all the stupid boy band music that Katie has. I won't ever have to listen to that crap again," he said, pumping his fist.

"I will kill you!" Katie yelled.

"Boy bands?" Allora said, lifting her eyebrows.

"So what?" Katie said, crossing her arms. "That's me. Take it or leave it."

"I'm not judging," Allora said. "I just never figured you for a boy band lover."

"Focus here, guys," Mr. Swan interrupted. "This is serious. You need to protect this orb with your lives. I can't describe to you how important that orb is to our struggle. Everyone needs to stay sharp. Okay?"

They all acknowledged their teacher.

Mr. Swan knew he had to start preparing them for what they were going to face. This meant that the four teens needed to grow up faster than they most likely wanted to. He had to start somewhere. The Sonorian rebellion now relied on these four to lead it against the onslaught of Titan aggression that had plagued their past. Now, they had the one tool to shift the balance of their campaign.

As Mr. Swan watched them leave his classroom, he thought back to night that had sent him to Earth. The painful memory had never left. It had stayed dormant in all those who witnessed the atrocities of that evening, and thereafter. Mr. Swan watched as Allora looked back and smiled before she left. He knew that the outcome of the future lay in his star pupil. Guilt engulfed him as he looked at the innocence still glowing on Allora's face. He had set her destiny in motion, and there was no stopping the coming events. She was now on a path to either save them from destruction or lead them to the demise of their entire world.

Chapter 27

Dreams

"Surprise!" a crowded room screamed as Allora came through the front door of her house. With everything that had happened over the last few weeks, she had totally forgotten about her birthday. Everyone she cared about was there. The house was decorated, and presents filled the kitchen table. Allora stepped into the room.

Katie ran over. "You are going to love my present!"

Even Sas had shown up. He had to bend down because the ceiling was too low. "Happy Birthday, Allora," Sas said, giving her a big, hairy hug.

"What are you doing here? You don't normally come out in public during the daylight."

"I had to come and see you," he said. "How does the saying go? 'Birthdays come but once a year'?" He looked proud that he had gotten the saying right.

Allora smiled. "Well, I'm glad you came."

"I actually have to leave," Sas said. "There is a lot of activity going on right now near the Gateway."

"Is that bad?" Allora asked, unsure of what that meant.

"I can't really talk about it right now. I'll try to update Milly when I can."

As he said that, Sas took off toward the forest. It only took him a few strides to get across the field.

Allora turned around and went back to the party. After a while, they gathered around the kitchen table to watch Allora open her presents. Katie insisted Allora open hers first.

Allora pulled back the wrapping and opened the box to reveal a beautiful purple top that put a huge smile on her face. She had found the same top in a magazine, and had talked about it to Katie for hours one day. Now, it was hers. She rushed into the bathroom to put it on. It was the perfect size. Allora came out of the bathroom to show it off. Then, she ran over to Katie and gave her a big hug. Milly wasn't so happy.

"Isn't that a little revealing?" she whispered to her daughter so that she wouldn't embarrass her.

"Mom, it's not that bad," Allora said. "I've wanted this shirt for so long."

Katie had heard what Milly said and leaned in to Allora's other side. "Your mom may not be a fan of the shirt, but I can see someone who is," Katie said, directing Allora's attention to Tanner, who quickly turned away when Allora looked up at him. She started to blush.

Allora thanked Katie again, and then went back to the kitchen to open the rest of the presents. Cake came after presents. It was a vanilla layer cake with purple frosting. Once they were done eating, the group of four went to the backyard and made a fire in the fire pit. They sat around by themselves while the adults talked inside.

"Have you started softball yet?" Allora asked Katie.

"Actually, I'm not doing it this year," she replied.

Allora was shocked. Katie loved softball.

"I'm not doing lacrosse, either," Tanner added.

"Am I missing something?" Allora said, confused by her friends. They loved spring sports.

"We were talking while we waited for you to get home," Katie said. "After what happened at Crater Lake and everything else that has happened to us, we want to train more this spring."

Allora was relieved to hear it. She had planned to go train with Sumatra by herself while the others were at practice. Now she could have company.

"We were thinking that every day after school we would go up to the orchard and work on our combat skills. I need more work with my staff," Dax said.

"What do you think?" Katie asked.

"Sounds good to me," Allora answered.

They sat there, gazing at the fire. The stars were beginning to shine, and the crescent moon was touching the tops of the trees. Every few seconds the firewood popped and a burst of sparks flew upward. It was a perfect night, and an even better birthday. Allora was glad that she had close friends to share it with.

~~~~~~~~~~~~~~

Weeks went by without any sign of the assassins. Sas remained at his post, but nothing out of the ordinary happened. Allora was relieved, yet determined to make sure that if anything did happen, she would be ready. Training resumed every day after school. Focalization practice was followed by weapons instruction. Progressively, they all got better with the use of their weapons. Allora was hesitant about focusing hadrons, though, after the ice cave. Sumatra tried to work with her, but her mind blocked any attempt to focus her hadrons.

Every time she thought about the night in the cave, doubt sprang up and caused her to stop. Frustration led to anger. One day, she threw her bow down and stormed out of the orchard. The rest of the group looked at each other for answers, but no one came up with an explanation. Tanner went after her, but Katie stopped him.

"She needs to figure this one out on her own," she said, pushing Tanner back. "You're not going to get anywhere with that girl when she is upset.

Trust me."

Allora spent the rest of the day with the animals in her backyard. They had a way of calming her nerves. She sat in the grass, petting her overeager dogs while they licked her face. Allora could feel her mood changing with every passing minute. The weight of responsibility seemed to become heavier. She couldn't understand why everyone looked to her to end the war. What was it that made her so special? More than anything, she longed to be normal. The excitement of her new life was fading. Doubt, confusion, and fear overwhelmed her mind. She had never felt so alone.

After it got dark, she went inside. Milly was standing in the kitchen. Allora ran to her mother and gave her a strong hug.

Milly pulled her daughter back. "Are you alright?" she asked.

"I just needed a hug," Allora answered.

Milly's eyes darted back and forth. Her daughter hadn't been this affectionate since she was little. Milly pulled Allora in and they held each other for a while. Allora thanked her mother and then went to her room. Milly stood, perplexed but happy with being able to embrace her daughter. She could tell that something was bothering Allora, but she knew her daughter too well to investigate.

Allora decided that she needed to create the hiding place for the Eye. It was lying in the back of her closet, next to her shoes. She pulled it out, looking around with caution. She took a deep breath and tried to focus her hadrons to her palm. Her emotions were a little calmer. It took her a while, but she was able to send a spark into the wall. Then, she twisted her hand clockwise and counter-clockwise, as Mr. Swan had instructed. The combination was tricky, but she made sure to repeat it in her head in order to remember it.

Allora opened her eyes and pulled her hand away from the wall. The wallpaper began spinning like water into a drain. She touched it with her finger to see what it felt like. Waves of liquid moved like the reaction to a pebble dropped into a pond. The texture felt like mud. Allora pulled her finger back and placed the obsidian orb into the wall. The wall sucked it in without Allora having to push it. It disappeared. The wall slowly became solid again. Allora ran her hand across the wallpaper. It felt like a normal wall.

Allora threw herself onto her bed and stared up through the skylight above her. The stars twinkled in the night sky. They had a mesmerizing effect. Her eyelids became heavy. Pretty soon, she was asleep. Training, along with the emotional roller coaster from earlier, had tired her out.

Her dream took her to a large lake that was surrounded by white-capped mountains. Allora stood in the middle of the lake. It was as if the lake was an inch deep.

"Hello, Allora," a voice said from behind her.

Allora spun around, almost losing her footing. She had to put her hand to the wet ground to keep herself from falling. Standing a few feet away was Uncle Ben. He wore long, flowing white robes that seemed to glow in the mystical environment that enveloped her dream. He had a calm, gentle demeanor. Allora stood up, wiping her wet hands on her pants. It all felt so real.

"Where am I?" Allora asked.

"We are in between your world and mine," the old man said.

"I don't understand," Allora said.

"Allora, there isn't enough time to explain. Our connection only lasts what amounts to a short time. I came here because it is important for you to trust in yourself. This journey that you are on will be grueling. You have the inner strength to become more; just believe in yourself."

"What if I don't want to be more? What if I just want to be normal?"

"Is that what you truly believe? Have you not dreamt of something more? There are no coincidences. We are who we want to be. You need to decide whether the life presented to you is where you want to go. If not, you have the ability to make a choice."

"I don't feel like I have a choice," Allora said.

"Destiny can change. Just remember, every choice to act or not act has its own set of consequences, whether they are good or bad. No one can dictate your life except you."

Uncle Ben faded away. Allora opened her eyes to find Bell hanging over her bed again.

Allora squinted to make sure that she wasn't in a dream.

"You realize that you talk in your sleep?" Bell said.

Allora lifted herself on her elbows. "You realize that if you don't get out of my room I'm going to kill you?" Allora said, launching herself at her sister. Bell quickly sidestepped to miss Allora's arms.

Allora crashed to the floor as Bell ran out of the room.

"I'm going to get you!" Allora yelled.

Milly replaced Bell in the room.

"Hey, you're up," Milly said, drinking her coffee. "Good. School starts in about fifteen minutes. You're late. I'll give you a ride."

Allora sat on the floor, flustered by her dream. Since the dreams of Sumatra, she had been taking note of her dreams. Somehow, her uncle was able to connect with her while she was asleep. Or was he just a figment of her imagination. It felt so real, though.

Allora dressed for school quickly and then went out the door. She was about twenty minutes late, but the teacher didn't mind since Allora was generally punctual. During class, Allora wasn't herself. All she could think about was what her uncle had said. This was the case in each one of her classes. Her teachers tried to snap her out of it, but it didn't work. Allora daydreamed the entire school day.

School ended, and Allora found Katie in the front lobby. She was glad that her best friend was in a talkative mood, because she didn't want to have to say a thing. She needed time to herself to absorb everything from her dream.

Tanner walked down the senior hall toward the front lobby, but Kim stopped him. She waved, and stopped everyone she could see to have them take notice.

"Tanner? Will you go to prom with me?" she asked, with a crowd watching.

Tanner looked back and forth. An answer wasn't coming out, which made things awkward. The truth was that he didn't really want to go with her. Dax finally shoved him in the shoulder, and he blurted out, "Sure...."

Everyone clapped, except for Katie and Allora. They were standing in the back of the crowd. Allora stared at Kim, who stood facing the crowd, as if victorious. Tanner turned and said something to Dax. Kim turned and parted the circle of students.

Allora walked up to Tanner. "You're going to prom with her?" Allora asked, aggressively throwing her arms in the air.

"What was I supposed to say?" Tanner said defensively. "She cornered me."

"Oh, I don't know, maybe that two-letter word that starts with 'N' and ends with 'O.' " she said, waving her arms.

Dax jumped in to his friend's defense. "I personally think it's a great choice of dates. I'm pissed that it wasn't me that she asked."

"That girl is evil," Allora said.

"I have to agree," Katie interjected.

"I don't understand why you're so mad at me," Tanner said. He knew why, but said it anyway. As soon as the words came out, he regretted them.

Allora had been building up tension all day. The stress was too much. She screamed and stormed off into the bathroom.

The students in the hallway turned to Allora when they heard the scream.

"I wonder if I'll ever be able to figure out women," Dax said.

"Maybe that's because you have the emotional capacity of a robot," Katie said to her brother.

Meanwhile, Allora threw open the bathroom door and went straight to the sink. Jenny stood next to her. Allora splashed some water on her face and leaned over the sink, letting the water drip down. Jenny was applying lip gloss.

"What happened?" Jenny asked.

Allora hesitated. Jenny was, after all, Tanner's ex-girlfriend. She would be giving away the fact that she liked Tanner.

"Come on," Jenny pleaded. "I know that we weren't the best of friends earlier in the year, but I can be a good listener."

She seemed very genuine, so Allora told her. "Kim asked Tanner to prom."

"I knew you liked him!" Jenny exclaimed. Allora turned back to the sink, regretting her decision.

"Hey, it's fine," Jenny said, placing her hand on Allora's shoulder as a reassurance. "That new girl is crazy. I think Tanner is smart enough to eventually figure it out. I wouldn't worry yourself." Jenny backed up and went into the stalls. "Besides, what's the worst that could happen? It's just prom," she said, closing the stall door.

Allora splashed her face with water. She heard someone else walk into the bathroom. When she came up and looked into the mirror, Kim was standing behind her. Allora twisted around suddenly. Kim inched closer to Allora's face with an evil grin.

"What do you want?" Allora said aggressively.

"I want you to know that I have my eye on you," Kim said, inching a little closer. "Tanner is mine, and if you even think of messing that up, I'll kill you."

Kim backed away and exited the bathroom. Jenny was awkwardly trying to pull up her pants while she came out of the stall.

"Was that Kim?" she asked.

Allora just nodded her head.

"Damn, she is such a bitch," Jenny said, buttoning her jeans. "I would have come out here to help, but I was a little busy."

Allora was gazing at the door where Kim left. "I don't trust her, Jenny.

That girl gives me the creeps."

Jenny followed Allora's gaze toward the door. "Yeah, I got the same feeling."

Chapter 28

Prom

Aggressively brushing her long brown hair, Allora sat in front of her mirror, dreading the evening's events. Prom was only hours away and Brandon had asked her to go. Without having any other prospects, she had reluctantly accepted. He wasn't the worst choice of dates, but she'd had her mind set on a different guy. Thoughts of Tanner in his suit drew a smile. The smile quickly faded when she thought of who he was going with. She stopped brushing her hair and sat back in her chair with a sigh. Looking across the room, she stared at the wall where the orb was hidden. Allora got up from the chair, walked to the wall, and performed the combination to open the hiding spot. When it melted through the wallpaper, Allora grabbed the orb and sat back on the bed.

Why is this piece of rock so important? she asked herself, twisting the orb in her palm. A black glint sparkled against the dim light. Staring into the almost-liquid interior, Allora felt a surge of energy flow into her hand. Something was missing. Now was not the time to dwell on it. The bedroom doorknob twisted, and Allora quickly shoved the orb in her purse right before Milly opened the door. Allora turned around, trying to act like normal.

"You alright?" Milly asked.

"Yeah, fine. Why?" Allora said rapidly.

Milly just stared at her daughter for a moment. "You should probably get ready. Everyone will be here soon," Milly said, closing the door.

Allora slouched forward, letting out her breath. Milly would have exploded if she knew what they had done during spring break. As much as Allora wanted to share her discovery with her mother, the consequences were too much. She was finally getting along with her mother and she didn't want to ruin it. Katie came over while Allora was putting on her dress. She walked in with her white dress in hand.

"Oh my god, you look hot!" Katie said.

"Shut up," Allora said, pulling up the middle of the strapless dress. It was a short dress that had ruffles, pinned at sporadic spots on the bottom. The middle was tightly wrapped with a purple band that fit snuggly around her waist. The dress beautifully accentuated Allora's long muscular legs. Her high heels were black with the toes expose. A web like pattern covered the heel, and strapped on top of her foot.

"It looks amazing," Katie said. "Brandon is going to love it." She put her stuff down, and began putting her dress on.

"I'm not trying to impress Brandon," Allora said, looking into her mirror. She pulled the sides of the dress down to pull out any wrinkles in the dress.

"Well then, you're going to make Tanner very jealous," Katie said, pulling up her dress. Like Allora, she had rented a strapless short white dress that flowed outward. There was a satin sash that tied in the front. It matched Katie's personality. She had never really liked clothing that inhibited her ability to run.

Allora ignored Katie's last comment and went to the bathroom to put on her makeup. A part of her wanted Tanner to be jealous. She knew that it wasn't the right way to go about getting Tanner's attention, but Allora was still hurt that she wasn't going with him. Allora applied her lip gloss and then joined Katie in the living room.

Katie noticed her friend pulling at her dress. "What are you doing?"

"I hate thongs," Allora said, still pulling the side of her dress. "Who invented these things? I don't know how you convinced me to wear this."

"You never know what might happen tonight," Katie said with a wink.

Allora turned to Katie, who was smiling really big. She knew what Katie had meant and decided to show her how she felt about it. Allora pointed her finger at Katie. Then, she sent a small purple spark, shocking her friend.

"Hey!" Katie yelled.

Allora smiled at Katie. "Serves you right."

"Girls, the rest of your group has shown up," Milly said as she walked in from outside.

Katie rubbed her side while she greeted her classmates.

The first to arrive were Jenny and Tanya. Allora couldn't believe that two of the girls that she despised in the beginning of the year were now going to prom in her same group. Behind Jenny was Allora's date, Brandon. He had on a nice black-and-white tux, with a black bowtie.

"You look amazing," he said, walking up to Allora.

"Thanks," Allora responded without much enthusiasm. She had never been able to take compliments very well.

Katie's date, Dirk, came in with an eighties-inspired retro red suit. He walked through the door with a huge smile on his face. He strolled up to Katie, who was holding her hand to her mouth. She couldn't believe what he was wearing.

"Are you kidding me?" Katie exclaimed.

"I know, right. It's awesome, huh?" Dirk said, while holding his jacket sides outward and spinning around.

Allora couldn't help it; she burst out laughing. Katie sneered in Allora's direction. Robert Mondrach came in minutes later looking incredibly handsome, which made Katie even angrier with her situation. Robert was wearing a black Armani suit with a matching black vest. The tie was silver, and perfectly even on his chest. In his left front pocket was a silver handkerchief that matched the tie. His shoes were nicely polished. They shone, even in the dimly lit room.

Tanya's date, Chris, who was the football team's starting center, came in next. Chris was six foot five and very muscular. He had received a scholarship to play for the University of Oregon in the fall. Chris was one of the reasons that Mondrach had such an amazing season rushing the ball. Allora thought that he cleaned up nicely, though.

Dax came in with his date moments later. Allora recognized the girl. Her name was Erin. She was a sophomore on the cheerleading team. Erin had also been at the rock quarry the night of the Rover attack. She looked as incredible as any of the other girls in the room. Her dress was pink, tight, and very elegant. Allora figured she was a little nervous about being one of the youngest in the group, so she went to greet her.

"Hi, Erin," Allora said.

"Hi, Allora," Erin responded. "That's an amazing dress. Where did you get it?"

Allora looked down. "Oh, this thing? My mother and I went into Portland to go shopping. They had a little better selection."

The adults congregated in the kitchen with their cameras in hand. Milly appeared around the corner to address everyone. "Okay, guys, picture time," she said, holding up her camera.

Everyone filed into the front door. When they were all outside, they huddled up with their dates. Boys were in the back, and girls were in the front. They lined up along the rhododendron bushes. The flowers were blooming, which made for a great backdrop.

"Hey, we're missing someone," Allora said, looking side to side. "Where is Tanner?"

Dax popped his head forward. "Tanner sent me a text saying that he was with Kim and that he would meet us there."

Allora faced forward again, yet she felt uneasy. There was something wrong. With every flash of the camera, she caught a glimpse of Tanner being beaten and tortured. The flashes became more intense. Allora could feel her heart beating faster. Her mind was swimming in her skull. Her limbs felt a tingling sensation.

Allora closed her eyes. Then she heard a scream come from within.

"Allora!"

The voice was Tanner's. Once the adults were done taking pictures, Allora ran to the bathroom. The only one who noticed was Katie. She ran after her, wondering why she was so upset. Katie rounded the corner to see Allora over the sink, splashing water on her face.

"You're going to mess up your makeup." Katie said.

"I don't care," Allora snapped.

"Well, I thought that Brandon looked very nice. I think that you should at least give him a chance."

Allora grabbed Katie by the shoulders. "That's not what I'm talking about." Katie had never seen her friend this intense before. "I can't really explain it, but I need to go check on something."

"What do you mean?" Katie asked.

Allora let go of Katie. "I need to borrow your car. My mother is leaving soon, to go help prepare for prom. Once she leaves, I'll go. Just tell people that I had to take care of something."

Dax came around the corner to go to the bathroom.

"Allora is leaving for some reason," Katie told him. She turned back to Allora. "What about dinner? And where are you going?"

After a long pause, Allora said, "I have to go check on Tanner."

"Why do you scare me like that? Can't you let it go? Tanner is fine," Katie said.

"Yeah, Allora, he's probably getting some pre-prom nookie as we speak," Dax said, smiling.

Katie turned around and smacked her brother on the shoulder. "Why do you always have to be an insensitive jerk?" Katie said.

Allora ignored both of them and snatched Katie's purse from her grasp.

Katie didn't even notice. She was too busy yelling at her brother. Allora removed the keys to the car and dashed out the door. Milly gave her daughter a good-bye hug. Then, the parents left. Allora got into Katie's car and turned the key. Suddenly, the passenger door opened.

"I need to go, Katie," she said, but the individual who hopped into the seat next to her wasn't Katie. It was Jenny.

"Let's go," she said.

"How do you know what I'm doing?" Allora said, confused.

"I overheard you talking to Katie. I don't trust this girl either. Something is not right with her and I want to be sure that Tanner is alright."

"No, I'm doing this alone," Allora responded, frustrated by this intruder who was holding her up.

"If you don't pull this car out, I will call your mother and explain what you're doing," Jenny said, with a stern expression.

Allora thought about it. Her mother wouldn't like Allora going off on her own anyway. She didn't have much time to argue with her. After a few seconds, Allora placed the car in reverse and drove out of the driveway. Katie came out as her car exited the property.

Allora sped through traffic with a sense of purpose. She didn't understand the images that flashed before her, but she wasn't going to take a chance. The house where they had dropped Kim off wasn't that far away. Allora pulled the car into an area that couldn't be seen, and then both girls silently crept along the road. They found a bush that gave them a perfect view of the house without exposing their whereabouts. Allora knelt down next to Jenny, and both of the girls waited, not knowing what lay behind the dark red door of the Nelson's house.

Chapter 29

The Storm

Allora's phone rang. The noise was loud. Frantically, she fumbled through her purse. After an exaggerated minute, Allora answered.

"Hello?" she whispered.

"Where are you?" Katie asked. "We are about to leave."

"I'm at the Nelson's house," Allora answered. The front door of the house crept open.

"Katie, I gotta go." Allora could hear Katie's voice on the other end of the line as she closed the phone. Both girls ducked down behind the bush as Kim strutted out of the doorway. Between the bush's branches, Allora and Jenny watched Kim carefully scan the front yard. They remained silent, hoping she would leave. Slowly, Kim stepped off the porch, glaring at the bush that the girls hid behind. Allora's heart beat against her chest, pounding faster with every step Kim took. The crunch of leaves beneath her feet got louder and then stopped at the edge of the bush. They held their breath. Kim's shiny red high heels stood between the branches. The feet snapped around, dancing around as if in pursuit of a potential victim. After a few agonizing minutes, she went back to the house. Jenny popped her head up in time to see Kim lock the front door, turn, and then walk out onto the road. Allora peeked around the bush to see her rounding the corner.

"Where is she going?" Allora asked.

"Where is Tanner?" Jenny said.

The question hit her gut and her breath escaped at the thought of something dreadful happening to Tanner. Panic stricken, Allora became more determined.

"We have to get into that house," Allora replied, standing up. Jenny had to hike up her long yellow dress to keep it out of the rain-soaked lawn. The grass was browning and thick. No one had cut it in a while. Inching toward the front door, they peeked into the windows. Allora grabbed the windowsill, and flakes of paint fell to the ground.

"Does anyone even live here?" Allora asked, pulling her heel from the mud.

"How are we going to get in?" Jenny whispered. "I saw her lock the door."

Allora confirmed it by trying to twist the doorknob. They tiptoed around the porch, searching for an access point. The floorboards creaked and shuddered underneath their mud-covered heels as they made their way to the back door. With every minute, Allora was becoming more stressed. The pained images of Tanner being tortured kept flashing in her mind. Frantically, she scanned the windows on the first floor. One of them was slightly open, but difficult to get open further.

"Jenny, lift me up," Allora said, after muscling the rusty window up. "I think I can get through."

Jenny clasped her hands together. Allora removed her shoes and placed the arch of her foot in Jenny's palms. Then, Jenny lifted her up to the window and pushed her through. Crawling on the washing machine, Allora caught her dress. She pulled awkwardly, ripping the synthetic fabric down the side. Off balance, her hand slipped from the edge of the appliance, sending her crashing onto the linoleum floor.

"You alright?" Jenny whispered through the window.

"Yeah, fine," Allora answered, examining the tear on her dress.

Allora unlocked the back door. Jenny wiped off her muddy heels, and they slowly walked through the kitchen and into the living room. A layer of dust covered the shelves and cupboards. Cobwebs hung at the corners of the room. At the bottom of the stairs, a putrid smell wafted down from the second floor. It was nauseating.

"What is that?" Jenny whispered, squeezing her nose.

Allora shrugged her shoulders. She had to plug her nose as well. The two girls inched their way up the steps, trying not to make a sound. Jenny's heel got stuck, causing her to fall forward. The sound reverberated against the walls. Allora cringed, snapping around. Jenny looked up with an apologetic look. They remained still, listening to the silence in earnest, wondering if they had been caught. Nothing happened. Continuing their ascent, they soon stood at the top step, staring intently down the darkened hallway as if expecting a ghost to appear. The shutters on the hallway window were shut. The air was cold and dank. The smell had grown stronger. Everything was eerily quiet. A chill shot up Allora's spine, causing her to shake.

Allora grabbed the doorknob of the closest room and twisted the brass handle. The rusty knob clanked and squeaked. She bit down on her teeth at the sound. If someone was in the house, they would have heard it. The house was old, and none of the hinges had been oiled in years. The wooden door opened into the master bedroom.

An inescapable stench blew outward. The only thing pushing Allora forward was the fear of losing Tanner. Regret consumed her mind. She had never told him how she truly felt. Now, she was terrified that it was too late. The bed was in the corner, and they could see lumps in the sheets. Jenny tried to pull at Allora's arm, but she kept going. Her legs became heavy. Every step increased a dreadful feeling of trepidation.

Allora apprehensively grasped the sheet that covered the bed. Jenny moved closer. Curiosity had beaten out her fear. She walked to the edge of the bed and gave a nod. Allora swallowed hard. Then, she yanked back the sheet. Both girls jumped back. Jenny tried to get her hands to her mouth, but she couldn't stop herself from the unavoidable reaction. The muffled scream echoed in the stillness. Allora was too grossed out to move.

Lying in the bed before them were Mr. and Mrs. Nelson. Their bodies were decomposing, suggesting that they had been dead for a while. The grotesque images of their bodies were burned into the forefront of the girl's minds. The smell of death overwhelmed them. They ran out of the room. Jenny gagged as if she were about to throw up. Once they were in the hallway, they heard a noise coming from one of the other rooms. It sounded like a groan.

Unsure of the source, Allora walked down the hallway with her ears trained forward. As she walked, the noise grew louder. The dark hallway was only illuminated by the light that shone through the slits in the shutters. Jenny was still behind her, bent over, with her hands on her knees.

"Where are you going?" she asked.

Allora didn't say anything. She was concentrating on the noise from the room. Jenny stood up straight.

"We have to call the police!" Jenny whispered emphatically. She hurried over to Allora. "The Nelsons are dead. We have to go!"

"No!" Allora said, shifting her attention back to the closed door. "I have to find Tanner."

This time she swung the door open quickly. Allora braced herself for what lay waiting. What she found was a boy sitting on a chair with his head down. The boy picked his head up.

"Tanner!" Allora ran over and hugged him. "Oh my god. I thought you were dead."

Tanner had his hands bound behind the chair. He couldn't speak. There was a rag tied around his head and mouth. Allora removed it, allowing Tanner to let out a breath.

"I'm so sorry!" was the first thing out of his mouth. Allora shuffled behind the chair to untie his hands. "You were right. Kim is evil. I should have listened to you."

He was in his tuxedo, but it was cut up and dirty. Around his neck, a bowtie hung loosely. Blood trickled down his cheek, and his right eye was blue and swollen. His hair was damp and disheveled.

"Tanner, what did she do to you?" Jenny said, finally coming into the room. Both girls frantically pulled at the rope. The tight knots took a while to get loose. "We have to get out of here before she comes back. Who knows what she'll do to us," Jenny said, pulling the last of the rope away. Tanner rubbed his wrists as he got up. The three were about to leave the room when they heard the front door open.

Fear stopped them at the doorway. They froze, not sure what to do. Tanner grabbed Jenny's arm and closed the door as quietly as possible. He swung Jenny to the other side of the room.

"We have to escape through that window," he said, unlatching the lock and yanking it open.

Tanner held Jenny's hand and helped her up onto the windowsill. She stepped onto the roof, sliding down the shingles to the gutter. Allora heard footsteps on the stairs. There were two sets. They quickly shimmied through the window and looked back to see the doorknob turn.

Two figures walked into the room with shocked expressions. Kim and the Rover from the rock quarry stared back. There was a moment of pause, as if time had stopped. Seeing her prey escaping her grasp, Kim's eyes turned blood red. Her body became tense and shook in an unnatural spasm of anger. Allora recognized what her next move would be, but couldn't communicate it in time. Kim pulled her hands to the sides of her body. A red glow grew at her waist. Allora pulled Tanner down the roof, just as Kim sent the red glow shooting into the wall. An explosion of wood and glass shot out, propelling Allora, Tanner, and Jenny into the air. Luckily, the ground below was soft when they landed. Allora hit the ground, rolling on the grass. Shards of wood rained down, covering the backyard. Jenny landed awkwardly. Her ankle twisted. Allora got to her feet in time to see Kim's silhouette in the large hole on the second story of the house. Allora focused, absorbing hadrons and shooting them toward the house. The purple ball of energy exploded into the roof. Kim and the Rover were forced backward. This gave Allora and Tanner enough time to help Jenny up and run off through the corn stalks that filled the yard. They weaved through the brown, withered corn, zigzagging away from the house, toward the forest. Tanner held Jenny up with her arm around his shoulder, while Allora held her other side. They angled their path in order to make it harder for their pursuers to follow. The sharp edges of the dead corn kept cutting their arms, leaving long slits of red. Once they made it to the edge of the farm, they let Jenny down to take a break.

"We have to split up," Allora said between breaths.

"No, we are not going to be separated," Tanner said.

They didn't have much time to argue.

"Tanner, we have to get Jenny to safety," she commanded. "You take her into the forest, while I distract them."

"No way, you take Jenny and I will lead them away," Tanner argued.

Jenny was holding her ankle on the ground. "Guys, just leave me and save yourselves," she said. The pathetic gesture was almost comical. Jenny was in obvious pain. Her ankle was bruised and ballooning. It was probably broken. This was no time to be stubborn.

Allora picked Jenny up and gave Tanner a look of confirmation. Tanner held the tips of her fingers, and then slid away as he moved back into the stalks of corn. Allora scurried into the woods ahead, listening to Tanner yell behind her. The light from the sun was dimming. The girls pushed through the darkening forest. Every move was painful for Jenny.

They stopped for a moment to rest. Blood covered her toes. Her bare feet were exposed to the sharp branches on the ground, but there was no time to clean up. In the distance, thunder filled the air. The ground vibrated with every boom. Ahead, the trees opened up. Both recognized the bright unnatural green covering the ground ahead. It was the school football field. They were almost out of the woods when they heard a branch crack from behind them. Someone was catching up to them. Their movements quickened.

Allora wasn't sure what to do once they made it to the field. The girls broke through the edge of the forest to feel the soft turf beneath their feet. They had made it about twenty yards across the field when something crashed through the trees. Allora turned her head in time to see the streak of red. Her movement sent Jenny flying to the right. The red ball split between the girls. Allora landed on her arm, knocking the wind out of her. Jenny rolled to a stop on the fifteen yard line. Allora tried to pull herself up to defend against the next attack, but it was too late.

She recognized the dark figure approaching. It was the same creature that had attacked them on Halloween. His dark sinister red eyes glowed as the creature pulled his hands to the side to fire again. Jenny was able to get to all fours. The creature pushed forward, launching another burst at Allora. Jenny leapt in front of Allora, taking the full impact of the attack.

Jenny was knocked back into Allora, and both of them slid along the turf. Allora pulled Jenny to the side, but the Wraith was upon her. He yanked the back of her dress and tossed her back toward the forest. Again, Allora's breath escaped. She got to all fours, gasping for air. Jenny wasn't moving. Allora couldn't tell if she was alive.

The night was approaching. Darkness seemed to consume the football field as the Wraith prepared for an attack. Allora wasn't about to give up. She got to her feet and focused two purple hadron balls in her palms. The Wraith mimicked her move, attacking in kind. The hadron balls detonated between them, exploding outward like fireworks bursting. The force pushed Allora back. She braced her right foot behind her to get traction. Then, she ran forward, readying herself to strike. The dark creature sent another shot. Allora angled her body, twisting around like a gymnast performing a floor routine. The red streak missed by inches. Launching her own attack, Allora skillfully fought the Wraith, punching and kicking in short bursts. The Wraith flipped around to avoid Allora's high-swinging leg. This gave him an opportunity to attack, which he capitalized on. The punch hit Allora on her side. She pulled her feet back in order to evade the creature's next move. The kick came at her head. She ducked and spun around. A hadron burst hit her in her back. The impact was painful. Electricity spread throughout her body. She blacked out for a second. Dizziness followed. Suddenly, she felt a forceful hand grasp the back of her dress. Whoever it was pulled her up and slammed her against the metal goalpost. Her vision was blurry, but images began to come into focus. A hand seized her neck and then clenched, causing Allora to choke. As she struggled for breath and blinked her eyes, the figure of a short, black-haired girl in a red dress came into focus.

"Hold on!" the Rover said. Kim put Allora down, but kept a firm hold on her neck. The Rover put his hand on Allora's forehead. She could feel something slimy sniffing her. After a long minute, the Rover's eyes grew wide and sinister, like he had finally found a treasure chest. Then, he pulled back.

"We found her!" he said.

Kim snapped her head around, as if she had heard the worst news of her life.

"This thing?" she questioned. "It can't be. She's so weak."

"It's her. I'm positive of it."

"There is no way I'm letting this one go. I've been waiting a long time to kill this one."

"The king was very strict about his orders," the Rover said. "You are to capture this one and bring her back to the palace."

"But, Taneous..." Kim began to protest.

"Do you know how long you will last if you disobey him?" Taneous said.

The Rover's words were final. Kim snapped her head back to look upon Allora. Anger seeped from her pores. Her red eyes looked as though flames were protruding forward. Through the space between the Kim's and Taneous' heads, Allora saw someone running on the field toward them. No one could brace themselves for what came next.

A bright blue streak hit Kim in the back. They were all knocked down. Tanner pulled back and shot two more balls of hadrons that burst into the Rover and the Wraith. Tanner grabbed Allora's hand, pulling her along as they sprinted to the other side of the field. The three creatures launched after them. The field's exit was in sight, but the creatures were fast. Tanner shoved Allora sideways and flung a burst at the Rover, who was attacking from above. Tanner was able to hit him, but the Wraith had caught up as well. Allora positioned herself and sent a burst that struck the Wraith as he was attacking Tanner. The creature flew into the bleachers, leaving a trail of splintered wood. The two got up, only to be knocked backward by two red hadron attacks. Kim had maneuvered herself to catch the two when they were vulnerable. They weren't able to defend another attack. Kim grabbed them both.

"Nice try," she said. "You're not getting away this time."

The other two creatures picked themselves up and joined Kim.

"Is this the one that you were talking about?" Taneous asked Kim.

Kim turned and smiled. "Yeah, this is him."

"You can probably kill this one," the Rover said, grinning and laughing.

Allora could feel the emotion boiling deep within. She was overcome with the thought of losing Tanner. The thought became stronger. She began to breathe louder. The creatures stopped laughing when they noticed a ball of light floating in the air. It floated toward them, and then streaked through the air, striking Allora in the chest and filling her with glowing light. Amazed by what had happened, the creatures just stood with their mouths open. Strength filled her body. She moved fast, swinging her arms downward, releasing them from Kim's grasp. Then, she pushed forward, striking Kim in the chest, forcing her into the air and across the field. Then, she launched two hadron balls into the Wraith and the Rover.

"Allora!" someone yelled behind her.

Katie and Dax had popped out of the forest. Tanner and Allora ran to them, still eyeballing the area where the creatures were picking themselves up. Katie was still wearing her dress, but holding Allora's purse in her hand. Dax had weapons as well. It looked odd to see the pair in their prom outfits and weaponry, but Allora was just happy to see them. Katie hugged Allora once they got to each other.

"You've looked better," Katie said. Allora's hair was protruding in all directions. Her dress was ripped all over, and she was covered in cuts. Katie handed Allora her bow.

"Is that Jenny over there?" Katie asked, looking at Jenny's limp body across the field.

Allora thought back to Jenny's unselfish act of bravery. "Yeah, she saved my life," Allora said.

"Is she..." Katie asked.

Allora looked over at Jenny's body. It wasn't moving at all. "I don't know."

"What's going on?" Katie asked. "We went to the Nelson's house, which is destroyed."

Dax gave Tanner his sword. "Yeah, we saw the Nelsons dead in their bed. I don't even want to know what happened there."

"That's when I found your purse in the backyard," Katie said. "And then this round glowing ball shot out of it and flew into the forest. We followed it, and that's how we found you guys."

"There isn't much time to explain," Allora said, strapping the quiver of arrows upon her back. "Kim killed the Nelsons and we think she might be one of the assassins sent here to kill us."

"Yeah, dude, she's evil," Tanner said, grabbing his sword from Dax.

Kim exploded through the bleachers and onto the field. Her dress was torn all over.

"Whoa, I can see what you mean," Dax said, placing his staff in front of him. "Tanner, you really know how to pick them, don't you?"

Dax always did know how to lighten the mood, even with the possibility of death. Katie pulled out her katanas. She almost relished the moment. The excitement of combat was a challenge that she revered.

The four spaced themselves along the football field's twenty yard line. The Wraith and the Rover joined Kim, standing to either side of her. Standing at the edge of the field, Tanner, Katie, Allora, and Dax each took a deep breath, feeling the fear subside, replaced by a mature confidence that they had never experienced before. All of their training had come down to this moment. The final test was here, and they felt ready.

The sun had dropped below the mountains, and the sky darkened. The thunderclouds were now above them, crashing and sounded violently. Allora drew an arrow from her quiver. She placed it in the bow. The arrow glowed as she placed it in the notch. Light moved down the wooden shaft of the arrow and accumulated at the metal tip. Hadrons were focusing at the end of the arrow without Allora even noticing. Allora focused her attention to the arrow. Kim glared at them with evil red eyes. She was intent to capture or kill. They also couldn't allow any of them to get away. If the assassins were able to inform others that the rebels were here, the safety of secrecy would be compromised.

The night sky growled, and a raindrop hit Allora's forehead as she stared down her opponent.

"You're not going to come away from this alive," Kim said in a sinister tone.

"If I'm going down, then I'm taking you with me," Katie said, pointing her sword at Kim.

Kim laughed. Her voice became deeper. "Get them!" she yelled.

Allora pulled back her bowstring as the Rover launched himself into the air. They pulled their heads up, not noticing the Wraith sprinting forward. Allora focused her sights on the Rover and let go of the bowstring. The arrow split from its core, forming eight separate purple arrows. The Rover tried to angle his body to avoid them, but there were too many. The impact of the purple arrows was like a salvo of hadron bursts that kept hitting the Rover, knocking him into the gym on the home side of the field.

Tanner ducked when he saw the Wraith swinging his staff at him. The Wraith had a long wooden stick with metal knives at each end. Dax was able to block the Wraith's downward swing, which was intended to cut Tanner in two. Tanner spun around, launching his own attack. Dax shifted his feet for a better position, pulling the staff around his body and clipping the Wraith on the knee. His legs buckled, and Tanner went high. The Wraith pulled his weapon up, blocking Tanner's strong downward strike. Rain began to fall harder as they clashed.

Seeing the boys handling the Wraith, Katie decided to take on Kim. No one in the group was more skilled than Katie at hand-to-hand combat. As she increased her speed, Katie swung her blades in a circular motion. Kim pulled up her own swords. Sparks flew when the two girls' blades connected. Allora pulled an arrow back to prepare for any opening for a shot, but there was no room for error. The last thing she wanted was to hit Katie.

Kim was far more advanced than Katie had predicted. She had to bend her body backward to avoid Kim's swinging blade. Her balance escaped her and she went into the ground. Kim went up for a strike, leaving her abdomen open.

Allora fired a shot. The arrow sliced through the air more quickly than normal. The arrow was halfway to its target when it erupted into fireball. Kim stopped her attack in time to see the orange ball hitting her stomach. Kim's body went flying into the other end zone. Allora rushed over to check on Katie.

"She is way too strong," Katie said, clasping Allora's hand. There was a slight fear in her voice that Allora had never heard before. "I don't think I can beat her alone."

Allora pulled her up. "You won't have to," she said.

Tanner and Dax were fighting the Wraith brilliantly. Every move that the creature made was blocked and countered. Their footwork helped to allow them to strike forward when the Wraith was vulnerable. Katie handed Allora one of her swords, and they ran into the fight.

Lightning lit the sky. Rain pelted the four as they stabbed, sliced, and blocked. The addition of the girls was too much for the Wraith. They had him surrounded. He tried to escape to the other side of the field, but Katie blocked his path. Dax saw the opportunity and swung his staff around, knocking the Wraith on his upper back. Tanner came in with the final blow. He thrust his sword into the creature's chest, which instantly caused it to go limp. The Wraith was dead.

Its red glowing eyes faded, becoming as black as its skin. Suddenly, the Wraith turned into ash, melting into the turf with every drop of rain. A heart-stopping screech came from the forest behind them. Allora heard the crack of a tree breaking. Kim had split a tree from its roots and hurled it onto the field.

"Move!" Tanner yelled. They all dove in different directions to avoid the large trunk flying at them. The turf was slippery. Allora slid about ten yards before getting her footing. Kim came into view on the other side of the field. She was breathing hard. Immediately, she started to change. She expanded to twice her original size. Her red eyes became brighter, bursting into balls of flames. Her teeth grew sharper, and her bones protruded outward. She also grew two more hands that jutted out from her sides. The sight was terrifying.

"I guess that's why they call them Shifters," Dax said.

Allora joined the rest of her friends as they prepared for the inevitable assault by the hideous creature. Kim didn't waste any time. She ran at them. Allora pulled back a purple burst and sent it streaming toward the Shifter. The creature deflected it as if it were nothing. Then, swords clashed. Tanner took the blunt force of the creature's first strike, which sent him backward. Dax swung low. Katie swung high. Both attacks were blocked. The Shifter hit Dax with a quick hadron burst, propelling him into the four foot wall at the base of the bleachers next to the gym. Seeing her brother hurt, Katie made an acrobatic turn and swung her katana. The strike sliced off one of the creature's arms, triggering Kim to hit Katie with a free arm. Katie flew back and hit the same wall as her brother, slumping unconscious onto the track. Allora initiated her own assault, enabling her to slice off another one of the creature's arms. The infuriated creature bellowed from the injury. The Shifter swung around to hit Allora, but she was able to roll out of the way. Tanner gained his footing and ran back into the fight. He got there just in time to save Allora from a swinging sword. The Shifter dropped the sword, crossed one arm underneath the other, and hit Tanner with a hadron burst to the chest. Tanner soared through the air and plummeted to the ground.

His body didn't move. Allora thought the worst. All of her friends had been taken out. She was left alone to fight this monster. The two opponents circled each other, each awaiting the other's move.

"You will never win," the creature said in a low, frightening voice. "No matter what you do, you will die. We are too many."

"You're wrong!" Allora yelled back through the constant beads of rain that pelted the ground. Thunder roared overhead.

"It's only a matter of time!" the creature shouted back. "All of your friends are going to die, and this world will be ours."

Allora couldn't take it anymore.

"*No!*" The emotion and inner power inside propelled her high into the air. Her body filled with strength, glowing with a bright light from within. She pulled her sword above her head. The Shifter reeled back, modifying her position for the assault. The energy within Allora flowed into the blade of her sword and burst into a yellowish orange. It trailed through the air, like a comet shooting through space. The Shifter pulled her sword up to block as Allora came down. The inflamed blade cut through the creature's weapon like a knife through butter. The force of the attack sliced through the creature's body, cutting it in half. The blade smoldered on the ground as the creature's severed body fell lifelessly onto the turf. Allora keeled over in complete exhaustion. She looked up to see Katie waking up her brother. With what was left of her strength, Allora turned her head to see Tanner's body to her right. She picked herself up and sluggishly crawled to Tanner, falling at his side.

"No, Tanner, you can't be dead," Allora said, shaking him. "I need you." She bent over his body and put her head on his chest. "I love you, Tanner. I love you," she said, her tears blending in with the drops of rain.

Dax and Katie limped across the field. Both knelt down at Tanner's feet. Allora wondered how a day of youthful happiness had come to this. Their innocence had gone, and now they had to come to terms with the gravity of their lives. The responsibility that came with it was painful.

Just as all hope had gone, Allora's skin began to glow. The light dropped into Tanner's body, filling him with light. Then the glow floated out, forming into a ball. It was the Eye of the Titans. The light quickly dissipated, and the orb fell onto the ground. Tanner's hand squeezed Allora's, jolting her upward. His eyes flickered open to see Allora's cheerful expression. She jumped on him, hugging his body as hard as she could. Tanner winced at the pain from the burst that had hit him earlier. His whole body was sore. Katie and Dax smiled from ear to ear when they saw their friend alive. They had made it.

They thought that they were in the clear when they heard something blast out of the gym, aiming toward the woods. The Rover had come to. He had seen the Shifter killed. This had made him realize that these Sonorians were obviously more powerful than they originally had thought. The four had no chance of chasing him. Rovers were known for their speed. The creature looked back, grinning at the thought of coming back with reinforcements. He leapt into the forest and was gone.

"We have to go after him," Allora said.

Tanner had pulled himself up.

"We won't be able to catch him," Dax said.

"But if he gets away, then..." Allora argued.

They turned when they heard a commotion from the woods. Sounds of battle were followed by yelling. They sluggishly limped to the other side of the field. They were almost at the edge of the woods, when two blurry creatures sailed over their heads. One was Sas. He had caught up with the Rover. Sas pulled the Rover down, making sure that the creature didn't break apart and escape. He slammed the Rover to the ground and pinned every limb down. The creature wiggled and jerked to get loose, but he was trapped. Finally, the Rover gave up fighting and stared up at them. He began laughing sinisterly.

"You have no idea what's coming. You may defeat me, but they know. Oh yes, they know."

Sas wasn't about to hear anymore. He lifted his leg and stomped down on the Rover, crushing him. After a few seconds, the Rover dissolved into the ground. A crowd of people erupted out of the woods. Allora had never been happier to see her mother. Behind her were Aunt May, Tanner's Aunt Lizi, Bell, Mr. Swan, Principal Winters, Mrs. Ferris, Sheriff Newton, Jarrod, Maureen, and Sumatra.

"Oh my god," Milly said, running over and hugging her daughter.

Family and friends exchanged hugs with each other. Everyone commented on the cuts that were randomly placed all over their bodies. Allora remembered about Jenny, but Sumatra was already on it. She was alive, but badly hurt. Mr. Swan picked her up, and then vanished through a portal that Sumatra created.

Milly checked her daughter to see if she needed immediate medical attention, but Allora only had minor bleeding. Milly decided that it would be best to get them out of there before Sheriff Newton had to call it in. There was so much death and destruction that it couldn't be covered up completely, but they already had plans in place in case something like this happened. Sumatra created a portal and they all left.

Allora was pulled inward, and reappeared in the field behind her house. The nightmare was over. She was now safe within the confines of her home. Those whom she loved were right there with her, thankful to still be alive.

Chapter 30

A New Beginning

A searing pain greeted Allora as she sluggishly entered the hallway, still in her pajamas. Every time she moved, her muscles fought back. The bruises on her body were becoming much more accentuated, and she could still feel the stinging cuts littering her torso. Her legs were stiff, which made walking out to the living room difficult. When she entered, Katie sat up on the couch, wiping the sleep from her eyes. Allora searched through the couch and found the TV remote in between the cushions. Aunt May entered the living room as Allora turned on the television. Milly was nowhere to be seen, which was strange because she was always the first one awake, making coffee.

"May, where is Mom?" Allora asked her aunt.

"She had to run out to take care of a few things," Aunt May replied.

Allora oriented herself to listening to the morning news.

"Thanks, Jim. In Sandy, police found Barbara and Randy Nelson deceased in their home. Initial reports say that the couple had died in their sleep during the winter. Neighbors say that they kept to themselves. They didn't have any children or close relatives," the woman said.

"So unfortunate, Mary. In other news, Sandy High School is getting a remodel. It looks like the school will be getting a new gym and football field. I

wonder if this has anything to do with the school's recent state football champi-onship. Principal Jodie Winters said that the project had been set to begin after the school year ended, but other factors pushed the project ahead of schedule. Principal Winters assures everyone that this will not affect graduation. Now let's take it to Pete for a weather report."

Aunt May disappeared into the kitchen without looking at her niece. Rushing to follow, Allora winced at the pain her steps caused.

"How is that possible?" Allora asked.

Aunt May started to answer, but Milly came trudging through the back door. She took off her shoes and went straight to the kitchen.

"So, I'm guessing that you watched the news," Milly said, preparing her morning coffee.

"Mom, how did you do that?" Allora asked, completely flabbergasted by the cover-up. "The field was destroyed. Not to mention the Nelsons house."

Milly poured water into the coffee machine and then directed Allora into the living room, where Katie, Dax, and Tanner were now wide awake. Sunlight was piercing through the window, making the living room glow. Allora sat down, waiting on her mother, and taking another look at the paintings that adorned the wall. They each seemed to take on a new shape, as if they were no longer far-off lands, but portraits of a world that seemed closer than ever. Milly patiently sat down in her armchair, taking her time to sip at the warm coffee.

"First of all, I'm so glad that you four are alright. Luckily, Katie had called me before she got there." Milly paused. "I thought the worst when I heard you scream, Allora. We must have gotten to the Nelson's when you had killed that Shifter. I'm honestly very proud of all of you. There aren't that many who can take on a Shifter, let alone a Wraith and a Rover at the same time. I knew that this day would come, but I was dreading it all the while." Milly changed her focus to Allora. "I guess it's time for me to start treating you more like an adult now. You will always be my baby, though." Milly blinked quickly against the tears that were forming in her eyes.

"Mom...."

"Sorry." Milly pulled her tears in and rubbed her eyes. "We have had contingency plans in place for this kind of incident. It's not like this hasn't happened before. They just haven't been this brazen before." Milly paused, wondering if it was going to get worse. She already knew the answer, but didn't want it to be true. "These sorts of incidents have happened throughout humankind's existence on Earth, but they have been relegated to myth or folklore. We have a duty to keep that secret, because this world isn't ready for that kind of revelation. It happened once before, thousands of years ago, and set our two worlds on a collision course that could have destroyed both."

Milly let that part sink in. She had sworn to protect the secrets of the Gateways, and knew the consequences of failing to do so. Forces in Sonora had no care for order and peace. They wanted this world for their own, and they would stop at nothing to conquer all. There was only one thing stopping their progression into Earth, and they were closer than ever to achieving their goal. Milly would give her life to stop them.

"What about Jenny? Is she okay?" asked Allora.

"She is in the hospital, but only as a precaution," Milly explained, glad to be distracted from her ominous thought. "The doctor said she will be fine. I was just there."

"You know, she saw almost everything," Allora said. "How did you?"

"Keep her quiet?" Milly said, interrupting her daughter. "I had Sheriff Newton take care of it. He can be very persuasive at times."

Allora looked to Tanner, who seemed to be thinking the same thought she was. "Can we go see her?" Allora asked.

"I'd actually prefer you did," Milly said. "She is probably pretty upset right now."

Allora quickly went to get changed.

"Here, Tanner, you can take my car," Milly said, tossing him the keys. "Remember, Allora, you have to remain cool. You can't let Jenny think you know more than you do."

Allora nodded, and they left the house. Tanner had borrowed some of Allora's uncle's clothes. The shredded tuxedo would have looked bad. He almost looked like Uncle Ben in the oversized sweatshirt, baggy ripped jeans, and worn-down baseball hat. They hopped into the minivan and took off to the hospital. They found Jenny's room in the intensive care unit on the second floor. Jenny's parents were in the room when they arrived. Tanner gave Jenny's parents a hug, and then the adults left to let them talk. Jenny had a sullen, confused expression.

Once her parents were gone, Jenny erupted with words. "Okay, am I going crazy? What happened last night? I'm almost thinking that I dreamt it. I thought that this stuff only happened in movies," she blurted out.

Allora went to say something, but Tanner took the lead. "Are you alright?"

"I'm fine," Jenny answered. "A little sore, but I'll live. How are you guys?"

"We're good," Allora said, trying to think of what to say next.

Jenny could tell that something was amiss. "I should have known," she said, glaring up at Tanner and Allora as they sat awkwardly on the bed. Allora thought that she had figured out that they weren't exactly human. Tanner thought the same thing. Jenny sat up a little more.

"Sheriff Newton got to you two as well, didn't he?" Jenny said.

Allora tried to hide her relief. She nodded her head, along with Tanner. "Yeah, he came to our house and told us the same thing."

"Oh my god, we are totally in some kind of conspiracy. This is crazy," Jenny said.

They talked for a while about that night. Jenny asked about how Kim had gotten away. Allora told her that she simply took off. Jenny asked about the Wraith. Tanner told her that it was some drugged-out guy dressed up in some kind of costume. Jenny looked like she believed it. They were about to leave when Jenny asked one more question.

"How did the Nelson's house explode?" She glared at Allora. "I looked up and thought I saw some kind of purple ball hit the roof."

Allora fumbled around her mind for an answer. She felt cold chill run down her body. They had been caught. Tanner stepped in front to look at Jenny.

"They threw an explosive that didn't get out of the house. The purple thing you saw was probably just a color spot from hitting your head on the ground."

Allora bobbed her head up and down in agreement. Jenny stared back as if contemplating the plausibility of Tanner's explanation. After a painstaking few seconds, Jenny let it go.

"Well, I'm glad you guys came to see me," she said. "I'll see you at graduation."

With that, the two left the room, exhaling while they walked down the hospital hallway.

"That was close," Allora said.

"Tell me about it," Tanner said. "I'm not so sure that it was entirely convincing."

When they got to Allora's house, Milly let them know that Katie and Dax had gone home while they were at the hospital. Tanner had to take off as well. He hadn't seen his aunt since the night before. Once Tanner was gone, Allora confronted her mother.

"This isn't over, is it?" She already knew the answer.

"No, Allora, it's not." Milly placed her hand on her daughter's shoulder. Allora looked up from staring at the floor. "I know that I have been protective of you. It pains me to say this, but you showed me last night that you can take care of yourself. I have never been more proud of you in my entire life. I can see that this has been a tough transition for you. Most would have cracked under the pressures that you have faced this year. I've always tried to shield you from this life because I have seen the destructive powers that fight against us. I know now that I can't shelter you from it any longer. Do not doubt yourself. You are more special than you could even imagine," Milly said, embracing her daughter.

Her mother's words were soothing. Allora had a deep respect for her mother. Even though they fought a lot, Allora always listened to what she had to say. Milly embodied wisdom that was beyond her age. People could sense it when she walked into the room. Allora never questioned the idea that her mother was far more experienced and knowledgeable than anyone she knew. Her mother was, at times, the most frustrating woman she had ever known, but she also knew exactly what to say when Allora was upset.

~~~~~~~~~~~~~~

Weeks went by without incident. All of the students at school believed what Principal Winters had announced over the intercom and what was said in the news about the gym renovations. Jenny talked about it in private, but didn't show any sign of knowing that they were involved. Graduation was approaching.

Allora, Katie, Dax, and Tanner went to the graduation ceremony, reveling in the fact that they were now seniors. After graduation, Katie drove Allora to her house. Tanner and Dax came over an hour later. They had decided to pay Sas a visit and thank him for what he had done the night of the fight. It took them a while because Sas' cave was so far up the mountain. They arrived to find Sas talking with Sumatra.

"Hi, guys and gals!" Sas said, running over and giving them all a big hug.

Squished together in his furry arms, they tried to reciprocate, but couldn't get their arms free. Sas let go and stepped back.

"Nice to see you, too, ya big furry ape," Dax said, sucking in air.

"We wanted to come up here and thank you for what you did the other night," Allora said.

Sas' mood changed when they brought up why they had come. "You four are like family to me. I wouldn't let anything happen to you. I don't think that Sumatra would either," he said, looking at the old man leaning on his staff at his perch on a large boulder.

"You all performed brilliantly," Sumatra said in his usual monotone, smiling slightly. "I couldn't have asked for any better."

The six of them talked for a while as the sun dipped into the western sky. Tanner, Dax, Katie, and Allora hiked to the lookout at the top of Sas' cave to look at the sunset. The four of them stared in silence at the beautiful landscape, relishing the peaceful serenity of the moment. The familiar orange orb dipped into the western horizon, and the warmth subsided. They knew there was a fight ahead, but somehow it seemed less scary knowing that they had each other. The dying sunset glowed with a purple hue, soon replaced by a dark blue night sky. In the distance, they could see a dark cloud hanging low, like a spy waiting for the right moment to strike. Though the evening was clear and the storm had passed, another was brewing in the distance. It was a storm like no other, fueled by the events of the past, and aimed toward the unsuspecting town residing in peace at the base of the mountain.

THE END

Made in the USA
Charleston, SC
02 December 2011